The Lost Daughters

Wildside Press Books by Leigh Grossman

The Green Lion

The Golden Thorns

Sense of Wonder: A Century of Science Fiction (ed.)

www.wildsidegame.com

The Lost Daughters

A novel of Ananya

Leigh Ronald Grossman

The Wildside Press

Rockville, Maryland

The Lost Daughters
daughters.swordsmith.com

Special thanks to Seameus Bethel
Ebook ISBN 978-1-4794-1892-3
ISBN 978-1-4794-1893-0

Published by:
Wildside Press LLC
www.wildsidepress.com

First Wildside Press edition: November 2018

10 9 8 7 6 5 4 3 2 1

For Cara

Contents

Prologue

"This is going to be a god-sucking fiasco," said Bhales. She wiped an oilcloth along the magical etchings that grooved her blade, but her heart wasn't in it.

"Can't argue with that," I said. "Think the general has any idea what he's doing?"

Nemias shook his head. "Not likely. You heard his orders?"

"I heard."

Nemias glanced at the heavy cloth flap that kept outsiders from the tent which had become the unofficial captains' mess and planning area. "Even if he did, it wouldn't matter. Koros got orders from the governor-general. Break the defenses immediately or be relieved. I heard from a channeler friend. The Empress told the governor-general it was his head if Davynen didn't fall by the end of mud season, so the city could be used to stage a spring invasion."

Bhales looked angry. She was one of the oldest captains in the Ananyan Army, but her company fought as hard as any. "The whole army is chewed up from two months of fighting in the mud. We barely have enough healthy channelers to keep the war-engines running at half speed. And he wants us to take the place by storm. It can't be done."

I shook my head. "It can be done."

"You really think so?" Bhales looked doubtful, but I saw a sort of ferocious hopefulness in her eyes. Her company would do its part in the morning.

Nemias cleared his throat. "So how do we fix this, Sperrin? You're the strategist. Tell us what we need to do to make Koros's plan work."

I looked down at the big map of Davynen's outer defense works pinned to the floor of the tent in front of us. Casualties among the senior officers had elevated Overcaptain Koros into an acting captain-general's role far beyond his talents. His well-intentioned floundering might yet kill us all. But maybe not. "Depends. Any word on whose company will be first through the breach? They'll have to hold steady."

"I heard it will be Averell," Nemias said. "He has one of the heavy companies of the Downmeadow Panthers. They're steady enough."

"They are," I answered. "He may need a little more help to keep going through the breach, though. I'm close to full strength, since I got some survivors from Jathra's company after she and her subcaptains died. I can send a few to help reinforce Averell."

"I'll try to find a few to help him in the Threecastle Tomcats," said Nemias. "I can't spare more than a few, but I'll talk to the other line company captains and see what we can scrape up."

Bhales just shook her head. She barely had enough combat-ready troopers left to keep her company's two bulky war-engines from being overrun by enemy skirmishers.

I looked back at the map. "Here and here"—I pointed—"We will need to overrun their skirmishers and hold these points. Even better if we can get a channeler or two there as well to help hold off magical attacks. They don't look bad on the map, and I doubt Koros is paying much attention to a few skirmishers, but if the light companies are taking losses from those points before they can reach the main jump-off point, they'll bog down. And this advance needs to be fast to work."

"Scout companies?" Nemias looked dubious, even as he made the suggestion.

"That should be enough. Koros never uses them in his assault orders, so they should be available. If we can scrape up a few channelers from the sick list that will help too."

Bhales shook her head again. "Some of those channelers aren't going to make it through the campaign. Whatever they've got is getting in their lungs. Some sort of mud fever, but channelers get it a lot worse around here. Some of the ones still fighting can't draw much power anymore. The fever hurts their link with the Empress."

"I don't care if it kills them in a month, we need some of them fighting tomorrow. A lot of them." That sounded harsh even to me. My wife would not have approved.

"The enemy's channelers seem to be doing just fine," said Nemias.

Bhales shrugged. "Their channelers grew up around here. Maybe they have a way to cure it. Or maybe they just don't catch it. Seems like our channelers are just so damned fragile sometimes." She caught herself. "Sorry, Sperrin."

I smiled. "Sefa's not very fragile. But she's not a combat channeler, either. I don't think she'd do well in mud."

"Not much else but mud here," Nemias said, laughing. "You'd better watch out, Bhales. The mud fever preys on the old and the weak and the channelers."

"Are you calling me weak?" Bhales's hand went reflexively to her blade, although her eyes had an amused crinkle.

"Nooooo," said Nemias. "I don't think anyone would call you weak."

"I'm not *that* old," she said, and then we all laughed, not because it was funny but because we needed something to laugh at. Nemias had half a dozen ready jokes about Bhales's age, and we laughed until Bhales started coughing so hard she couldn't stop. Which would have led to another joke if so many of the army's channelers weren't already coughing in a sick tent as their lungs slowly filled with fluid.

"So, the battle tomorrow?" Nemias said, a little tentatively.

We all turned back to the map, and I pointed out a few more places where Overcaptain Koros's battle plan needed shoring up.

"On paper this should work," I said. "But it all depends on Averell."

On paper the whole campaign should have worked. The Empress had sent more than enough troops and channelers. We had taken the outer defenses and opened a breach in the city wall two months ago. On paper it looked like an easy victory with one final push. But with the mud and the sickness and some timely Alliance counterattacks, Overcaptain Koros and the whole campaign seemed to be foundering together in the mud fields that now surrounded Davynen.

Nemias looked at the map again. "Anything else we need to watch for, Sperrin?"

I shrugged. "If we hit those two points and keep everyone moving fast we may be all right. Their channelers are accurate, but the crews on their war-engines are slow. If we move fast, no one will get hit too hard before we get to the breach. That's where the real fighting will be, anyway." I stood up, and adjusted my belt so my blade hung cleanly by my side. "I'm off to check the lines. I want to talk with the late watch officers before they start their rounds. Pass the word to the other captains. If the gods don't meddle and Koros keeps his head, we should be fine."

"That's a lot to hope for," said Nemias. He clasped my shoulder in farewell. I returned his gesture, then passed through the tentcloth into the night.

EVEN BEFORE THE signal whistle blew to start the advance, the battle didn't look good. That morning, Overcaptain Koros had summoned all the captains to join him for breakfast. Reluctantly, I turned over the final preparations to my subcaptain and sergeants and jogged over to the overcaptain's pavilion. I could see a sergeant of engineers and some borrowed troopers helping prepare a battered harrowflame thrower; they'd strapped a wan-looking channeler into her chair, wrapped in a thick layer of blankets. Her skin looked unnaturally pale, even in the early morning light. But her eyes still had a deep blue intensity and she nodded solemnly as she met my gaze.

OVERCAPTAIN KOROS SAT at the head of a long table, while the oversergeant who served as aide and bodyguard sliced pieces of yellowfruit into a bowl. Bowls of yogurt and goat-milk already sat on the table, along with two big trays of small loaves still steaming from the ovens.

The overcaptain looked calm and confident, as he did before every morning's fight. If he knew the stakes of today's actions, Koros's face betrayed nothing.

Maybe he really doesn't know, I thought, not for the first time. Everyone knew Koros was grand-nephew to the Empress, but the wife she'd selected for him was no great favorite. He had to know he had very little margin for failure. More margin than a field captain like me, but not by a lot. The Empress valued success more than she valued nephews.

Koros sat with some odd companions. Ranvera, a ragged bandage over his wounded head and lost eye, sat with both his subcaptains at Koros's right. Ranvera's subcaptains looked angry, but the wounded captain looked happy.

Happier than I would be. Ranvera fought hard, but his company did not. He had lost an eye leading his troopers into the fighting at the breach—but more to the point, he'd lost his company. They'd broken and fled the field in the chaos of the assault, leaving two unprotected channelers to be killed and a gaping hole in the middle of the army. Jathra and half of her company had died filling that hole, buying time for the army to reform its lines and fall back.

Ranvera's company had been reassembled—his losses had been light, considering—and they had been sent behind the lines to refit and retrain. Now, apparently, they had returned.

"Captains"—Overcaptain Koros stood and gestured with both hands to silence the growing disgruntlement in the pavilion—"I have an announcement to make before this morning's advance. You all know Captain Ranvera of the Willow Valley Sand Vipers. His company had an unfortunate time in the last attempt on the breach, so he has asked for a chance to finish today what his troopers couldn't then. Therefore, I have given Captain Ranvera the honor of leading this morning's advance. Captain Averall's company will switch position with Captain Ranvera's troopers and serve as principal reserve. Captain Ranvera, you have a few words for us?"

Ranvera looked around the room. We all stared back, a little grimly. His two subcaptains looked at Ranvera bleakly; the request clearly hadn't come from them. *If they're here, who's helping prepare his company for the battle?* I wondered.

Ranvera stood, looking defiantly at all of us. "All I have to say is that my troopers will be in the breach by midmorning. I swear it in the name of all that the gods betrayed."

"Well spoken," Koros said. "Captains, you have your assignments. See to your troops."

We all filed out, the breakfast untouched.

"Do you believe that?" Nemias said to me quietly, when we'd passed out of hearing of the pavilion. "If they couldn't make it in the last two months, how are they going to make it this morning?"

I shrugged. We had our orders. Nemias was right, of course. But it wasn't the sort of advice Overcaptain Koros would have appreciated.

"So what do we do, Sperrin?" Nemias persisted.

"What we always do. We fight. We watch each other's flanks. We follow our orders. Who knows, maybe Ranvera can pull it off."

"Can we win if he does?"

"Let's find out." I clasped Nemias's shoulder as we parted ways to our separate companies' lines.

THE SAND VIPERS lined up passably well. I could see them from the front of my company; we would be third through the breastworks at the center of the line. I would have felt better if Koros—or anyone—had inspected them, maybe given them a speech to gauge their courage. Ranvera's company hadn't replaced its lost channelers yet, so they would be advancing in the face of magical fire, with nothing but courage to help them make it across the muddy field that separated our defenses from the breach in Davynen's walls.

I looked to either side and saw Ananyan scouts occupying the positions I'd marked on the map last night. So that part of the plan had worked; the Sand Vipers would still face fire from the walls of Davynen and the skirmishers in front of them, but at least their flanks would be protected.

Ranvera stood in front of his company, holding a signal stick, his blade still sheathed at his side. His subcaptains stood at the left and right flanks of his company. Nodding once, Ranvera raised the signal stick high. The whistle for the advance screeled loudly. The crack of throwers releasing their payloads sounded as our channelers fired at Alliance positions to help cover the advance.

With Ranvera at their head, the three companies of the Sand Vipers regiment stepped out from the entrenchments and began to dress their lines for the advance. Sky flashed as a bolt of harrowflame landed at the right edge of the formation. A subcaptain and three troopers dissolved into screams and charred flesh.

"Advance!" Ranvera called out.

The soldiers behind him lifted their weapons. Then one of them cracked the butt of his halberd against Ranvera's skull.

The captain pitched to the ground.

A bolt of harrowflame splashed into the mud nearby, exploding just short of the front rank. As if that had been a signal, Ranvera's company melted away, troopers dropping their weapons and turning their backs to run. The Sand Viper companies to either side faltered and then began to fall back as well, clogging the breastworks as they tried to retreat into the companies moving up behind them. The fire from the Central Alliance lines increased, as their channelers sensed easy targets.

I saw our scouts falling back from the positions they'd taken forward of the flanks, choosing retreat rather than being left unsupported in front of a collapsing front line.

A double whistle blew from the rear, from Overcaptain Koros's command post: the command to return to defensive positions and hold. My troopers, still set for the attack, watched silently as Ranvera's company fled around them. Other than the three companies of Sand Vipers at the very front of the line, the panic hadn't spread. But that had been enough.

The whole advance stalled before it had even begun.

"KOROS HAS BEEN relieved." As usual, Nemias heard the news before any of the rest of us.

I hadn't even seen the overcaptain in the twelve days since the aborted battle. A handful of couriers had come and gone from his pavilion, but the rest of us had settled into a sort of sodden truce. A deluge from the skies had soaked everyone and made the field between Davynen and the Ananyan Army completely impassable. Only in the last few days had hints of sun returned. Soon the province would enter the hot, dry season before which Davynen needed to be won if the river guarded by the city was to be a roadway for invasion.

"The governor is on his way, but his lieutenant got here early and relieved Koros."

"So who's in command?" I asked.

"The lieutenant-governor, at a guess," said Nemias. "At least until the governor gets here."

"Why is the lieutenant-governor even here?" Bhales asked. "This is the one with the beautiful wife, right? The way I heard it, he comes from a family of diplomats, but none of them talk to him anymore. He's too ambitious even for them."

"From what I heard," Nemias said, "he's here because his wife is here. They needed a channeler powerful enough to perform an execution. He came along, and because he beat the governor here he gets to take command."

"So he's here to play governor-general?" Bhales asked.

"It looks that way," said Nemias.

"Let's hope he's better at it than Koros," said Bhales. She coughed, deep and hacking. "I want to win this fight and get out of the mud before this cough gets any worse."

THE SOLDIER HAD to die, of course. Even Koros would have seen that, if he'd still been around. Camp rumor had it that Koros had been sent back to the Drowned City to answer to the Empress herself, but more likely the overcaptain had been rotated to some forgotten mountain fort as far away from the front lines and serious command responsibility as could be managed. That was how the army handled well-connected officers who fell out of political favor.

When the order to assemble for the execution came, they lined us up by companies instead of regiments. With Koros gone, none of the four overcaptains originally assigned to the expedition remained, and Koros—himself an

overcaptain serving in a brevet captain-general's role—didn't have the authority to promote anyone to regimental command. Not that the lieutenant-governor or his beautiful executioner-wife was here to promote anyone.

I noticed her first on the platform: I think we all did. She looked as beautiful as advertised, wearing the same sort of city clothes as my wife Sefa.
Beautiful and comfortable for wearing in theaters and palaces, but not especially practical in mud. A small brown-haired girl about my daughter's age,
dressed in the same sort of impractical clothing, clung to the executioner's leg
possessively. *Why bring her here?* I wondered. I missed my daughter fiercely, but I would never have brought her to a fever-infested wasteland like this
one.

They'd bound the soldier who'd struck down Ranvera to a post at the center of the platform. He'd been stripped to the waist, presumably for dramatic
effect, but didn't look otherwise mistreated. What was the point? Beating him
wouldn't make him any more of an example than he was about to become. I
didn't even know his name.

Once the lieutenant-governor started speaking to the assembled army, I
didn't notice anything else. None of us did. He looked unassuming: chestnut
hair and neatly trimmed beard more-or-less indistinguishable from a dozen
other diplomats I'd heard speeches from. We expected something fiery and
inspirational, but that wasn't what he did. He spoke for an hour without notes,
and by the end of it we felt terrible—every one of us ashamed. I don't think I
could remember a word he said, but I've never been as ashamed of myself as
I was that day—and *my* company had held its assigned position.

He turned away from us at the end, said a few words I couldn't hear to the
soldier bound to the post, and nodded to his wife. The soldier had looked defi-
ant up until that point, trying to put up a good front for his former comrades.
But whatever the lieutenant-governor said drained the defiance from him.
The soldier sagged against his bonds, as if in surrender.

And then his head exploded. Blood and flecks of bone and brain spattered
the front ranks of the drawn up soldiers, though none of it touched the lieutenant-governor or his executioner-wife or to the young girl who still clung
wordlessly to her mother's leg.

That speech made the lieutenant-governor famous, but afterward in private he made a shorter, grimmer speech to us captains. "I am not a soldier,"
he told us, in a way that made us ashamed that we were. "You know who
among you is the best tactician. You will make a plan, and you will attack in

the morning and you will carry the enemy defenses. I will leave the details to you."

He took a breath. "You think you have accomplished something because each of you has fought bravely and your company didn't break. I want to tell you that it means nothing. No one will speak of you or remember you unless you win tomorrow."

He stared at me—I suppose every one of us thought he was staring at them. "You think I am exaggerating to upset you, to make you fight harder. But I am not personally concerned with how hard you fight. If you fight poorly, another will replace you who fights better. What I tell you comes from the Talisman of Truce itself. If you fail here, you will be forgotten by man and god alike:

Let those who fall in battle be celebrated if their fall be brave. But if
They fall through misdeed among their comrades, or through
failure of their comrades to fight steadfastly, there shall
be no need for celebration: Their kin shall mourn them if they choose but
their fall incurs no obligation among their foes.

I had heard the Truce quoted before, mostly in dry history lectures. But the lieutenant-governor used the words like a lash. He turned and left with those words, and we turned to planning—this time planning how to win the battle, not just how to minimize Overcaptain Koros's mistakes.

I hated the lieutenant-governor. I cursed his name, which I can't even remember anymore: It vanished from my memory years later when he gave it up in the Empress's service. Mostly I hated him for being right.

We hated ourselves but we fought brilliantly. We broke Davynen's principle defenses the next morning, and took the city while the poor fool of a soldier's magic-blasted body was still sagging from its post on that terrible stage.

I was in the thick of the fighting and they promoted me, but I felt dirty about the whole thing. I hated the lieutenant-governor for that speech, but I couldn't help respecting his ability and his oratory. I wasn't surprised when he was named a governor, then continued to rise in the Empress's service. He would be chancellor of all Ananya the next time I saw him, the Empress's closest adviser.

That moment outside the walls of Davynen was the first time I saw the way nothing touched him, how even death avoided the man.

Part I

The Executioner's Daughter

Chapter 1

When I was a boy we played gods and heroes, just like kids everywhere. I was the only one who didn't really care which side I played, so I got to play a god a lot, while everyone else wanted to play the Holy War heroes. I wasn't any less patriotic than anybody else. But I think in some ways I was playing a different game than the rest of the neighborhood kids fencing with our linen-wrapped sticks.

I don't think I realized it at the time, but I was learning to kill. I did care who won or lost, and even then I was the best tactician of all the kids in the town. But really, for me the games were personal. It wasn't just that I wanted my team to win: I *needed* to beat the players on the other side.

I could tell the difference between play and real life—I never killed anyone in the game, except in a pretend way. But I wanted to. After the game they were my friends, but during the game, if they were on the other side, I wanted to kill them.

Later, as an adult, I started to think that might have been a little unhealthy.

But the whole time I was a child, and then when I was a soldier, no one else ever seemed to be the least bit bothered by it. My wife even felt jealous of it, I think: She wanted me to have the same passion for her that I had on the battlefield. Or at least that's what I thought she wanted at the time. Ironically, trying to do that is how I lost her.

I KILLED FOR the first time when I was fourteen. I was in a pioneer unit— kids with shovels and axes sent to keep mountain paths clear. I managed to get separated from the others. Our channeler was an old drunk, which was why she'd been assigned to a pioneer unit instead of somewhere useful. If she hadn't been sleeping at the main camp she would have noticed I was gone and found me. I wasn't worried; it might mean a night spent out in the mountains, but she'd find me in the morning when she sobered up. Except that I ran into an Alliance scout instead. He must have separated from his group too. He had a blade and I had a trench digging tool, but I struck faster.

After I stabbed him we found ourselves stuck in a roadside ditch together for the night while he slowly bled to death internally. He wasn't going to make it out of the ditch alive, and we both wondered if his friends would show up before mine did—in which case I wouldn't, either. I didn't speak any Alliance languages then and he didn't speak any Ananyan, so we spent half the night talking without understanding each other. Then at some point he stopped responding and I realized he had died. I always wondered what his name was.

I guess it was the right thing to do, because the next morning after the pioneer troop found me the subcaptain in charge had me sent to Officers' Academy, and I never had to do any more shoveling.

Sperrin
Officers' Academy: Twenty-six years before the Loss

"So what's the academy bladefighting champion doing here in the library studying instead of out on the practice fields in the heat like the rest of us?"

I looked up at the speaker: scrawny kid with red hair, slated for the scouts. Passable with a blade as well, though he didn't really have the size for his straight-ahead fighting style. It took me a moment to place his name.

"Nemias, right?"

The redheaded kid nodded. I could see a touch of nervousness in his eyes, wondering if he'd overstepped himself.

I met his gaze squarely. He was sweaty from the practice field, while I felt cool, though I hadn't come in all that long ago. "I'll tell you what I'm doing in here. The same thing I'd be doing out there—practicing."

"Practicing? Maybe you told the blade-coaches that, but I don't see how you'll improve your footwork from a book." He gestured to the lavishly illustrated volume on the table in front of me.

"Well, I'm not going to improve my footwork working with you," I said, smiling to show I meant no offense. We both knew it was true.

He smiled back, a little ruefully. "So what's in the book that's more useful than working out with me?"

He actually seemed to want an answer, which surprised me a little. I usually had the two tables in the small academy library to myself. I had finished just over half its volumes so far—mostly history, tactics, strategy, fighting techniques, and the occasional treatise on logistics or engineering. Or in this case, anatomy.

Nemias looked more closely at the book. "That looks ancient," he said. "Are those pictures hand drawn?"

I nodded. "It's older than anything else I've seen here. But it's a copy, not an original. There's a note in the front that said it was one of a dozen copies made by the sorcerer Juila herself. She made them near the end of the Holy War for the use of generals, before the old magic was banned. At least one of the copies survived and ended up here."

The pages in front of me depicted an adult male silverwing in several positions: resting, flying, diving, as well as an anatomical view with wings fully outstretched. Each pose had vulnerable areas and strongest points marked, while copious notes originally handwritten by several different authors described the fighting techniques to expect from silverwings and the best counters to them.

"So it's a guide to fighting creatures that nobody has seen in eight hundred years."

"Basically, yes."

"And you think that book on fighting extinct creatures will teach you more than working out with me."

I shrugged. "Maybe you should work on your footwork."

He faked being hit by a blade thrust, as if I had wounded him. "Seriously"—and he did seem serious about the question—"what's in there that's useful to you?"

"I'm not sure. Maybe nothing. But you never know what you're going to encounter. There are plenty of fey in the mountains, even if there aren't any godservants. Why do you think there's still so much cold iron used in building mountain forts? There are giants in this book, and a giant took out half a company of the Westerly Whipsnakes and their channeler a few years ago, and got away clean."

"Really?" Nemias asked. "I hadn't heard that."

"The commander's report is in that volume," I said, pointing to one of the bound volumes of annual action reports from various regiments. The library's selection was haphazard, but useful.

Nemias looked back at the open book on the table. "You can really learn to fight one of those godlings just from these drawings and notes?"

"I won't really know unless I meet one, will I?"

He laughed, then realized I was serious. A different look crossed his face. "Can you show me then?" he asked. "If I run into one, I wouldn't want to lose because of my bad footwork."

"Sure," I said. I moved the tables aside, and I spent the next half hour analyzing silverwing strike techniques and counters for him.

"Don't you need to refer back to the book?" he asked at one point.

"No," I answered honestly. "If it's about how to kill something I usually get it the first time."

The lesson seemed to leave an impression, and I thought he might come back to learn more. But our paths didn't cross again for seven years, as it happened.

Sperrin
Glass Desert Campaign: Nineteen years before the Loss

"You there! Sperrin! I know you."

"You do," I said. It took a moment to place the spare frame, filled out since I'd seen him last, and the narrow face. His hair had gone from red to red-brown. "Nemias. Congratulations on your promotion, Captain."

"Yours as well, Captain Sperrin. You're making a bit of a name for yourself. Even more of a blademaster than you were at the academy, I hear."

"I suppose," I said. "I think I've had some lucky assignments."

"Right. The Alliance troopers just fall dead in front of you, the way I hear it."

I shrugged. "Nice to see you in the line infantry now. Last time I saw you, they wanted to make you a scout."

He smiled. "I didn't make much of a scout. I don't like running, and I don't know how to avoid a fight."

"I guess your footwork's gotten better, then."

"It has," he answered. "Someone told me to spend more time in libraries."

"It worked for me."

We clasped shoulders. "You'll like it here," Nemias said. "There's a lot of killing to be done, and I hear you're a good killer."

I didn't really know how to answer that, so I just nodded.

He was right, though: I was a *really* good killer by then. I'm not a bit ashamed of all the killing I've done. All of it was in the name of the Empress— or later, in the name of survival. But a part of me had started to wonder if I should be ashamed of how much I *liked* it. At twenty-three that distinction hadn't crystallized yet, though.

As newly minted captains in the Glass Desert campaign, Nemias and I really got to know each other: fighting in the same battles, eating in the same mess, and more and more called on to plan fights together. We led a reinforced company together on a scouting-in-force before the battle at Camalyn Brook. When the action got hotter than expected and our channeler went down we fought back to back, and left a heap of dead Alliance troopers around us. He swore for me at my wedding. I pinned the insignia on him when he was promoted to overcaptain, two weeks after my own promotion. I used one of the silver overcaptain's leaves the Empress herself had pinned on me.

We weren't like brothers exactly, but we fought well together, and enjoyed each other's company. Mostly we enjoyed the fighting, and planning the next fight. When I realized I needed to do something that would destroy my career, he was the one person I went to for advice. Though I would never be able to tell even Nemias the real reason I had to abandon a family and career that I loved. That would have destroyed everything he loved as well.

Sperrin
Glass Desert Victory Garrison: Nineteen years before the Loss

It took a few minutes to register that I was engaged to be married. I didn't have any idea it was coming. I was sitting in my office, filling out duty rosters, when a tall, thin channeler entered. My future sister-in-law as it turned out— the same one who would send me away later, but I had no way of knowing that at the time.

She said something, but it didn't register. It must have been the traditional words of engagement, but all I could do was stare at the golden object she held. She put it on my desk on top of the pile of duty rosters. Then she turned and must have left, but I never saw her go.

The token looked like a piece of golden fruit, covered with spiky outer leaves. I know a lot more about them now—my wife created and delivered many of them while we were together—but at the time I had no idea. Naturally, I picked off the first leaf, and the first few memories filled my mind: Sefa as a teenager, diving into a river to rescue a drowning sheep; Sefa at the Empress's Academy, organizing a Memorial Day ceremony; a young Sefa lost in the woods, but determined to find her way home without having to be rescued.

They tell you that the memories are random, a way of getting to know the person you've been chosen to marry, but I know now that isn't true. The memories are chosen to play on your emotions and vulnerabilities, to make you need each other, to feel like you complete each other. You fall in love, not with the person as they really are, but with the parts of the person that most appeal to you, which are the only parts you see before the marriage. I'm told the engagement pieces are not hard to make if you know what you're doing—perhaps half a day's work. The hardest part is keeping the chosen subjects from realizing their memories are being magically copied. Not that it would change anything, but it would ruin the surprise.

So if you ask me, were Sefa and I in love when we married, of course I was in love, and the thought Sefa might not be never crossed my mind. What alternative did we have? Who knows, the couples the Empress brought together might have come to love each other anyway, but it wasn't the sort of thing the Empress took chances on. Besides, as I later found out during my years in the palace, the Empress got a lot of enjoyment from what she saw as matchmaking. Most Ananyan rulers since the Truce delegated all but a few upper-level marriages to local officials, but the Empress took a personal hand in a surprising number of them.

Sperrin
Boldwater Province: Eighteen years before the Loss

I had always heard there was no way to tell the gender of a baby before it was born, but it turned out that wasn't true, at least not if your wife was a channeler who had the Empress's favor. The process just uses a lot of magical energy that could be better used to heat an herbary or plow a field, and I gather the channelers decided it was easier to tell people it was impossible than to tell them the Empress thought their pregnancy was a low priority. Sefa's pregnancy, as it turned out, was an entirely different story.

Sefa's sister, Nolene, took us under her wing from the time Sefa knew she was expecting a daughter. It almost seemed like Nolene didn't have any other duties during that time, she was around so much. I was nervous as a trooper on his first campaign and some days Sefa wasn't much better than me, but Nolene always seemed to know how to make us feel better.

I was home on leave a lot during the pregnancy: My regiment was quartered nearby and doing a lot of retraining new recruits after the battles of the Boldwater Campaign had depleted us. My overcaptain at the time probably preferred to have me fretting at home than fretting in front of the recruits. And he wanted me focused when the time came to fight again. So when Nolene would tell Sefa and me to get out of the house and do something, we did. Sefa and I hadn't really spent a lot of time together over the years we'd been married, and pretty soon we would both be back at our careers, but for that one magical season we went to concerts and explored all the parks and forests nearby. We went boating and even spent some time taking cable-carriages to cities we had never been to and spending a few days exploring them.

The tension between us was gone for that season. Whenever I would turn to her and say something that would normally lead to a misunderstanding, she would say "We're going to have a baby," and that would be much more important than whatever either of us had been thinking. I did the same thing. We met with tailors who made baby clothes, interviewed what seemed like dozens of potential nurses, and planned the nursery together. We agreed on very little other than how excited and nervous we were about the arrival of our daughter-to-be. I have never been happier when I wasn't in battle.

When Nolene handed me our newborn daughter and I held her for the first time, I had never before loved anyone so much as I did Lynniene. But I also never loved my wife so much as in that moment, when we shared something that hadn't been pushed on us by the Empress. Maybe the feeling didn't linger, and soon Sefa and I again found ourselves happier apart than together. But no one can say we never loved each other, no matter what Sefa convinced herself of later.

I don't think of Sefa as she was the last time I saw her—an empty, angry shell. I think of her as she was during that one season we spent together caring about each other first, sandwiched between all those years of caring for the Empress's wishes first.

Chapter 2

I was probably six or so when my mother first explained magic to me. Up until then I'd just taken it for granted, as all kids do. My mother told it like a fairy tale, and forever after, even the most everyday magic has had a sort of fairy tale quality for me. I think it was the only fairy tale she ever told me—my mother was very proud of how focused she was on real-world problems, and she left dreaming and storytelling to my nurses.

But I guess you can't explain magic to a six-year-old without a bit of dreaming.

"Once," she told me, "the gods walked among us, and people worshipped them. Some of the gods even lived in the same lands as people, in huge palaces filled with giants and pixies and other fey creatures.

"But after a long time, the people and the gods quarreled, and it turned into a long war, the one we call the Holy War. After many years of fighting, most of the places where people lived had been destroyed, but the gods still couldn't make the people give up and go back to worshipping them. And some of the gods had been crippled or lost their power as well. So the people and the gods finally decided to end the war.

"The gods agreed to leave the lands of the people, and never come back unless they were invited. And they agreed to provide people with magic, which would flow through the queen or empress of each land. In return, the people agreed that they would give up their own magic, the kind they had hurt some of the gods with. And they agreed that the ruler of each land would have the blood of a god in her veins, so she would have a connection with the god who was giving up his or her own power to provide magic to a human land. And she would give up her own name to the gods in return for the gift of magic—the gods got extra power from human names, and tricking people into giving them up was one of the things the war had been fought about. But in the end giving up a few names was a small price to free our land from the gods."

"How do we know the gods won't come back again, Mama?"

"Because they promised and they have to keep their promises. Gods aren't like people. They can't tell lies." She was wrong, but at six, I believed her.

"Why would a god give up her own magic for us? Are names that important?"

"I don't know: It happened a long time before I was born. We had worshipped them once and maybe some of them still cared about us, even after all the fighting. I know that some of them volunteered to give up their powers for us. There's a sad story in the Book of Gods about Senne, who had to leave her lover Kedessen so that she could give her powers to our Empress. And the Empress passes magic along to women like me, who have been trained as channelers."

"So only girls can use magic?" I asked.

She pushed my hair back out of my eyes. The gesture felt a little unnatural: She rarely touched me, and wasn't really used to reaching out that way. "Only women in Ananya," my mother answered. "The training takes many years. The Empress chooses who will become a channeler, and where she is assigned. If a woman has a lot of channeling power she might help with wars and fighting, or move cable-carriages and ships between cities. Or if she's less powerful she might light buildings and streetlamps, or keep water heated in a bathhouse or mansion. The more experienced a channeler is, the more things she can do at once, but she will never get any more powerful than that first day the Empress gives magic to her."

That was getting a little over my head. I knew my mother was a channeler and that she was important, but I didn't really know what she did.

"Will I be a channeler like you someday, Mama?"

"Of course you will. You will be a very powerful channeler, just like your mother." She was mostly wrong about that, too, although in the end I guess maybe she wasn't.

But by that time my mother had been dead for years, and she was the one member of my immediate family who died before finding out that gods could lie to you. Or that there were betrayals far worse than being lied to by a god.

Ketya
The Siege of Davynen: Thirteen years before the Loss

I hate to say this, because it turned out to be so important in retrospect, but to a seven-year-old who got dragged to a lot of battles and state occasions, Davynen didn't make much of an impression on me. Especially since it was what happened after the battle that really ended up changing everything for me and my family.

I remember there was mud everywhere, and some crumbling walls in the distance where the fighting itself must have been happening. There was a big encampment in the muddy fields, with a lot of soldiers everywhere whom my parents didn't seem to like, which made the soldiers seem scary to me, even though I knew they were supposed to be on our side. In the middle of the whole thing was a big wooden stage, which my parents climbed up the stairs to since it was the only place out of the mud.

I was bored and clingy and no one stopped me from climbing up after them. Once I was up there I held on to my mother's leg and wouldn't let go, especially when row after row of scary soldiers lined up in front of the stage. The rest of it was all kind of a blur until the prisoner's head exploded and then I just buried my head into my mother's leg until it was time to go.

We left for home right after the battle ended, before the celebrations finished, even before the governor arrived. Only years later did I realize that was a deliberate stratagem on my father's part. Leaving so soon didn't really surprise me either—I was old enough to be used to arbitrary comings and goings. What *did* surprise me was the news that we would be taking a vacation at my mother's family's chateau.

Although both of my parents traveled a lot, we didn't travel as a family much: Even overnight trips were rare, special things. I think this might be the only long trip with both parents that I remember.

If my parents ever told me the name of the place I didn't remember it, just that we were going to the lake. My mother's extended family owned a spa for the use of family members on the lake; Years later when I returned to a place that might have been it, all the family members who might have confirmed it were either dead or trying to kill me, so I never did find out for sure.

My mother's family, all descended from the goddess Bayinna, was large and powerful, with spas and bathhouses for family use scattered across the provinces where most of them lived. But after my mother died, my father didn't get along with her family anymore, so I never got to go back, or ask about it. Even if he had gotten along with them, there was no more time for vacations after she died.

This trip was before my mother even got sick, though. We were going to have a genuine family trip, for a whole month. The packing went on for days, with my nurse and her assistant and a man I didn't really know—one of the gardeners, I think—all working together to pack the big trunks with everything from the nursery that I would need.

I had been to the big cable-carriage station before: Sometimes my nurse took me there to meet my father or mother when one of them was coming home from a trip. And sometimes we just went to watch the massive carriages come and go, sliding along beneath the great metal cable that supported them high above the ground and carried the magic that moved the network of cable-carriages over mountains and between cities. A good channeler could move a cable-carriage more than a tenday's walk before another relay had to pick it up; my mother had sent carriages half as far again when she had worked the great stations as a young channeler.

Usually we took a streetcar to the station, but with all of our baggage, my family rented an ox-cart instead. The cart plodded along slowly, much slower than the magically powered streetcars. I loved it because I got to ride high at the top of the pile of trunks in the open back of the cart with a broad view of the wide streets and white stone houses, instead of in a crowd of people on the streetcar where the window seats were always taken. It seemed like the ox-cart would never make it up the steep road to the hilltop cable-car station, but somehow it did. Then porters were unloading all of the trunks and I got to go into one of the giant cable-carriages for the first time.

We had a sleeping compartment for my parents and one for the servants with a sitting room between them. I was supposed to sleep on a couch in the sitting room, but I think I barely dozed the whole trip. I spent most of it kneeling backward on the couch with my nose pressed firmly to the window as the ground went by far below. The carriage rocked slightly from side to side as it moved along the cable. I would count pylons as we passed them; then the carriage would seem to go gently downhill until it reached the halfway point to the next pylon and began to climb again. My father spent most of the trip working and sorting papers at the gilded drop-leaf table in the center of the sitting room, and normally I would have wanted to know what he was doing and gotten underfoot. But this trip I just watched the scenery and enjoyed the way the carriage rocked like a swimmer as it moved. I even saw my father smile at me when he glanced up and saw me playing on the couch. I don't remember ever seeing him happier than on that trip. From time to time he even got up and briefly pointed out features of the terrain passing beneath us before returning to his table.

I could see the broad lake like a mirror while we were still a long way off. When the cable-carriage arrived, someone at the spa had sent a private street-car for us, with its own porters in spa livery to take our trunks and bundles. The streetcar had velvet-covered seats at the front for us, and I got a window all my own for the ride downhill to the lakeside spa.

From there things turned into a whirlwind. Dinner was in a huge, glittering room filled with thick red carpets. Chandeliers of cut glass, each piece glowing with channeled magic, slowly revolved above us. We sat at the longest table I had ever seen, surrounded by strangers who all seemed to know my mother. By that time my head was spinning, and I'm not sure I even made it through dinner awake. I remember course after course, each one fancier than the one before, and I think the last few I may have dreamed.

I woke up in a soft featherbed. It swung gently as I moved, suspended by ropes from the bedframe, and the swinging made me feel like I was back in the cable-carriage. Both of my parents had already gone for the day by the time my nurse brought me down to the same plush dining room for a late breakfast. My father was lecturing at some sort of school near the lake—one of the academies for civil servants, I think. He couldn't bring himself to just take a vacation—he needed to be working, loved to be working. That didn't start when my mother died, it just intensified. And my mother had dozens of friends and relatives she hadn't seen for years, and only a month to catch up with them before more years of separation. As it turned out, because of her illness, it was the last time she saw most of them.

We soon settled into a routine. During the days I mostly spent time at the lakeside beach with my nurse, where I played with other kids. Sometimes we would go in groups to the bathhouse or to see other attractions nearby: a woodland maze, fields of bright red jellflowers that snapped shut if you touched them, a hall filled with gilded statues of my mother's ancestors. Mostly there were no parents around, just nurses and kids. In the evenings, before dinner in the glittering hall, I would see my parents and tell my father about all of the adventures I'd had during the day. My mother would sit near-by and write letters while she half-listened. I was used to spending evenings with my mother, but I was so excited to get to see my father every night. At home even when he wasn't traveling he often had to work so late I wouldn't get to see him before I had to go to bed. He idolized my mother, but when I think back now, I think they didn't spend much time together, even when they were both home. Not until she got sick, anyway.

There were side-trips with my mother too, and visits to relatives who told me how much my mother meant to them, most of whom I never saw again. But mostly I remember the beach, and the sparkling dinners, and telling my father about my adventures. It was like a trip to another world, to what I thought the land of the gods must look like, filled with incredibly costumed people and spectacle. I had a lot of misconceptions as a seven-year-old, but it turned out I wasn't entirely wrong.

When we boarded the cable-carriage to return home, it was like leaving a faerie world to which we could never return.

My father didn't make the trip back with us. He took a different carriage in a different direction, on royal business. I didn't see him again for weeks, which is when I found out that he'd been named provincial governor, in place of the one who had shown up to the victory celebrations at Davynen just in time to give the impression that he was taking undeserved credit for his subordinate's good work.

Sperrin
The Kelpie Aqueduct: Twelve years before the Loss

Nemias looked grim as he entered the low blockhouse that had become the senior officer's mess and our more-or-less official battle planning room—even though the battle had supposedly been won already, before the Empress had sent me here. He said a few words to the sentry outside the blockhouse, then closed and bolted the door behind him.

"How bad is it?" I asked.

"It's bad." He shook his head. "I keep wondering why the Empress hasn't given me a pretty little wife like you have, when we've fought in as many battles together, and then something like this happens and I know."

"That's not fair. You won a pretty little battle. If I were Empress I'd give you whatever wife you wanted." I don't think I'd ever seen Nemias upset like this. I hadn't seen him in more than a year, but while I'd been breaking up an attempted Alliance combined land and sea attack at North Harbor, he had beaten back a diversionary attack in the mountains that formed Ananya's spine, holding two passes with his Threecastle Tomcats, one other regiment of regulars, a scout regiment, and some hastily formed companies of pioneers.

Several weeks of guerrilla attacks and skirmishes threatened to undo his victory, however; a worrisome enough possibility that the Empress had asked me to leave the mopping up at North Harbor to my senior captain and take the fastest transportation I could to the fortresses that protected the vital aqueduct, picking up a fresh regiment of reinforcements on the way.

"It's not a victory if I lose the peace."

I shrugged. "Then I guess we'll have to win. What's going wrong? You're the best campaign planner there is, so I know there's no problem with training or logistics."

"Not yet there isn't," Nemias said. "There will be soon, at the rate we're bleeding soldiers and supplies now. What we really need is a tactician, and you're a better one than me."

I nodded. "So what can I help with?" Technically, since my promotion to overcaptain preceded his, I could have taken command. Which I suppose was what the Empress expected by sending me here. But Nemias and I were so used to working together that we fell automatically into the same sort of joint command that had won the Glass Desert campaign.

"Do you remember that book you showed me that first time we talked in the library? Must have been almost fifteen years ago now."

"I remember."

"I laughed at you for studying that book, but I wish I'd come back and read it with you."

"Why is that? As I recall, you needed to work on your footwork more than you needed help learning to fight ancient opponents."

"That's what I thought, too. But we're fighting an ancient opponent now. I beat back that alliance army, but apparently they have friends among the fey. They're getting bolder, and it's going to start scaring the troops. Tonight I found four sentries replaced by bundles of twigs. Still in uniform at their posts and weapons sheathed. They never saw whatever got them."

I smiled. "Sounds like fun."

Nemias opened his mouth to make an angry response when he realized I wasn't joking. Instead, he asked "What do you need?"

"I need your best company of scouts. Line soldiers won't do: I need troopers who are fast and agile, like you used to be in your scout days. And the scout company with the regiment I brought isn't good enough."

He nodded. "The scout company attached to the Tomcats is good. Use them."

"I will also need weapons. *Old* weapons. What's the oldest depot you have here? Is there anything left from the Holy War fort?"

Again he nodded. "There's the museum. The storeroom underneath it still has barrels of old blades soaking in oil. No one ever bothered to move them out after the war." That didn't surprise me. It would have been easier to build a new storehouse than to haul hundreds of barrels of old supplies out of the mountains when the war ended, just to dispose of them somewhere else. And the Army never got rid of anything if it could help it, not when it could be secreted away somewhere just in case it was needed again someday.

"That will do fine," I said. A museum was more than I had hoped for. "Have the scout officers meet me at the museum storehouse. I'll go there as soon as you can find someone to show it to me."

"Anything else?" he asked.

"I'll need about a week."

"A week." He seemed unsure of how to respond to that.

"No reason to stretch it out any longer." I started for the door. "If you can send someone with keys to the museum, I'm sure I can find it. I'll see you at mess this evening. I should have a plan by then."

Actually, I already had a plan. I just wasn't sure yet whether it would work.

BY THE TIME the clerk in charge of the museum arrived, I was already looking through the exhibits, accompanied by a scout captain and oversergeant—the other scout officers were on patrol until morning. The museum displayed a reasonably impressive collection of weapons from the time of the Holy War on, along with models of the aqueduct and the forts that had defended it at various times in its history. A few uniforms in glass-fronted cases filled out the collections.

The clerk caught up to me next to a prominent case in the center of the museum, which held an old-style blade on a padded velvet display area. The blade's cutting surface looked slightly broader than modern designs, black from the cold iron that jacketed its steel spine. It had no sheath, just a worn baldric of woven gut which sat beside it in the case.

"This is our most important artifact," he said. "It holds—"

"Open the case, please."

"But 'captain, it contains—"

"I know what it contains. I read the description. Fannin, consort of the first Empress of Ananya, fought here, before he became the model for the Snake Slayer in the festival pageants. They have another of his blades at the palace, I'm told, though I haven't seen it. I want to see this one more closely."

"Impossible, 'captain. I must insist—"

"Insist all you like, but open that case."

He sputtered, but complied.

I lifted the blade out, tested its weight and balance. Lighter than it looked: lighter than an iron-jacketed weapon had any right to be. The blade felt slightly point-heavy. A few practice cuts revealed the techniques it had been weighted for: I remembered them from the essays on various fey in the book of anatomy I'd read in the academy library so long ago. I tested the edge with a finger—still sharp.

"I'll take it," I said.

"What? You can't just take the Snake Slayer's sword. It's the very soul of the museum."

I shrugged. "I need something that's killed fey before, and his blade's done plenty of that. Do you have any more like it?"

"We have barrels of this design. But none of the others so famous," the curator said. "Perhaps you would be satisfied to take some of them?"

"I'll take all of them. You can have the ones we don't need back afterward."

"And the Snake Slayer's sword? Will you give *that* back?" he asked.

"I'll do better." I unbuckled my sword belt, and put the sheathed blade and belt in the case. Then I pulled the Snake Slayer's baldric over my shoulder and slid the sword into place by my side. It hung comfortably. I tested and it drew smoothly.

The curator looked down balefully at the standard-issue officer's blade, its only adornment the overcaptain's stripes on the sheath. "It really isn't the same, 'captain," he said. "You presume a lot by comparing yourself to such a great hero."

I smiled grimly. I could see the scouts smiling as well; they were enjoying this. "Why don't we play a little game, then," I said. "I will take this blade and leave mine behind. You wait until I'm dead like he is, and we'll see who's more famous. In the meantime, I have things to kill. Sergeant"—I nodded to the scout—"please be kind enough to follow this man to the storage room and secure enough blades for the scout company. And a few extras, perhaps."

I turned and strode off, the scout captain with me, while the curator stood sputtering next to the sergeant.

AFTER THREE DAYS of training, most of the scouts looked comfortable with the blades, and with the new drills I'd shown them. They were as good as promised: mostly on the small side, but fast and tough and able to run for hours at need. More women ended up in the scouts than in line infantry, and scout units in general seemed to be a lot more diverse than line units, which tended to be mostly composed of soldiers from their home region.

I had picked out the comparative handful of scouts I planned to take with me in the active part of the fight, stationing the others at crossroads and a few other places I thought would be likely places for fey to cross, letting the cold iron in the scouts' blades act as a deterrent and, hopefully, encourage the enemy to head for the trap that I was baiting with myself and a blade famously hated by fey. I liked setting traps: I had a knack for knowing what people would believe. This would be my first chance to see if it worked on fey as well.

I had surprised Nemias when he asked how many channelers I needed for the fight and I said *none*. But I did borrow a channeler from the town beforehand, one who had created a fair number of engagement tokens.

The fey swarmed us before I knew whether the trap would work. An isolated group of scouts marking trees to cut for fortification-building, led by a lone officer with a famous fey-killing blade, must have been too much temptation to pass up. Especially since being silent, magical, and all-but invisible unless your target knew what to look for did give them a natural advantage despite their small numbers and smaller stature.

What had been an empty clearing suddenly filled. Giant ravens swooped from above, aiming for eyes and faces. Woodsprites leaped out to grab at axes, jumping from trees onto troopers' backs, long knives slicing at exposed necks or knees.

Seemingly exposed, anyway. I had thought the fey might see through disguised blades to the lethal layer of cold iron, even magically disguised ones. But the thin layered strips filled with memories of cutting wood and blazing trails seemed to have hidden them effectively. The fey barely had time to recoil as the disguises fell from the blades.

I smiled as I lifted the Snake Slayer's blade—my blade now. Time seemed to slow down as I stepped forward. I felt like I had time to plan each cut precisely: beheading the first woodsprite, severing a raven's wing, slicing the hand from another woodsprite before its knife could connect with a scout's neck.

The fight took only seconds. Two of the scouts were wounded. Eleven fey lay dead or writhing from the pain of cold iron. The others fled or flew.

We took no prisoners, after what they had done to our soldiers. Afterward, I marked each of them with the Snake Slayer's blade, for whatever fey recovered their bodies to see.

Eleven fey dead would have been like losing a regiment to us; their numbers were few in the mountains. For all of their hatred of the humans who had expanded into their forests and mountains after the gods they fought beside had abandoned them at the Holy War's end, fey rarely attacked unless sure of a relatively painless victory. The attacks on Nemias's troops and supply lines ceased, and within a few weeks I had been recalled to another battlefield.

Sperrin
Mud Otter Crossing: Eleven years before the Loss

"This is going to be a god-sucking fiasco," Nemias said to me under his breath. That had become something of a catch-phrase for Bhales, and very nearly managed to be her last words. (Her actual last words had been the more soldierly "Don't let the beer go to waste.") Of course we'd told her husband, a scholar and poet who'd become famous for a book of children's verses he'd written before it became apparent that the Empress wasn't about to let a company commander with a reputation for coolness under pressure leave the service to raise children, that his name had been the last thing she'd said.

A channeler or bureaucrat could raise children and continue to do the job the Empress had assigned, with the help of nurses. For a field soldier that simply wasn't possible. Which was why I saw so little of my own daughter, whom I had to practically become reacquainted with every time I took leave.

Bhales had been a soldier for forty years, since she'd been a teenager, but Nemias and I were practically the only soldiers at her funeral. If Bhales had died fighting at the head of her company, her soldiers would have been given a few days to mourn, rotated off the line and allowed to hold a burial ceremony. But she had died after a long sickness, eventually sent home to convalesce when the cough she acquired at Davynen set into her lungs. Rotating a company off the line for a few days was at worst a minor inconvenience for the new governor-general. Giving a company two weeks leave and alloting transportation to a funeral was unthinkable to the governor who had browbeaten an army to victory at Davynen, and who personally oversaw the army's logistics with complex schedules of his own devising. The army ate better and traveled faster than it ever had, but leaves no longer occurred outside of precise timetables, and commanders who used more supplies or took more casualties than the schedules provided for found themselves swiftly transferred elsewhere.

For Nemias and I, promotion in the wake of that campaign had removed us from the governor's command and sent us to other fights, only the one at Kelpie Aqueduct together. But our work together in bleak causes had led to a new posting: After the funeral we would be serving a different governor and his appointed captain-general by taking joint tactical command of an expedition along the Powder River, where we were expected to clear defensive emplacements along both banks of the river to allow troop transports safe passage. Command of the expedition had been declined by a number of more senior officers as operationally hopeless. Even the captain-general in nominal charge of the expedition had chosen to remain behind with the rear guard at the fortified river port where we would begin the expedition. The better to ensure our supply lines, he explained, but also the better to avoid blame for the expedition's failure. It had been ordered by the Empress against the advice of her senior military advisers; it would be carried out.

Having found two successful overcaptains willing to take the tactical command—and the responsibility—for the expedition, the captain-general was more than willing to grant us leave to attend an old comrade's funeral while he massed supplies and troops at the depot. We spent the trip poring over maps and supply lists and gaming out tactics, along with the pair of sublieutenants who'd been dispatched as aides. We'd given them the morning off; they would attend enough interment ceremonies for friends over the next few months without asking them to mourn a captain they'd never served with.

That was how we'd gotten to the funeral. Now a part of me was wondering why. Military funerals tended to be short and to the point. An officer spoke about the service the soldier had rendered for the empire and the army, recited the soldier's service record, or at least the interesting parts of it, and comrades might share some memories. Then the body was interred while a band played the "Dead Trooper's March" (which had another name that no one ever used) and perhaps a few favorite songs of the deceased, then closed by playing the company and regimental themes. Then everyone retired to a mess tent or restaurant, depending on where the funeral took place, got gloriously drunk, sang a bit more, and told exaggerated stories about the dead soldier.

At this funeral, no one but Nemias and I even wore blades. People recited poetry, and most of them barely seemed to have known Bhales. Unless she had a very different sense of humor on leave than she did with the army. Mostly, people comforted the husband, who I gathered had written or translated most of the poems people were reading. Bhales *had* loved poetry, so it wasn't totally inappropriate, but the ceremony was a lot more reflective and less celebratory than I expected. With a lot less drinking.

I never had much of an ear for poetry, and couldn't really tell a good poem from a bad one—something Bhales had mocked me endlessly about. I suppose these were good ones, but the only ones that really stuck with me were a series of translations and modern renderings from old verses. Toward the end a young man with a beautiful baritone voice sang a haunting version of "Keir's Lament." The traditional version, which I'd read in school but never cared for, mostly focused on the politics of the Holy War's end, and on social mores that no longer existed. The husband's adaptation cut to the heart of the story: General Keir's stunning victory in battle, tempered by the loss of his sons and the disappearance of his wife Juila, herself a major figure in the war; his search for the missing Juila, hampered by enemies and allies alike who didn't want wounds reopened that the treaty negotiations had barely papered over; and his embittered marginalization at the very moment that a triumphant empire celebrated his exploits and made his name synonymous with victory. While the young man sang, I understood for a moment Bhales's love for poetry, and the clarity it could bring to emotions that otherwise defied description. But then the next speaker started reciting something about children bathing that I'm sure was a metaphor for something in this curious world outside the army that I visited sometimes but didn't live in.

By the end of it, Nemias and I were sitting in the back row, heads bowed to look respectful, while we planned out skirmish tactics for the river campaign.

Ketya
Delamyen Province: Eleven years before the Loss

I was eight years old when I first realized my mother was sick. By then she must have been pretty far along, but she lived another year. It was one of those diseases that preys on channelers, one of the side effects of magic if you're really unlucky. It affected a lot of channelers who had served at Davynen, and even though she'd only been there a little while, she caught it too. Her lungs gradually solidified and it was harder and harder for her to breathe. But I didn't know any of that at the time. I just know that my mother had less energy, and walking from one room to another would wear her out.

Until I realized there was something really wrong, it was a sort of golden age for me. I had never been so happy. My mother had always been so busy with her duties for the Empress that my moments with her were precious and fleeting. Now we spent hours together: I would sit cross-legged next to her on her giant bed, pink satin coverlets swirling all around us, and she would help me with my reading and history. She would tell me long stories when I asked her questions. Now I can see that she was trying to teach me all she could in the time she had left, but at the time I just felt glad for the attention.

For a while my father was around a lot, too. Then he was gone all the time, and more and more easily provoked when he was home. I had never seen my father lose control before, but when he was in the room with my mother sometimes he would forget I was there and cry. Usually he would send me to the nursery, unless my mother asked me to stay.

Then he was away for a long time, and by the time he got back, my mother had faded badly. She could barely shuffle across the room with me helping, and she gasped for breath at every step. I had finally realized that she was really sick, that it wasn't something that was going to get better. I still had no idea that she could die from it, and nobody told me that. She just spent all the time with me that she could.

When my father came back, he took me for a long walk, and explained, sort of, how he had spoken with a god—he didn't say which one, even when I asked—and traded my name for my mother's healing. I remembered what my mother had told me about gods wanting human names, so it made sense to me. The part about trickery hadn't really registered. It was a very good thing that I had done, my father told me, even though I hadn't done anything. Everything would be all right now, he said. I would have a new name when my mother healed.

Then she didn't heal. She didn't fade any faster, but by then she was close to the end. Finally she couldn't breathe at all, and her own lungs drowned her.

There were no more walks with my father. No more gentle explanations. When he gave me my mother's name after her death he told me it was to honor her memory, but I knew better. He gave me my mother's name to punish me for failing to save her.

I don't know how he adjusted all the records or if he even had to. Ananya's history was riddled with people who had lost or changed names, so the channelers who administered the records surely had ways to deal with it. If anyone knew anything about my name changing, they never said it to me.

I know I didn't literally kill my mother. She spent so much time with me that year, and I was so happy. I wonder if she had any time left for herself, or for my father. When the god accepted my name as a sacrifice and then failed to heal my mother, I think it broke my father's heart. He had to face my mother's death for the first time. He had already had to face not being able to save her himself. When my name wasn't enough to save her either, part of him just withdrew from us. He focused on saving the empire because he couldn't save her.

My father had learned how to speak with gods, but that still wasn't enough to save the person he loved most in the world. What chance did I have? I didn't have my mother's gifts or my father's wisdom. Why would the gods think my name was worth my mother's life? It wasn't, of course. If I'd been a prodigy, or had more of my mother's raw channeling talent, my name might have been enough. I was only nine years old. What else did he have to trade? They kept the name. But it wasn't enough.

If I'd been a little more talented I might have saved her. I might have saved our family. Up until that point, I think my father had high hopes for me, but when the god didn't give him back my mother in return for my name, he must have decided that I didn't have the potential to become as talented as he and my mother were. I tried to earn back his trust, but what could I do? Every time he looked at me it must have reminded him that my name wasn't worth enough to redeem the life of the woman he loved.

Sperrin
Whitmount: Eleven years before the Loss

At the end of a successful fighting season, the captain-general sent Nemias and me on long leaves while he took on the logistics of staging supplies and reinforcements for the following spring when the offensive resumed. I think he was concerned that all the fighting I had done over the last seventeen years would eventually impact my effectiveness as a commander. He was more right than he knew, although before that winter, the possibility had never occurred to me. I enjoyed what I did—as someone who had become one of the Empress's favorite officers, I had the freedom to plan and execute battles as I saw fit. I had the freedom to participate in those battles on a personal level as well. I killed a lot of enemy soldiers, directly and indirectly.

Not until that winter did it occur to me that just how much I had come to enjoy killing might become a problem.

I had never had any problem differentiating between the time I spent soldiering and the other parts of my life. Somehow, that winter, the barriers that separated the different parts of my identity began to break down.

At first, the leave went normally: visits to the families of fallen soldiers, a special party for my daughter to celebrate all the holidays I had missed spending with her, a formal dinner with my wife and her sister and several other prominent channelers. Our marriage hadn't been especially close for a while—both of us had so immersed ourselves in our careers that we seldom exchanged messages while I was at the front, beyond a few lines I would enclose with the letters and packages I sent to our daughter. But it had been comfortable enough, like any Ananyan marriage. Now, however, I sensed a greater distance between us, and wondered if years of fighting had begun to change me. It felt as if my wife had been replaced by one of the fey from the Kelpie Aqueduct. As if my wife, the woman I loved with all my heart despite our differences, had been disconnected from my life and an alien creature left behind.

A day later, when the idea of killing her entered my mind as if from nowhere, I knew something had changed. Later, when I found out the secrets she kept from me, it would have been easy to blame Sefa for the urge to murder that I could barely restrain. But that wasn't it. Her secrets may have increased the emotional distance between us, but the feelings that threatened to overwhelm me came from too many years on the battlefield, not from any choices my wife made. She hadn't changed, I had. I could return home, but I could no longer leave the battlefield behind.

We were out walking in an indoor winter market, my daughter skipping beside me and holding my hand while Sefa walked ahead to browse stalls that didn't interest Lynniene. Something felt off. I found myself looking at Sefa the way I looked at an enemy soldier I was stalking, my mind providing kill moves each time she took a step. The other people in the market felt like alien strangers, not targets but not potential friends either. Only Lynniene, skipping beside me, happy to finally have me home, seemed normal to me. I loved my daughter as much as ever.

So why did I suddenly feel the urge to kill her mother?

More horrifying: Was this an urge I might give in to in an unguarded moment? So far it felt abstract, something I could do, not something I had to do. But why was I feeling it at all?

That evening after I'd put Lynniene to bed, Sefa and I found ourselves alone together in our bedroom. The room looked like it had barely been slept in during the months I'd been gone; I knew Sefa often stayed with her sister or other friends during our long separations. Tonight she seemed friendlier, though, as if she sensed that the distance between us had grown too wide and we needed to find a way to come closer together.

We talked a little, mostly about shopping and about our daughter. Even when we had felt closer, the first days together after months of living separate lives felt disconnected. But tonight I found myself reluctant to ease the disconnectedness. Eventually, drowsiness began to catch up with us. We lay together in the center of the big bed, not quite asleep but not talking anymore. I couldn't shut my mind off: Every time Sefa shifted I automatically thought of the easiest move to kill her, as if I slept next to an enemy rather than the person who loved me, and whom I loved. The person whom I couldn't help loving, ever since my first, magical introduction to her.

Why did my mind want me to view her as an enemy?

Drowsily, Sefa snuggled back against me. "Make love to me," she said.

Sperrin
Powder River Campaign: Eleven years before the Loss

I slipped into the headquarters tent so silently that nobody noticed me at first. Then Nemias looked up sharply.

"Sperrin! You're hurt!"

"No, I'm fine. I needed a long walk."

"You're covered in blood," he said.

I lifted the baldric over my shoulder and hung my blade from one of the pegs on a free-standing rack. Then I stripped off my sodden shirt and hung it from another hook, careful not to let the bloody cloth touch the blade.

An aide stepped forward with a towel and a bowl of warm water. I scrubbed off my chest and arms, soaking my face for a long moment in the warmth of the wet towel before looking up at Nemias.

"What happened out there tonight?" he asked me. The aide had vanished, to find me something to eat and give us some privacy.

I shrugged. "There are fourteen alliance troopers and their covering channeler in a forward ambush post who won't be troubling us when we advance tomorrow. I left the post in possession of some troopers from the Silvercoast Sharks."

Nemias looked concerned. "Again? This is the third time this week you've gone off like that."

"And each time it's made things a little easier for our troopers. What's the problem?"

He seemed to pick his words carefully. "Sperrin, you know I love you like a brother. And we've fought together for years. I love nothing better than fighting beside you…" He trailed off.

"But?"

"But you're the co-commander of this expedition, and our battle planner. what if you died out there? Then what would we do?"

"But I didn't die."

He sighed. "Sperrin, I think you're a little out of control."

I snorted. "This is how I find control."

Nemias shook his head. "Most people go on leave to recover themselves from what we do in battle. But you just came back from leave."

"I'm fine," I said. "I'll be fine. We have a campaign to win."

"You can't win it all by yourself, Sperrin."

That sort of missed the point, although I couldn't say so to Nemias. The almost-daily fighting along the Powder River was only part of the campaign I was fighting. I saw my wife in the face of every Alliance soldier I killed. Sometimes I had started to see friends and neighbors as well. But always my wife, the woman I loved more than anyone other than my daughter.

I could win the fights in the Powder River campaign. But sooner or later, we would win the last battle, and then I would be sent on leave again. And then what would I do?

IT TOOK TIME for me to admit Nemias was right. I couldn't sustain the path I was on, despite my efforts to burn the awful desire out of me by killing soldiers who really *were* enemies. Some days for a few hours I could lose myself in the joy of fighting and winning against a strong foe. But always my thoughts would circle back to the inevitable end of the campaign and where it would lead. To my wife and all the others I cared about, who I was becoming a danger to.

That didn't mean I would do anything to slow our victory. I wouldn't let myself or any of the soldiers under my command lose focus as we forced a retreat, beat back a counterattack, and now faced what most of the army saw as the climactic battle of the campaign. For me the climax had been months ago when the Alliance commander first fell into the trap Nemias and I had set up, a trap that would draw shut tomorrow. But if that had been apparent to anyone else, the Alliance would never have fallen into it. At the time, and for weeks afterward, they thought they had taken the initiative in the campaign.

I hoped I would still be able to savor the victory. In the meantime, I needed to find a solution to the problem tearing me apart.

Or I had to follow through on the solution I had already decided on, however painful it might prove.

I waited until every detail of tomorrow's battle had been set into place. I wouldn't be fighting hand-to-hand unless the trap failed—unless a lot of things failed, actually. In this battle, troops and terrain would be holding the Alliance army in place while our channelers hit them. Among other things, my activities since returning from leave had exacerbated a shortage of channelers in the Alliance army we faced: Unless all of the scouts I had sent misread the situation, it would be difficult for the Alliance to counter the trap that was about to close on them.

The last troops posted in position, I walked off the wall I'd marked as observation post for Nemias and me tomorrow and strode toward the channelers' quarters to see Khemme.

AS SENIOR CHANNELER for my regiment, Khemme enjoyed private quarters, one of the few privileges of her position that she took advantage of. I had known her since I'd been a junior subcaptain in one of my first postings. Khemme's husband commanded the regiment—such pairings were uncommon, but not unknown. As the newest subcaptain with the regiment, I commanded the detail assigned to protect the engineers and channelers, not a safe post exactly since every enemy attack targeted the channelers if at all possible, but a relatively easy one for an officer whose capabilities remained unknown to his overcaptain. Plus, I'd been assigned to the regiment because of the death of the previous subcaptain holding that job.

This was at the Battle of Perrilen Fields, just before the big Alliance counterattack. Our regiment broke through the enemy's front in that first, mad assault and then the salient collapsed around us as the Alliance poured in reinforcements. We had to abandon the war-engines and fall back fast, with Khemme's husband and what had been the vanguard of the regiment the only thing protecting our rear. In the end it came down to hand-to-hand fighting, with me and a handful of troopers holding a swarm of attackers off us—and Khemme protecting us from magical lightning bursts boiling down from the sky. We held until the Alliance attack lost its fury, and finally until we were relieved. Three days later, we received her husband's body back in an exchange of prisoners and remains.

Khemme never remarried—sometimes people did, but it seemed to be less important to the Empress than arranging first marriages. And Khemme didn't seem to be inclined to push the process.

She answered the door in trousers and an undertunic, comfortable clothes for around camp. "Good evening, 'Captain. I was just having dinner in my quarters. Would you care to join me?"

"Thank you, I would be happy to." We shared meals sometimes. Her husband had saved us both, and we'd saved each other's lives more than once, so we felt a certain connectedness even in the years we'd spent in separate regiments. I'd been glad to have her serving with me this campaign: There were more powerful channelers in the army—and my wife was a *much* more powerful channeler—but Khemme knew soldiers and engineers and how to work with them. She never created friction and with her as senior channeler, no one else did either.

After a few pleasantries we ate in silence while she waited for me to tell her what I'd come for. Khemme had a stocky, soldier's frame, unlike most channelers, who tended to have a more willowy look. She wore her blond hair cropped short.

"I need to ask advice in confidence," I finally said. She nodded, and I already trusted her. "After the battle tomorrow, I think I need to ask for a transfer away from the front. I think I need you to ask the Empress for me."

That didn't seem to be the question Khemme expected, but she didn't look shocked, either. She asked a few questions, and I found myself describing what had happened, and my growing inability to separate loved ones from targets.

"It happens sometimes," she said. "You have been at the front a long time. You may need a longer rest than a leave can give you."

"That's what I think," I answered. "If I can take time away from it, my mind will stop playing these games. Things can be better with Sefa again." I think that was more hopefulness than what I actually felt, but at the time it never occurred to me that Sefa and Lynniene and I wouldn't be together if I could work out the problem. For all my battlefield tactical skill, it never occurred to me there might be deeper problems I couldn't see.

I think it may have occurred to Khemme, but she didn't say so, at least not directly. "The Empress values your service very much," Khemme said instead. "I think she will be very reluctant to let you go."

"I'm not sure how much my service will be worth if I can't solve this. It's hard to give my best when I'm afraid of what I'll do when I go home."

She nodded. "True." Something seemed to occur to her. "Why not talk to Nolene? She has the Empress's ear, much more than I do."

"What would I tell her? 'I want to kill your sister. Soon I may want to kill you, too'? How do you think that will go?"

"Also true. I will do what I can."

I could tell she had something else she wanted to say, so I waited.

"I once felt the same way. When my husband died, after Perrilen Fields, I felt very angry for a long time." She waved away my response. "I know I didn't show it, but for a long time, I killed people for my husband's sake. Like you, I saw his face instead of the people I killed. I didn't want to kill him, but I wanted to kill *for* him. And like you, I didn't like what it did to me after a while."

"What did you do?"

She shrugged. "It passed. Your problem is deeper than mine was, I think. Perhaps you should focus more on the people you kill—their names, their faces. Kill who you need to, but don't give them your wife's face."

I nodded. "Will that help?"

"Not really. It will make it easier for you to keep going until the Empress responds to your request, though. These things don't always happen quickly. I don't have Nolene's influence, but I will make the case for a transfer away from combat."

"Just for a little while, until things settle down with Sefa." *If they settle down*, I knew. But I couldn't say that. Khemme knew, though.

"I will do my best," she said again. "Try to be patient."

"I've been trying," I said. "I've been trying to get through it in other ways, but it's not working. And now I feel like I'm out of time. We're going to win this battle tomorrow, and if we win it well, the Alliance army we're facing will be destroyed. And after that, in a few months at most they're going to send me home on leave again. I'm just not sure I can handle it."

"For a little while you can," Khemme said, but her eyes were sad.

Ketya
Ialanye City: Ten years before the Loss

It wasn't quite true that I didn't see my father at all between the speech he made at my mother's funeral and his ascension to chancellor of Ananya, but mostly I saw him at a distance. He had always worked intensely, and now he threw himself into his role as provincial governor even more intensely, as a poor consolation for the wife he had lost, and the daughter who had been unequal to the task of returning her to life.

I think it was too painful for him to even look at me sometimes. He would stay at work until long after my bedtime. In the morning he would already be at work when I breakfasted; the nurses would give me pitying looks and tell me that he had looked in on me while I slept, and that they could see in my father's eyes how much he loved me.

By then the nurses and other servants felt almost like family to me. My parents had maintained a very formal household, but with my father gone most of the time things relaxed a lot. Many of the servants had kids around my age, and I was allowed to play with them as long as all my lessons and all their work was done. It also meant I got to run around town with them, and meet some of their friends. I hadn't really been out of the house much since my mother had gotten sick: not that anyone was trying to hide me away, but at the time I was too young to go out without someone supervising me, and no one was willing to suggest it with my mother sick. So it felt great to actually have a chance to play outside with other kids again, instead of spending all my time in the nursery with the same toys I'd had since I was eight, or in the library with my tutors.

My father did tell me about his promotion to chancellor firsthand, though. He had been summoned to the capitol immediately, but took the time to stop by the house and order lunch set for both of us. He even asked the cooks to serve my favorite foods. It was funny; we'd seen each other so little since my mother died that he didn't know what I liked to eat anymore, but he knew that the cooks would. So we sat, just the two of us, at the huge dining table, and I nibbled on all of my favorite things—there was too much to do more than nibble—while he spun stories about how wonderful things in the capitol would be, and how much I could learn there and how I would be meeting the Empress herself.

"I can't wait to tell my friends!" I said. Somehow it didn't occur to me that I wasn't going to see them again.

"You will need to pack," my father said, unusually patient. "The nurses will need help closing up the household and packing the things that will be going on to the city. I will be leaving tonight, and you will be following as soon as our things are packed. You will be traveling with our things. Someone from the palace will be coming to escort you."

"Why do we need an escort? I'm sure the nurses can get me there. I'm not a baby anymore."

"Of course not. That is why the nurses will not be coming with you. The household staff has been reassigned by the Empress, at my request. They will be leaving as soon as the house is packed. The new governor who replaces me will want his own staff, and we will have new servants at the palace in the Drowned City."

The implications of all these changes were too big to take in. I ventured a question: "What about my friends? Will I see them again?"

Tears welled in my eyes, and my father must have noticed them. "Don't cry," he said. "This is a time to celebrate, not to cry. I know that you think this move will be painful. But the people you are leaving behind are servants. You don't have any real friends, so it won't hurt to move the way you think. At the palace there will be more appropriate friends, and your life will be better."

That didn't make me any less sad, but I knew my father would be happier if I held back my tears, so I did. I didn't want the last thing he saw as he walked out of the house to take on his new responsibilities to be the crying daughter he left behind him.

Chapter 3

Sperrin
Powder River Campaign: Ten years before the Loss

After the massacre at Powder Gap that all-but ended the Powder River Campaign, Nemias and I were both decorated again, and put on the short list for promotion to captain-general. But that battle had burned the killing out of me—or at least that's what I tried to convince myself. It let me pretend that I wasn't on the edge of becoming a monster. I hadn't lost my love of killing, or the enjoyment I got from it, but what I felt it was doing to me terrified me in a way no enemy ever had—the kind of husband and father I was afraid I was about to become. Nemias was the only one I told about my conversation with Khemme asking her to request my transfer away from the front.

I didn't really expect him to understand, and he didn't. He told me he thought I was an idiot and why he thought so. Then we got gloriously drunk, and he told me he'd support whatever I decided, idiot or not. "Go if you need to," he said. "You'll be back." We were both drunk, but the words stayed with me. Then we didn't say another word about it over the next few months of mopping up, while I waited for the Empress's decision. When I went on leave to see my family I dreaded my homecoming, but I had no idea I wouldn't be coming back to my command again.

Nemias and I didn't meet again for ten years. I think he kept his distance out of respect for my choice. Mostly what we had in common was killing, and I think he knew it would be too easy for him to draw me back into that life, despite everything I had given up to get away from it.

Besides, he had already told me he knew I would be back.

As it turned out, he was right.

THE LAST NIGHT before my leave began, I received an unexpected visitor. The junior officers had thrown me an unofficial "sendoff party," knowing that I would be leaving in the morning, and that the extended victory celebration of soft duty that the campaign's end had become would be over. Nemias had left early, pleading morning duties, but I had stayed to the end.

I stepped into my quarters, a little tipsy, definitely more relaxed than I had been in some time.

Immediately my blade was in my hand. "Who's there?" I said.

"It's me. You know me." A familiar voice.

A light came on without my touching it, illuminating the room.

Nolene, my sister-in-law, sat in one of my two chairs, leaning against the back wall of the small room. "We need to talk, Sperrin," she said.

"Why?" I asked warily. I lowered my blade, though.

"I think you know," she said. She didn't look angry, exactly. Disappointed. Her eyes darkening like a storm waiting to break. "You are about to destroy my sister's life. Maybe mine as well. Isn't that something that merits a conversation?"

"Destroy?" I said. That didn't sound anything like what I had done. "I am trying not to hurt her. All I asked is to leave this place, with her, and to heal. Together."

"And what makes you think she would want to leave with you?" asked Nolene, one eyebrow arched.

Again, the question baffled me. "We're married. We go where the Empress orders. Together."

"Just like that. Has it occurred to you she might be happier when you are away?"

It hadn't occurred to me. How could it? Since the day I had opened the first leaf of the engagement token, I had never thought that we would do anything but spend our lives together. Weren't we meant for each other? That was exactly why the violent impulses I felt toward her disturbed me so much.

"Oh, come now," she said, seeing my disbelieving expression. "You can't be *that* naive, can you?"

I continued to stare.

She laughed bitterly. "You really *are* that naive. Brilliant soldier, toy of the Empress, able to read the enemy's mind. And you honestly believe Sefa loves you."

"But…how could she not? How could anyone not? We were engaged."

"You were. I made the tokens myself—a special honor from the Empress, because she favored me and my sister. Not for much longer, after what you've done. Something you may not know: There's a charm on the tokens that makes the person they're intended for want to open them. Only, if the person *does-n't* want to open it and she's the person you love most in the world, maybe you don't put the charm on." Her eyes grew stormier as she talked, though the anger still didn't show on her face, only in her voice and eyes.

"She never opened the engagement token? How is that even possible? Don't they check?"

"They check if the token has been opened, of course. But I made it, so of course I could unmake it. It was easy enough to discharge the magic. Who would question me when I said my sister discharged it herself? They heard what they expected to hear."

That stumped me. "Why wouldn't Sefa want to be married?" I asked.

"Because she already loved someone else, you idiot. You think she want-ed to forget the love of her life just because some soldier-of-the-week has won a few battles and caught the Empress's attention? Sefa already knew her heart. She married you because she had to, and pretended to love you because you weren't home very often and didn't ask for too much. And every time you went back to battle she could be herself again." Nolene held up a hand to forestall a response. "She didn't hate you, if that's what you're thinking. She even came to like you a little, I think. Respect you at least, which is more than I would have. And as long as there was no hope, she could act the part well enough that you believed it."

"But…?" None of this made any sense, but why would Nolene lie? Why would she tell me she'd lied to the Empress and cheated on her orders? Why ask for a death sentence?

"But last fall, her true love finally managed to leave his wife behind and move near Whitmount—near enough for a channeler whose husband only came home twice a year. I had made his engagement token too, you see. And I discharged it the same way I did with Sefa's. Once he lived nearby her duties let her travel a lot"—duties that Nolene arranged, as the senior channeler in Whitmount, I knew—"and she was finally happy again. And then last winter you came home and you knew. I don't know how but she could see it in your eyes, in the way you looked at her. You knew and you never said anything, just glared at her like you wanted to kill her."

I did want to kill her, I thought, but didn't say it. "I didn't know." Which was true, as far as it went.

Nolene looked at me disbelievingly.

"If you didn't know, why send what you did to the Empress? And why send it through some regimental half-channeler instead of through me so I could make sure it never got any farther? Because of the way you sent it there will be an investigation, and everything will come out."

"Why would it?" I asked. "And why should I help keep your secrets if you've been lying to me for all these years?"

Now she smiled, like a feral cat looking at its intended prey. "Because," she said, "you don't know the official reason I'm here. And if you say a word of what I've told you, it won't just destroy Sefa and me, it will destroy your favorite comrade in arms."

"What are you talking about?"

"The Empress's order that brought me here. The order that will already be carried out when she hears what you did. The order that will save my life. Tonight I was engaged to the most recent unmarried war hero to catch the Empress's fancy. Your friend Overcaptain Nemias opened the engagement token when he returned from your going away party." She didn't even try to hide the disgust in her voice.

Neither did I. "What happened to your token?" I asked.

"I still have it," she said. "Channelers are given a lot of latitude—it's assumed no one needs to fool us into looking at the tokens, as long as they're discharged afterward. And I've had practice at discharging one undetected. I'm sure if Sefa can fool you for so many years I'll have little difficulty fooling your dance partner. Especially since he'll love me as completely as you loved Sefa, and be home just as little."

"You're right," I said. "He will believe you. He will love you utterly."

I lifted my arm swiftly. The dark edge of my blade touched her throat. We both held utterly still. A trickle of blood dripped down her neck and onto her shoulder.

"Now, very slowly, take out the token," I said. "I know how magic works. I am very good at killing enemy channelers, and right now, you are an enemy. Try to use your magic and this blade finishes you." I applied the tiniest pressure. More blood flowed.

Slowly, she took the token out from the folds of her tunic.

The storm had passed. I saw real fear in her eyes.

"Now take the first leaf," I said. "You know how."

Her face widened in shock as what I wanted her to do hit her. More blood touched her shoulder.

Slowly, she lifted the first leaf.

Involuntarily, she relaxed.

"Now the next one," I said.

After the third one, I didn't need to say anymore. Nolene never noticed as I withdrew my blade and wiped the edge clean of her blood. She was too caught up in her blossoming love for my friend, my friend who could never, ever know that I had done this, or that his wife's love was anything but willing.

He deserved that. She—I wasn't sure what she deserved, but I felt no sympathy for Nolene. Especially when she left my quarters filled with love and excitement at the thought of marrying the man she now knew to be her soulmate.

In spite of everything, in spite of the secret about my own wife that I would have to pretend not to know for Nemias's sake, I slept better than I had in months.

Chapter 4

Much of the Drowned City hadn't survived the Holy War. It had another name then, Seacliff, but people stopped calling it that after gods sunk the great cliffs into the ground in an attempt to shorten their siege. They summoned great waves that swept walls away, and massive sea creatures that ravaged the city's fishing fleet. Still, the Drowned City continued to fight. When the war ended, the city, still half-submerged, was named capital of the Ananyan Empire as a last act of defiance to the withdrawing gods.

The sea creatures never left, so the city's residents fortified the harbor, and replaced the fishing fleet with a seaborne hunting fleet. They built great levees to hold back the tides from the remaining neighborhoods, and built massive walls to withstand storms and sieges. Bounded by ocean and river, they built upward instead of outward: The city's heart became a sea of towers and tall houses, in the shadow of a massive palace—built on top of the half-ruined structure that had withstood the worst the Holy War could throw at it.

The series of wars Ananya had fought with the surrounding nations since the Holy War had taken place far from the Drowned City. Over the years the empire's capital had prospered, had been made as beautiful as a half-submerged, sea-monster-infested city could be made.

That much, every kid my age in Ananya knew. Before my mother died, the capitol had been a faraway, exotic place. Now it would be home.

AS IT TURNED out, my journey to the palace in the Drowned City took a lot longer than my father's. Cable-carriages carried people quickly throughout the developed part of the Ananyan Empire but an almost-ten-year-old girl accompanying a household worth of possessions had no need to travel fast. I took a flatboat downriver to the sea, where my guards and I became the sole passengers on a refrigerated vegetable transport ship traveling between the vast farm belt on Ananya's eastern coastal plain and the capital city at the edge of the jagged cliffs to the north.

Much as I loved the sea voyage at first, it got monotonous after a few days of slowly churning along the coast. The soldiers and the ship's sparse crew didn't really want to talk, and the ship's channeler, an ancient woman who crocheted endless pairs of mittens in the ship's bridge while staring straight ahead into nowhere, couldn't talk and keep the huge screws that propelled the ship turning at the same time. She would talk a little at dinner, after the ship had anchored for the night, but mostly she wanted to talk about how much I looked like her grandchildren. By the second day of the trip I had unpacked some books from one of the trunks so I could study them whenever the scenery faded from captivating to dull.

By the time we approached the great city the landscape had turned to bands of farms and orchards, and the seascape had become crowded. Freighters, warships, transports, and hunting ships scudded back and forth across the ocean in front of the distant towers that slowly grew against the cliffs on the horizon. Almost everything seemed to move faster than our slow churning crawl. I hadn't wanted to leave home, but by now I was anxious to get away from the dullness of the ship and into the new city, even if it meant meeting a whole palace-worth of new people.

We spent most of a day lined up to enter the wide harbor mouth that fronted the Drowned City. Towers on either side of the harbor and interspersed in the harbor channel itself bristled with war-engines, and each ship had to stop and be inspected by guard-cutters before being given a path into the harbor. Bouys would flare magically along the path that had been temporarily cleared and then wink out in the ship's wake. Each ship was given a different channel through the harbor defenses, not in any pattern that I could figure out in an afternoon of watching.

Apparently, my father had come to regret my slow journey with his household baggage: When the officer on the cutter who boarded us realized that the ship contained me as well as vegetables, he sent for two channeler-powered tugs, and we were escorted directly into the harbor before a dozen ships lined up ahead of us. Crew members lowered my father's luggage onto one of the tugs even as the ship entered the harbor, and let me clamber down a rope ladder after it. By the time the vegetable ship turned to approach its assigned berth, the tug had detached and churned rapidly toward the palace docks.

The channeler who powered the tug looked decades younger than the one on the ship, younger than my mother had been even. She smiled and laughed as the tug cut smoothly through the harbor. She even let me stand beside her in the open-air pilot house, out of the way of the bustling crew, and pointed out the theaters and bathhouses and most famous towers to me. "Have fun tonight!" she said as I disembarked.

I followed the carts of luggage and the servants who'd been sent to fetch them into the stone-lined tunnels behind the docks that marked the seaside entrance to the palace.

Part of me hoped to see my father waiting on the docks for my arrival, but I knew how foolish that was. My father had an empire's worth of responsibilities, and I was in the safest place in the whole empire, in the care of skilled palace servants. I followed the luggage through endless wide, stone halls filled with people scurrying everywhere, everyone seeming in a rush. Everything sort of swam together—I felt incredibly tired. I remember seeing some sort of blue streaks on the walls out of the corner of my eye, but when I tried to focus on them the streaks disappeared. I saw only polished stone walls illuminated by the magical glow from what must have been thousands of decorative wall sconces.

I arrived in the barely furnished chamber I'd been assigned and found a pair of maids not much older than me waiting. A formal tunic and trousers had been laid out on the bed for me. The maids seemed just as rushed as everyone else: I'd hoped for something to eat and a quiet afternoon taking in the overwhelming new surroundings, but instead found myself being combed and cosseted and ornamented like a sheep at a fair.

"We have to hurry," one of the girls said, in a tone that made it sound like her life depended on it. "We barely have any time before the ceremony!"

IT'S JARRING TO suddenly forget your father's name, even if you're expecting it. This was the day I found out how much the Empress loved ceremony. The day I first met the Empress. As it turned out, she had thought I needed to be at the ceremony for it to be as special as possible. The Empress had made my father wait around the palace for more than a week until I got there and she could hold the accession ceremony. Until the ceremony, he wasn't formally the chancellor, just another advisor getting to know the ins and outs of the palace. But there was nothing he could do about it since she was the Empress. And once she told him what she wanted, he was responsible for bringing it off without a hitch. So he got to plan his own accession ceremony, on the condition that I was there.

At the time I didn't know he'd had a week to plan the ceremony, though. So the size of the crowd in the Presentation Chamber astonished me. Once they finished dressing me and preparing me, the two maids led me downstairs and more-or-less left me by the doorway. My father had probably appointed someone to make sure I got into the chamber correctly—it wasn't the sort of thing he would leave to chance—but no one except the two maids actually knew what I looked like, and they only knew because they'd been waiting in my room. So I stood around near the doorway watching the crowd swirl around me, until one of the young channelers who acted as ladies-in-waiting to the Empress realized who I was and walked me through the throngs in the vast chamber toward the Empress's throne.

Everything in the room glittered. I caught a glimpse of my father, resplendent in his formalwear, his face expressionless, his eyes taking everything in. I wanted to wade through the crowd to go to him and show him I had arrived, but palace ministers surrounded him and took all his attention. I realized I was being silly; of course he knew I was here safely, that would have been reported to him as soon as the ship reached the harbor.

I watched my father for as long as I could before the lady-in-waiting nudged me forward. He spoke elegantly and generously to everyone, and only someone who had grown up in his household would ever sense that he wanted to move things forward rather than linger in the glamour of the accession forever.

Suddenly I found myself in front of the Empress's throne, the Seat of Ananya itself. The throne sat on a raised platform with a semicircle of chairs around it, facing outward, where the Empress's consort and favorite ministers and attendants sat. An empty seat next to the throne would become my father's after the ceremony concluded.

I'm sure the room was still filled with people talking, but suddenly I felt as if I stood in a cone of silence, just me and the Empress. My parents had drilled the correct greeting and signs of respect on meeting the Empress into me from the moment I could talk, long before my mother was sick. Both of them knew I would meet the Empress someday, even if she seemed like a faraway fairy tale figure to me. At that moment, I was so glad that I didn't have to think. I started saying the ritual words of greeting, my voice barely above a whisper.

"Aren't you precious," the Empress said, leaning forward. Rich blonde hair framed her face. "You're so much quieter than your father." That just made me more self-conscious. Everyone was staring at me and it was supposed to be my father's party.

The Empress knew just what to say, though. "Come, sit with me for a minute." She gestured to the empty seat that would become my father's. "You can watch the ceremony from here. You must be very proud of your father." I nodded in agreement and walked to the seat. I couldn't make any words come out.

And then the room really did fall silent, as if there had been some sort of signal that I missed. Someone, a female voice I didn't recognize, called out my father's name and the sound resonated through the room. He stepped out of the glittering crowd, into the space before the throne that I had vacated. I heard him repeating the same phrases of greeting and respect that I had said, but they sounded so much more polished coming from him, more right. I was so glad the attention was on him, not on me anymore.

Then the Empress spoke: "Are you ready?"

"I am," he said.

"And you give this up willingly?"

"I do."

"Then speak your name, for the last time until you leave my service. Your name shall be a token to the gods that you serve your Empress. From this moment forward, when you speak, you shall speak with my voice, in accordance with the laws that govern us and the Talisman of Truce that binds us and allows us to live with gods in peace, where once there was only fighting."

I expected my father to speak his name then, but he didn't. He quoted from the Talisman treaty on the importance of names, and why the Empress and chancellor had to give theirs up as part of the bargain through which the magic flowed from the gods. He spoke of the goddess Senne, from whom Ananya's magic flowed, and of how she had offered to give up her magic and her life with her lover Kedessan in order to make sure that the treaty succeeded, and that the lives expended and the land laid waste by the war could finally begin to heal. He spoke of the ways that humans had healed the land and rebuilt also, and the great empire in Ananya that grew from Senne's sacrificed magic. I felt so proud to be Ananyan by the end of his speech. But I felt even prouder that people like my father and the Empress had sacrificed their own names to the gods so that the Ananyan Empire might continue to enjoy prosperity.

No one stirred when he stopped speaking. The whole glittering crowd stood silent.

And then he spoke his name.

The word echoed and filled the room. And it filled my mind, but I couldn't grab hold of it. I heard the sounds but the word eluded me. And then the sounds faded and the word was gone. And though I searched my mind, my father's name had vanished from my memory as if it had never been.

For a moment I wondered if the same thing had happened with my own name, the day he had come home and told me it was gone. But I don't think anyone noticed it going, not even me.

With the accession complete, the celebration began. The room filled with noise again, and performer after performer took the open space in front of the throne: dancers, musicians, puppeteers, mimes, a water spirit in a great glass vase wheeled in by liveried servants. More servants in livery brought in trays of food, and I saw more food heaped on the sideboards. I didn't stir from the chair, just tried to watch all I could. I don't think I could have moved if I tried. Someone brought me a plate of food—I'm not sure who. I guess I must have looked like I was going to pass out. My father had disappeared somewhere, probably working on the problems of the empire already. He wasn't one to stay at a party when there was no more business to be done there.

My head swam with it all. In all the dancing and glitter and music and intermingled conversations, I started to think I saw the blue streaks on the walls again, but once more they disappeared when I tried to focus.

I don't remember the end of the party. Like the feast at the lakeside chateau, at some point the dancers and performers merged with dreams. I woke up in my new room in my new bed to find myself surrounded by familiar objects. Someone had unpacked my trunks and hung up my clothes while I slept.

Sperrin
Whitmount: Nine years before the Loss

For years I couldn't remember my last day with my wife and daughter. Now, of course, I can remember it with painful clarity. It's hard not to assign extra weight to that day, because of what came after, but really it was just like every other day of that long leave, spending as much time as possible with my daughter and as little as possible with my wife. Somehow, Nolene's revelations had made the urge to kill Sefa subside somewhat, as if knowing what had triggered my initial reaction made it easier for my mind to cope with it. But if anything, the knowledge made a solution to the problem farther away. I knew I needed time away from fighting more than anything: Sefa's actions hadn't caused my reaction, and it could easily have been triggered by something else, regardless of anything she did or didn't feel for me. But when I asked Khemme's help in appealing to the Empress, I imagined that removing myself from the battlefield would allow Sefa and me to regain our feelings for each other and heal. Now I knew I would only be removing myself to another battlefield, a battle with the woman I couldn't help loving. A battle I had no desire to fight. Sefa's actions baffled and confused me, and I felt hurt that she didn't share my feelings for her, but she hadn't betrayed me. Her choice had been made before the Empress had arranged our marriage, and the soldier in me couldn't fault her loyalty to her first love, for all that the idea of disobeying an order from the Empress felt utterly alien to me. My tactical abilities failed me: I had no idea of how to fix these problems. All I could do was spend time with my daughter and wait for the Empress's solution.

I spent that morning playing with Lynniene, who was almost seven. My wife was working at the ministry offices. In the past sometimes she had taken time off when I was home on leave, but less so recently, for reasons Nolene had made me painfully aware of. I knew Sefa could sense how guarded I was around her, how I kept my distance, and she took it for something other than me trying to control my worst impulses. Wartime duties kept her busy as well. She and I had quarreled the night before, not over anything significant, since we both pretended not to sense the strain between us. It was easier to pretend that because we lived in different worlds, we didn't have anything much to say to each other. We would try to talk and end up fighting, mostly as a way to avoid really talking. The only thing we didn't fight about was Lynniene. Sefa was a good mother to Lynniene and, when I was home and not thinking about killing her mother, I think I was a good father to her.

I had no idea what, if anything, was being done about my request to the Empress. Enough time had passed that I suspected Nolene had managed to have it quashed by some friend at the palace before it reached the Empress's ear.

I had a week of leave left. Lynniene had a long list of places she wanted to visit and things she wanted to see that her mother was too busy to take her to. We were working our way down the list, methodically. With my status as a war hero on leave and my wife's position as a channeler in the ministry, very few places on Lynniene's list were closed to us: Life could be frustrating for a girl her age, so she looked forward to the rare times when I came home on leave, when all sorts of doors that were normally closed to her opened as if by magic.

When the messenger came saying that the Empress had responded to my request for a transfer, Lynniene and I were on our way back from a menagerie: a hothouse filled with a hundred kinds of flying lizards and poisonous reptiles collected by a retired captain-general whose son's life I'd saved on two occasions. He'd led the tour effusively and in person, finishing the visit with flavored ices, and Lynniene was telling me all about her favorite parts as if I hadn't been right there beside her the whole time.

Messengers from the Empress don't wait. I left Lynniene at the house with her nurse, giving her a kiss that I wish had been longer. Then I pulled on a dress cloak and the baldric that held my blade, and followed the messenger to the ministry building and the channeler representing the Empress in this matter: my sister-in-law, Nolene, which made things a bit uncomfortable.

She gave no sign that there had been any investigation, and seemed very much in control of herself and her position. I nodded to her in greeting, perhaps a little too grimly.

My request had, Nolene told me, been approved, effective immediately. There was, she said, a catch. She and my wife were best friends as well as sisters. She had already explained to me the price she and Sefa would pay for my request to the Empress. So I didn't understand why her smile looked so sincere.

"What is the catch," I asked.

"This," she said, and I found myself in a room full of strangers.

A coach awaited me outside, and the same messenger guided me to it, though I had no idea I'd ever seen her before. In twenty minutes I was at the carriage platform, waiting for the next cable-carriage out of the mountains. In a little more than a day I reported for duty in the Drowned City.

The Empress had left me with most of my memories: childhood, youth, battles, promotions, glory. Only marriage and fatherhood were gone, excised smoothly enough that until the night the Empress died I never knew they had existed.

Ketya
The Drowned City: Nine years before the Loss

When I first came to the palace, some of the kids would use the old theater as a sort of clubhouse. No one else ever came there, and something old and oppressive permeated the atmosphere. Despite the theater's huge cathedral ceiling, somehow the air felt like it was pushing down on you. Unlike the other old parts of the palace, I never saw a hint of dust or decay anywhere in the theater, but old age and echoes of thousands of performers soaked the air.

We would play on the stage, singing popular songs and pirouetting like Fireday dancers and giving long monologues that Gertin, the palace rhetoric and public speaking tutor, had forced us to memorize. Somehow, delivering the speeches to the mass of empty seats in the theater made the old words seem relevant—as if we really spoke to rapt audiences, instead of standing at an ancient lectern waiting for Gertin's sarcastic corrections.

The one thing in the theater we never touched were the costumes. Racks and racks of them lined the walls of the cavernous backstage. In front of each rack stood a pair of seamstress's dummies garbed in elaborate festival pageant costumes: the Mouse King, or the dancing Spectral Princes, or the silver-armored Snake Slayer, or dozens of others. When I was younger I had loved to dress up in my mother's fancy clothes, no matter how huge they hung on me. You'd think I would have buried myself in the racks of furs and wolfskins, but I barely touched them. Ancient as they were, the costumes remained immaculate, not a moth-hole or worn patch on any of them.

On stage we danced and shouted heroic monologues to imaginary audiences. But in that backstage dressing area, we spoke only in whispers.

I only went there when I was young, usually with my friend Mala. By the time I was eleven or so, Mala was gone and most of the other palace kids wouldn't have much to do with me out of fear of my father. Then when I was twelve I met Tenia, who didn't have much interest in play-acting. I know the younger kids in the palace still went, but for the next few years, while I spent time with Tenia and then we went off to the Academy together, it was as if I had forgotten the old playhouse existed.

I WASN'T SUPPOSED to go in the kitchens when I was at the palace—my father thought it was beneath our station—but of course I did anyway. Mala worked in the kitchens, and both of her parents were cooks. And with all of my various lessons and my father's schedule, he would forget about meals a lot, so I was a little hungry all the time.

I would sit at a big prep table with Mala and her parents, help them cut up or peel whatever they were cutting up or peeling, and they would bring me a bowl or a plate with something delicious on it. While I ate, Mala's parents would explain how it was made, demonstrating cutting techniques or how to squeeze out dough at the table while they talked. Mala and I soaked it all in while we ate, dipping hunks of the brown kitchen-bread in the leftover sauce and gnawing on them while her parents performed.

Once, after a long discussion with the minister of agriculture about resource allocations, my father began demonstrating cooking techniques on the spot to prove his point. I was nine and always wanted to impress him, so I kept wanting to join in and show him what I knew. But then I would have had to admit how I learned it, and he would have been furious that I'd gone against his instructions to visit my friend in the kitchens. It was a little jarring watching a lesson from him in a subject performed by people it was beneath him to associate with. But my father was like that: He always had to understand everything, and couldn't stand the idea that he didn't know a subject better than the person he hired to do it for him.

Perhaps that was why he seemed to dislike soldiers. He couldn't do most of the things they did, but he had to rely on them for protection.

"AND *THAT* ENDS your east defense!" Mala played the blue god card triumphantly, paralyzing my blue empress card for a turn and disabling the channeler card that protected my until-now impregnable east flank.

Mala was really good at talisman games. I scanned my remaining cards for countermeasures, but Mala had timed her attack perfectly.

We heard a loud footstep in the hall.

"Quick, hide the deck!" I was supposed to be studying, and Mala was supposed to be working. Mala had to work in addition to taking lessons; as a child of servants she was only allowed to study with us if her work in the palace was done. Whenever I could, I helped with her work so we could study together, as long as no one could see me helping so I didn't get in trouble with my father. If my father caught me dusting! Right now we had finished both Mala's work and our studying, but if we got caught doing something as frivolous as playing talisman games we'd both have more work piled on us.

I reached for my books frantically, while Mala scooped up the cards.

No time to case them! If we lost them it would be no more talisman games for a while. Gertin had already confiscated my talisman deck, and told me he wouldn't return it until I memorized another seven hundred lines of Old Ananyan poetry, ten lines for each card in the deck.

The red-whiskered harbormaster, Burren, swept into the room a moment later. He didn't usually go out of his way to cause trouble for us kids like some of the ministers, but I saw him a lot since he often had business with my father. Any senior bureaucrat in the palace was allowed to assign us more tasks if they caught us shirking. Burren glanced at me more-or-less at work with books strewn around the table, while Mala dusted the sideboards.

"At work, are you?" Burren looked doubtful. "I heard giggling. One might almost think the two of you had been playing."

"No, Master Burren," Mala said. She knew I had a hard time lying, so she jumped in to forestall me from having to.

I had no idea where her talisman deck had disappeared to.

"If I searched you, would I find anything I shouldn't?" Burren asked.

"Of course not," Mala said. Lifting her arms, she twirled around slowly, as if to demonstrate her innocence.

"I just have my books and memory stylus," I chimed in. That much was true at least. The stylus had been one my mother had used for practice in her own school days, given to me by my father last New Year's. Normally he didn't care for family gift giving, but since he attended most palace ceremonies as part of his duties and the Empress loved gift ceremonies, the quality of my birthday and New Year's presents had increased a lot. Of course I wouldn't be able to use the stylus to record songs or memories until I was actually a channeler, but I could at least mark up books without causing any permanent changes.

Burren grunted skeptically but didn't question us further. Either he was in a hurry or he didn't really care how hard we were working.

"How did you make those cards disappear?" I asked Mala after he'd gone.

"Easy," she said. "Watch."

She reached back and plucked the deck from the small of her back, where I would have sworn she'd had nothing concealed.

With a practiced flick of her wrist, Mala opened the clamshell case and riffled the cards across the table. Then with her other hand she swept them back toward the case where the seemed to fall neatly all by themselves. Then another flick of her wrist and the case seemed to disappear under her open hand. The barest twist of Mala's hip and it vanished again, her hands empty.

"Magic," I breathed.

"No, just a trick, like festival clowns do," said Mala. "My father showed me how to do it. He says it's useful for a cook to be able to make things disappear, but I'm sure that's not where *he* learned it."

"Can you show me?" I asked, entranced.

"Of course," Mala said. And she spent the rest of our talisman time that afternoon patiently coaching me until I could make small objects disappear almost as effortlessly as she. I never did learn to riffle the cards as smoothly as she did, though.

"WHAT'S YOUR BIGGEST secret?" Mala asked. We were backstage in the theater hiding from Gertin, who had decided to add an extra session of recitations from *The Book of Gods* to what was supposed to be our afternoon off. I was good at reciting and a quick study—my father made sure of that—but who wants to spend a precious free afternoon reciting? Luckily one of the palace runners was in earshot when Gertin mentioned his plans to the dancemaster. The runner's warning spread quickly to the kids in the palace that we needed to disappear before Gertin could find us.

"You first," I said.

"Okay," Mala answered. She looked both ways as if to be sure no one was watching. "My mother lived with someone else before she married my father. She and the man she lived with were both up for jobs at the palace and you need to be married to work as a servant in the jobs they wanted, so they asked to be allowed to marry each other. But then she was accepted for the palace and he wasn't, so the Empress had her marry someone else and forget the guy she'd been living with. So she doesn't even remember that she loved someone else before she knew my dad."

"Wow," I said. "The Empress did that herself? Why would she care about who your mother married. Isn't she too busy?"

Mala giggled nervously. "That's what I was told. I don't know if it was really the Empress or someone acting in her name. But it really happened."

It was tough to take in. "How did you find out? I thought they took all the memories away when that happens."

"They're supposed to," Mala said, "but sometimes they mess up, especially in the countryside where records aren't checked as closely. I was visiting my grandmother when I met this old guy who kept telling me I looked just like my mother. It was creepy. He told me the whole story but made me promise never to tell my mother. He smelled bad, like he drank a lot."

"That must have been strange," I said.

"It was." Mala's eyes glittered. I wanted to ask her more questions, but she shook her head. "Now you tell me yours."

I thought for a moment. She knew most of my secrets already except the ones my father didn't want me to talk about.

"Well, there is one," I said.

"Tell me."

"I had another name when I was little. But then when my mother got very sick, my father sacrificed my name to a god, with the promise of even more if she recovered."

"Which god?" Mala asked.

"I don't know. My father never told me. But after that, I couldn't remember the old name and neither could anyone else. When my mother died anyway, my father told me to use her name, Ketya, to remember her by. And that's the one I've had ever since. But it's not really mine. I don't have a real name anymore."

"Like the Empress and her chancellor? They don't have names either."

For a moment I felt bitter. "I guess a little like that. But at least they got something in return for giving up their names. My name wasn't good enough to bring my mother back."

Mala opened her mouth to ask another question, but then we heard Gertin coming, and we had to burrow back into the costumes and stay absolutely quiet until he gave up looking for us.

As it turned out, that afternoon was the last time I ever saw Mala.

Chapter 5

Something felt off in the kitchens. The bowls were arranged differently on the shelves. The big pile of tamiya roots on the table didn't have the normal shape. I didn't recognize the people sitting at the table, cutting the tamiya roots.

I didn't recognize the people sitting at the table.

"Where's Mala?" I asked. Was something wrong? Was she sick? She always told me when we couldn't meet in the kitchens at the usual time for some reason.

The two men at the table didn't look up. They continued cutting and sorting the roots as if completely intent on the work. Even I didn't have to concentrate like that on tamiya roots, and I'd never spent time in a kitchen before I met Mala.

"Is everyhing okay? Is Mala okay?"

Neither of them would meet my gaze. I stood waiting while they stared uncomfortably at the tamiya. By now they had abandoned all pretense of working.

One of the men finally looked up, glancing around as if wary of predators in the kitchen.

"You should leave," he said, his accent thick from a lifetime in the countryside.

I don't know how my father found out about the secret I'd told Mala. I don't know how I knew that my father was the reason she and her family were gone. I just knew.

I ran through the palace, dodging messengers and servants. People called out to me but I ignored them. By the time I got to the top of the stairs that led to my father's tower chambers I felt lightheaded and out of breath but I kept on going, pushed right through his door and into the central room of his chambers.

My father looked up from his table. I hadn't thought about what I would say if there were people with him, but he was alone, studying maps.

"How did you find out?" I said. I didn't ask why. In my heart I knew why Mala was gone. I had told her the secret. But I had thought it was safe, had thought that I could tell someone and not have to keep it so completely inside.

He gave me an indulgent smile. "You really think an eleven-year-old girl can keep a secret? Of course I found out." *I kept a secret,* I wanted to say, *I kept the secret for all these years,* except even as I thought of the retort, it hit me that it wasn't true anymore.

He must have read the words on my face, even though I hadn't said them. "You are growing up, daughter. It is time you understood that words have consequences. Sometimes when you reveal something you shouldn't, the price isn't paid by you, but by the people you care about."

"What...what did you do with her?" It suddenly crossed my mind that he might have had her killed. I didn't know if I could live with the guilt of knowing that something I said had gotten my only friend killed, along with her parents who had been so nice to me.

"Realize that what I did is purely my decision, caused by your indiscretion. And it would have been perfectly fitting for you to pay a harsh price for what you did. But because I am not ungenerous, I did no such thing. And I will not have you sneaking around the palace asking about them, either. So I will assuage your curiosity."

"What did you do?" I asked again, my voice barely a whisper.

"I sent them away to the colonies. To Elessethe. They will be running a dining room in the government plaza in Elessethe City, serving Ananyan food to soldiers and clerks who miss the taste of home. I might have punished them, but I gave them a better opportunity instead. They treated you well, and the fault of what happened did not lie with them. As I said, I am not ungenerous."

My father looked back down at the map, supposing he had said all that he needed to. I tried to parse his words. I felt numb; the impact hadn't hit me yet. Then it started to:

"Elessethe City? That's a month away, by cable-carriage and ship. And you can't even go there without special permission. I'll never see them again."

He looked up again and smiled. "That is correct," he said agreeably.

"Why couldn't they have stayed here? You even said it wasn't their fault."

"Fault does not matter. They had knowledge that could cause damage—

to me, to the Empire. They could not remain here where that knowledge would spread. Cooks talk, and that talk would have spread through the palace. In the wrong ears, that talk might have been the end of everything."

That puzzled me. I didn't see how the story of my name and my mother's death was so important. I was just a kid, and my mother was gone. What did that have to do with the empire? But even at my most upset I knew better than to ask. So I tried to ask a safer question to see if I could get him to explain.

"Is there anyone I can ever tell secrets to? She was my best friend, I thought it would be safe to tell her anything."

I thought he would answer me with some sort of platitude, but he actually paused to consider his words carefully.

"For now, while you are young," he said, "you must never tell secrets to anyone. Someday you may have a soulmate whom you can tell anything to, but until then you must tell no one your secrets."

"Not even you, father?" I expected an *of course you must tell me everything*, but he shook his head.

"Not even me."

I almost didn't have the courage to ask the next question, but something made me do it. "Was mother your soulmate?"

Surprisingly, my father didn't seem bothered. He got a faraway look in his eyes.

"She was," he answered. "You only have one soulmate. I will never have another."

"So who do *you* tell secrets to?"

"No one. And neither should you."

Aren't you lonely, I wanted to ask, but didn't. Instead, I tried to make a final plea for my friend and her family.

"But maybe Mala was my soulmate!" I burst out. I didn't really know what he meant by *soulmate* at the time.

And his answer didn't enlighten me:

"She was a cook's daughter. Cooks' daughters can't be soulmates."

I sobbed. "I don't know if I can keep secrets the way that you do. I already left all my friends behind when we moved here and now I've lost my best friend, too. I lose everything." Tears ran down my face uncontrollably, but he didn't seem to notice. He still had that faraway look.

"No, you haven't lost everything," he said, his tone almost musing.

"Someday you will lose everything, and you will realize that all you will have left is me."

My sobs stopped abruptly and I felt a shiver on my arms. I knew he was right, somehow.

"But what will you have left?" I asked my father. At age eleven, I still didn't know what a hopelessly naive question that was. I wanted him to say that he would have me, and a part of me thought that he would.

But he just looked at me sadly.

"I will have duty, and the memory of your mother." He said the words with no hesitation, as if he had thought about them a lot. And with that he turned back to the maps, and never said another word on the subject.

At the time I never questioned what he told me, that he had sent them to Elessethe. And I never did see them again. Sometimes later, after I'd grown up a lot, I would wonder if he really had gone to so much trouble for a family of cooks, or if he had just had them killed. I never knew the answer, and any records which might have revealed that particular secret perished in the disaster that still lay eight years in my future.

MY FATHER SENDING Mala away didn't keep me out of the kitchens. We all still went there. As kids we were were perpetually starving, at least in our minds, and our adventures around the theater and other little-used parts of the palace invariably took us through the kitchens at some point to see what food we could scrounge up. Even after Mala's family was sent to another place, some of the cooks had kids my age, and a few times we would play together. It never lasted, though. The next time I would go looking for one of the cooks' daughters to join in an adventure she would be nowhere to be found, or if I could find her she would avoid eye contact.

Their parents were forbidding them from playing with me: I realized that much at the time. What I didn't realize was that they were doing it out of fear of my father. As far as I know he never said a word to them—for all his enjoyment of cooking, my father wanted very little to do with palace cooks and servants—but any servant family whose children seemed too friendly with me was soon sent elsewhere, to a less desirable location than the palace. He started with Mala and her family. The others got the idea quickly.

That was his way of teaching me to make what he thought were suitable friends, I think. The lesson never really took. My next close friend turned out to be suitable, but that was just an accident. All I learned from my father's lesson was that friendship was fleeting, and that someone who was friendly one day was likely to be gone the next.

Ketya
The Drowned City: Seven years before the Loss

I sat at my usual table in the library studying the same passage in two different translations of *The Book of Gods* when I heard a girl's voice say, "Hello there."

A girl about my age, maybe a little older, stood in front of the table looking at me. She wore her blonde hair in long ringlets, a style I had never seen before.

I glanced around to see that my father wasn't watching, then said, "Hello, I'm Ketya."

"I'm Tenia," said the blonde girl. "Why did you look around that way before you answered me?"

She seemed very self-assured for a girl I had never seen at the palace before. I wondered who she was. I couldn't imagine anyone else asking so direct a question. Which may be why I answered it honestly.

"Sometimes my father doesn't like it when I make friends with other girls in the palace. If he sees me talking with them he has them sent away."

My words seemed to amuse Tenia. "Oh. Well, I don't think he will mind you talking with *me*. And I just got here, so I don't think he will send me away." She extended a hand. "You must be the chancellor's daughter. I'm pleased to meet you, Ketya."

I took her hand. "I'm sorry, I don't know who...."

That seemed to charm her. "My mother is the Empress, silly. One day I'll give up my name and be Empress too, so best be nice to me now." She said the words with a smile but a little tiredly, as if she'd said the same thing too many times.

My hand flew to my mouth and I felt my face coloring. "I'm sorry! I didn't know...."

"You didn't even know that Empress had a daughter? I was away at school but now I'm home on holiday. It seems like the sort of thing your father should have told you, though."

"He's very busy. Maybe he just forgot."

"I'm sure he did. Daughters aren't very important at the palace. Only when they make the wrong friends." This time her smile looked more genuine. She pulled up a chair and sat opposite me. "Now show me what you were reading in *The Book of Gods*. I'm good with most things but I can't make any sense of poetry, so maybe you can help me. Maybe you should be my chancellor just like your father is for my mother."

"NUMBER 178, PLEASE," my father said. He sat at the small table in the alcove of his chamber. The table was set for two, and the dishes of food in its center steamed delectably.

My stomach growled. *Don't look at the food! Just concentrate on the verse*, I thought. *I know that one. It's one of the easy ones, he asks that a lot.*

I still hesitated a moment, making sure I had the words right in my head.

"Number 178?" he asked again. "I would hate to have half of this delightful lunch go uneaten."

"'Concerning Speaking with Gods,'" I started, then recited:

Wear clothing appropriate to the occasion; if you wear
false clothing or false names the god may refuse
to speak with you or may speak falsely without penalty.
But if you dress aright the god must speak truly,
and promises may not be unmade without penalty.

"Not bad," said my father. "Except for the hesitation. Of course that is one of the short ones. Perhaps something a little harder, before we share this meal. How about number 249?"

I breathed a sigh of relief. I knew that one. Having Tenia help me drill with the cards that held the Truce really helped: She would sit across from me on the big bed in my chambers and hold a card in front of her while I recited, stopping me at every missed word. It was good chancellor training, she told me, and I was going to be her chancellor someday.

"Hesitation again?" my father prompted. "I would hate to have to send you back downstairs to your room to study some more instead of enjoying this meal together."

"No," I said. "Just gathering the words. And now I have them: 'Concerning Worship'"

The gods must be spoken of with respect
nor may their contributions be minimized
save when they failed to fight beside their brethren.
But no one may be compelled to worship a god
or encouraged by promises true or false.
If one chooses to worship a god that person
shall expect no favor in return:
Worship confers no obligation
and worship unasked for confers no glory.
The gods' names shall be remembered
and their deeds spoken of at festivals
but in no other ways shall their words be marked
save those required in this treaty.
The magic that the gods confer
is provided only to secure an end to fighting
and to pay for the magic that people now forswear.
Worship and the desire for worship has brought
both sides to ruination;
it shall be discouraged from this day forward.

I didn't really understand that one. Why would anyone want to worship a god? And why were there obligations—was someone paying to be worshiped? Both sides seemed pretty concerned about it in the language of the verse, so they must have been worried about something.

Sometimes I could ask my father to explain one of them, but usually he would send me to another book, or get angry that I hadn't picked up what he saw as the clear meaning of the verse. I certainly wouldn't risk ruining his good mood.

Besides, I was starving.

"Good enough," he said. "Your new friend does seem to have helped your learning. I quite approve of that friendship. Now sit here and have lunch with me. We can spend a little time together before I return to my duties."

Days like this I felt so proud: living in the palace, with a new best friend, and studying for a chance to be a part of the work that my father and the Empress were doing to make Ananya a better place. Someday, maybe when I was grown up, I knew I would be able to make him proud without working so hard at it. But days like today, when he took time out from his work to help me learn and even shared lunch with me, gave me hope for the future.

"WHY DON'T YOU like the theater?" I asked Tenia once. We were in her chambers pretending to study history together, so of course I was thinking about the theater.

"It's an old place," she said. "I'm not comfortable there. My mother says it's filled with the old magic, even if no one can see it now."

"What do you mean?" I asked. "Isn't the whole palace filled with the old magic?" I knew about old magic, at least in theory. Between history lessons and all the mentions of it in the treaty that my father was making me memorize, I knew more than I wanted to about the magic that people had used to fight the gods to a standstill, and even kill some of them. But the old magic had been given up in the treaty that ended the Holy War, in return for the "new" magic channeled from the gods for the last eight hundred years.

"The oldest parts of the palace are, but a lot's been rebuilt since then," said Tenia. "The theater used to be used for something else, I'm pretty sure. I know a lot of the treaty was negotiated there, so it was filled with wards and with the most powerful magic people could manage because everyone expected the gods to turn on us during the negotiations. All those suits they used to use as festival costumes started out as the formal wear used to speak to the gods."

"Really? Someone dressed up as the Mouse King to talk to the gods?" I wondered if that was what Clause 178 of the treaty was about, that odd bit about wearing "clothing appropriate to the occasion" so the gods wouldn't lie to you.

"I know, really." Tenia's blonde ringlets shook as she laughed. "But the suits symbolized something different back then. They were really important."

Tenia seemed to know about everything. I'm not sure I was much of a chancellor to her, but I loved to listen to her explain things, and I seemed to ask her the right questions. I let her do most of the talking, which seemed to be fine with her. I still wasn't used to the idea of having a friend whom my father couldn't send away if I said the wrong thing.

I'd asked her about that once, too, not directly of course. I asked her, hypothetically, if she thought my father could ever be wrong, or if I should trust everything he said.

"I think you should trust him completely," Tenia answered. "My mother does. She says he's the only person she's ever known who doesn't care about power, just about serving his Empress. And if the Empress trusts him completely, I wouldn't question him. I mean, we're smart, but we're just kids. If he says to do something it's because he knows better."

So that settled that. Once my best friend and the Empress both said to trust my father, my doubts seemed pretty foolish. I found myself studying harder, trying to really understand what it was he was trying to teach me by having me memorize the Talisman of Truce. As a twelve-year-old the meanings of many of the clauses escaped me, no matter how many times I studied them. I could follow the basic meaning, but I knew there were implications that I wasn't seeing hidden in the verses. I told myself that as long as I memorized every word of the treaty to my father's satisfaction, I would gradually understand the hidden meanings as I got older and learned more. Which actually turned out to be true, although not in any way that I expected.

I HAD THOUGHT that it was impossible to learn anything much about magic before you were admitted to the Empress's Academy, and that was probably true for most people, but it wasn't true for people living in the palace. Or at least it wasn't true for people living in the palace who were friends with Tenia.

Whether because she was just naturally gifted in magic or because her mother had shown her how to find them, Tenia could draw small magics from what she called "practice threads," bits of magic that had been connected to certain rooms or objects, but remained malleable, unlike other magic once a channeler finished molding it. Later I would encounter similar places at the Empress's Academy, but when Tenia showed them to me it seemed exciting and new and almost forbidden. Except that if Tenia said it was okay I knew we wouldn't be punished for it.

She worked the magic easily, changing the color of the lamps on the chamber walls and making their lights flicker, calling up a faint breeze. Nothing big but it was magic! Real magic. And we weren't even channelers yet.

She showed me how to relax my focus and let my mind touch the practice threads, but I couldn't do it. On the fourth try, I started seeing blue flickers out of the corners of my eyes again, and then, on the wall in front of me, a startling glimpse of a whole rune the size of my hand. Then my eyes refocused and the blue disappeared.

On the sixth try I was able to raise enough breeze to tousle Tenia's ringlets for a moment. I barely felt the thread, but at least I had managed something.

Tenia remained patient and gently coached me; I think part of her liked how much more easily magic came to her than to me, the way memorization and recitation came so much more easily to me.

We did this a few times a week: whenever all our other lessons were done and she got tired of helping me recite treaty verses and we could sneak away. Practicing on the threads wasn't exactly forbidden, but we weren't sure if it was allowed, either. The threads hadn't been created for kids to practice on, but for the use of channelers convalescing from illness or injury. I don't think we were even supposed to know they existed, much less be able to sense them.

Of course, without all Tenia's coaching I never would have sensed them at all. And I still felt more of the elusive blue streaks and rarely glimpsed runes than I did of the Empress's magic.

Finally I asked Tenia about it, hesitantly.

"Do you think anyone can still see the old magic?" I asked her. "I know there's plenty of it in the palace, lingering."

"Of course not," she answered. "I certainly can't, and I know my mother can't, and no one has more powerful magic than her."

"But what if someone could?" I persisted.

"Nobody can. Even if someone knew how to use it, what's left is hundreds of years old and faded. A few people can sense it maybe—that's why the the-ater bothers me—but no one can see it."

"What would you say if I could see the old magic? Not really see it, I mean. But maybe little glimpses of old things. More than I see of the new magic, anyway?"

"If that was true—and it's not true, is it?" Tenia looked at me sharply, and I knew enough to shake my head vigorously.

"No, of course not. I'm just asking because it would be exciting, like in a fairy tale. I just wondered what someone would do"—I didn't say *I* this time—"if they could see it."

"I'd say to keep it a secret. Do you want to be a channeler or an exile? The old magic is forbidden in the treaty, right? So anyone who can see it has to be exiled or punished."

"I guess." Actually, Clause 119 of the treaty, which was the appropriate verse, seemed pretty ambivalent on the subject. It was one of the longer clauses:

All magic shall be channeled through the gods and
the practice of any other magic is forbidden. Let the practice
of magic that comes not from the gods die with this generation
of practitioners, who
will live long enough to stand guard against betrayal.
Those who persist in practicing magic
after the first generation has died shall
be punished by exile or
turned over to the gods for punishment or
thrown from cliffs to their deaths,
at the discretion of their rulers.
No books on the practice of magic may be written
save those on the use of magic that flows from the gods.
Any books that now exist may be kept but not sold
or passed to the next generation: They must be interred
with their owners or destroyed at the time of the funeral.
Such magic as now exists outside the gods
must be destroyed or allowed to fade away;
it may not be renewed but only replaced
by magic that comes through the gods.
If any god shall violate the treaty in a material way
then this clause shall be held in abeyance
even though the remainder of this treaty remain in force.

My father hated that verse. "Poetry written by a committee," he had called it the last time I recited it for him, but I knew that I didn't have enough knowledge about either poetry or treaty negotiations to understand his mockery. And I knew that asking him to explain would just call attention to my lack of understanding instead of my successful memorization.

I never brought up the old magic again, and Tenia pretended I had never said it at all. She was a great friend that way; she never held missteps against me and she let me help her on the things that came more easily to me, like history and recitation.

It seems weird to say it, but having Tenia to confide in meant I actually got along better with my father. Having Tenia as a friend meant that I didn't hold things inside until I couldn't stop myself from blurting them out to my father. I could hold back more until I was sure of my words, so I didn't say as much to my father that made him mad.

I just wished I was better at the magic. No matter how good I was at other things, magic was the one way he couldn't help but compare me to my mother.

"I'M NOT GOING to be very good with magic, am I?" I asked my father one day in a moment of doubt.

"Probably you will not," he answered. "You are an acceptably quick study at history and law, better than many I have known, but you have very little aptitude for magic. Certainly nothing like the abilities your mother had."

That was as close as my father ever came to a compliment, but it still stung.

"Does that mean I won't be able to go to the Empress's Academy? Tenia said I might not be good enough. I'm trying my best, I think."

My father thought about the question for a minute, then looked at me directly.

"If life was fair, you would not be allowed at the Empress's Academy," he said, meeting my eyes directly so I couldn't look away. "Were you nearly anyone else's daughter, Ketya, you would be politely but firmly declined at the Empress's Academy and encouraged to attend a civil service academy where you might be more successful. But you are my daughter, and because I am the Empress's closest adviser, you will be accepted. Even if I were a nobody, your face looks enough like your mother's that it is not unlikely the examiners would fool themselves into thinking you will someday wield the power your mother carried with such ease."

The power that killed your mother. He didn't say the words, but I could see the thought in his eyes.

"Even your friendship with Tenia might be enough," he said. "She will be Empress someday, when her mother tires of ruling and takes back her name. When Tenia is Empress, the examiner who rejected her friend might have cause to regret it. Some Empresses have long memories for slights."

"Is there nothing I can do to earn a place at the Academy for myself?"

My father made the annoyed expression he got when I asked a stupid question. "Why waste energy fighting a battle that you have already won? Your father is the Empress's chancellor. You befriended the Empress's daughter to make your success certain. Work on winning the next battle as decisively as you did this one. The best victories are in battles your opponent never realizes they've fought."

I didn't make friends with Tenia just to get into the Academy, I wanted to say. But I kept silent, since it was the one thing he seemed to think I had done right, even if I hadn't done it for the right reasons.

So instead I said, "If I go to the Empress's Academy, I will be far away. I won't see you much for years."

"That is true," he said. I waited for him to say more, but he turned to some deployment reports on the desk in front of him instead and I knew the conversation was over.

Chapter 6

Ketya
The Empress's Academy: Four years before the Loss

Tenia laughed. "You can stop gaping now. Everyone will think you've never been here before."

"But I *haven't* been here before. And it's amazing. Can't I gape a little?"

"Always act self-possessed, just like the drama teacher said."

"He never said that. You made it up." I couldn't help smiling; Tenia's playfulness had a way of infecting me.

"Well, he should have said it. It's true."

We had just gotten off the cable-carriage. The academy had its own platform, floored with sparkling blue tiles. Even though we had arrived at night, rows of lanterns on tall poles lit the platform as brightly as a summer day. The air smelled of jasmine, though I saw no plants. More magic? Everything here seemed magical.

Downhill from the platform, more lampposts illuminated a path across a broad green. On the other side, the pearlescent walls of the academy buildings glowed in the night as if struck by moonlight, though the moon had not yet risen. Light shone from every window. Most of the places I'd lived had been built for defense; the series of wars that ran through Ananyan history had colored its architecture as well. But the Empress's Academy had been built for light and beauty and exuberant displays of magic. Even at night, the oversized doors of the academy buildings stood open—inviting and brightly lit. The slight chill in the air would not penetrate them, I supposed.

I hadn't seen anyone unloading our luggage—perhaps it had been done magically while I stood gaping—but now a cart with all the trunks and bags from the cable-carriage rolled gently downslope along the path. *Now they're just showing off*, I thought. *So much magic for something that doesn't really need it.* Wordlessly Tenia and I fell into step behind the cart and followed it slowly down the hill and across the green.

It felt odd arriving to an empty platform. Perhaps this was part of the transition to adulthood we would be making? Once we finished our studies and connected with the Empress, we could be sent anywhere—to fight in battles, to clear swamps, to power ships across the sea to the colonies—and would be expected to perform as fully skilled channelers. A channeler who failed at her job could not claim inexperience as an excuse. Only sickness and weakened powers excused less than perfection.

Which, given my lack of channeling potential, meant that I had a lot of hard work ahead of me.

We didn't meet another soul that night. We followed our luggage as it floated up a flight of stairs and down a long hallway—not so bright upstairs as in the entryway or the front of the building—to our rooms. We received our own rooms, next to each other, which surprised me for some reason; I'd heard stories about bureaucrats' academies and officers' academies, where even the highest ranking officers sent to prepare for a promotion were expected to share a room. For the lower ranks and would-be bureaucrats, barracks of eight or more seemed common. But privilege felt inevitable at a school for magic, even one like this where each student might, in theory, be drawn from the poorest family as long as she had talent.

In practice, almost every girl I knew at the academy was the daughter of a channeler, or at least very well connected. Like me, of course.

But most of them turned out to be a lot more outgoing than me. Most of them were used to being the most important kids in their schools or circles of friends. Here, almost every girl in the school had been the most popular girl in her town. A lot of them had to adjust to being just another student at the Empress's Academy.

WHEN I WAS a girl, I loved to dance. Not just country dances, I mean formal, festival dances. I'd picked up a little bit as a kid, and then when we moved to the palace I pursued it more seriously. I was trying to fit in and meet other kids my age, but my father was very conscious of his position in the palace, and didn't want me to do anything that would reflect badly on him. Formal dancing was one of the things my father approved of, so he wrote a note to the palace dance instructor asking him to add me to the junior-level class. I loved it. I never got past junior-level—I was nowhere near ready to perform in an actual festival, and the dancemaster rarely had spots open for new performers anyway—but we performed at a lot of children's festivals and palace garden parties and such.

Then, when I got to the Academy, I saw they had spots open for the dance class—and I could actually learn senior-level dances. I was pretty astonished to get into the class as a first-year student.

It didn't take long to find out the reason. Dulcet, the dancemaster, had…wandering hands. Nothing that would leave a mark or that you could prove when it was your word against his, even if you'd had the courage to pursue it. He would never have dared to try anything on Tenia, but she wasn't in the class with me. And I couldn't tell her about it: Her mother had handpicked the faculty, and Tenia had told me more than once about how elite they were, and how if we didn't learn from them the problem was us, not them.

After I joined the class lots of other girls warned me about him, at least elliptically, but no one said anything before. People had a lot of strategies for surviving his class. Girls who tolerated some but not too much seemed to do best—you learned to do what you needed to survive.

We'd all heard the stories of girls who had tried to report him and gotten terrible assignments as channelers, cleaning up disease-ridden swamps or working on drainage projects in the colonies. Everyone knew he had some sort of influence. Besides, he was a teacher. At the Empress's Academy. Looking back, I have no idea if any of those stories were true or not—whether he even had any influence at all, or if anyone had ever complained. Or whose side the Empress would have taken if someone had complained. You hear a lot of rumors like that when you're in school, and you take them as fact.

I would, as it turned out, meet him again later, in a very different situation.

But for that year, we all kept our heads down, worked on our dance steps, and tried to ignore everything else that was going on. We did what we needed to survive.

After that first year I left the class, as soon as I was able. I knew that it meant I would never have an opportunity to dance again. I missed the dancing, but it wasn't worth the price.

TENIA WASN'T THE leader of the girls at the academy, but she could have been if she wanted. Magic came easily to her. She excelled at everything athletic as well. (She joked with me that if she didn't have to follow her mother as Empress she would have loved to be a general.) The other girls wanted to follow Tenia's lead, and not only because they knew that someday the Empress would take back her name and turn the job over to her daughter.

Tenia just didn't have much interest in schoolgirl politics and intrigues. Maybe it was her personality, or maybe it was because when you're preparing to take over as leader of a great empire, schoolgirl squabbles don't seem all that important. I don't think the other girls understood that. And they definitely didn't understand why Tenia's best friend was me: a quiet, studious girl who kept to herself and said little, except to Tenia.

I think Tenia and I both helped each other. At the academy we really became close friends, not just the inseparable playmates whom our parents approved of that we had been at the palace. At the academy we had other choices, and became closer friends. I helped Tenia study, served as her adviser and confidante, and learned to keep both my secrets and hers. Outside of classes, I didn't talk to others much, but I watched everything, and told Tenia all that I saw. For her part, Tenia helped me get through my struggles with magical theory and sheltered me socially. We also played a lot of talisman games together, and socialized with the other girls as much as Tenia thought appropriate.

"I'm going to have to tell some of them who to *marry*," she reminded me. "I need to know something about them, even the ones I don't like. And I need you to know enough about them to advise me. You're my chancellor, remember?"

"How could I ever forget?"

We were sitting on her oversized bed talking about marriage. She was promising me a good one, to someone I would like. "Well, I mean, of course you'll like him once the engagement is settled and the engagement tokens have been created, but I mean someone you would like anyway even if there wasn't any magic involved."

I told her I hadn't ever given much thought to marriage. It was true, too. I just hadn't been around a lot of families since my mother's death. My father took me to state occasions when it was called for, but otherwise, I had spent my childhood in the company of governesses and sometimes friends. The only family I had really gotten to know in the last few years had been Mala's parents, and of course that had ended badly. Abstractly, I knew that channelers married as the Empress dictated for reasons of state. I always figured I would deal with that when the time came. Hopefully the memories that came with the engagement token included some instructions on what marriage and family life were like when wars and death didn't intervene.

"You don't need to think about it. That's my mother's job."

I sat up a little straighter "So your mother really picks everyone who's going to get married? How does she ever have time to do anything else?"

"Well, technically she picks everyone. But really other people do a lot of the picking, especially in the countryside. There are a lot of people needing marriages whom she doesn't really know or care about, and that's what local bureaucrats are for. And probably some people never get picked, and just stay unmarried. But anyone from a good family, or any channeler or war hero, my mother decides on personally. She puts an incredible amount of time into thinking about who to put together—it's funny, almost like a little girl playing with dolls, except she's the Empress. But my mother really likes deciding who will match up well, and how she can make the kingdom stronger. It's like a big talisman game." Tenia smiled thinking about it, maybe anticipating when the decisions would be hers.

"What about people who love each other?" I asked. "Doesn't who they love have anything to do with how they're matched up?" My words came out as almost a wail, and I wasn't sure why. I thought back to Mala's story about her mother and the man she'd loved before she had been engaged to her father.

Tenia gave me a strange look, like *get it together*. "Of course love matters. But really making sure people love each other is up to channelers like us. Haven't you been paying *any* attention to Lehnire's lectures?"

"I've been paying attention, I just don't understand them. It's all pretty abstract, *measuring strength of memories* and *evocativity scoring*. I'm not sure what a lot of it means."

"It's how you make someone love the person they're supposed to marry, silly. It's how you make sure marriages work the way they're supposed to. If a channeler gets it wrong and a marriage starts to fail, my mother gets furious, so you're going to need to learn to get it right." I must have had a grim expression on my face because Tenia gave me a silly smile. "Oh, don't worry about it. You'll be great. Why do you think you're going to be my chancellor? You read people better than I do, even. You'll be perfect at making marriages work."

"I suppose," I said weakly. I couldn't let go of the conversation. "But it feels like love should be important. My father really loved my mother."

"Of course he did," answered Tenia patiently. "He hardly had much choice about it, if the engagement token was well done. And if the channeler assigned to it didn't want to spend the next few years using her magic to unplug clogged sewer pipes, she would have made sure it was well done."

Tenia could look at things unemotionally, the way my father did. Maybe that's why I admired her so much. I was as smart as anyone at the academy, but sometimes I couldn't control my emotions the way a channeler needed to.

"WHAT HAPPENED TO Rhenne?" I asked Tenia. The small redheaded girl in the next room kept to herself even more than I did, usually buried in studying that almost made me feel lazy. She had joined us in a few talisman games on rainy afternoons or study days, but she always seemed preoccupied and anxious to get back to her studies.

Now her room stood empty, the bed neatly made up but all personal touches gone.

"She didn't make it," Tenia said. "They're cutting down the class size. They always cull a certain number. She couldn't handle the magic, so she'll be transferred to a different academy. I'm sure she'll make a good bureaucrat somewhere."

I felt myself flush. "But she was better than me! Does that mean—"

"It doesn't mean anything." Tenia smiled. "My mother knows you're struggling a little, but I've told her you're going to be fine. She's not going to transfer you, and you'll learn the magic. We just need to keep working at it. Which you have been. You'll get it."

I hadn't realized that Tenia's long letters to her mother contained reports on our performances, but I suppose it made sense. She wasn't just here to learn magic like the rest of us: She was here to learn to be a future Empress.

And I supposed I was here to learn to be a future chancellor, though that always felt more like a fancy that Tenia would outgrow than like a real promise. She would need someone more like my father than like me, I knew. But until that time, I could still give her good advice.

I felt more than a little guilty about Rhenne losing her place at the academy while I kept mine. But I wanted to be here and Tenia wanted me here and she genuinely seemed to think I would learn the magic.

"Come on," said Tenia. "If you're worried, let's work on your magic some more. The talisman game will wait."

"Thank you," I said. I knew how much she loved talisman games as a way to relax. Instead, I sat on the bed in front of her, tried to empty my mind, and focused on the first of the finding exercises, to draw on the threads of magic that student channelers could use for practice.

I picked up the thread on the third try. That was better than I used to do, but most girls here could do it in one. I didn't have the blue streaks distracting me here, at least. Whatever they were, they seemed related to the old magic: common enough in the palace and other structures that dated back to the Holy War but nonexistent in newer buildings.

"Relax," Tenia said. I could feel her hands massaging my shoulders. "Does that relax you?"

It distracted me a little, but I didn't want her to stop. I focused harder on the magic so she would think her hands helped me relax.

It never really went beyond backrubs and close friendship and long talks about our futures together. At the time I was so sheltered and had so many trust issues that I was only dimly aware that going further was a possibility, even though all of us had private rooms in a mostly unchaperoned hall: I had to be in serious denial not to realize some of what went on. And Tenia never pushed, although I'm pretty sure I would have done whatever she asked.

But I think it was wanting her to touch me, however innocently I conceived it, that finally motivated me to learn to channel magic. I would never be a great channeler, I knew. But by the end of our stay at the Empress's Academy, I was pretty sure I would be a competent one. I was proud of that, even if I suspected my father wouldn't be.

Chapter 7

We took special cable-carriages back to the palace from the Empress's Academy, the outsides freshly painted in the academy colors. Tenia had her own carriage; it had a large, central compartment with a couch and a sitting table, and bowls of yellowfruit and red-brown fawn nuts still warm from boiling, and spiced meat pastries, and sweetmeats on the sidebar. She'd invited me, as her best friend, to ride with her.

The rest of the graduating class rode a few minutes ahead of us. They shared a large two-compartment carriage with two chaperones sent by the academy, though what sort of trouble they expected us to get into on the cable-carriage I had no idea. The faculty hadn't much cared how we behaved at the academy, as long as we attended classes and learned quickly enough, but once we left the glittering campus they expected us to look and act the part of earnest, newly graduated channelers.

"They're going to hate me for not riding with the rest of the group," I said to Tenia, but I was glad to be riding with her.

"They hate you anyway," said Tenia, "and none of them will dare show it as long as your father is chancellor. Besides"—she smiled, her blond ringlets catching the light—"you have powerful friends."

We spent the ride eating too many sweetmeats and playing marathon games of four soldiers with her beautiful talisman deck, whose golden case exactly replicated the case in which Ananya's actual copy of the Talisman of Truce was stored. I liked to watch the scenery go by when Tenia dozed; but she'd traveled a lot more than I had and wanted to talk or play talisman games, both of which had been severely restricted by the intensifying workload during our last year at the academy. My own talisman deck had been confiscated by Dulcet the unpleasant dance instructor and never returned—I knew better than to go to his office and ask for it back, which was what he'd hoped for when he took it—but of course no one would touch anything belonging to Tenia, so we just used her deck in the infrequent moments when we had enough time for a game.

"Do you think your father and my mother will be waiting for us at the platform?" Tenia asked when we saw the towers of the Drowned City approaching.

"They probably forgot we're coming back," I said, giggling. Over the last few months, when I'd finally been able to finish the compulsory magic exams with relative (for me, at least) ease, I'd found myself more relaxed. I finally felt like I belonged at the school, not just like I had taken the place of someone more qualified because of my family connections. Which I had, of course. More than one friend of Rhenne and the other girls who had been dismissed had let me know as much—though never in Tenia's presence.

"My mother will remember," said Tenia. "The whole royal family is going to be there in the Presentation Chamber to celebrate when I become a channeler. It's the first time the entire family has been together in the same room in all the years since the talisman was first accepted. It was your father's idea to bring them all to the palace as a special celebration—my mother loves it. She sent me a long letter about how he managed to get everyone here. Some of the stories were pretty unbelievable."

I wonder if I'll get any celebration? I thought, then realized I was being incredibly unfair to my father. *What is it about leaving the academy and going back to my father that makes me start acting like a little kid again?* Besides, did I even want a celebration? Tenia and my father thrived on being in the middle of things but my happiest moments had been quiet ones, that no one but me remembered much afterward.

WHILE WE DIDN'T see the Empress waiting for Tenia on the platform, several royal cousins stood waving as the cable-carriage approached. We had a chance to take a long look, while we waited for the lead carriage with the other graduates to unload before we could approach the platform.

Tenia practically squealed: "That's my Aunt Marta! And my cousins from the Silver Coast! I haven't seen them since I was twelve! And my Aunt Harenne! Oh wait—"

She suddenly went a little white. The cable-carriage had begun its final descent to the platform.

"What's wrong?" I asked.

"Aunt Harenne hates talisman games, and she *really* hates this deck. She saw it once and said the case was 'an ugly reminder of an uglier time.'" Her voice dropped an octave in imitation of her aunt. "She'll have fits if she sees it and I can't hide it in these clothes."

She thrust the golden case at me. "Here, you take it. I've seen you hide things. You can give it back to me after the ceremony. Or the next time you see me when I'm not surrounded by aunts."

I smiled, trying not to feel wistful at my father's absence. After all, Tenia's mother was too busy to be at the platform, too. "Of course," I said. I liked using Mala's trick to make things disappear. I had gotten good at it, and had tried to show Tenia, but she hadn't been interested. "Empresses have other ways of making things disappear," she had said. But apparently not from their aunts.

The case disappeared into the small of my back, where it sat snugly between my shirt and overtunic, all but invisible. "Don't worry, I'll keep it safe."

"Thanks. Hopefully we'll have time for a few games after the celebrations, before you get sent on your first assignment."

"Oh that's right!" My hand went to my mouth. "I might not see you for—"

"Stop," said Tenia. Her hand covered mine, shushing me. "You're my chancellor. I'll make sure you're always close to me. Don't start worrying on me."

She leaned forward and kissed me on each cheek as her hand held mine, pulled it against her. Her mouth brushed my lips softly. And then the cable-carriage shuddered to a stop. We both pulled away suddenly as if shocked. I could hear cousins and well wishers boiling outside like frothing surf about to flow into our sandcastle.

"After the ceremony"—Tenia waved and blew a kiss back at me as the door opened—"we'll talk then. I'll ask my mother to let us celebrate with a trip together before your first assignment. Just the two of us. You've always wanted to spend time in the mountains, right?" Then the surge of cousins and baggage porters flowed all around us, filling the carriage and sweeping Tenia away with the undertow. When the tide receded, I found myself alone in the carriage, all my baggage and Tenia's cousins gone.

Looking around first to make sure nothing had been missed, I stepped out of the carriage. Reflexively I touched my back to make sure Tenia's golden talisman case remained secure and hidden. *Not much of a thief you'd be, giving away your hiding place like that*, I thought, but I stood alone on the platform. I paused at the edge of the stairs and slowly twisted around in a circle, taking in the Drowned City skyline and the towers that had been my home for so many years, the salt-smell of the ocean as the breeze came from the seaport side of the city.

I didn't know how long I'd be here, but it felt nice to be returning someplace comfortable and familiar, with new skills. *I'm a channeler*, I thought to myself. *I really did it. I'm a channeler in the service of the Empress.* Even in my thoughts, I had to correct myself. *Or at least I will be in a few hours.*

Taking a last deep breath of the salt breeze from the solitude of the platform, I started down the stairs toward the palace. It was time to find my father.

Ketya
The Drowned City: The day before the Loss

At the Empress's Academy it was easy to forget Ananya was at war. Situated far from any fighting, the academy focused on theoretical and everyday uses of magic, on gaining control and precision rather than on specific techniques. Although many of the girls I had studied with would soon be assigned to military service, they would train on the big war engines with their engineering units. I knew in theory what it took to work a thrower or a lightning bear, but to actually use one effectively I would need to learn to coordinate with the engineers who aimed and loaded the engines, and also learn to control the precise amount of force used. It took a lot more teamwork than moving a cable-carriage or powering irrigation rigs on a farm.

At the palace, however, no one could forget the war. Partly because the palace itself bore the scars of so much fighting, but also because soldiers seemed to be everywhere: directing traffic, keeping factions of the royal family who didn't get along with each other discreetly separated, guarding pantries and works of art and entrances to areas where people needed to be left alone to get work done. At the academy we'd had a lot of freedom to explore, and as children at the palace we'd found ways to make ourselves invisible to adults. But being an adult in the palace meant having to stop and explain yourself frequently, especially if you'd been away at school for several years. The guards appeared festive rather than martial, with glittering uniforms and light ceremonial blades that looked more like dance props than weapons. But even wearing the festive uniforms the Empress (or my father, who planned for her) had decreed for the occasion, the guards seemed scrupulous in making certain that I really had a reason to be in the heart of the palace's administrative wing.

It had taken me more than an hour to make my way from the suite where the candidate channelers (except for Tenia) had been quartered to the landing below my father's tower room; now I would only have a few minutes to spend with him before I had to make my way back through the crowds and checkpoints so I could change into ceremonial garb.

It seemed like the whole palace had been decorated for the festival. Even here, in an administrative area, the ring of columns that supported the landing's high ceiling bore garlands of silver ferrin bark worked into fanciful shapes and dotted with colorful berries.

Up the stairs, I could see the door to my father's chambers propped slightly ajar, while a worker knelt in front of it applying a coat of paint. For all his planning skill, it seemed like at least one decoration wouldn't be complete before the party. Or at least the paint wouldn't be dry yet.

I knocked on an unpainted part of the lintel, and stepped into the room, easing my way around the half-open door.

I still felt a little giddy from Tenia's almost-kiss, even a few hours later. I had to compose my expression or my father would want to know why I was smiling.

Inside my father's chambers heavy wooden crates covered half the floor, like the ones people used for a move or an ocean voyage. The crates completely blocked the shelves of books and bound archives that covered the near wall of his central office. On the other walls about a third of the volumes I remembered seemed to be missing, presumably packed in the boxes. A large cabinet where he kept formal clothes stood open as well, with half its contents gone. Incongruously, the Mouse King costume, the same one I'd seen in the theater a hundred times, hung from a rack on the side of the clothes cupboard.

My father sat at a table, sorting through a small box of what looked like keepsakes. Next to the box sat a card case that looked just like the one hidden at the small of my back. With a start I realized it was the *real* talisman case, the one that held Ananya's original Talisman of Truce. As chancellor, my father had access to it, of course, but seeing it sitting at his elbow like a register of births or food production ledger startled me a little.

"You're early," he said, without looking up.

"Excuse me?" I asked, not sure how to interpret his words. "The cable-carriage arrived hours ago."

Then he did look up. "It's you," he said. "I was expecting someone else. How was your trip?"

"It was pleasant enough. Tenia told me you have a big ceremony planned for tonight."

He smiled at that. "There will be a few surprises, I think. I apologize for not sending someone to meet your cable-carriage when it arrived. I have been caught up in last minute plans and work—" His hand swept around the mess that filled his normally tidy office.

"I see you're packing. Are you redecorating? Is that why the door is being painted?"

"If I wait for a day when I am not busy, it will never be done," he answered. I took that for a yes.

Then the Mouse King costume caught my eye again. I had to ask. "Is that for talking with gods? That's what Tenia says they're used for."

He looked almost angry for a moment, then composed his face. "Remember," he said "a long time ago I told you that some secrets were not to be spoken of."

"I remember." *How could I forget. That's the same day you sent Mala and her family away.*

"That, and its uses"—he gestured to the costume—"concern one of those secrets. Understand that I can tell you no more."

"Of course," I said. Only my father could make a festival costume hanging in his office into a state secret. I wondered suddenly if he was seeing someone. As chancellor he couldn't marry, but that didn't preclude... the thought was too incongruous. He had loved my mother so intensely he had bargained away my name to try and save her. I couldn't imagine that intensity would allow him to share himself with anyone else. Not that I knew much about love.

I wondered if I could ask, elliptically.

"You said once," I ventured. "You said once that there would come a time when all I would have left is you. What did you mean by that?"

He smiled again, but this time it seemed a little sadness crept into his eyes. He looked a bit wistful when he spoke. "I think that meaning will become clear sooner than you think, daughter." He glanced down at the box on the table, then back up at me again. "I must bid you goodbye. You have a ceremony to dress for and I"—he looked around at the boxes—"I have many preparations to make for this night."

I nodded. "Will I see you at the ceremony?"

"If I can make it there," he said, in a tone that meant he couldn't. "A lot needs to happen behind the scenes that won't happen if I'm not personally looking after it."

"I understand." And I did. "I'm sure I'll see you afterward then."

But he had turned back to the box of keepsakes, and the Talisman next to it, and didn't look up at me as I left his chambers.

Ketya
The Drowned City: The evening of the Loss

I managed to speak to Tenia briefly before the ceremony, amid the mob. All around us royal family members and loved ones of other initiates celebrated among tables of food and cases of ancient documents in the giant, museum-like anteroom outside the Hall of Ceremonies. Tenia looked radiant, her blond ringlets elaborately styled. Her skin practically glowed with excitement as she danced from relative to relative, treating each one like a long-lost friend. I had never seen her happier; I wondered if even the Festival of Initiation itself could make her any happier.

"Ketya! This is amazing!" She gave me a big hug. "Did you see the harbor procession at sundown? Every ship in the home fleet in formation, throwing off streams of colored magic as they left the harbor just as the sun went down. Then they sailed south for a sea monster hunt tomorrow. Tomorrow night at sunset there will be another procession back into the harbor and then a midnight feast for the entire city. And your father organized it all!"

I smiled. "He said there would be surprises."

"He's an amazing man," she said. Then pitched a little lower: "You're going to have a lot to live up to as my chancellor." She winked, which was as intimate a gesture as anyone could make in this crowd.

"Will everyone fit in the hall?" I asked.

"They should. I'm sure your father worked out all the numbers." Then in the low voice again. "There was even a scandal this afternoon. I guess Burren isn't harbormaster anymore, and whoever is, didn't want to lower the harbor defense chains the way your father wanted for the sunset procession. Something about not being able to raise them again quickly enough and breaking procedure. Your father ended up having to go down to the harbor himself to make sure the procession went off the way he planned it."

Tenia looked around. "Is he here?" she asked. "I wanted to thank him again, and introduce some of my relatives to him."

"I don't think so," I said. "It sounded like he would be too busy doing things behind the scenes."

"That's too bad. But I suppose he would have to be busy to avoid the limelight. He loves to be at the middle of every ceremony—even ours." She smiled impishly. "*My* chancellor does things differently."

"She does," I agreed, but by then the crowd of royal relatives had swept her away. We exchanged a few glances across the crowd, but didn't manage to get close to each other again before the guards began ushering us in for the ceremony.

TENIA HAS A *lot of relatives*, I thought to myself. The bejeweled crowd filled the room so tightly that even the guards barely had room to move. I had so little family—or at least so little that I'd seen since my mother's death—that the sea of excited people who surrounded us at the initiation ceremony seemed unfathomable to me.

I thought the Empress would call Tenia up last, but she actually called her daughter first.

Tenia glowed as she stepped forward toward the Seat of Ananya where her mother awaited her.

"You are my jewel," the Empress said as she opened her arms. Tenia stepped forward into her mother's embrace.

The air crackled with magic. Tenia's expression changed as the magic flowed into her, and her features took on a calmness I'd never seen. She stepped aside as the Empress called the next girl's name, and stood looking at her family with utter serenity.

Magic filled the air as the Empress embraced each initiate. Her magic suffused the room. Colorful streamers of light danced and spun in the air as if the initiates couldn't contain all the magic that flowed from her. Underneath it I felt a faint humming, and blue light flickered at the edge of my vision: the barely visible glow of ancient runes beneath layers of paint and paper that covered the walls of the Hall of Ceremonies.

Nearly everyone had been called to receive the Empress's magic and I wondered why she had chosen to leave me for last. Then I realized she was giving my father as much time as possible to make it to the ceremony.

I didn't see him anywhere in the room. A few of his fellow ministers had glanced my way sympathetically—pitying me because official duties meant my father hadn't been able to attend his own daughter's confirmation into power.

I still didn't see him when I approached the throne for the Empress's embrace. And then I didn't care, as the Empress held me and power flowed into me. For the first time since my mother's death, I knew what it meant to feel whole and complete.

"Aren't you precious," the Empress said, echoing the first words she'd spoken to me. Colorful streamers of magic flickered around her blonde hair. "You are still much quieter than your father. But tonight I think you have made him proud." She embraced me a second time, holding me tight the way my mother had, or the way I wished my mother had.

I felt an odd sensation—something magical, but like nothing I ever felt at the academy. Then the runes on the walls winked out.

The Empress stiffened and spat blood on me. The colors vanished from her hair. Another channeler screamed. Then they all started screaming. A guard at the door clutched his throat. Something flashed in my head.

The magic ripped itself out of me even more swiftly than it had flowed in. I couldn't move. Couldn't breathe.

I heard Tenia call my name, an agonized wail. Her mother collapsed onto me, gushing blood.

Then the palace faded into darkness.

Part II
The Drowned City

Chapter 8

Sperrin
The Drowned City: The night of the Loss

I never knew her name, but the dead girl changed everything. On my rounds as commander of the Early Watch, I had seen the girl arrive in the palace the previous morning with the other channeler-initiates from the Empress's Academy. Not routine exactly, especially with all the celebrations surrounding the return of the Empress's daughter, but as long as they could be kept out of trouble until then, the group of girls would assume their powers with the Empress's touch in the midnight ceremony that completed the Festival of Initiation.

At the time, I didn't give the girl a second thought.

I spent the day mostly guarding introduction parties and keeping virile junior palace guards separated from doe-eyed new arrivals. By the time the actual ceremony started, I was asleep in the West Tower room I shared with the commander of the Late Watch.

The screams weren't what woke me: I was half a palace away from the first attack. I woke when the lights went out.

The lights never went out in the Drowned City. Darkness never touched the palace here at the heart of the Ananyan Empress's magic. Even from a deep sleep, when the wall-lamp flickered and died I woke instantly.

I had been a soldier for almost thirty years—changes in environment meant danger.

Danger had passed silently on its way to the Empress's glittering Presentation Chamber. Fifteen steps from the door of my chamber, I saw the same girl dead on the floor at the foot of the tower stairs, in the hallway that linked the guardroom with the kitchens and guest quarters. Likely, she'd been on her way to the ceremony after visiting someone she shouldn't have. A slice through her shoulder blade had cut her almost in half.

She'd been dead an hour, meaning she had died before the lights went out.

No light palace blade had caused that wound. Maybe not even a human blade.

The girl looked about the age my daughter would have been. The age my daughter *was*, I corrected myself. As far as I knew, my daughter still lived.

Only, I hadn't known about my daughter when I'd fallen asleep. By order of the Empress, she wasn't my daughter anymore. Her mother was no longer my wife.

My family, and all my memories of them, had been the Empress's price for accepting me into palace service. Had been her price for letting me leave the battlefield and put an end to the killing I had started to love too much. Memories of why I had left, of what I had done, remained fuzzy. I could remember only bits and pieces about my wife.

But at that moment, standing over a dead girl's body in a dim hallway lit only by moonlight through the high windows, I remembered my daughter's name for the first time in a decade: Lynniene.

That was the moment when I knew the Empress must be dead. *Not just the Empress*, I realized. *The whole royal family had been gathered for tonight's celebration.* Empresses had died before. When an Empress died before abdicating, the magic passed to her closest blood relative. Which tonight, seemed to be…*no one.*

Lifting my blade, I moved noiselessly through the hallway toward the Presentation Chamber. Like the memories of my family, battlefield reflexes returned quickly. I found myself smiling, even now at the moment that my Empress was dead and my whole world dying along with her: It was time to find something to kill.

Ketya
The Drowned City: The morning after the Loss

I woke groggy and disoriented. Sticky blood covered me.

Water lapped at my feet.

I held a dead woman in my arms. *The Empress.* The thought only slowly registered, as if it came from far away. As if I wasn't soaked in the broken woman's blood.

The body and I lay curled together across the huge gilded bulk of the Seat of Ananya, the Empress's throne. Early morning light shining through high, arched windows lit the Presentation Chamber dimly, even with the wall-lanterns darkened. Several women floated facedown in knee-deep water, which lapped gently at the base of the Seat. Barbed darts protruded from the floating women's backs, like museum pieces from the Holy War.

The truce must have been broken, or betrayed: After eight hundred years of exile, gods had returned to Ananya. For a moment after I regained consciousness, the scene felt oddly abstract. I wondered who had let the servants of the gods into the palace. The passages between worlds were sealed. Only a few people had the skills to even see the seals, much less open them. Who had broken the seals? Who had invited the gods back into this world?

Then I looked at all the dead around me, and the bodies suddenly became real.

All of my academy classmates, dead. The Empress who had done so much for my family, dead. Her consort—Tenia's father—sprawled alongside the throne, his head split open. The magic that flowed through the Empress, lifeblood to Ananya, gone.

Tenia!

She couldn't be one of them—the cold, floating bodies. She had to be alive.

I thought of her as I'd just seen her a few minutes ago—no, it had to be a few hours ago, from the light coming through the windows. In my mind I saw her alive and glowing, colors flickering in her blonde ringlets as her mother embraced her.

Then I saw her.

She floated face-up, apparently unmarked. An anguished look had replaced the easy smile I remembered. I remembered hearing a scream as I had passed out.

Dead, all dead.

The Empress and her whole family. All of them had been in this room. The only movement other than me came from bodies gently rocking in the rising floodwaters.

Many of the channelers' bodies looked unmarked, killed by the magic torn from them when the Empress died. The bodies of the guards and relatives had been hacked apart. *What could do such a thing?* I answered my own question: *The gods, or their servants, nothing else.*

My father had drilled that into me, the same way he'd made me memorize the treaty. The gods were to be feared and respected, but never trusted.

Only the treaty and its guardians—the Empress and her chancellor, who'd surrendered their names for the privilege—stood between the people of Ananya and the brutal return of the gods.

And now the Empress and the entire royal family lay dead around me. If my father had been at the ceremony the way I had asked him, he would be dead too.

I couldn't avoid the question any longer. *Is my father alive?*

But he had to be. I knew he had to be. He had told me that someday I would have no one left in the world to turn to but him. he had repeated the words just this afternoon.

He had to be alive tonight. I would die if I lost him to.

He would be crushed, though. My father had brought all of the royal family together for the first time in generations. His grand gesture had been used by someone as the means to destroy Ananya, to strip the empire of magic. What would happen when he realized that his actions had so badly failed his Empress?

He would need me too, I realized. He would need me as much as I needed him. I focused on that, as the water sloshed around Tenia and I looked at the dead face of the girl who had called me her chancellor, who had blown me a kiss across the room and promised we'd be together forever. *My only friend.* I focused on my father's need. He would need me. I had to live for that. He needed me.

I felt an ache in my chest where the Empress's magic had been torn from me. It hurt, but it wouldn't kill me. Absurdly, I thought about Rhenne, the small redheaded girl who had lost her place at the Academy while I was kept in her stead, because my father was chancellor to the Empress. Rhenne's latent ability to channel the Empress's magic had been stronger than mine, but not strong enough to keep her place. Tonight, she was still alive because she had lost that place.

For years at the Academy I had struggled with the awareness that I'd only been admitted for my political connections, for my father's position and my friendship with the Empress's daughter, rather than for the just-barely-good-enough strength of my gift. Now, as I looked at the bodies of the students who had mocked me lying dead in the water, I knew that weakness had saved my life. I felt numb and empty from the loss of magic, but not dead.

Gingerly, I untangled myself from the husk of the Empress and stood up.

My legs wobbled as I stepped down from the Seat, holding the massive gilded arms for support.

Water covered the last two steps. I shivered, unable to control my reaction. I squatted on the step and rinsed the blood from my hands and face in the brackish water. I scrubbed my face hard, as if it would make the reality around me go away.

No one can see you, I thought. *You're just wasting time.*

I didn't care. Even if no one else was alive in the palace I had to wash off the Empress's blood.

I'm only still alive because I'm a terrible channeler. And now there's nothing to channel.

I took another step in my ruined shoes, sloshing through lukewarm water.

There's only one person in this palace who will have answers to what's going on here, and that's my father. He knew I could turn to him when I had nothing else left. He said so.

I knew he was still alive. I needed him to be. He hadn't been at the initiation ceremony. I clung to that. Remembered the people who had glanced my way—pitying me because official duties had meant my father hadn't been able to attend his own daughter's confirmation into power. Hadn't been there when I approached the throne, when I felt the Empress's embrace. For a moment I tried to savor the feeling of connection, of acceptance, of power again, but I couldn't. All I could see was Tenia. *What will I do without you, Tenia?*

Trust your father, she had told me. And that's what I would have to do. If I could find him.

Hours had passed since the attack. I might be alone in the dying palace. If there had been a counterattack it would have already happened.

For a moment I thought the counterattack might have failed already, or passed through and left me for dead. But then I realized that Ananyan soldiers would never have left the Empress's body behind. There had been no counterattack.

I knew my father's duty as chancellor if the palace faced a catastrophic attack: My father would have led an evacuation through the sally tunnels to safety. I knew his duty meant he couldn't risk others' lives to try and find me or save me, not when so many were dying. So I would have to find him myself.

Water sloshed at my feet as I began to wade forward. With the Empress and Tenia and the royal family dead, all the magic in the Drowned City had faded away. Binding magics had strengthened the levees holding back the sea from the half of the Drowned City that remained above water. Those bindings had vanished with the harbor defenses and the lights on the walls and in the streetlamps. As I sloshed toward the door of the Presentation Chamber, circling to avoid the floating bodies of my classmates, I could feel the water rising, slowly but perceptibly.

My father would most likely have been in his office in the South Tower when the gods had struck. He might have gone any number of places since then, but his office, I decided, was where I should start looking—if for no other reason than that it meant ascending, away from the rising floodwater.

Sperrin
The Drowned City: The night of the Loss

My first two kills were god-sent: an slender silverwing with glossy marks around its wingtips and green eyes, and a hulking ironback with black-and-red chains tattooed around its neck and shoulders. I committed details of their features to memory, so I could write them down accurately later. A decade after Khemme's suggestion, it still helped me to hold onto myself since I had gotten myself so lost in killing—the details were still murky in the just-returning memories.

The ironback I took outside the Hall of Ceremonies, in a presentation area filled with display cases. It had killed two guards with its heavy, back-curved stillsword and was tossing heavy darts at a pair of fleeing servants. The ironback half-turned as it noticed me coming into the chamber, flexing its shoulders so the tattoos rippled on its iron-gray skin. The creature didn't look very worried. It threw another dart, shattering the skull of the last servant, then turned to face me.

The guards' palace swords had shattered against the ironback's stillsword. It seemed surprised when my blade held. *They never know how to fence*, I thought, meaning the guards and the creature both. I remembered reading that in the book at the Officers' Academy, so many years ago.

The ironback didn't seem to have a plan for when its strength and power failed to overwhelm me. I deflected an overhand slash, then severed the creature's spine with a slash through the gap in its collarbone, where ironback armor was weakest. Apparently, the information in the book could be trusted.

By the time I had worked my way to the central guard station, I found myself sloshing through ankle-deep water. The city engineer had once bragged to me of the levees' ability to hold for up to a week in a magical failure, but that had clearly been optimistic. I had passed the man's corpse on my way through the dining hall.

The silverwing attacked from above. I heard the slight whir as it flapped its wings twice before diving.

Jumping out of the path of the silverwing's dive, I wheeled and slashed its right wing tendon, crippling the wing and throwing it off balance. Ignoring the tough skin on the creature's exposed back, I stepped inside its guard on the crippled side and gutted it. The silverwing splashed facedown into the water. I pinned its head underwater with my foot until it stopped thrashing.

Those two messengers of the gods—I had no idea which god they served—seemed to be outliers. Most of the palace attackers must have moved on to other targets in the city. Not until I reached the Presentation Chamber did I find another sign of life.

Ketya
The Drowned City: The morning after the Loss

I had seen the older guardsman before, though I couldn't remember his name. Most guards were in their mid-twenties, four or five years older than me—veterans, but not graybeards. This one was closer to my father's age than to mine. I recognized him because he always carried a big, clumsy-looking blade on a worn baldric. It looked jarring hanging across the breast of his tai-lored palace guard uniform. He had some sort of scandal in his past, but I don't think I had ever heard the details. After what had happened to Mala and her parents, people were very reluctant to pass gossip or rumors on to me. My father had a way of intimidating people.

It wasn't like my father told me anything much, either.

Grizzled or not, right now I was glad to see the guardsman. He carried the blade unsheathed in his right hand: It looked black, like seasoned iron, rather than the silvered inlays of the palace blades. Here and there I could see odd grooves and studs, though whether they were for bladework or to facilitate magic I had no idea. It struck me as strange that even as a just-initiated chan-neler I didn't recognize the design of the blade. It must be very old, I decid-ed. It looked a little like some of the patterns in the old theater costumes but I didn't know what it signified, if anything.

Sperrin

"Have you seen anyone else alive?" I asked the girl. It took me a minute to place her, soaked in blood and bedraggled as she was: Ketya, the chancellor's daughter. A little shy perhaps. Just returned from the Empress's Academy but I'd seen her around the palace for years before that. Not one of the girls I had to keep away from the guardroom. "You came from the Presentation Chamber, correct?"

Ketya shook her head. "No one," she managed to say. "The water is getting deep there."

I nodded. "Are you hurt?"

"I don't...I don't think so. The blood is...the Empress...I..."

I didn't wait for a coherent answer, patting her down quickly. "You're right, you aren't hurt. Nothing cut or broken, anyway. You are sure no one is alive back there?"

"I'm sure. I hoped I would find someone..."

"Me too. But I'm not surprised. We need to get to the sally tunnels. I don't think they will be flooded. And as far as I know they are the only place in the palace safe from the godlings."

To my surprise she shook her head again. "We can't," she said.

"What do you mean, we can't? Why not?"

"I don't mean we can't. I mean we have to go to the South Tower first. My father's there. Or at least, he might be. Have you seen him?"

You're father's dead, I wanted to say. But I didn't actually know that. Not surprisingly, there weren't any standing orders for what to do if the royal family and everyone else in the palace had been massacred. As far as I could tell, my duty was to find whatever survivors I could and get them out of the palace to safety, then worry about what to do next.

I could check the South Tower, but there was a good chance that doing so would get the one survivor I *had* found killed.

But I couldn't ask her to leave the palace not knowing whether her father was alive or dead. I wondered if my own long-forgotten daughter thought I was dead.

"Stay behind me," I said. "Close, but not too close. If something kills me, you don't want it to get you on the same blow."

She smiled wanly, as if she thought I was joking.

Ketya

The whole thing felt like one of those dreams where nothing makes sense but you can't wake up. Things got progressively stranger on the way to my father's chambers. I was following the soldier—Sperrin, I'd finally remembered his name was—"close but not too close" when he stopped at one of the bodies. I'd been trying not to look at them—so many of them were people I'd known for years—but he had spotted something that seemed important to him.

Steeling myself against the sight of yet another dead friend, I edged closer—hoping it wasn't "too close." Then I saw what had stopped him.

This body didn't belong here.

The corpse wore a green-and-gold Central Alliance uniform.

By the dart in its back, the soldier had been killed by the godsent, so at least the gods weren't teaming up with Ananya's strongest enemy. But what was an Alliance soldier doing here in the palace?

Two attacks at the same time went beyond coincidence.

After a moment or two of checking the soldier's body, Sperrin seemed satisfied with what he'd found and we moved on. I wondered what he'd been looking for, but didn't want to ask. He hadn't said a word to me since the "close but not too close" comment.

I wanted to hear another living human voice to help push the dead ones out of my mind, but even in my current bad-dream-you-can't-wake-up-from state that sounded stupid and dangerous. Sperrin was probably still alive for a reason, while only a combination of blind luck and my lack of magical aptitude had saved me so far. I would have to wait to ask questions until we were out of the palace.

I kept reminding myself of that, but I still had trouble not calling out to Sperrin as he walked ahead of me, never seeming to look back.

As we approached the South Tower stairway, Sperrin held his left hand up to stop me. He went completely still. A moment later I heard a footstep on the stairs.

Quiet as a serpent, Sperrin edged forward, disappearing into the doorway that led to the stairs.

Do I stay here? I wondered. *It might be my father on the stairs.* I waited for what I hoped was long enough to let him find whatever was up there, then followed after as quietly as I could.

Sperrin stood behind a column at the edge of the main landing, watching.

In front of him on the landing six Central Alliance soldiers lounged in that pose soldiers got between duties with no officers nearby. All of the soldiers were male, and husky. Piled in the center of the landing were empty pack frames and poles. They planned on carrying something out of here. A fairly substantial something. But what? The South Tower held administrative records and the living quarters of the chancellor and his staff. Not the sort of records people would kill for, either—mainly birth and marriage and employment records. Maybe the soldiers were lost, or in the wrong place?

Like a serpent, Sperrin uncurled and struck. The first soldier fell before he realized Sperrin was on the landing. Two more died reaching for their weapons. Then three of them circled Sperrin, blades in hand. Their weapons crackled slightly with the sound of magic. I could see slight green flickering on their blades.

I didn't see Sperrin's hand move but suddenly one of the soldiers fell. Dark blood welled from the fallen man's side. The other two came at Sperrin, one high and one low. Sperrin pivoted and chopped. His heavy black blade sliced through the first man's neck and lodged deeply in the second attacker's back. Both of them pitched to the ground, unmoving.

Sperrin glanced back at me as he cleared his blade, then cleaned it. Something looked different about him. It took me a moment to place what had changed.

In all the years I'd seen him in the palace, I had never seen him smile before.

His blade secured, Sperrin walked over to the man whose side he'd cut. The Central Alliance soldier lay in a pool of blood, still moving slightly.

Squatting, Sperrin bent over the man, and said a few words in one of the languages of the Central Alliance. The dying soldier grimaced and spat. Sperrin said a few more words, sounding a little regretful. Then he calmly stood up and wiped the bloody spittle from his face.

He motioned me into the landing. Carefully, I stepped around the bodies. The Alliance swords lay on the stone floor, magic gone with their wielders' deaths.

"Where will your father be?" he asked. The smile had faded, replaced by his usual neutral expression.

I pointed up the short flight of stairs. "There. He'll be in there if…if he's here."

"Thank you," said Sperrin. He began walking.

The injured soldier had died, I noticed.

I walked fast to catch up with Sperrin. Probably "too close," but there was something I needed to ask. "What was it you said to that soldier?" I asked. "What made him so mad?"

"His name," Sperrin responded. "I asked him to tell me his name before he died."

Sperrin

I knocked on the heavy door. Painted decorative edging scrolled around the door like a trellis, distinctive from all the other doors in this section of the palace. Fresh paint, too. The chancellor had picked a poor time to have his door redecorated.

Knocking seemed an oddly formal gesture, under the circumstances.

A bolt slid back and the door drew open slightly. Faint light backlit the chancellor as he appeared in the slight crack of the doorway.

"Overcaptain Sperrin. It is an honor to see you, as always." The chancellor wore well-tailored traveling clothes, just worn enough to look comfortable and yet somehow formal. His short chestnut beard was neatly trimmed, despite the earliness of the hour. Even in the half-light his personable green eyes seemed to twinkle. His daughter has the same eyes, I thought. If you hadn't been forced to watch him officiate at an execution, it was impossible not to like the chancellor. Which was why he was chancellor, I supposed.

I still despised the man.

That wasn't really fair, I knew. I had a soldier's distrust for politicians and their insincerity, and this was the highest-ranking politician in Ananya who wasn't actually a member of the royal family.

Which meant, I realized, that at least in name the chancellor was the highest ranking person left in the Ananyan Empire, since all of the royal family was now dead in the Presentation Hall with the Empress. Until a few hours ago, the Empress's magic had made the palace the brightest building in all Ananya. The darkness in the halls around us was all the proof I needed that none of her family still lived.

Something felt off about the chancellor's clothing and demeanor. More than off: Much as I disliked him, the chancellor may have been the most fearless and aggressive man I ever knew. The man who had forced a broken army to take Davynen, just by sheer force of personality. The man who had ruthlessly destroyed every obstacle in his path. The only man whom the Empress had trusted utterly, and who had carried out her policies with a wolfhound's fierce devotion.

So why did the man whom I would have expected to be taking charge of a counter-attack not rally an attack? If even he saw a counter-attack as helpless, why was he not leading an evacuation? This was the last person in all Ananya I would have expected to find hiding in his chambers at a time of danger. And he was dressed as if he intended to leave on a pleasure cruise at any moment. Where was the commanding personality who had forced his way from the mud of Davynen to the height of the Empress's service?

In all the years I had known the man, I never knew the chancellor to do anything without reason. I had hated him for it since I first encountered him at the siege of Davynen, but he was brilliant at his job. He was brilliant at every job the Empress ever gave him. But now he seemed cowed, just another bureaucrat in a dead palace. *What happened to him?*

One possible answer dawned on me: Had the savior of Davynen lost his mind? I'd seen it happen to soldiers who couldn't face the reality of what they had done, or of what they had failed to do. They seemed normal and pleasant, but utterly disconnected from reality. I'd had my own disconnection with reality, as I was only now rediscovering. Maybe the demons that had driven me from the battlefield had taken hold of him.

The chancellor was perhaps the last person I ever expected to see that way. But as I knew from my still-incomplete memories, bravery and cleverness were not always enough to prevent doubts and fears from taking possession of your mind.

Some of those broken soldiers healed, I knew. And the chancellor would be needed in the upcoming war—war not just with the armies of the Central Alliance, but apparently with the gods themselves.

"Lord Chancellor, you need to come with us," I said.

"Out of the question. My place is here in the palace. My duty is to remain here."

The clothes belied that, I thought. But I chose my words carefully. "It is not safe here, your lordship. The palace is flooding. We need to take you to safety."

"I will be perfectly safe." The chancellor still hadn't opened the door fully.

I could see sealed crates and packages on the floor behind him. Wherever the chancellor thought he was going, he hadn't planned on traveling light.

Ketya came up from behind me. "Father," she said simply, and pushed her way through the door.

The chancellor opened his mouth to say something, but Ketya and I had entered his chambers already.

Candle lanterns lit the main room dimly, though it seemed bright after the near-darkness of the rest of the palace. What had been an immaculate chamber looked untidy now; if the chancellor had been packing for a trip he hadn't bothered straightening after the lights went out. A pile of boxes and bundles stood just inside the doorway, ready to be carried downstairs for whatever trip the chancellor fancied he was taking. Lying across the topmost bundle I saw an elaborately worked golden card-case, a fancier version of the kind used to protect field manuals and nautical charts.

"Father, we have to go," Ketya said. The chancellor's expression shifted from puzzlement to displeasure.

"You will not go anywhere dressed in those rags," he said. "Go into the other room and change. Some of your old clothes are still here. I burned the ones you had outgrown."

Ketya looked at him blankly and touched her tunic. Her hand came back wet with the Empress's blood. For a moment her face welled up as if about to cry. Then she swallowed hard, nodded, and walked into the other room without a word.

After a few moments of rustling, she emerged wearing drier clothes: a belted tunic over a shirt and loose trousers. A pair of well-worn low boots replaced her ruined formal shoes. She had scrubbed her face and hands, and pulled her long hair back out of her face and bound it with a bit of black velvet.

"Now we need to go," she said to her father.

"I will go nowhere," he said, his back to her. The chancellor faced the front door, as if waiting for another knock. Ketya walked toward him, past the pile of crates and packages. Then she lifted one of the candle lanterns. "Sperrin, help him please."

I took the chancellor's elbow and guided him toward the door, nudging it open with his foot. The chancellor shook me off and took a step, then froze.

He stood transfixed in the open doorway, staring at the bodies of the dead Central Alliance soldiers on the landing below.

Ketya followed his gaze. "Father, it isn't safe. We have to go."

This time the chancellor didn't resist when I took his arm.

Ketya

I couldn't understand why my father seemed so different. He hadn't foreseen this disaster, but it wasn't like him to wilt in the face of a reverse. This couldn't have been the first cataclysmic event he'd been surprised by, and he'd turned the others into victories. Why, this time, wasn't he rallying support, fighting back, finding some way to turn defeat into victory that even a god would never have thought of? That's what my father always did.

What made tonight different?

Then I noticed something missing. The Mouse King suit no longer hung on the armoire.

He must be wearing it, I realized. The implications of that took a moment to sink in. *Those are the suits Tenia said were used to speak to the gods. And he didn't deny it when I asked him about it. So he* did *see this coming. He must have somehow anticipated the attack and been sure he could stop it. And he failed, and the Empress died as a result.*

Not just the Empress. The Empress and the whole royal family.

My thoughts were running away with me now. *He might even have said something that made it worse. This must have crushed him.*

All my life, ever since my mother died, my father was the one strong figure I could count on. He was the one who was going to protect me when everyone else was gone.

Now everyone else is gone, and he is the one who needs protecting. It's time I grow up and do my duty to my father. If I can't serve the Empress, I will have to serve him instead.

I scrubbed my face and hands again—I hadn't actually gotten much of the blood off when I tried to clean them in the throne room—and dressed carefully in traveling clothes. I returned Tenia's talisman deck to the small of my back, where it had hidden all night. The cards were soaked, I was sure. But what else did I have to remember my best friend by?

I saw my father's eyes and the guardsman's eyes on me as I stepped back into the cluttered main room, with its stacked crates of books and personal effects that we would be leaving behind. And then I saw the Talisman of Truce itself, sitting on top of a crate as if forgotten.

He means to leave it behind, I realized. *Has his mind been so shattered that he's forgotten how important it is?*

Up until that point, I had assumed that we would get my father out and nurse him back to health and then he would talk to the god or gods who had done this and fix things. But he would need Ananya's original copy of the treaty to do that. Without it they would never talk to him.

For the first time, I realized that he might never heal. That for once in my life, my father might not be able to fix a problem. As I passed by the crates I palmed the Talisman and replaced it with Tenia's talisman deck, disguising the motion by picking up one of the candle lanterns so they followed my other hand. Mala would have been proud: Even with their eyes on me, neither my father nor the guardsman saw a thing. In the dimness of the candlelit room, the two cases looked identical. And picking up a lantern was sensible enough that it raised no questions.

Leaving behind the only keepsake I had from Tenia hurt almost as much as having the magic wrenched from me.

It took all my strength to keep my eyes forward and not glance back at the deck as Sperrin took my father's arm. Both of them were smart and decades more experienced than me. I didn't dare give them a hint that I had the Talisman until I knew how they would react. If my father made a scene it could kill us all. And it might reveal to the guardsman the real motivations for what I was going to have to do next.

Somebody is going to need to talk to the gods if we're ever going to get out of this, and it probably shouldn't be me. But if I leave the Talisman behind it won't be anybody. And I'll need a suit that someone can talk to the gods in, too, because my father may not recover, and if he doesn't he isn't about to give up the one he is wearing to whoever is able to do the talking. In spite of everything, for a moment I felt something closer to pride than sadness. *And I know just where I can get another suit.*

I hated to leave Tenia behind, but in that moment, I felt almost as if she was there. *What would you do, Tenia?* I wanted to ask. But then I realized that was the wrong question, if I wanted to survive and do my part to help fix this disaster.

What would you expect your chancellor to do, Tenia?

Forcing myself not to take a last glance at the gilded card case on top of the packing crates, I followed Sperrin and my father from the chamber.

Sperrin

Ketya hooded the lantern except for the barest sliver of light. It illuminated just enough for us to silently make our way through the dark, windowless galleries that led toward the tower bridge. From within the stoneworks that enclosed the bridge we would be able to see most of the city without being seen ourselves. More important, several sheltered stairways led downward to the High Road, the raised causeway that ran along the inside of the city walls. Built up over generations, the High Road would still be above the level of floodwaters, even if the levees had failed completely.

If the levees had failed completely, there were a lot of people dead in the city tonight. I'd grown more pessimistic as I'd worked my way through the castle, finding only the two survivors. Most of the attacking godservants had already moved on. There had been whole cities massacred in the early years of the Holy War, I knew. That had been done by armies of gods and their servants, not by the comparative handful I'd seen signs of here. But that didn't mean there weren't others I hadn't seen.

The view from the bridge would tell me if the High Road would let us get to one of the inland gates. If we could get to an inland gate, we could escape the city on the river side, where we could count on cover from attackers.

We moved quietly. Ketya ranged slightly ahead with the light while I guided her father. I noticed when she'd concealed the card case in her clothes, replacing it with an identical one she'd already carried. She'd taken it right in front of me, so whatever the case contained, she hid it from her father, not from me.

The chancellor followed along pliably as long as I kept a hand on him. All of us knew this part of the palace well; heavily trafficked during the day, it fell quiet during evening and overnight hours. Now, in the early morning, it would normally be coming back to life, full of servants with bundles and carts and messengers on their two-wheeled scooters rushing through the passages to prepare for when the palace would awaken.

We met nothing alive in the galleries that led to the tower bridge. Even the bodies lay widely separated, a handful of servants cut down from behind while fleeing. All bore the marks of godsent blades, not Central Alliance weapons.

Nothing I saw added much to my understanding of the twin invasions of the palace.

Ketya

Every child in Ananya knew the story of the Holy War and its aftermath. Both sides had claimed victory, with some justification. The gods and their servants had withdrawn to their own homeland, reachable only through passageways that no one without the blood of gods in their veins could find. In exchange for this withdrawal, every human land would be ruled by a queen or empress descended from one or another of the gods. The rulers would live and die as humans, and each kingdom would benefit from the magic of the gods, flowing through each of those queens. No god or godservant would return to the lands of humanity, except by the express invitation of one of the five principal empresses or her chosen representative. Each of those five was given a copy of the Talisman of Truce. The symbol of the war's end, the cards that made up each Talisman contained the complete text of the truce with the gods. They also served as a symbol of the compact that even the gods would have to honor if it were presented to them.

Most girls learned the story and perhaps had to memorize the preamble to the treaty to recite at Talisman Day festivals. That was the end of their education in the peace settlement that ended the Holy War. But my father was very proud of his role as guarantor of the treaty. As chancellor, he held the physical Talisman in the Empress's name, and was responsible for making sure that Ananya upheld its obligations to the gods under the treaty. To impress his daughter with the magnitude of his duty, he'd required that I memorize all of the treaty's 267 clauses. It took me more than a year, but I had done it. Even now, years later, I could quote most of the Talisman from memory.

Which didn't really explain why I now had the Talisman concealed between blouse and tunic, at the small of my back. I didn't really have an explanation for that—in the dimness I had begun to doubt my motives again. I knew that we couldn't leave the treaty behind in the tower when we left. But wouldn't a word to my father have sufficed to remind him, no matter how upset he was? Instead I'd picked up the case and hidden it from him, almost like lying to him.

Despite the near-lie, I drew a certain comfort from feeling the Talisman against my back as we approached the bridge. I could almost pretend I still carried Tenia's deck, that I still had a part of her with me. Barely any light remained from the guttering candle. Entombed in this dead palace, I needed every possible comfort.

The tower bridge had been added to the palace more than a century ago. The bridge connected the towers that housed the then fast-expanding Ananyan Empire's administrative officers without impeding the flow of information by forcing messengers to descend from one tower and climb another to pass documents between ministers. In recent years bridge traffic had fallen dramatically, replaced by a magically powered network of polished wooden tubes along which laquered cylinders containing documents sped more quickly than any messenger. However, the bridge remained a convenient passageway between towers, and the sweeping views of the city combined with its comparative seclusion made it a popular lovers' walk.

The white stone blocks that made up the bridge causeway glowed faintly pink from morning sunlight coming through tall, narrow window bays. The harborside windows overlooked and defended the High Road. Sperrin strode quickly to the nearest window bay, releasing my father, who stood like a wax-museum statue in the middle of the covered causeway.

Sperrin took a step back, his face grim.

I knew what that expression meant, but I stepped forward into the nearest window bay anyway.

Through the window I could see the submerged neighborhoods between the harbor and the city's walls. A few taller buildings poked through the surface, but most houses had sunk beneath the water. The levees seemed to have been swept away entirely. In the city's walled sections the streets had flooded, but parts of most houses stood above the flood. Several of the great towers had collapsed completely, undermined by floodwaters. A cable-carriage had smashed into the top of the same berthing tower I had arrived on less than a day ago: The cables had snapped, leaving the tower sagging and the carriage floating upside down beside it.

But I could see people clinging to roofs, and rescue boats rowing through the flooded streets.

Three great warships floated at anchor in the inner harbor, flying the four-colored flag of the Central Alliance. Soldiers crowded the decks, and longboats crewed by soldiers rowed back and forth filled with looted treasures from the city. Someone must have released the great chain that blocked the harbor to large ships, I realized. That berricade was designed to remain even if all the city's magical defenses failed. Who could give such an order? I wondered briefly if it had something to do with the commotion that Tenia had told me about right before the ceremony. My father would know, but I couldn't exactly ask him.

But more than mere chains protected the harbor. The magic that had protected the Drowned City held back more than just ocean waters. As I watched, one of the longboats listed suddenly and then capsized. Soldiers floundered in the water, only to be pulled under.

A mast on one of the warships creaked loudly as a great black tentacle wrapped around it and began to pull. A second tentacle emerged from the harbor depths. Flicking back and forth across the warship's deck, it threw a half dozen soldiers into the water before wrapping around another mast. Soldiers on the deck chopped frantically at the tentacles with their blades and sea-axes as the deck began to tilt. The other two ships cut their anchor cables and began making their way out of the harbor, wakes churning behind them as the ships' channelers started their screws turning. The Alliance ships left their longboats behind as more dark tentacles emerged from the thrashing water to capsize the beleaguered ship and pull it under.

Nearer to the palace walls, refugees clogged the High Road. Water lapped against the walls beyond the road. Now and again a tentacle reached over the wall and grabbed some luckless refugee from the road, pulling them screaming into the water. But for the most part the sea creatures concentrated on the feast in the harbor, and on the floating corpses of people caught in their beds when the floodwaters burst through the levees.

The godservants seemed to have departed with the coming of the dawn, the only hopeful sign. With the retreat of the Central Alliance ships, the survivors would be able to rescue the living, and dispose of any dead that evaded the sea monsters.

"Should we help with the rescues?" I asked, my voice shaky.

I knew the answer, but didn't want to be the one who said it out loud.

Sperrin shook his head. "We leave. You may be the only channeler left alive in the country. And your father, despite his present condition, is an important official. We get you to safety, to someplace where you won't be killed before we've figured out what happened and can launch a counterattack."

That seemed like an odd use of *we*, until I realized Sperrin meant the army. He still thought of himself as a field soldier, not a palace guard. *Which is probably the only reason we are alive*, I knew.

Reluctantly, I nodded. It felt like we should be helping, but I had no idea what I could do to help here. I had certainly trained in disaster assistance at the Empress's Academy—but everything I had learned required magic. I had no idea how to move debris or perform rescues without magical assistance. Somewhere else, with a little time to think, I might be able to help piece together what had happened, and how to start fixing it. But here and now, my father and I were liabilities, people who wouldn't be helpful in the recovery efforts but who would need to be guarded and fed at the cost of precious resources.

None of this made any sense.

The gods were forbidden to come here without an invitation. That prohibition had stood for centuries. Fickle as they were, gods did not break their treaties. And the Empress and her family were of the gods' own blood, in a direct line from the goddess Senne, who had given up her own powers so that her descendents would enjoy her magic instead.

And why would the Central Alliance attack on the same night, but send only three ships, with their own channelers unprepared for the creatures that haunted the harbor? Why was the harbor chain not in place?

More important at the moment was the question of how to get out of the palace alive. Sperrin seemed to be thinking the same thing.

"Will the old sally tunnels be dry?" he asked us both.

My father ignored the question.

I thought back to a dozen history lectures. "They should be. They were built for the Holy War, and they were used to launch attacks when the city was flooded originally. I think there's some special way of keeping water out."

"That's what I thought," said Sperrin. "But how do we get to them? The entrance I know is in the foundation of the West Tower, down the back stairway from the guardhouse. That will definitely be underwater by now."

This was the chance I had been waiting for. I pretended to think over each of the other entrances to the sally tunnels. Sperrin and I both knew that all of the ones in the newer parts of the palace would be inaccessible. But perhaps somewhere in the old palace. "The theater," I said finally, trying to put a note of hesitation in my voice then seeming to gain confidence. "It was built on a hillside originally for the natural light, so it will be above floodwaters. And there is a tunnel entrance from the old dressing room. I don't know why it's there, but I've been in it."

I looked at my father, wondering if he would give a more authoritative answer that would ruin my chance to recover another costume. Of all the city administrators, he knew the escape routes and emergency plans better than anyone. I had seen the heavily annotated maps and copies of emergency plans in his offices, even though I'd never been allowed to read them.

My father wore a neutral expression, but still said nothing. He just listened to us silently. I had a feeling he knew why the theater connected to the sally tunnels. But it would be pointless to ask him directly—the best we could hope for, till he regained his old self, would be that he continued to come with us quietly.

I looked out the window again at the refugee-clogged road and the flooded city. The sun had fully risen over the harbor. A slight cool breeze off the sea ruffled my hair.

I wondered if I would ever see the city where I'd spent so much of my life again.

This wasn't the way I wanted to remember the Drowned City. The only thing I carried with me to remember it by was the cased Talisman hidden at the small of my back. The last, failed symbol of my dead city, and my dead friend.

Chapter 9

We approached the theater through a side passage. Although deep underground now, the hallway had once been an open atrium filled with artwork and cut flowers when this had been the hillside annex of a younger, smaller palace.

I led the way, surefooted even in the dimness of the passage. The candle in the lantern had almost burned out, but even in its barest flickerings I knew the way from a hundred childhood memories.

Sperrin held his blade righthanded and gripped my father's elbow firmly with his left hand. He pulled the silent chancellor along with little resistance.

The old part of the palace felt dry; even the air smelled dry, although we had crossed below the waterline outside. We would have to go lower still to reach the tunnels, but after the flooding above I found the dryness of the air refreshing.

We'd seen no signs of godsent attackers since entering the old part of the palace—not even bodies left behind by them. Whether that was because so few people spent any time in this part of the palace at night when the gods had struck, or because of some innate warding power, I didn't know. But out of the corner of my eye I glimpsed the familiar blue of the runes Tenia had told me no longer existed. I sensed them in places I never had before, as if the long-dormant old magic now reacted to the unwelcome intrusion of gods.

"This way," I said, turning into an alcove. The white door with its gilded decorations looked gray in the dimness. "This door leads to the seats on the right side of the hall. It's quicker than the main entrance. Be careful, there are three steps down."

The tiny details about the theater that I remembered after all these years surprised me.

I pushed the brass handle downward and the door swung inward silently, same as always.

"This is…different." I hadn't meant to say the words aloud.

The theater had transformed. The seats in front of me looked plush, their worn flax covers replaced by rich velvet. A warm blue glow radiated from the walls—from everywhere, really. The stage shone most brightly: A wide ring of blue runes glowed on the center of the stage floor.

There was nothing elusive or half-glimpsed about these runes.

Tenia had told me they didn't exist. And I had just spent several years at the Empress's Academy studying all there was to know about magic in Ananya, and I had never seen anything like those runes. I might not be a very good channeler, but I *was* a very good learner. I knew that if anything like this had been touched on at all by the Academy instructors, I would have remembered it.

Stepping down the stairs, I started toward the stage, slowly. I couldn't help myself.

Behind me Sperrin entered, still holding my father firmly by the elbow. He closed the door behind us.

"It looks like the magic in the theater is not quite so dead as the rest of the city," Sperrin said. "Why is this room lit?"

"But the magic *is* dead," I answered. "I don't know what the light and these runes are, but I don't feel anything like magic inside me. This isn't Ananyan magic."

My father laughed drily. It was nearly the first sound he had made since we left the dead soldiers and the tower. "Ananyan magic is exactly what it is. It is the very heart of Ananya's magic. You think there was no magic in Ananya before the Holy War ended? Do you think we always suffered with what little magic the gods doled out to us? Fools!"

"Why can I see it now? No one can use the old magic anymore."

"It was a gift from your mother," said the chancellor, the words coming out sounding more like a curse than a statement. "A gift from beyond the grave."

I had no idea what he meant. I just gaped at him.

"What do you mean?" asked Sperrin.

My father turned. He looked Sperrin up and down slowly, as if seeing him for the first time.

"Did you address me?" my father asked, for a moment every bit the chancellor. He shook his elbow free of Sperrin's grip and took a couple of steps back from the soldier.

Sperrin gave my father a puzzled look.

"What did you call me?" the chancellor repeated.

There was no stopping my father when he got that tone, I knew. I'd certainly heard it often enough. Even if this seemed like an odd time and place for it.

I had a feeling that Sperrin wouldn't defer to my father the way I did. The way everyone else in the palace who wasn't royal did, too. I didn't want to hear an argument. I hated the way my father crushed people who disagreed with him. It was the job of the chancellor, he'd told me often enough. But sometimes I wished he wasn't quite so rigorous in performing that part of his job.

He's still my father, and a great lord of Ananya. I would love to stand up to him sometimes, but I can't. Even if it is my place. I thought the words, but I didn't really believe them. I didn't want to stand up to my father. A part of me just wanted to be the kind of girl who would, like Tenia. The same way a part of me had wanted to be a *real* channeler, like all the dead women back in the Presentation Chamber.

I waited for the onslaught.

Sperrin spat on the floor, as if to clear dryness from his mouth.

"This doesn't seem like the place for titles." Sperrin emphasized the word *titles*. "I would have used your name, but you don't have one. Did you ever have a name?"

The chancellor gave him a look that would have withered me. "I did. My wife, my parents, and my Empress had the privilege of addressing me by that name. All of them are gone now. You may address me by title, as all others do."

So he knows the Empress died, I realized. *At least a part of him is still here with us in the present.*

Sperrin seemed unmoved by the words. He glanced at me before he spoke. "Even your daughter?"

"Especially my daughter."

Except I never call him by title. I call him "father." So what is he talking about?

I brushed a loose strand of hair out of my face, checked to see my ponytail was secure, and tried to keep walking toward the stage and ignore the brewing tension. I felt the cased Talisman snug at the small of my back, scratching a little against the fabric of my shirt, and it calmed me. It let me pretend I could ask Tenia for advice.

Has my father gone crazy? No, Tenia would have told me. Angry and upset by a situation beyond his control. And frustrated because he has no one to take his anger out on. But he's still sane. He's still my father. I still have to trust him, even if he's lost his way.

Sperrin shook his head and took a guard position, watching my father as carefully as he watched the doors. Sperrin had a look on his face like someone's pet dog had just tried to bite him.

I wondered if the big soldier thought my father had gone mad. I wondered if that was what my father wanted him to think. But mostly I wondered why this room was lit and filled with glowing blue runes, while everywhere else in the palace the magic was gone.

Reaching the stage, I pulled myself up onto the polished wooden planks.

Blue light radiated upward from the wide circle of runes that filled the center of the stage. The runes themselves glowed steadily; they didn't pulse or flicker like flames. Something about them felt tremendously old.

They've been here all along, I realized. All the time my friends and I play-acted on this stage we were dancing on a nexus of magic. We just couldn't see them before. Something hid them. *Were they hidden by the Empress's magic?*

Then whose magic is this? I had no idea. Who in Ananya had magic before the gods? How did it work? I knew the old magic existed, that it had been used to injure or even kill some gods, but the history books said nothing useful about it—they were banned from saying anything too specific by the treaty itself.

Carefully, I walked around the circle of runes.

Within a few moments I found myself wandering backstage. A wall of silence descended; for a moment I didn't have to think about saying the wrong thing or about my father's cutting words. I didn't have to think about Tenia's body in the water or the Empress's blood covering me. For a moment I was twelve years old again, wandering in a thick forest of costumes that none of us had ever dared to touch.

I needed one of those costumes.

My hand reached out and touched the Snake Slayer's glittering armor lightly. Blue light flashed. I pulled away suddenly at the unexpected warmth.

What is happening here?

The costumes looked the same as I remembered. Immaculate, as if they'd been freshly mended and cleaned and put on the racks a day ago.

One of the seamstress's dummies stood empty. I'd seen it in my father's room: The Mouse King was missing.

I turned back to the glistening armored scales of the Snake Slayer. The blue flash had surprised me, but it hadn't hurt. The silvery cloth had given off an almost soothing warmth.

I put my right hand on the sleeve and held it there.

This time the warmth came slowly, soothing my palm and spreading as far as the back of my hand but no further. Blue wisps wrapped like tendrils around my wrist and hand, slowly spreading along the sleeves of the costume. Blue pulsed gently outward from within the Snake Slayer's shirt of silver mail, till it seemed covered in a fantastic blue filigree.

Slowly, as if in a dream, I put my left hand on the other sleeve, and lifted the blue gossamer from the dressmaker's stand. The costume felt barely substantial, like a shirt of spiderwebs.

I want this, I thought. *It's stupid, but I want to know what's going on.*

I pulled the oversized garment over my head, putting my hands through the sleeves. It seemed to settle on top of my clothes and then slowly sink through them, shrinking to fit me closely. I felt warmth against my skin, like an armor of snakeskin. The Snake Slayer's armor felt substantial and insubstantial at the same time, as if I wore a weightless coat of mail. I shrugged my shoulders, getting used to the feel.

Should I take it off? I wondered. I didn't even know how. And we did need to bring it with us, so someone could talk with the gods if my father's recovery took too long.

The blueness faded from around me, leaving me alone in the dressing room again.

How long have I been here? I wondered why Sperrin and my father hadn't checked on me. It felt like I'd been backstage for a while.

But when I reemerged onto the stage, they were just climbing up the brief flight of stairs at stage right. Had it been only a few moments?

I walked forward, my foot touching the ring of runes before I realized it.

Sperrin yelled and rushed toward me. At the same time, my father pulled away from the soldier and shrank back from the circle.

I looked at my hands and saw silver gloves over impossibly long, thin fingers.

"What is…?" I started, but my nose tickled from bushy mongoose whiskers. I sneezed.

I took a step back, out of the ring of runes.

I was a girl again, no longer the festival Snake Slayer. Sperrin stopped, a few steps short of me. He stood in the middle of the circle of runes.

"What happened?" he asked. "Are you safe?" He looked puzzled, unsure what he had just seen.

"I don't know. I think so. But is it safe for you standing inside the ring?"

"What ring?"

"The runes on the stage. You're standing in the middle of them. They changed me when I touched one of them by mistake."

Sperrin froze. "I don't see any ring."

At the edge of the stage, my father laughed hollowly. "Of course he doesn't," he said to me. "This man is just a common soldier. He has not a drop of uncommon blood in him. *You* have the blood of two gods in your veins." He laughed. "There are many things you and I can see that this man cannot.

But that doesn't explain it, I thought. Tenia had the blood of gods and she couldn't see them. She insisted that no one else could, either. But for some reason I could.

Sperrin slowly edged back toward my father, who didn't seem inclined to say any more.

I looked again into the runes, taking a long gaze this time. They felt intensely magical and old. *Why have I never seen this before?*

But a part of me had always known it was there. Wearing the insubstantial armor of the Snake Slayer's costume against my skin, momentarily I felt the same joy I had experienced dancing onstage and speaking to the empty chairs.

I wonder which gods I'm related to? I knew I carried the thinnest tinge of the goddess Bayinna's blood on my mother's side. It wasn't uncommon in Ananya to have a trace of god's blood, especially in a family of channelers. My father had never mentioned that he too had the blood of a god. Had he needed it to become chancellor?

I felt young and foolish, realizing how many things that I thought I had understood remained almost unknown to me. I wished Tenia was here. She would have known the answer, or how to get it.

Somehow, asking my father to expand on his words seemed like a bad idea.

Silence spread through the theater.

Finally, Sperrin broke the emptiness. "We had best get to the sally tunnels," he said to me. "Since you know where the entrance is, can you lead the way, please?"

If Sperrin noticed anything amiss with the missing costumes, he didn't mention it as we walked backstage.

BY THE TIME we reached the entrance to the sally tunnels, the Snake Slayer armor felt like a memory, the barest presence against my skin. The tunnels smelled earthy and dry. As I reached the bottom of the ladder that led to the tunnel, blue streaks glowed on the walls, the same blue as the runes of the stage. The same blue I'd been almost-seeing for years, but now vivid and luminous. Each of the three tunnel branchings that met here had a distinct blue symbol.

"Can you see it?" I asked Sperrin. "There's magic down here."

"What kind of magic?"

"Old magic." I reached out a finger and almost touched one of the streaks, then pulled back.

"All I see is dirt."

"But you can see a little bit, like in the theater?

"Yes," Sperrin answered.

I lowered the dying lantern to my side.

Something slammed into my back, and I hit the floor. Metal flew over my head, clattering into the far wall. Half dazed, I rolled over and looked up.

Sperrin faced off against a silvery scaled creature with luminous golden eyes. It had legs like a human, but spines up its back like a mane. Its face looked more fish than man, with gill slits and whiskers like a catfish. The axe in its hand looked manmade. I saw the axe's twin against the far wall: It had been thrown at my head, I realized. Sperrin had pushed me down to save me.

He and the merrow circled each other warily. Sperrin had a little bit more height, but the sea-creature outmassed him. *What's it doing in the tunnel?* I wondered.

The merrow lunged, and Sperrin blocked its advance. The axe blade clattered against his sword with a shower of sparks.

The creature lunged again, as if trying to force Sperrin to give way by sheer weight.

That's exactly what it's doing, I realized. And then it hit me: *It's not trying to get at Sperrin, it's trying to get past him.*

But what's on the other side of him that's so important?

Behind Sperrin, my father huddled against the far tunnel wall.

The creature seemed to get angrier as Sperrin kept blocking it. It mouthed words—at first they sounded like howls, but I gradually realized they were in my own language, just distorted by the merrow's facial structure. Something about the harbor, and betrayal. Betrayal in the harbor? Harboring betrayers? If it was a warning about betrayal, it seemed a little late. And coming from a golden-eyed sea monster swinging an axe, it hardly seemed like the clearest message. I'd read accounts of merrows before, but none had said anything about those eyes.

Sperrin struck suddenly, opening up a wide furrow down the creature's side. The axe clattered to the ground. The merrow sat down hard, dark liquid pouring out around its hands where it tried to hold its insides in. It glared, first at Sperrin and then at my father.

"Harbor. Betrayer," it said again, the words harsh and guttural. Then a longer phrase, spoken this time to me. It took me a moment to puzzle it out. "What gods take, only gods can return." I couldn't ask what the creature meant: By the time I had figured out the words, the luminosity had passed from its eyes.

WHEN I HAD explored the sally tunnels in the past, I'd emerged high up on the riverbank, with a steep slope between me and the wide river. This time we went further, by a different branching. I'd explored by lanternlight as a girl, and had missed many branches in the flickering candleflame. Now, with the passage marked by the glow of ancient runes, finding the right path proved easier.

Afternoon light pierced the tunnel ceiling as we neared the passageway's end.

The passage widened into a sort of storeroom, with a rough-cut plank floor laid over the ground to keep dampness off the stacked barrels and crates. A ladder led upward to a trapdoor in the wooden ceiling. Light passed through the ceiling unevenly, presumably through windows in a room above.

Sperrin seemed to know exactly what to look for. He quickly pulled out clothing, boots, oilskins to keep off rain, traplines, and a variety of knives in different sizes. Raider supplies. Even packages of food wrapped in dried leaves and string. I hoped the supplies were restocked regularly; I had a brief but horrific image of trying to eat food left over from the last war.

"Can you use a knife?" Sperrin asked me.

I looked at him. "If you mean on food, yes. If you mean, do I know where the pointy end goes, yes. If you mean, do I have your back if the gods attack, then no."

He nodded. "That's about what I thought. Same for your father?"

Would you trust a madman with a knife right now? Even if it turns out he's just angry and frustrated instead of out of his mind? Apparently my expression answered Sperrin well enough. He handed me a pair of longish, slim knives with sheaths and thigh straps.

"Wear these for now. I'll try to teach you to use them while we're on the road. Don't try to use them against any gods—they won't help and will just get you killed."

So will not using them, I thought, but I didn't say it out loud.

Motioning for us to wait, Sperrin climbed silently up the ladder. After looking through the floorboards for a long moment, he seemed satisfied. Knife cocked in his left hand, he pushed the trapdoor open with his right, set the trapdoor down all but silently, and clambered into the room above.

With a loud clatter my father bolted away from us, back toward the castle.

He disappeared up the tunnel before I could react.

What's he doing? I wondered, and then, *What should I do?* By then Sperrin was down the ladder and past me, into the sally tunnel after my father.

TEN MINUTES LATER, Sperrin returned, pushing my father forward by the scruff of his neck. The chancellor looked like a housecat caught making a break for the garbage barrels.

"Restrain your father," said Sperrin, pushing him toward me. "Before he gets all of us killed. Count to fifty and then send him up the ladder. You follow after him." Without another word, Sperrin climbed the ladder to the room above.

I thought my father might refuse to go up the ladder, but he ascended pliably enough.

We emerged into a shack lit by late-afternoon sun, no different than any of the dozens of fishermen's houses that dotted the slope on the cityside riverbank. Somewhat fewer shacks occupied this stretch of the river, which faced the massive graveyards of the Westbarrow. The shack was completely bare, just rough-cut pine plank walls and floor. The door stood open; presumably Sperrin had gone outside.

I closed the trapdoor and stood with one foot on top of it. My father seemed docile enough, looking out one of the eight-pane windows, but I saw no reason to take chances. I could see a little bit out the front door: a small porch, with a flight of weathered wooden stairs leading downslope to the river and a decaying dock. Sperrin squatted on the dock, looking more like a fisherman than a soldier. I supposed that was deliberate.

I glanced at my father and followed his gaze out the window. Half a mile upriver, I could see the cable from the ferry had been snapped or cut. The near side hung limply in the river. Refugees crowded the shallows there, wading the river in hopes of reaching the Trade Road that circled the Westbarrow. At least nothing seemed to be menacing the refugees. But watching people flee our hometown wrenched me. My father seemed strangely unaffected, whether from madness or from having already lost everything he cared about losing.

Sperrin
Downriver from Westbarrow Ford: The day after the Loss

I closed the door as I reentered the cabin. I noted Ketya unobtrusively blocking her father's potential escape routes. I hadn't wanted to leave them alone, but I had needed to scout the river crossing.

"You might as well sit and rest," I told the two of them. "Sleep if you can. We will be rowing across after nightfall."

"Why not just wade?" Ketya asked, nodding at the crowd of refugees at the ford upriver.

"I think we don't want to draw that kind of attention," I replied. "Anyone looking for surviving channelers or government officials will start there. We would be making things more dangerous for them as well as for us. Unless the gods return again, those refugees will find food and shelter a few miles up the Trade Road. If the gods return, they'll die anyway."

"So where are we going if we're not taking the road?"

"We'll cut through the Westbarrow and link with the Mountain Road on the other side. No need to take the Trade Road at all. I know the Mountain Road well enough to get us to one of the mountain forts, and from there to Whitmount eventually. We can be helpful there." I looked over to the chancellor, staring out the window unmoving. "You and your father should try to sleep," I said again.

"Sleep? How are we supposed to sleep?" said Ketya. "I don't dare close my eyes." She shuddered at some memory from the last few hours.

"You learn to rest when you can," I answered. "Mourn later. Now you need rest, whether you want it or not." That would have been good advice for a soldier. Which she wasn't, of course.

"What about you? Don't you need rest? Why don't you sleep instead?"

I nodded to her father. "Because I think I would wake with one fewer guest. I will rest when I need to." I didn't feel tired, despite the fighting of the day. Part of that came from soldier's training, and years of fighting. But mostly it came from the surge of energy from the killing I'd done. I had missed the fighting. After trying to leave the things I'd done in the war behind, a part of me hated the reminder of how much each kill energized me. But a bigger part of me loved it.

We would need that energy tonight, I knew.

Eventually, I managed to get Ketya and the chancellor more-or-less bedded down. While they slept—or rather tried to sleep in Ketya's case and pretended to sleep in the chancellor's case—I went through each of their packs, adding from the stores below and repacking as necessary for the journey into the mountains.

Chapter 10

Ketya
Downriver from Westbarrow Ford: The evening after the Loss

The second time my father bolted, he didn't make it as far. Sperrin's hand shot out from his bedroll and grabbed the chancellor's foot, sending him sprawling. My father hit the cabin floor hard and sat up slowly, clutching his elbow.

The glow of fires lit by the mass of refugees camped upstream illuminated the cabin dimly.

"I don't know if you're mad or not, but I will tie your hands if I need to," Sperrin said. "Even if it means—"

A scream cut off the rest of his words.

Something momentarily blotted out the light from the campfires.

"They are...the gods are back, aren't they?" I asked hollowly.

My father laughed, but said nothing.

By now screams had spread through the encampments. Fires flickered as refugees tried to fight horror with torches.

Sperrin let go of my father's foot, stood up, and walked to the window. He watched for a minute, saying nothing as he studied the situation.

Finally he replied. "I don't think so, Ketya. Those aren't godlings attacking the camps, anyway. They may have returned to the city but not here."

"What's attacking them, then?" Something else swooped down and carried off a pair of screaming refugees.

"Fey, I think. Allies of the gods, like the merrows. The gods had a lot of allies who were left behind after the war. The Empress's power restrained them. Whichever god attacked the palace also made sure that every hill creature and hidden sprite knew that nothing was restraining them any longer. The fey want this land for their own, I believe."

"The gods promised it to them," I whispered, though we all knew that much already. I had memorized clause 116 in the Talisman, where the gods backed away from that promise. But they never broke it exactly—just suspended it for the duration of the peace. The terms of the treaty bound none of the hill creatures and other faeries. As long as the Empress's magic held and the gods withheld support, they dared not attack openly. But clearly the situation had changed.

"I don't suppose you want to tell us what is happening?" Sperrin asked the chancellor. My father smiled improbably, but said nothing.

Turning from the window, Sperrin walked to our packs and picked his up. "Come along, you two," he said. "Horrible as this distraction may be, there's no point in wasting it by not crossing the river while we can. We only have an hour until moonrise. We need to be across before then."

I nodded, and even my father seemed a little shaken by the thought of passing so close to the carnage upstream.

"Will there be merrows on the river?" I asked.

"Probably not, if we're quiet enough. They prefer salt water, and there are richer targets. I need you both to be absolutely silent while we cross, though."

"Of course," I said.

We walked quickly and silently down the stairs, following Sperrin's shadowy movements. As we passed our packs down to him and stepped off the dock into the rowboat, I could see that he had already loaded it with blankets and provisions.

As soon as my father and I took our seats, Sperrin unstepped the oars and cast off. He sat facing us, his back toward the opposite shore as he rowed. Sperrin had muffled the oarlocks with extra blankets, I noticed. That must have been what he was doing while kneeling on the dock earlier.

Except for the almost imperceptible dip of the oars, we sculled silently on the wide, slow river. In the darkness the far bank seemed invisible.

The screams upstream gradually fell silent as well, and the fires vanished. Perhaps a bend in the river hid them, I hoped, but after the events of the last day I didn't really believe that.

A faint, cool breeze came from upstream. The air smelled like blood.

I hadn't expected such utter blackness. I couldn't see my father beside me, or the black water an arm's length away.

Sperrin and my father didn't seem to be bothered by it. My father's breathing relaxed, and I realized he slept.

I couldn't even hear the oars dipping into the water anymore, couldn't hear Sperrin's steady breathing.

The air closed in, worse than in the tunnels: even darker with no light and no idea if we were even going in the right direction.

Finally I couldn't take the silence any longer.

"They used to call this the River of the Dead," I whispered. It sounded impossibly loud. I expected Sperrin to shush me, but I needed to hear my own voice, to know that I wasn't alone and lost in the darkness.

He didn't respond, just kept rowing silently.

"They renamed it because no one wanted to buy fish from the River of the Dead. It was my father's idea. No one fishes across from the graveyard, though."

This time he did silence me, with the briefest gesture to my forearm. I couldn't see his hand in the darkness, but somehow the touch of his fingertips felt reassuring.

A faint edge of moonlight glinted on the horizon.

"How close?" Sperrin barely breathed the words, but I heard them clearly. *How does he do that?* I wondered.

I looked over my shoulder. A dark line indicated the shore, only a few boat lengths away. Beyond that, I saw the edges of a stone wall, and glimpses of glowing blue behind it.

"Almost there," I said, trying to imitate Sperrin's quiet voice. The words came out as a hoarse whisper instead.

He seemed to already know, perhaps sensing a change in the water's depth. He let the boat glide to the bank, then leaped out to grab the bow and bring it noiselessly to shore.

"Quickly," Sperrin said in the same quiet voice. "There is cover in the barrows. But we need to pass the wall before we are noticed."

The moon had risen a little further, enough to illuminate the stone line of the wall more clearly beyond the irregular shadows of the rocks and scrub trees along the riverbank.

I touched my father's arm and he woke instantly. He followed me from the boat without complaint.

"Make for the wall," said Sperrin. "I will be right behind you." He took the packs from the boat, then kicked the bow away from the bank. Slowly, the boat drifted out into the river, until the current and darkness took it.

Sperrin
The Westbarrow: The night after the Loss

The chancellor feigned sleep for most of the river crossing. Beside the chancellor, I could hear Ketya's ragged breath as she grew increasingly terrified.

I focused on keeping the oars steady and silent.

It took all the self-control I had not to leave the two of them and join the fight upstream. Not that it was much of a fight, but there would be something to kill. I might make a difference.

There will be plenty of fighting on the Mountain Road, I told myself. *My duty is to protect these two*. It didn't really make me feel any better, not when I could hear screaming and the whirring of wings not far off.

I forced myself once again to focus on the oars.

By the time we reached the far bank, the noise had stopped. We had made it across without the girl's nerve breaking entirely, and without any more disruptions from the chancellor. Better than I had expected, really.

I wasn't completely sure what Ketya had seen in the theater and the tunnels. Other than the odd blue light, I had seen nothing. Perhaps what she had seen on the stage really was an older form of magic that had been reported extinct for centuries, and that she had never noticed in all her previous visits to the theater. Or perhaps it was her mind showing her what she wanted to see after a night filled with desperate losses. And maybe my mind too—there was that moment where she'd looked oddly transformed, before shifting back to herself.

One of those losses she mourned might have been her father. I didn't know what to make of the chancellor's condition. Someone would have to make some tough choices in the weeks ahead, if the chancellor didn't return to his old self. I hoped I wasn't that someone. My gift was for battles and tactics, not grand strategy.

The moon had barely begun to rise, but the night promised to be bright. We would need to find shelter in among the barrows: Too many of the godsent creatures and their allies hunted by night.

Ketya and her father moved quietly enough; the noise of the river covered what sounds they made. I stayed a little behind them, waiting until they had reached the slight shelter of the wall's cemented stones to catch up to them.

"Can you climb the wall?" I asked them. "We can find a gate if we must, but we might not be the first to find it."

Ketya eyed the stone wall dubiously. "If you can boost me," she finally said. Then after a pause: "Perhaps you should boost my father first."

Whatever impulse had caused the chancellor to run before seemed to have quieted, at least for now. Docilely he accepted my boost and scrambled to the top of the wall.

"Stay low," I said when the chancellor looked like he might stand on top of the wall.

"I would like to see the fate of the refugees," the chancellor replied. "They are in my care, even if I cannot care for them at present."

"We'll get a good view of that spot when we reach Longhold Hill. It will have to wait until then," I said. "Right now if you stand you will be backlit by the moon. And most likely eaten."

The chancellor seemed about to muster an indignant response, then thought better of it. He slithered across the flat top of the wall and lowered himself to the other side.

By then, I had already boosted Ketya. She scrabbled for handholds, but finally pulled herself to the top.

"Stay there," I said. "Stay very still." I waited for any sign we had been noticed. When I felt satisfied we hadn't been, I carefully handed our packs up to her.

"Lower them to your father on the other side, then climb down yourself."

When she had cleared the wall I scrambled up and over as silently as I could. I landed softly in a springy patch of moss beside their packs.

"Don't get too comfortable," I said to the chancellor and Ketya, sitting nearby on the moss, backs tight against the wall to keep themselves out of sight. "We are nowhere near safety yet. Don't relax just because we didn't die on the river. Still plenty of time to die tonight if we're careless."

Ketya

Was that supposed to be a pep talk? I wondered. *Don't relax. We'll probably all be dead soon anyway.* Thanks, Sperrin. Thanks lots.

I pulled myself to my feet, still stiff from the river crossing. Picking up my pack, I adjusted it carefully—he was watching to make sure I did it right, of course. *Do you think we're idiots?* I almost asked. But we were still alive, and most of my friends weren't, and he was a big part of the reason why. *That and your stupid incompetence at magic*, I reminded myself.

I felt angry as we started to walk through the Westbarrow—angry at myself, at Sperrin, at the gods who had destroyed our world on what was supposed to be the happiest night of my life. A part of me was even angry with my father.

Angry enough that I almost missed the flash of blue where there should have been only barrows and memorials to the Drowned City's privileged dead.

A lot of the Holy War dead were interred here, so I had been hearing about the Westbarrow on Memorial Day since long before I'd lived in the palace. Once my father had moved us to the Drowned City I'd taken part in the annual memory walk through the Westbarrow. It really wasn't optional for the chancellor's daughter: I and all the other kids who were old enough not to have nightmares afterward were given baskets of flowers, and we would follow some old soldier or other through the rows of barrows while our guide would tell us which ones to leave flowers in front of. Some of the guides told stories about the inhabitants of particular barrows. Others just pointed and never said a word; it mostly depended which of the old soldiers got sent that year.

It took a while to get used to the idea that people weren't actually buried here, but lay inside the barrows on raised platforms. That made sense given the Drowned City's high water table and the river's occasional habit of overflowing its banks, but it still seemed odd. I had never been in any of the barrows—I assumed the doors were kept locked—just stood in front of them on the memory walks and scattered flowers wherever the old soldiers told me to.

None of them had glowed blue at the time.

Runes covered one entire barrow, while others bore only a symbol or two on the door. Comparatively few of the tombs glowed: only the oldest, I realized as we began walking among them.

I could tell Sperrin wasn't sure whether to believe me or not when I told him about the blue runes. His expression changed when I pointed out which barrows had marked doors.

"Those are all Holy War veterans," he said. "Those aren't just the oldest graves, they are all soldiers. All significant soldiers, I would say. People whose names you will have heard of."

People whose names even you will have heard of, is what he means. I'm not an idiot. I studied history like you. Just because I'm not a master of killing like you are doesn't make me stupid.

I knew better than to say the words out loud, but some of my feeling must have shown on my face. Sperrin moderated his tone:

"What I don't understand is the one that you say is covered with blue, not just on the door." He gestured, though I knew he couldn't see the blue himself. "It's an old barrow but it doesn't belong to anyone particularly heroic. Why would they mark it?"

Both of us startled at my father's quiet laugh. We had gotten used to his silence.

"The soldiers' barrows are protected from people trying to get *into* them. The barrow you are looking at is protected from things coming *out*."

I looked at the runes on the door. They looked jagged, unlike the ones that covered the sides and top of the barrow. "But the seals are broken. They broke some time ago, it looks like."

Sperrin looked at me, then at the door. "Can you tell if they broke from the inside or the outside?"

"From the outside," I said. "Why do you ask?"

My father gave both of us a hard look.

"No reason," Sperrin said. "I thought it might be nice to know if someone was visiting the gods before they visited us."

That's what it is! It's a passageway to the land of the gods. I had known there was one in the Westbarrow, but had never made the connection. I felt a little silly that Sperrin had realized before I had, even without being able to see the runes.

My father had known all along, of course. I wondered if him not saying anything was some sort of test.

"Let's get moving," Sperrin said. "I would rather not stand around waiting for straggling silverbacks to come kill us."

"You don't know that the gods came out of this barrow," my father said.

"No, we don't know that," Sperrin answered. He started walking down the row of barrows, away from the portal between worlds.

We walked a long way in silence before Sperrin finally stopped us in front of a blue-runed barrow door.

"You know this tomb?" he asked me.

"Of course. This is Captain-General Keir's tomb. I had to put flowers here."

"He deserves them. He earned those flowers by winning a battle he had no right to."

"You know a lot about him?" I knew the name, and that he was a war hero, but not much else. He'd had some connection with the truce negotiations too, I remembered, but I couldn't recall what exactly.

"I studied his campaigns. We played heroes and gods a lot as a kid. I was always trying to beat him. Whenever I played the gods' side I always trounced the rest of the kids who were playing his campaigns. They shouldn't have been winnable. But he won them. I read that he was the reason the gods were willing to negotiate in the first place."

"Really?" I had never heard that. I glanced at my father for confirmation, but I couldn't read his eyes in the darkness.

"It was in another general's biography, written not long after the Holy Wars ended," Sperrin said. "I can't say whether it's true or not, or whether the diplomats would agree, but soldiers thought so at the time."

Sperrin reached for the door.

"Wait, we're going inside?"

"We need to take shelter for the night somewhere. This seems like the sort of place where a godservant or one of their allies is very unlikely to come looking for us. Especially if it's glowing with magic that doesn't come from the gods—or at least not from the Empress, so it doesn't come from *our* god."

"Aren't the doors locked?" The rune wasn't a lock, I could tell. Some ward against godservants, I suspected. *That would have been useful to know how to do yesterday. Not that there's anyone who could teach me how to use them...even if I wasn't terrible at magic.*

"Not anymore," Sperrin said. "They were sealed magically. The seals died with the Empress."

"Oh," I said. *I should have known that.*

As we crossed through the threshold, I felt a flare of warmth against my skin. The Snake Slayer's armor seemed to harden into real metal as I passed the rune, then went back to its gossamery near-nothingness.

Sperrin closed the door, leaving us in darkness.

"Welcome to a hero's grave," he said. "We should all hope to die so well."

AFTER A MOMENT, Sperrin struck a light and lit a stub of candle from it. Taking another candle stub from his pocket, he lit it and placed it in a small alcove. Between the two candles we had a flickering measure of light.

"Is that safe?" I asked.

"Safe enough," Sperrin said. "I think the worst of the danger for tonight is past. There will be enough danger tomorrow."

"Thanks. That's very comforting." I couldn't help myself.

"Watch your tongue," my father said. The first words he'd said since we had left the portal. "Do not speak that way to your elders, or in front of me."

"Yes, father," I answered. What else could I say? *How about: Is this really the time to quibble about manners?* But it wasn't the time to pick a pointless fight with my father, either. He would win, and I would feel even worse.

Sperrin waited till my father and I had quieted. "I thought it would be safer to risk a little light than to blunder around a tomb in the dark."

Somehow I had almost forgotten the purpose of the chamber. For the first time, I looked around.

Part of me expected to see the glowing blue runes that had been showing up everywhere, but only the flickering candles lit the space. We stood in a small outer room, with a wooden couch on either side and a small stone-topped cask in the middle. A small doorway led to an inner chamber, where desiccated bodies in martial garb lay on a pair of stone platforms.

I walked over to look more closely, though I didn't step into the inner room.

Black blades lay alongside the bodies, similar to the one Sperrin carried, but nothing like the silver-bladed swords I'd seen carried by the palace guards. I'd seen firsthand that those light swords weren't really designed for war. But I hoped Sperrin wasn't trying to protect us with a centuries-old sword.

"Why are they all men?" I found myself asking. "There are no women in this tomb, only men."

Sperrin answered from behind me. "Keir's wife, Juila, was a soldier and sorcerer—they called them sorcerers in those days, before there were channelers. She was taken by the gods during the war. Keir said she was a prisoner, not dead, but the gods insisted they didn't have her. She was never returned with the rest of the prisoners on both sides who were exchanged at the war's end. I don't know if she really was dead, or if there was some other reason."

"You know a lot about him. I thought you only cared about battles."

"I heard a song about it once, at a friend's funeral. It stuck with me. Keir never remarried, because he expected his wife to return someday. That's why only he and their two sons are buried here."

"Weren't any of his sons married? They look old enough." From the size of the bodies, anyway. I didn't consider myself much of a judge of dried corpses.

"I wouldn't think so. None of the ones here survived the war. Their father didn't join them until later."

"Oh," I said. "I didn't know." For some reason I felt sadder about that than about some of the bodies we had walked past in the last day, even though these were strangers and some of the bodies had been friends. Perhaps I would be able to mourn the friends later, but now that part of me felt empty— as if it had been ripped away along with the magic. Just like Sperrin had said: I would need to survive now, in order to mourn later. *And you will probably lose more friends before later arrives*, I reminded myself.

Looking away from the bodies of the dead boys and their father, I saw Sperrin had spread out a little buffet of dried food from our supplies, and three cups of water. Somehow the food seemed so oddly ordinary that I had no idea what to make of it.

"I THINK," SAID Sperrin after we had all eaten sparingly, "that now is the time to discuss where we are going." He sounded oddly hesitant. "I have given the matter some thought, and wanted to give the two of you my suggestions."

Glancing over, I saw light in my father's eyes, the excitement he always got when he sensed weakness.

Sperrin

Now came the hard part.

We needed to go to Whitmount, deep in the mountains, and I needed to tell them the reasons why. All of which were true, but none of which were really my reasons.

"I think we should take the Mountain Road for Whitmount," I began.

"Whitmount? Really?" said the chancellor. "So you are saying we should bypass the easy coastal roads and walk for three weeks over some of the most difficult and mountainous roads in all Ananya, wihout benefit of magic. That makes sense to you?"

I felt myself flushing slightly, but pushed on. "For a number of reasons, yes. We will be exposed to attack on the coastal roads. I know the Mountain Road well. Whitmount was specifically hardened against attacks by godser-vants in the Holy War; it was the temporary capital for part of the war, and it is a regional seat of government now. It is a likely place to regroup and launch whatever counterattack is decided on by the...war government."

The chancellor snorted.

"Captain, there was a saying where I grew up, 'Don't lie to a liar.' It was often used with respect to games of chance, I believe. Now I am certainly no liar, but in my years of service to the Empire I have come to know more than a few of them, and I think I have a credible knowledge of lying. I think perhaps there is something you are not telling us, Captain."

"I think it is our safest course," I said. "It will be safer—I can get both of you to safety on the Mountain Road. If there are dangers on the way, we will be much less exposed."

"Come now, Captain. Surely you do not expect me to believe that is your true reason for subjecting us to this arduous journey."

The chancellor has chosen a strange time to begin talking again, I thought. *How much does he know? Too much, I suspect.*

I started again: "After the attack here, I think the seacoast is unsafe. We do not know how widespread the godservant attack was. Perhaps they only attacked here, but it's just as likely they attacked more broadly. And even if they didn't, with our armies stripped of magic, forces from the Central Alliance will be raiding along the coasts and attacking the northern border crossings, at the very least."

"Perhaps," said the chancellor. "And perhaps not. There is much that you do not know."

What a bizarre answer, I thought. *It's as if he wants us to take the most dangerous way, for no real benefit. That's not like the chancellor at all.*

"Would you care to enlighten me?"

"None of it concerns you especially. You are a mere soldier. Brave, but ignorant."

"If there is something we need to know, I would appreciate your telling me. It might save your life, and your daughter's."

"Not as long as I am your prisoner. Release me to return to the city, and be on your way."

For a moment I actually thought about it. *That man is far too convincing.* I wondered why the chancellor was so anxious to take the coastal road. We'd seen the Central Alliance ships raiding in the city already—there would certainly be a fleet raiding along the coast. And the Ananyan Home Fleet, which had left the Drowned City's harbor with such fanfare and fireworks, would be crippled without its channelers to provide propulsion and power their war-engines, making them easy targets if they couldn't find shelter before the Alliance fleet found them.

"I'm sorry, Lord Chancellor. But I can't do that."

"You certainly can."

"My job is to take you and your daughter to safety."

"Your job is to obey my orders, just like it is hers"—his eyes touched Ketya—"and anyone else left alive in that city. Taking me prisoner is not part of your job."

"If I had obeyed those orders, we would all be dead now."

"Perhaps *you* would be. I certainly would not. And your *job* as a soldier is to die when ordered to do so."

"I don't think you have so many soldiers left under your command that you can afford to spend their lives freely," I said. In spite of myself I heard a warning tone come into my voice.

"Your lives are nothing to me. Stay or go as you please. But I will return to the palace."

"No, my lord, you will not." I realized my hand was on the hilt of my blade. *Would you kill this man?* Oh, how I wanted to. Right here in Keir's grave. But I had more control than that. Mad or sane, the chancellor was still an important man and my duty was to keep him alive, however reluctant we both might be about it.

"Then we must take the coastal road. North or south, as you choose."

"I am sorry, my lord. We take the Mountain Road."

The ghost of a smile touched the chancellor's face. *This man thinks he can break me,* I realized. *He thinks I am like a spirited horse, to be broken to his will.*

"I will tell you why you wish to take the Mountain Road," said the chancellor. "You wish to take it because you think that a woman whom you abandoned a decade ago and forgot about until yesterday might still be there, and might care for you, now that you have lost your new life. You think that the daughter whom you were so quick to abandon might half-remember your face, and might even be able to convince herself that she loves you. You are a fool, Overcaptain Sperrin. You know nothing, and you will take us only to disaster."

The chancellor moderated his tone, mockingly. "Am I correct?"

Hardening my voice, I deliberately took my hand from the hilt of my sword.

"I think, Lord Chancellor, that I am not the only ignorant one in this chamber." I took a breath. "I think you should sleep. Do not attempt to escape again. I saved your life once from duty and once from respect. If you were a friend, I might save it a third time, from friendship."

"I did not ask for your friendship," said the chancellor. "I do not befriend sheep. Sheep are to be herded, and worn, and eaten."

"Even so," I said, unsheathing a knife from his boot. "I will sleep across the doorway. Try and cross it while you think I sleep, and I will cut the tendon in your leg. You will never walk straight, or swiftly, again." I spread my blanket in the flat space across the doorway, folded it once, and lay my blade and knife next to it.

I realized that I had enjoyed the exchange.

"Ketya," I said. Her face looked very pale, even in the dimness. "Please be kind enough to snuff out those candles before you go to sleep. We have a long way to go before we reach safety, or a fresh supply of candles." With that I lay down on the blanket and closed my eyes.

Tomorrow, we would begin the road to where I last saw my daughter. To where we used to live. *What will you do if you find her?* I wondered. The Empress might well have given my wife a new husband, my daughter a new father. They probably wouldn't have remembered me at all, until yesterday. It had been almost ten years.

Right now my memories were still maddeningly incomplete, returning in bits and pieces. I tried to piece together how our relationship had ended from the memories that had returned so far.

Far too many of my memories of Sefa were unhappy, and I wished I could remember more of the good parts, the feeling of being in love with her. I had loved Sefa the whole time we were together. I couldn't help it with the memories I'd gotten at our engagement. When I asked to leave the front, it never occurred to me that doing so would mean leaving Sefa, even though we spent very little time together by then. What I hadn't realized, though, was that the memories from the engagement piece were never really mine to keep. When the Empress died and my other memories returned, the memories from the golden fruit that had signaled our engagement didn't. So all I could remember, when I found out that Sefa still lived, was the marriage as it was in the years we actually shared, not the stolen memories that made me fall in love with her before we ever met.

I was a much better soldier than husband. I had shown a lot of promise as a young officer. I was a decorated war hero with a gift for tactics and a knack for being in the middle of the action against the Central Alliance. So the

Empress chose one of her favorites to marry me. But it was never really a great match. We came to love each other, I thought, through the incomplete memories—and we both loved our daughter, but we didn't have a lot else to talk about. I was a soldier and she was a channeler. Our work consumed both of our lives. We weren't home at the same time enough to learn to talk to each other.

Maddeningly, the pieces surrounding the end of our time together were missing. I remembered telling Nemias that I had asked to transfer to the palace because of how all the killing was affecting me. But I don't remember actually making the request, or whether Sefa and I talked about it first. Given the problems in our relationship already and my wife's status as a favorite of the Empress, Sefa may have talked to the Empress about the problems in our marriage. Perhaps when I asked about transferring to the palace, the Empress saw a chance to fix her mistake.

I wondered how many of that last year's worth of memories would return. Often, when a soldier received a head injury, the memories close to the incident were lost forever—sometimes days or weeks of memories. It occurred to me that having memories magically blocked and manipulated might have the same effect. Only time would give me the answer.

Chapter 11

Sperrin

I awoke once that night, to the sound of soft singing. I wondered if the chancellor even realized he was singing. As an officer, I had known soldiers who needed to sing in the face of tragedies they had no words for. For the chancellor, who always had the right words, the events of the last day must have been particularly tragic.

The man had a husky baritone voice, rough-edged but pleasing enough to listen to. Keeping my eyes closed I listened. I was sure the singing would stop at any stirring. From the sound, the chancellor sang from just inside the inner chamber, perhaps standing at the edge of a bier. There wasn't much room to pace in the tomb.

Softly as he sung it, the chancellor's tune sounded familiar. Nothing I had heard recently, but haunting. Finally I placed it: one of the ancient teaching songs from the *Book of Gods*. As a boy, I'd heard the tune sung at Fireday and New Year's festivals, in the afternoon ceremonies before the dancers started. I'd known boys who sang in the choir, always struggling to memorize page after page of Old Ananyan verses; they taught from a prose translation in history classes when they touched on the gods, but festival choirs always sang in the original.

The chancellor knew the *Book of Gods* by heart? It was hardly light reading, or the sort of thing likely to be helpful in his avocation. Singing ancient festival poetry seemed like an odd hobby for such a ruthlessly driven politician.

I continued listening with my eyes closed. I could read Old Ananyan passably, but not speak it very well. My vocabulary skewed heavily toward the specialized military vernacular of the Holy Wars, almost a separate language from the lush rhythmic lyricism of the *Book of Gods*. I strained to hear the words, hoping to at least recognize what part of the book they came from.

Something sounded off.

Then I realized it.

I understood the words.

I'd never heard them before, but I understood them. They weren't in Old Ananyan.

Had the chancellor done his own translation? The complex rhythm scheme was the same, but there were elements unfamiliar to me. Perhaps a part of the text I didn't know? But the chancellor was singing about Senne, who'd sacrificed herself to be the source of Ananya's magic. Certainly I knew *that* part of the book well enough. But the words were unfamiliar, building on the *Book of Gods*, but going further. Did *he* write this?

He sang about Senne's sacrifice, but mostly the chancellor sang about Kedessen, Senne's lover, left behind by her choice. *I wonder when he wrote this?* The chancellor had lost his own wife when his daughter was still young, I knew. Maybe the poem was how he dealt with his loss. Thinking of my own lost wife and daughter, I couldn't help but sense the loss in the chancellor's baritone voice more keenly.

At some point before the song stopped the words lulled me to sleep, so I never knew how long the chancellor stayed awake, singing a lullaby of loss.

Ketya
The Westbarrow: Two days after the Loss

As it turned out, we did leave for the Mountain Road the next morning. The argument between Sperrin and my father never openly resumed. But I could see on their faces that neither of them considered the matter settled.

My father's eyes looked sad, but he said little as we ate and packed.

We emerged from the tomb to a beautiful blue sky. The events of the last two days felt somehow unreal. In the brightness of morning, I could barely see the blue runes on the old soldiers' barrows. I could feel their presence, though, just as the Snake Slayer's armor reminded me of its presence with a surge of warmth as we left Captain-general Keir's barrow.

The brisk morning air cooled me after the closeness of the barrow, but the day promised heat to come.

Sperrin led us slowly toward the far end of the massive cemetery, always choosing the rows with the most cover and the tallest barrows. It would be impossible for anyone outside the Westbarrow to see us now, but perhaps he was concerned about enemies within, or in the air. The broken seals on the passageway to the gods served as a constant reminder of our peril.

"The gate is that way." My father pointed to our left.

"I am aware of that," said Sperrin.

"The Trade Road runs right by the gate. It can take us to the coast roads. It even connects to the Mountain Road, if you persist in taking us that way."

"We aren't taking the Trade Road."

"Why not?"

"Because it's watched."

"The godlings are gone by now. And why would they be watching a road?"

Sperrin's eyes never stopped moving as we walked—scanning the area around us, taking in everything. I wasn't sure if Sperrin had even heard my father's words until he responded.

"The gods are not the only ones to be feared, with no magic to protect us. There will be fey creatures looking for people to ambush. They might not attack us in the daytime, but they would strike while we slept. But I'm most concerned that those Central Alliance ships may have sent infiltrators to look for high-value targets escaping from the city. I don't know how or why they coordinated with the gods in attacking us, but I have no intention of allowing either of you to become their target."

My father seemed about to respond, but then he closed his mouth abruptly. That wasn't the response he'd been expecting, apparently.

We continued in silence until the sun blazed high overhead. Sperrin stopped us for lunch in the shadows of a tall barrow topped with stone sculptures, shaded from the early summer heat.

"Ketya, can you climb up there and tell me what you see?" Sperrin asked once we'd eaten.

"Is it safe?" *I ask him that a lot*, I realized.

"It should be safe for a few minutes, as long as you don't make much noise. It will be hard to see you in this light unless someone is looking right at that spot."

Carefully I worked my way up the barrow and then scaled the tallest of the monuments. From the top, standing on a pair of cupped stone hands and holding onto the crown on the stone woman's head, I could see all the way back to the riverbank, as well as a broad arc of the Trade Road.

I climbed down somberly, waiting to say anything until I'd reached the bottom.

"There's nothing there," I said. "No one in the road or on the riverbank. I could see debris where the camp was, but no people. Not even…" I couldn't bring myself to say *bodies*, but Sperrin and my father both took my meaning.

"Some of them will have gotten to safety," Sperrin said. "Some always do. More than you expect. As for the bodies, many of the fey that attacked like to carry them off."

He quietly cleaned up the remains of our lunch and made sure our packs were tied securely, as if his words had settled things for me.

I'm not a soldier, I wanted to say. I'm not used to seeing what you're used to seeing. I'm not used to all the killing and dying. And from the look in his eyes, I thought Sperrin would know what to say to make me feel better. But I could see the look in my father's eyes also, and knew how he would look at me if I showed weakness. *How he already looks at me*, I thought.

No use in confirming what he probably already thinks of me. If I can't be useful, I can at least be quiet.

I shouldered my pack wordlessly. But this time I felt grateful when Sperrin adjusted the straps so they didn't bite, knowing without asking where they would bind me.

WHEN WE CONTINUED, my father walked slightly ahead of us, his head sometimes bobbing from side to side like a visitor taking in scenery. He did not attempt to change our direction again toward the Trade Road, and if he walked less circumspectly than Sperrin had, the big soldier didn't seem to mind especially.

I didn't mind, either. Glad as I was that we'd saved my father, I hated the arguments he started, and knew that sooner or later he would pull me into them.

I walked more closely to Sperrin than I had dared before, and with my father out of easy hearing distance I finally worked up the nerve to ask him a question.

"Is it true what my father said…about your daughter?" I asked softly.

Sperrin seemed to consider the question from all sides before answering.

"It's not untrue. It's misleading, but the essence is there. I lived in Whitmount with my wife and daughter before the Empress required my services at the palace."

"You didn't visit them?"

He paused. "Until…until two days ago, I didn't remember that I had a daughter. Or that I'd ever been married. I don't know if they are still there, or if they remember me." He paused, then seemed to think he needed to say more. "I would like to see them if it's possible. But that's not why we are going to Whitmount."

"I understand." But I wondered if I really did.

We walked on toward the wall, still hazy in the distance.

"How old was your daughter?"

"She was just a little girl last time I saw her. She would be about your age now, I think. Maybe a little younger. Her mother was a channeler, like yours."

I wasn't sure if he realized what that implied. *He's not going to want to hear this*, I thought.

"You know that means she's probably dead, right?"

Sperrin nodded, slowly. "I hoped the distance from the capital might save her. And the protections in Whitmount. But I know what it means."

"Maybe. They might help, at least a little. Unless she was a very powerful channeler. The stronger her magic, the greater the loss will be. It's like a big wound."

I could still feel the hurt inside, both from losing the magic and from knowing I wasn't good enough to have died. Every word I said to him just made me feel worse.

At least Sperrin was nice enough not to point out my obvious lack of gifts.

"She was a very powerful channeler," he said. His voice sounded a little sad. "She was one of the Empress's favorites, I was told when the marriage box came."

"You hadn't met her before?"

"No. I was too busy fighting to meet very many people who weren't soldiers. I grew up in the mountains, where there aren't many people to begin with, and was sent to fight when I was younger than you. I met a lot of soldiers, but I didn't know many others until I got to the palace. Maybe I knew some through my wife that I...forgot. Even at the palace, I didn't make many friends who weren't soldiers."

"You didn't"—I wasn't sure if I should continue, but his look said it was all right—"You didn't exactly look the part. I always wondered why you were here. You seemed to try so hard not to fit in, while all the other guards looked sort of the same."

Sperrin nodded. "It wasn't that I wanted to be here," he said. "It was that I stopped wanting to be somewhere else. But I always did my duty."

That sounded cryptic enough that I expected him to elaborate, but he didn't say anything more. After a while I fell into his rhythm of walking and watching. The far wall gradually grew less hazy as the sun dipped lower toward the horizon.

"ARE WE SPENDING the night here?" my father asked. We had reached the wall at last, but only an hour or so of daylight remained. The sun glowed red against the edge of the stone wall.

Only a few barrows had been built this close to the Westbarrow's edge, newer ones mostly.

Sperrin wiped sweat from his brow. "No, we move on."

"We could spend another night in shelter." My father gestured to the nearest barrow. I hadn't seen any blue runes in almost an hour.

"I think it would be a bad idea to spend a second night in the same place, Your Lordship. If I didn't know better, I would say your advice has all been calculated to make us easy to overtake. Since I know that can't be the case, I believe it's just a reflection of your lack of time out of doors, or fighting. Perhaps this journey will be a useful experience for you."

My father gathered himself for a reply, but Sperrin cut him off. "In the meantime, please leave the guiding and the soldiering to me. I was kind enough to leave the governing to you. Fine job you did keeping the empire safe from gods and invaders."

He turned appraisingly to the wall. My father said nothing.

Sperrin must have prepared that response ahead, I realized. He knew what my father would say. He was even implying that my father was trying to get himself killed, or was at least indifferent to whether he lived or died. I wondered a little at the words: I had seen my father defeat many people with his words, but had never seen him fall into someone else's ambush. *He really isn't himself.*

We camped in a small clearing a few hundred paces past the wall. A narrow, fast stream ran nearby, and Sperrin refilled our flasks. Once again, he produced a small, neat meal of dried fruits and grains.

"We're nowhere near the Trade Road," Sperrin said. "No point in your running tonight."

"I could go back through the barrows," my father observed.

"Good luck climbing the wall by yourself without being heard."

"Better odds than getting lost and starving in the wild."

"No one is lost except you, Your Lordship. We're going to cut across country for two days on hunting trails, and then pick up the Mountain Road. Nice and easy. We may have to avoid the odd carnivore, but I don't think we'll be bothered by godlings or Central Alliance soldiers. Unless they're *very* lost."

That night, after moonrise, I heard wolves howl for the first time. Having lived in cities my whole life, I'd never encountered wolves except as metaphors in love stories. Now when I listened to them, they seemed unutterably sad.

Sperrin
Just west of the Westbarrow: Three days after the Loss

A part of me wished the chancellor would run again. There was a time for politicians to stop arguing and let the soldiers do their job. I supposed the chancellor and I differed on where that point was.

It wasn't that I regretted rescuing the man: No one deserved to die in that palace, especially after so many had already fallen. But I felt like someone who tries to rescue a drowning man, only to be pulled underwater by the poor fool he's trying to save.

I didn't actually have any reason to believe the Trade Road was being watched, either by gods or by soldiers. It was a possibility, though. And the chancellor seemed so determined to put us at risk that I decided to be cautious. Once or twice before, I'd run into officers who were just *unlucky*. It really did pay to do the opposite of whatever they wanted, no matter how reasonable their arguments seemed. Given the events of the last two days, I had decided to treat the chancellor the same way.

I would be glad to get us to Whitmount, where the chancellor would become someone else's problem. Whose problem, I wasn't sure, but the only way I could keep working with the chancellor was by focusing on a finite end to the assignment.

Unlike my palace assignment. Although that had, I realized, had a much more finite end than either I or the Empress had expected.

And after I turned the chancellor and the girl over...then what? I knew the answer of course: I would fight, and fight well. Ananya needed me now, even more than the empire had in all my years of war. I would fall right back into the life I'd given up everything to escape.

Some things weren't made to be escaped, apparently.

And I certainly *liked* the life I'd escaped from. I hadn't left it from fear or fatigue.

I'd asked for my release because I feared I liked the killing too much.

I WOKE CHILLED, in the pinkness of the early morning, just before sunrise. The others slept deeply, huddled in their blankets. Neither of them had rested enough since the horrors of the palace attack; no point in waking them early now.

I relieved myself behind a tree, stretched out my legs and arms to loosen fighting muscles, then paused by the stream to watch the sun rise.

It felt good to be alone again, away from the constant bustle and lack of privacy of the castle. Until I remembered my wife and daughter—the memories no more complete than they had been yesterday—I had thought that my privacy was the biggest sacrifice I'd made in coming to the palace.

While Ketya and the chancellor slept, I scouted the trail, making sure conditions remained as I remembered. We had camped amid a grove of young chestnuts, and the air of newness lingered on the trail. I moved quickly but appraisingly, looking for traps, wet spots that would mire boots, poisonous vines, and any other potential surprises to my castle-bred charges. On the way back I moved more slowly: Human travelers were scarce here, even when gods weren't attacking, and the hunting would be good. I caught two hares with knife throws on my return to camp.

The smell of cooking meat woke the others.

"Is it safe to burn a fire?" Ketya asked. From the look in the chancellor's eyes at his daughter's question, her father rather hoped that it wasn't.

"The smoke won't show from here. We can't risk fires at night, but it's safe enough now." I smelled the air, making sure I was telling the truth. "We'll be leaving soon, and we'll cross water that will hide our trail even if we are followed."

Ketya looked relieved at my answer, and very hungry. Her father acted more reserved, but seemed disinclined to argue this morning. They ate quickly, with better appetite than I had expected. As soon as I broke camp both of them followed me willingly enough.

The stream ran fast but not deep; we barely wet our feet crossing the ford a little ways upstream. For a while we walked mostly through young hardwood forest and meadow, scarred here and there by past fires. Gradually our path became rockier, as we entered the band of foothills that would lead us into Ananya's rocky spine.

Now and again I stopped them, and got on hands and knees to check spoor on our trail.

I pointed out bear scat to Ketya. Her father seemed uninterested.

"Should we be worried about bears?" she asked.

I shrugged. "There are other things I would worry about more. Bears will have easier food than us this time of year unless we're stupid. It's fey I'm worried about."

"That's the second time you've mentioned fey. Fey, like…faeries? Brownies and things you leave saucers of milk out for? Are they really worse than bears?"

"What do you think was attacking those poor fools upstream from us last night? Just because they drink your milk doesn't make them your *friends*."

Ketya looked offended. "I've never heard of faerie attacks before."

"There used to be plenty. I'm sure your father can tell you all about them." I nodded at the chancellor. "Usually they don't attack where magic is strong. During the Holy War and its aftermath, they attacked often enough, though. I've known soldiers who fell asleep on watch to be replaced with changelings: I had to explain to a husband once why one of my troopers—his wife—had been replaced by a badger in an exact replica of her uniform. Thanks to your father, there's even a form to fill out when it happens."

Ketya looked unsure whether to believe me or not. Her father chose not to contradict my exaggeration.

"The fey haven't forgotten that we were their enemies in the big war. Even if the gods left them behind when the war ended and the gods went back to their own lands. The fey have long lives and long memories."

Ketya
Northwest of the Westbarrow: Three days after the Loss

I had never been so tired before. My legs were holding up, but my hips and shoulders ached fiercely by the time we stopped for lunch. Sweat covered me and soaked my undershirt. Sperrin had made us stop often for water and brief rest breaks, but it hadn't seemed to help.

I had made it through the Westbarrow without getting too sore, and that

had left me a bit too confident. In retrospect I had made it through the previous day on a combination of fear, excitement, and the graveyard's mostly flat
ground. Today's foothills attacked my feet and hips in entirely different ways.
And we were still nowhere near the mountains themselves.

Sperrin seemed unaffected by the walk, even with the little hunting and
scouting expedition he had taken before my father and I awoke. *How does he
do it? He's been in the palace for years. He should be tired, too. It's not fair.*

And it's what's keeping us alive, I admitted to myself ruefully. *Stop com-
plaining to yourself about it and get in shape.* Not that I would dare complain
out loud in front of my father.

If he suffered like I did, my father showed no signs of it. As always, he
seemed cool and in his element, no matter what the environment or even the
state of his sanity.

We ate lunch by a racing stream, on a little patch of water-smoothed
stones surrounded by huge rocks. After he ate, refilled his water flask, and
rinsed off, Sperrin sat on the flat top of one of the big rocks and wrote in a
small book bound in red fabric.

My father had settled down for a nap, so I pulled myself to my feet, shook
away the soreness, and clambered up the rock.

"Do you mind if I join you?" I asked Sperrin.

He nodded to a spot next to him, flat and sunny. Crawling over, I lay on
my back, closing my eyes. Sun on my face felt more soothing than the heat of
the trail, somehow. A thin breeze from the stream cooled me.

"It's nice here," I said. If Sperrin answered I didn't hear it.

After a while, I opened my eyes and sat up. Sperrin continued leaning
over the book.

"What's that you're writing in?" I asked.

Sperrin glanced at me, then paused, as if deciding whether to answer.
Normally, Sperrin looked at me very directly when we talked. Now, I could
see he didn't want to make eye contact.

Finally he spoke. "It's a lifebook."

"A lifebook? What's that?"

"It's a sort of journal. I write descriptions of everyone I kill in it. Sort of a
life list of the people I've killed. I'm still trying to work my way back and
reconstruct some of the older deaths. With some of the memories that the
Empress blocked returning, I can remember some more details. I was filling
them in."

"What do you put in there? You list their names?"

"Names if I know them. That's why I asked the man in the palace before he died. Whatever I do know goes in there."

"Why? What would you use something like that for?"

"Not for any particular reason. It's a way of remembering." Again, he avoided eye contact. *He's a terrible liar*, I thought. *I guess he wasn't lying about the fey before, because he looked me right in the eye when he told me the badger story.*

"So it's just for you? Or are you planning to do something else with it?"

"I haven't decided," Sperrin said heavily. "Right now it's just for me. It gives killings more...weight. Heft. Lets me remember details that I might want later."

"I see," I said. *Hefty killings.* But I didn't. "Have you been keeping it all these years?"

"No. I wish I had been. I started after...a little more than ten years ago. A friend of mine suggested it, before I came to the palace. It had started to bother me that I didn't know very much about the people I killed. I tried to fill in as many from before as I could remember."

"That sounds like it would be very hard on you," I said. "Most people would want to forget."

"Most people would," said Sperrin.

I lay back on the stone, and let the sun soak me. I was becoming accustomed to the rhythm of Sperrin's silences, and was pretty sure he didn't want to talk anymore.

Closing my eyes, I listened to the breeze, and the birds, and the scratching of his pen on paper. Not a magical stylus like the now-useless one I'd lost in the palace, but a soldier's pen with a refillable well of ink. I didn't really know how to react to anything he had said.

Sperrin
Longhold Hill: Four days after the Loss

The guard tower at the top of Longhold Hill sat empty. The door had been ripped from its hinges. Blood covered the floor of the central hall. Up the stairs I found part of a guard, half-eaten, in the barracks. Only four soldiers and a channeler had been stationed here; it looked like the last two soldiers had made a brief stand on the roof. Nothing remained except some blood and a dropped blade. I'd seen the second soldier's blade at the base of the tower where it had fallen.

Ketya followed me up to the roof of the tower, while her father stayed below. She looked shaken.

The west side of the hill, behind us, overlooked the Mountain Road, where our journey would continue. In front of us, the tower had an unobstructed view of the Trade Road and most of the Westbarrow, as well as a partial view of the rear of the Drowned City. We couldn't see the harbor from this vantage point, but we could see enough. Flames licked at the great towers. Whole neighborhoods burned. A handful of refugees dotted the ring road, but only a handful.

I saw tears streaking Ketya's face.

"I thought there would be more people on the roads," she said, quietly. "There have to be more survivors. That can't be everyone."

"There will be," I said. "People are resilient."

"But not many."

"I don't know, Ketya."

Ketya

"We need to leave," Sperrin said suddenly.

The specter of the burning city still held me. I couldn't stop staring at the flames, lighting the horizon.

"Ketya, we need to go."

"Can't it wait one more minute? Maybe *you* can wait on mourning, but not all of us are like you." The tears wouldn't stop coming now.

"Whatever killed those troopers will very likely be back at nightfall. Did you see how the tower door was torn off? We have less than two hours until darkness. It can't wait."

I just shook my head and sobbed. I couldn't talk.

Sperrin stood there until it became clear that I wasn't moving.

"Just for a moment then. I need to bury the body anyway. Come downstairs as quickly as you can." Then he walked back down the stairs, pausing incongruously to take a ring of keys from a hook at the top of the stairwell.

By the time I pulled myself together, Sperrin had covered the partial body with enough dirt and stones to keep animals away. I didn't know where he'd found a shovel; presumably someplace he'd needed the keys to unlock. "It's not much of a grave," he said. "But better than leaving the rest of him to be eaten. Someday, he'll have better."

I just stared at him, my eyes puffy.

"We do the best we can." Sperrin sounded a little defensive. "We had to do this or worse after some battles that went badly, and send details back for the bodies later, so they could be treated properly."

I said nothing. I picked up my pack and fell into line ahead of my father as Sperrin started us down the steep trail to the Mountain Road.

I must look terrible, I realized. *My father hasn't said a word. Not even a look to remind me how to conduct myself.* I wiped at my face as much as I could on the rugged trail.

Here and there stairs had been cut into the roughest parts of the path, but it had never been intended as more than a shortcut to the Mountain Road. Assigning channelers trained in stonecutting to smooth the trail beyond its initial rough cut had never been a priority.

Sperrin walked down the path with almost catlike smoothness, but I found myself half-sliding at times. I scraped both hands catching myself from near-falls. Springy foliage spanked my legs and torso and sometimes my face. I kept reaching back to make sure the Talisman hadn't been dislodged, until I wondered if I was making it obvious to my father I was hiding something. But I feared losing it in the mountains without ever noticing I had dropped it.

Very little light remained when we reached the base of the trail; darkness came early in the mountains.

We found ourselves on a smooth-cut stone road, wider than a pair of army wagons. Despite my father's talk about its roughness, the Mountain Road had been designed for a marching army, with its supply wagons and channelers' battle-wagons. I knew it would be a lot rougher in some places, but now we might as well have been on one of the coastal highways that connected the Drowned City with the bands of farmland that had fed the Ananyan Empire. It felt awfully exposed. Sperrin walked us down the middle of the road, dim in the last fading daylight and emerging stars.

"Don't we need to stay hidden?" I asked. It seemed very different from the furtive way we'd traveled so far.

Sperrin shook his head. "Hiding won't help. Whatever destroyed the fort can probably smell us if we're close. We need to get out of its territory before it knows we're here. If we're lucky it's still on the city side of the hill."

I gave him a puzzled look. Fey had territories? "What do you think it was?" I asked.

"Some sort of giant, I think. Possibly a mated pair. Maybe stone giants, based on the strength and appetite for human flesh."

"You've read about them, too?"

Sperrin missed the sarcasm. "Of course. Soldiers have a lot of time to read. And Ananya had a lot of potential enemies for me to study."

"And you read about them all?"

Sperrin shrugged. "Enough of them, I hope." He gestured for me to stop talking. "Sound can carry oddly in the mountains. We can talk later, when we stop for the night."

It began drizzling as we walked, but Sperrin did not slow our pace. Once the moon rose, I could see a little bit, but it seemed like nothing but smooth road, with rocks rising high around us in the darkness.

Twice I tried to ask questions, but he motioned me to silence. We walked quietly amid the patter of increasing rainfall. Occasionally, I heard distant thunder.

After two hours, Sperrin turned off the road abruptly. I would never have seen the side trail in the steady rain. I followed closely; even a few paces away, I could barely see Sperrin's back in the rocks. I feared being lost forever in these mountains.

I almost ran into Sperrin's back when he stopped. He was feeling the flat rock surface in front of him. Then I saw thin, parallel ridges: wood, not rock. We stood in front of a heavy round door, fitted almost seamlessly into the wet rock.

I heard a keyring clattering, then the click of a key in the lock. Sperrin stepped back and the ironbound door gaped outward.

"Come inside," he said. "It will be warm and dry and we will be safe here until the storm passes."

An unexpected voice sounded behind me. "What is this place?" my father asked.

"Inside," said Sperrin. "Inside, we can talk in safety. You will find, chancellor, that the Mountain Road holds a few secrets that even you do not know."

Part III

The Mountain Road

Chapter 12

I expected the rain would last for days. Storms tended to linger here, in the vanguard of the Ananyan mounains. I rather hoped the rain lasted; finally, we could begin to make preparations without immediate danger.

As soon as the others entered, I shut the door and lit one of the candles from my pocket. With an audible click I locked the door behind us, then returned the keyring to my pocket. Holding the flickering candle carefully, I lit four large wax tapers that stood in unornamented wrought-iron wall-sconces. The tapers burned brightly and almost smokelessly—nowhere close to the brightness of magical lamps, but enough to work by.

Checking the stove, I found dry kindling already prepared. It caught quickly: We would have a hot meal and dry clothing soon enough.

I saw Ketya's wide-eyed look, and forestalled her question: "It's safe enough. Even without the rain outside, the smoke is ventilated in a way that can't be seen. Unless you know where to find the door, we might as well be invisible. And the door is warded and bound with iron, in a hillside of iron-filled stone. It would be difficult even for gods and their servants to look here. And it should be proof against fey."

"Even the ones that attacked the tower?"

"I don't think a stone giant could fit in that narrow corridor leading up to the door. And there would be no leverage to open it, even if it wasn't bound in cold iron."

"Who paid for this room?" the chancellor asked abruptly. "I certainly did-n't approve it."

"This hideaway has been here for centuries. It doesn't cost anything to replenish the firewood and supplies—an extra day of candles brought from Longhold Hill now and again, as a guard against disaster. I had hoped the troopers in the fort would have enough warning to use it."

The chancellor grunted in disagreement.

"How could they use it when it's so far away?" asked Ketya, mostly to fore-stall her father, I suspected.

"They would have needed to be lucky," I acknowledged. "Forts like Longhold Hill are built for strategic location—that tower guarded the approach to the rear of the city and watched the roads. Shelters like this need-ed to be built where the stone has a certain kind of iron content, deposits that fey are reluctant to approach." I shrugged. "It would have cost more money to seal it up than to keep it stocked. That's how the army thinks. We fought them before, who knows when we might fight them again. Politics and budg-ets may mean that big city defenses are disassembled. But what's the harm in keeping small shelters like this one intact?"

"How did you know about it?" Ketya asked. "Even my father didn't know it was here."

I shrugged again. "I spent a lot of time walking these trails, hiked and hunted in the mountains when I had to take leaves these last ten years. I stayed in Longhold Hill more than once. Soldiers like to talk, especially in postings where there's not much company. And with my rank and reputation, there was no secret they weren't allowed to tell me."

Racks for weapons, mostly empty except for a scattering of practice blades and wooden knives, lined the wall on the right. Food barrels had been stacked along the left wall. Shelves above them held boxes and jars and other supplies. Alongside the stove, a large, round, stone-lined basin cut into the floor filled the center of the room. It looked almost like a deep stone bath.

I picked a tin pot from a shelf and dipped it in the rain-fed basin, which was filled to the spillholes with water. Then I set the pot on the stove to heat. At the back of the room two doorways led into sleeping chambers lined with pallets. We wouldn't lack for space; the hideaway had been built to shelter twenty soldiers, from the days when Longhold held a much larg-er garrison.

I stripped off my wet cloak and hung it from one of the empty weapon racks to dry. Pulling off my boots, I set them near the stove, checking for signs of damage first. Then my socks joined the cloak drying on the rack.

I gestured to the sleeping rooms. "There's privacy if you need it. Change out of your wet clothes. We'll be staying here until the rain stops. Likely two or three days."

In an hour we had all changed into dry clothes. I served a porridge of grain and fruit, and steaming mugs of bitter chickory. I had added more fuel to the stove and set dried beans soaking for morning.

My two charges seemed headed in opposite directions. Ketya, with the resilience of her nineteen years, seemed to gain energy with the meal and rest. She had perked up visibly, and had spent time exploring the chamber and cleaning herself in one of the private rooms. Now she seemed almost meditative, as if puzzling over problems and solutions in her mind.

Which is probably exactly what she is doing, I thought. She might be young, but Ketya was the daughter of Ananya's cleverest administrator; her mother had been one of its most talented channelers. It wouldn't pay to underestimate her. She was young and inexperienced, but I knew that with the proper tools she could solve problems beyond my knowledge.

Her father, by contrast, seemed to be fading badly. Whether the strain of not showing weakness in front of his daughter and me had weakened him or whether the shock of the last few days had finally sunk in, I didn't know. But the journey—only the beginnings of our journey, really—seemed to have aged the chancellor. He wore the fatigue badly, his eyes drooping as we ate. As far as I could tell, the chancellor wasn't faking tiredness. Ketya had to support him when they walked to the bedchamber I had chosen for them.

I straightened the outer room unnecessarily for a little while, then wrote in my lifebook before retreating to my own room. I unrolled my bedding onto one of the ten pallets. I would have given a lot to have another professional soldier along with us. It would have added substantially to the chances of getting my charges to Whitmount alive.

I lay awake thinking for a while, but knew what I really needed was rest. *There will be time to think and plan tomorrow. You rescued who you could, and for tonight at least, they are safe.*

THE CLICK OF the other bedroom door opening and closing awakened me. I heard soft steps going into the main room, then the rustling of papers.

What is the chancellor doing now? I decided to wait a little while before investigating further. There wasn't much harm the chancellor could do from here. I could feel the keyring against my fingertips, so the chancellor couldn't unlock the heavy door we had come in by. Presumably the chancellor didn't know about the other, secret way out of the hideaway—but even if he did, my bedroll and pallet lay on top of the entrance.

The rustling of papers continued.

I listened for a little while longer before curiosity finally got the best of me.

Picking up my blade, I stood up silently and padded to the door. The door opened quietly.

Not what I expected.

Ketya looked up from a pile of papers with a guilty expression. Relief crossed her face when she saw me, and not her father.

She sat crosslegged near the stove, where the light from the candles illuminated most evenly. The case that I had seen her take from her father's chambers in the palace lay open next to her thigh. Card-sized sheets of ancient vellum, inscribed on both sides in neat, tiny letters, had been unfolded and lay strewn around her legs. She held one close to her face, looking at one passage, while her other hand marked a passage on a different card.

"Give me a few minutes," she whispered. "I'm trying to find something."

I nodded. Walking over to the stove I put water on to heat, then retreated to a bench and sat watching.

After those first words, she went almost silent, mumbling a little to herself as she read in the candlelight, referring back and forth to certain passages. Occasionally she glanced furtively at the closed door to her father's room. My presence didn't seem to bother her, though.

When she looked up, Ketya had an oddly inquisitive look. "I need to ask you a few questions about what you saw in the palace. Can you answer a few things?" she asked me.

"I can try."

"You didn't see any signs of gods themselves, right? Or their personal bodyguards?"

"No, just godlings. Messengers and soldiers, but no gods or high-ranking vassals."

"How many kinds of messengers did you see?"

"Just two. An ironback and a silverwing."

"Do you know if they both served different gods, or the same god?"

I thought back to the markings on the godlings. "The same god, I think. Although I couldn't tell you which one."

She asked many more questions, increasingly specific, to the point where I started to worry that her father would wake up. She had noticed a lot more than I realized in our flight from the palace. Terrified or not, she had paid attention to what was going on around us.

"What's this about?" I finally asked.

"I've been starting to wonder about what's going on. It may not be what we think it is. I wanted to check some things against the Talisman first before I made any assumptions. I was pretty sure I remembered the exact clauses, but I had to double check."

"You memorized the Talisman treaty?"

"Yes, of course." She brushed a hand through her long hair in a moment of shyness, knotting it back behind her head. "The important thing is what I think I found."

"What did you find?"

"Well, we've been assuming the treaty was broken—but what if it wasn't?"

I shook my head in puzzlement. "I thought gods had to honor their word? Is it one of those treaties where they can break the spirit of the treaty but not the letter?"

"Not exactly. They do have to honor the treaty, spirit and letter both, but if a god wanted to lie to your face, he could. As long as you didn't have standing in the treaty."

"I will keep that in mind if I ever meet a god."

She kept referring back and forth for a while, before carefully rearranging the cards of the Talisman and placing them back in their case. "I really wanted to work this out tonight, but my head is swimming," she said. "I need to think about it some more, and sleep. Thanks for sitting up with me."

"Glad for the company," I said. And in a way I was. Watching her, I could wonder what my daughter might be like, what my daughter might be doing right now.

Ketya
The Mountain Road: Five days after the Loss

The next morning, I finally felt ready to talk about it. It took longer than I expected, since I had to work up the nerve to talk about it in front of my father. We had already eaten breakfast and cleaned up. I could sense Sperrin's silent encouragement. Finally, I took a deep breath and forced myself to start speaking.

"So I think I've figured something out," I said. "At first I thought the…the attack on the palace was the start of a new Holy War. But it isn't. I think this was just one god and his messengers that did this. Maybe some god that hated the god our Empress was descended from."

"Hated her enough to break the compact?" Sperrin raised an eyebrow. "That's a lot of hate."

"That's if the compact was broken. Maybe someone with standing in the treaty invited them." I knew I was on dangerous ground here.

"Such as who? The Empress. Your father?" Sperrin turned to my father. "Did you invite gods to come kill all of us? Did the Empress ask them to kill her?"

My father gave him a look. "Do not mock our loss," he said, then turned away from them again.

"I'll take that as a no," said Sperrin. "What about withholding magic from us while still sending it to the Central Alliance? That way the gods could decide which countries rose and fell. That would fit what we saw, though I don't see why the gods would care for some of us over others. Maybe it's a way to get people to worship them, by giving or withholding gifts or weapons."

I shook my head no. "It's compelling, but if that happened all the gods would need to have been involved. Most of them, anyway. And the negotiators thought of that while negotiating the treaty. There's no way to reconcile that with clause 202:

"Magic shall flow evenly to all human lands herein.
By the terms of this treaty it may not flow
more fruitfully to one than another.
Nor may impediments be offered to some and held from others.
Neither worship nor favors may be required beyond those enumerated
    here.
Magic shall flow regardless of personal conflicts
as long as the royal line shall exist;
In the failure of that a new line may be established
provided a complaint is made by a party with valid concerns
(those parties enumerated above, c. 4)
and negotiated with the consent of concerned parties
with the utmost speed.
And it shall fall on the ones who have violated this clause
or caused it to be violated
to pay the utmost price of repairing it
no matter how dear."

"Does that mean there's a way to fix it?" Sperrin asked. "That's what it sounds like."

"Yes, but there's a list of conditions in clause 4 that apply," I answered. "You have to have been appointed to a position by the Empress or her designate, and you have to have given up your name to the gods like the Empress and chancellor do while they serve. For a long time after the war there were several assistant chancellors who were never allowed to be in the same part of the country in case a disaster like this happened, but the gods seemed to be keeping their word and the assistant chancellors kept trying to start civil wars or assassinate the chancellor or each other. Finally they discontinued them." Somehow I felt more confident when talking about the treaty. As painful and hunger-inducing as memorizing it had been, it left me without any of the self-doubts I felt in areas like magic where I knew I couldn't measure up to expectations.

"So who would qualify to actually talk to the gods?" asked Sperrin. "Is there a list somewhere?"

"Well…definitely my father." I thought about the language of clause 4 carefully. "I'm not sure there is anyone else. But there are contingencies for times when all the appropriate parties are dead. I guess it happened during the war a few times. I *think* that with the right dress and knowledge of the Talisman"—and with one of the original copies as well, but I wasn't about to say that out loud—"someone appointed by a powerful civil leader would be listened to, or at least heard out. But it would be best if my father could do it."

My father sat listening quietly, his expression unchanging. He seemed to stare past us, like a housecat ignoring its owners and staring at a tiny crevice that it knows prey will emerge from if it waits long enough.

"Whether your father can do his usual brilliant service in his present condition seems like an…open question," said Sperrin.

"That's why I am focusing on the question of what happened, and leaving the question of how to fix it until things are less unsettled." I couldn't help glancing at my father. "I just can't understand who outside of the royal family and my father would be able to talk to them, or who would want to."

"Could someone have impersonated a member of the royal family? Maybe someone from the Central Alliance, using magic?"

"Perhaps…" I started, then stopped. "It would be awfully hard to fool them with their own magic unless they wanted to be fooled. But perhaps the gods accepted someone as a speaker for the Empress who wasn't entitled to the position."

Sperrin didn't seem convinced, even though he'd offered the suggestion. "That would still be a violation, wouldn't it? Maybe more than one. Don't the gods require some proof of who they're speaking to?"

I knew exactly what proof they required. I could have quoted the passage from clause 242 of the treaty that specified how messengers would be verified. My father had made me recite it often enough. And they would also need the Talisman that I carried secretly. It would have had to be stolen from a guarded display case, or from my father's room. Even my father was never supposed to leave it unattended unless it was under guard, but I knew the Empress would never impose that kind of restriction on her most trusted adviser.

Could that carelessness have caused all of this? Those Alliance soldiers Sperrin had killed—had they been guarding the spy who had stolen the Talisman and then returned it to my father's room, perhaps while my father was outside dealing with the harbor mishap?

And I couldn't exactly claim that stealing the Talisman had been difficult when I'd done it myself, with no more training than a cook's daughter could give me in an afternoon.

I wished my father would help me figure this out. He knew the treaty and all the loopholes. He had studied the gods themselves. Had even spoken to one before my mother's death. He could solve this.

If he would talk to us. If he hadn't gone mad.

"Besides," Sperrin said, "someone would need to be mad enough to want to betray the empire, and sane enough to pull it off. And to fool the gods, no less."

"They might not have been that hard to fool," I tried. "As long as the terms were followed, if it was what a god wanted to hear, he or she might not have stopped to double check. If the spy chose the right god."

"I can see why a god might want to do that. Maybe out of revenge, or just for fun or out of boredom. But what would the person who approached the god get out of it? It doesn't make any sense," said Sperrin. "I'm sorry."

"No, you're right," I said. "There's some piece that I'm still missing. But I really do think it was just one god, not all of them."

"Maybe. That would change things. It might be possible to talk to the gods if only one of them attacked, since they would still be bound by the treaty. And there seems to be a procedure for fixing it, if you can interpret eight hundred-year-old poetry correctly. But"—he actually smiled as he said this, I think without realizing—"it also means that everyone else but us will still have magic. We already saw that in the palace and with the raiding ships in the harbor, but I didn't think much of it at the time. The Central Alliance will certainly try to invade, with no channelers to support our border troops. Probably they're invading already."

Why did he look almost happy about it? He was in his element, with a war to fight and people to kill, but did he have to enjoy it so much? But he was trying to help.

I drew a breath. "At the Academy…there were books on the Talisman. Is there a library like that at Whitmount? Maybe someone who can help figure this out?"

"I'm sure they're already working on it," Sperrin said. "Maybe they've already solved it. Or the information we bring may be the key to the answer.

And of course, we were just sitting here talking, not traveling at all. The satisfaction I'd felt in reciting the treaty melted away, like a prisoner under one of my father's stares. Frustration filled me instead. "How long will it take us to get there?"

"Depends when the rain stops. And on how well you and your father hold up in the mountains. Two weeks at the outside, I would think. Depending on what dangers are on the road."

He's doing it again, I thought, *talking about how we're probably going to die. And he's smiling.* Then I realized: *He likes the dangers. And my father has always thrived on risk too. Maybe Sperrin honestly doesn't think what he's saying is discouraging.*

In the corner, my father spat out the shell from a seed. Other than the one outburst he hadn't said anything to us since he awoke.

I desperately needed his help. And even though I seemed to always say the wrong thing and make him angry, I really missed him.

I wish he would come back to himself soon. I know what we lost was a huge blow, but I've lost as much as he has and I'm holding it together. Shouldn't we be able to draw strength from each other in the midst of our losses? But that's never been his way, however much I wish it was. The part of me that thinks that way came from my mother.

And really, that was the problem, I knew. Despite all the years that had passed and all the things I'd done—maybe even because I became a channeler and followed in my mother's footsteps—my father was always going to see me as a symbol of my mother's death. This journey would be much easier for him if I wasn't there.

I wish he could be comforted that his daughter somehow managed to live through this disaster alongside him. I wish we could work together to somehow restore some of what's been lost. Might as well wish that I didn't represent all of those losses to him.

I saw him look my way and dropped my eyes to avoid making contact. *At least I'll do what I can to avoid making things any harder for him.*

AFTER WE BREAKFASTED in uncomfortable silence, my father retreated to his room while Sperrin sat on a bench next to the stove and carved. He had taken a pair of the wooden knives from the weapon racks and whittled at them singlemindedly, dipping the wood in a pot of boiling water on the stove every few minutes.

Slowly, the practice knives took on a longer, more slender shape.

He held up a knife to test its weight and feel against the one he was carving.

Unsatisfied, he went back to shaping the practice knives.

I had a sudden suspicion. I reached down to my boot. The knives he had given me were gone. I hadn't even realized he had taken them. *How did he do that?*

I suspected that was something he intended for me to learn.

No point in saying the obvious. How many times had Tenia had to remind me of that? I wanted to say *something*, though, if only to break the uncomfortable silence. Uncomfortable for *me*, anyway—Sperrin and my father both seemed to be perfectly happy to spend hours arguing without words.

Finally, I settled for: "Why do you dip the blades in hot water?"

The question didn't seem to surprise Sperrin. He hefted the blades again to compare weight and feel before answering.

"These practice blades are made from *lein* trees. It's got the weight of metal, but a lot more give. It will bruise you but not break anything. The wood is tough to carve, but it gets malleable in hot water."

"I've never heard of lein trees."

"You wouldn't, unless you're a soldier or a gardener. The lein comes from the colonies. It only grows in hot, moist climates. They still import it, but lately most of what we've used in the Drowned City was grown in hothouses in the farm belt north of the city."

Not anymore, I realized. Without magic, there would be no more hot-houses, no more food trains to the city. For my whole life, I hadn't thought about how much of Ananya's food supply depended on magic. From the grim set of the soldier's face, I realized he already knew.

"Sperrin, how long until people are starving?"

"A few weeks, maybe. Your father would know better than me. The worst of it won't be for a few months. People will be able to get by until winter."

"Can we get to Whitmount any faster? Maybe there's something I can do there...to help."

"We'll get there as quickly as we can. Traveling in this rain won't help." He tested the weight of the blades again, and finally seemed satisfied. "Come on, here's something useful you can be doing now."

Sperrin

Rainfall always meant training days to me. Days spent indoors meant time to hone skills and learn new ones. So that afternoon I began teaching Ketya to use the knives I'd given her.

She seemed glad to be doing something potentially helpful, and just as happy to be away from her father, who retreated to the other bedroom and pointedly declined to watch. I wondered if Ketya would learn more quickly without her father watching, or if she was the sort of student who thrived on criticism. You'd have to be, with that man for a father, I suspected.

We worked in my room. I piled the other pallets on top of mine to clear a flat stone arena of sorts. After the fifth time Ketya glanced at the open door-way to make sure her father wasn't watching (he wasn't), I latched the door shut as well.

I started with stretching and some basic drills, and worked into simple slashes and thrusts, and even a few feints. Ketya took to the blades surprising-ly quickly; I had taught knife fighting to many soldiers and she learned more quickly than most. She moved with a dancer's agility, quick and lithe, not like the rough street-fighting power of most beginners. More power would have been helpful, were she fighting humans, but against fey it would likely be best for her to rely on speed and coordination and let the blade do most of the work.

Quick learner or not, she had best hope that her first opponent was also a beginner.

After a water break, I had her practice the moves I'd taught her, while I sat on the stack of pallets and called out steps. Again she responded quickly to the drills; but then she'd been drilled often enough by her father and teachers.

"Enough," I called out after an hour of thrust, slash, and counter drills. "Let's not wear you out. More later."

"I can keep going," she said. She fought in loose trousers and an oversized men's shirt, tied at the waist and sleeves rolled up. Sweat soaked her arms and forehead, and soaked through the shirt in patches. Her long hair, tied back with a black ribbon, hung slack and damp. She'd looked visibly heavier on her feet the last couple of drills; she might still feel good, but I knew she was tireder than she thought: tired enough to hurt herself.

"I know," I said. "But take a break. Walk it off, then drink some water. You learned a lot."

"Enough to stay alive?" She breathed raggedly, struggling a little for air.

"No."

"Then I want to keep going."

"You'll learn better with a little rest. Don't worry, I'll teach you as fast as you can learn. I want you to be helpful on the road."

"Thank you," she said, and seemed to mean it. How could the chancellor's daughter seem so straightforward and sincere?

Ketya paced around until her breathing eased. Unrolling one of her shirt-sleeves, she used it to mop sweat from her forehead and hair.

While she straightened herself, I checked the practice blades for damage or imbalance, to give her a bit of privacy.

"It's funny," she said when she looked up again. "I worked just as hard as this when I learned dances, and they ran us hard sometimes at the Academy. But I've never been this sweaty someplace where there wasn't a bathhouse waiting at the end of the day." She laughed. "I suppose I should get used to life without bathhouses for a while."

"Till Whitmount, I would think. Maybe one of the earlier mountain forts. There are towns we'll be passing by, but I don't know what shape they're in. Some of them will have evacuated to mountain forts."

She nodded. "What do...what do soldiers do? How do you stay clean?"

"Sometimes it's not a priority, I'm afraid. But here, you'll be able to take a sponge bath. Warm or cold as you prefer. There's a bucket by the stove."

The hideaway had cleverly engineered, if limited, sanitary facilities. The

174

previous night, I had found myself oddly reluctant to explain them to the chancellor's daughter, a girl around the age of my own child—even though I would have had no such reluctance explaining them to a teenage soldier of either gender. I'd been at a loss to explain the difference to myself—and eventually I'd showed her anyway—but something felt different.

After she'd walked off the muscle tremors, Ketya sat near me on top of the pallets, massaging her right forearm.

"So, I was wondering about something," Ketya asked, not looking up from her forearm. She worked at it like a cat worrying at its forepaw.

"Sure," I said.

"What's hidden under the pallets?"

This time I was the one glancing at the door. *That girl is too quick to notice things. I'm not sure if it will save us all or get us all killed.*

"Why do you ask?"

She looked up from her forearm. "It seemed odd that you wouldn't move the one you were sleeping on. It would have opened up a lot more space on the floor. And then when you put the other pallets on top I figured you were trying to keep it from being kicked out of the way by mistake. If there was nothing under there, you would just pile the others in the corner, so you wouldn't have to pick straw out of your bed all night."

"True enough," I admitted.

"So what's under there?" asked Ketya again.

"There's an escape tunnel. I thought it might be better to leave it concealed, until your father's condition is a bit more...stable."

"I understand."

Ketya walked over to the door and checked to make sure the latch remained shut. "Now will you show me?"

I smiled in spite of myself. Ketya did have a sort of irrepressible energy. "Sure."

Lifting the stack of pallets off my own, I dropped each one back in its old position. Then I pushed my pallet and bedroll aside to reveal the ironbound trapdoor beneath.

"There are stairs under here," I said, and went to lift it.

"Wait!" Panic edged her voice.

"What's wrong?"

"Have you been down there before?"

"A couple of times, yeah. I followed the trail out so that I could find it in the dark if I needed to. There are storerooms and a couple of branchings down there, along with a well that draws on an underground stream in case water is low. Mostly food and firewood in the storerooms, I was told. Why do you ask?"

"There's a rune on that trapdoor. Like the ones on the tomb."

"The soldiers' tombs?"

"No, the...other one." She meant the barrow that led to the land of the gods.

I let the handle of the trapdoor rest.

Ketya walked over and examined the door more closely—presumably looking at the rune that I couldn't see. "It looks like there's no actual seal. Maybe it's just a warning of some sort?"

"Warning of what? The rock around us is riddled with iron and uncomfortable for fey or gods. Why would they come here?"

Ketya shrugged. "I'm no expert on gods. I'm just telling you what I see."

"Do you still want to go down?" By way of answer she picked up one of the candles from its wall sconce and gestured for me to open the trapdoor.

We walked down the stone stairway warily, into a small atrium with a vaulted ceiling. I supposed it had been a natural cavern before a channeler smoothed it out. Ketya took the lead, handing the candle to me. "I can see," she told me. "The path is marked. The exit trail is that way, right?" She pointed, and I nodded. "And that way would be the storage rooms." Again, I nodded. "Then we need to go this way instead."

We walked toward the well. Circling around it, Ketya stepped into a smooth-walled corridor I'd never known existed. Fifteen paces later she stopped abruptly, and put up a hand in warning.

"Don't come any closer. This is what the rune above was warning about. This door is loaded with seals and runes."

"Any idea what they are?"

Ketya leaned closer. "I think so. Some of these I can read. Sort of. They're similar to the one in Westbarrow, but these aren't broken. The Westbarrow ones were opened from this side, too. I don't think anything in there can get through unless we open it first."

"Let's not try. It leads to the gods?"

"I think so. I couldn't tell you which god or where in their lands, but it's a passageway from the Holy War."

"Strange place for it." And then it hit me. "Wait. I know what this is."

"What do you mean?"

"Toward the end of the war, there was talk of taking the war to the gods. Launching raids into their own lands. The gods would never have opened a passage here—it would be too uncomfortable to pass through. Also, this has always been in the middle of nowhere, but the gods liked quick surprise attacks. Their tunnels always opened near population centers."

Ketya winced, probably remembering the night of horror.

"I think," I said, "that this passage was created by our side. This was a passage for launching attacks. They built it here amid the iron so it would be hard for the gods to detect. The war must have ended before it could be used."

"How could we have created a passage to the gods' world?" asked Ketya. "I thought only their magic could do that. At least, that's what I was taught at the Academy."

"I don't know," I answered. "I am beginning to think there are a lot of things about gods and their magic and the Holy War that it would be nice to know right now. Your knowledge of the treaty will help when we get to Whitmount, I'm sure."

Ketya sighed. "My father knows it a lot better."

"I've seen soldiers recover from the condition he has," I said. "He had the shock of his life. We all did. It will take him time to adjust and be his old self again."

"You adjusted. I adjusted. Why can't he adjust? We need him." She almost cried the words.

"I don't know, Ketya. Soon, he'll be his old self, I hope."

"I hope so too." This time I did see a tear in the flickering candlelight. "Let's go back," she said. "I want another knife lesson, if you think we've rested enough."

"I think so."

She led the way back up the stairs in silence. Only just before the door did she turn and say to me, "But I think you're right to hide the trapdoor from him."

Ketya

When I asked Sperrin to teach me how to use the knives, when he brought me into his room that day, I expected to be pawed the way Dulcet the dancemaster at the Empress's Academy had pawed me. I was prepared for it, physically and emotionally. At least I think I was. You do what you need to survive. And I needed to learn how to defend myself, more than I had ever needed to learn to dance.

Instead, he treated me as if he thought he was my father. I knew he had a lost daughter somewhere and that I reminded him of her. But the way he stared at me, and the way he showed me how to do things as if I was someone he really cared about—I think in some ways that was harder to take emotionally than what Dulcet had done.

I didn't show it, of course. I needed to learn, no matter how hard it was.

I was ready for him to hurt me. I wasn't ready for him to act like he was my father.

I wanted to scream. All I could do was take it out on the exercises.

I wanted to say, *I have a father.*

He's right next door.

I may fight with him sometimes, but he's still my father. He may not be gentle like you are when he teaches me, but he's still my father. I love him. And I know he loves me. Even if I haven't done much to deserve it.

Chapter 13

The first day back on the road, I could already see trouble coming.

We left the hideaway under cool weather and gray skies, but the air promised heat and humidity later in the day. Ketya had her knives back at her thighs, with the practice blades stowed in her pack. I had restocked our food and water from the hideaway's supplies. I wasn't sure how much hunting I would be able to do along the way, or whether we would be able to cook without drawing attention. A lot would depend on how far the trouble had spread, and how quickly. One vengeful god and that god's allies destroying the Drowned City and wiping out Ananya's magic was already an unimaginable disaster, even if the massacre was localized. But it was a disaster that could be countered, contained before the Central Alliance could attack in force. Perhaps the magic might be restored somehow under the Talisman of Truce: Ketya had implied as much. A more widely coordinated attack would leave fewer possible solutions. Would leave fewer people alive at all, and those few would be struggling for survival rather than solutions.

The scale of the losses at the Drowned City did not portend well, but one could hope.

Hope, but not foolishly: Soon after we left the protection of the hideaway, I took the three of us off the road as well. A narrow path led us through the rocky edge of the road and up a heavily forested hillside. The hilltop trail that overlooked the road was overgrown in places; it meant a lot more scrambling over rocks and encroaching underbrush than the barren flatness of the Mountain Road, designed for marching troops.

Unlike the Mountain Road—mostly a wide, level sunken track running between rocky slopes—the trail let us see a lot more of the steep wooded hills around us, and left us less visible to potential attackers. On the other hand, its narrowness and rugged contours presented plenty of ambush opportunities. I didn't feel the need to point that out to the others, even as the soldier in me couldn't help but pick out potential traps and ambush sites in front of us.

"What is this place?" Ketya asked, out of breath. We had stopped at a clearing surrounded by spindly mountainthorn trees, and the pungent fragrance of a century of fallen thorn needles filled the air.

"It's the old road, the hunters' trail from before they cut the Mountain Road. It's still used by hunters, and a few pleasure travelers—at least enough to keep it from being overgrown completely. Also, it's sometimes used for military training, or to teach a group of pioneers how to clear roads." I remembered my first kill, on one of those pioneer expeditions. "The trail used to link all the homesteads as well, but most of the folks who live out here are connected directly to the Mountain Road now."

"Is this safer than the main road?"

"It's hard to tell. I would rather be overcautious until we know more about what dangers are looking for us. If the danger has passed we'll know in a few days. Till then, best to stay out of sight as much as we can."

The chancellor sighed. While Ketya seemed to be growing more comfortable with the climbing, her father seemed less so. "I thought the point of your insisting on the Mountain Road was its obscurity. Now even that is too conspicuous."

For a politician known for his mastery of nuance and complexity, the chancellor seemed to have little patience for real-life winding trails, I thought.

"That's true for people," I answered. "Probably less so for stone giants, though. No point in making yourself someone's dinner."

Presumably I wouldn't need to remind them of the half-eaten soldier in the tower at Longhold Hill. I saw Ketya go a little green with the memory, and put her water flask down half-drunk.

She swallowed hard and asked, "When will we start to know? I haven't seen anyone but us on the road. Not even many animals. Is it always this quiet?"

No point in not being blunt. "You'll hear more when you learn to be quieter."

She nodded.

"But in answer to your other question, we may know a little more tonight. There's a fortified homestead not far from here. In an hour or so, when we've gone a bit farther, the two of you will hide for a little while while I go and scout it. If all is well, we may be able to spend the night there."

Ketya

Waiting in the hollow beneath the giant rock terrified me. *Am I being quiet enough?* I kept wondering. I had thought that I'd been quiet before, until Sperrin's comment.

As uncomfortable as the big soldier could make me, I felt a lot safer with him around.

Even my father seemed cowed by our isolation; the one time I went to whisper something to him, he silenced me with a gesture.

The wait dragged on. Sperrin had said to expect him back two hours before sunset. I watched the sun slowly creep toward the treeline, then cross behind the stand of grayleaves, reddening them briefly before the sky faded to dusk.

Should we do something? I wanted to ask my father.

He silenced me with a look.

I never saw Sperrin approach; suddenly he squatted there beside me under the rock, his breath steaming slightly in the evening coolness.

One look at his face and I knew we would be spending the night outdoors.

"I checked three different households," he said quietly. "The first must have been taken by surprise. The others had some warning, I think. They were empty; probably they'd made it through the first night and then fled for safety to the nearest of the mountain forts. Perhaps someone from the first house got a warning out. Not everyone who lived there was…inside."

"Can we stay here?" I whispered.

"We can stay the night here. I wasn't followed, and I don't think anyone is looking for us. No fires, no voices over a whisper. But this rock is a good shelter. It will be a cold camp, but we'll make it to morning, I think."

Sperrin handed me a satchel. "There are travel clothes in here that may fit you better than what you're wearing. In any event, they're made for the mountains, and not the palace." He saw my look. "They belonged to a girl in one of the households that fled, not…the other one."

Right. Because that makes it better.

But a part of me knew he was right. The clothes did fit better—and more important, they protected my arms and legs better. The walk from the Mountain Road to the hunting trail had left me scratched up from brambles. I hadn't realized Sperrin had noticed.

By then, night had replaced dusk. Sperrin portioned out food by feel, and we ate in near total darkness. Except for glimpses of starlight, nothing illuminated our sheltered hollow.

"So where do we go?" I asked, as quietly as I could manage. "I know we're going to Whitmount, but are there other stops along the way? Or will we be camping out every night?"

"You'll get used to the camping," said Sperrin. "There's a fort a day's walk from here, though. Bigger than Longhold Hill. If they had any warning, I think they will have held."

I nodded silently in the darkness. That seemed like a lot of ifs. Sperrin seemed to take my silence for approval, however, and turned away to make sure our hidden camp was secure.

That night I heard wolves again, closer than the last time.

Sperrin
The Mountain Road: Nine days after the Loss

Lorinhold had been designed as the first of a string of modern forts to defend the Mountain Road against a potential Central Alliance attack at the spine of the Ananyan Empire. Built low in the notch between two mountains, it incorporated the latest in anti-magical defenses. Lorinhold and other forts like it had been conceived to replace the older forts built when the Mountain Road was first cut, in the wake of the Holy War. Unlike the earlier forts built with the long war against gods and fey a recent memory, Lorinhold was geared to what had been seen, until a few days ago, as more contemporary threats. As long as at least one of the four channelers assigned to the fort remained in place, Lorinhold's passive magical defenses made it nearly impregnable. The fort, and the small village scattered around it, had been built for defense—an army trying to command this stretch of road would break upon it. With channelers in the fort, Lorinhold owned the mountains that surrounded it.

With its channelers dead, the mountains had reverted to their previous owners.

The roof of the fort had been torn off and scattered across the grass nearby, exposing the stone floors of the fort's upper story. Most of the village buildings had been pried open like oysters, their stone shells shattered and the contents pulled out.

From our hidden overlook point, I couldn't tell if anyone in the fort had survived. Most of the structure remained intact, including the lower two stories and the main door. Whether that meant the attackers had been defeated, had given up trying, or had found other ways into Lorinhold I couldn't tell without getting a lot closer.

"I'm going to need to go down there to see if there are any survivors. You two will be safe enough if you stay here."

I unbuckled my sword and put it on top of my pack. "What are you doing?" asked Ketya.

"A blade won't help against stone giants, and I don't know of anything else in these mountains that could take off that roof. I'll need to move quietly, in places giants can't fit. The sword will just slow me down, and tempt me into something foolish if there are still giants nearby. It looks like they're gone, though."

"Let me come," said Ketya. "I want to help. If we're avoiding a fight, an extra set of eyes will help. And I've gotten a lot quieter."

I nodded. I had to admit that she had. Her knifework had continued to improve as well; I worked with her when we took breaks on the trail, with her father watching skeptically but saying nothing. "All right." I looked at the chancellor. "What about you?"

"Not me. I stay here. I'll have dinner waiting for you when you get back."

The chancellor didn't sound sarcastic; I wondered if I was missing some hidden irony, but Ketya didn't seem to react to the words either.

WE AVOIDED THE main trail down to the fort. A hidden side trail soon led us deep into tall rocks. We saw sky above and a few overhanging scrub trees, but nothing else except tall rock walls. The fortress below and the overlook above remained equally invisible. I guided us downward mostly by instinct.

"This trail dates back to the old fort," I told her. "There are plenty of places on it where giants can't get you. If you see a giant, find someplace narrow and deep. They can reach a long way and they're fast. Don't wait for me if you see one, just run for cover." I sensed doubt in her expression. "Whatever you do, don't try to fight one. If you get close enough to use a weapon on a giant, it *will* find a way to kill you."

By the time the slope began to flatten, we had to walk sideways through the narrow rock corridor. Then the stones opened a little ways and we found ourselves looking down a shallow grassy slope, with the scarred wall of the fort directly ahead. Shingles covered the grass like patchwork, with an overlay of heavy, shattered timbers from the roof. Not just torn off, but torn and thrown. A few days ago, at least, I decided. The timbers had been rained on, and the grass no longer looked trampled.

"You wait here," I told Ketya. "Keep watch and yell if you see anything, but be ready to run for shelter. I think the giants are probably gone. I can't see any reason for them to stay, anyway."

"How did they know to attack?" asked Ketya. She hadn't missed the age of the torn roof either. "How would they know the magic would be gone? We're miles and miles from the city."

"I don't know," I answered. "Maybe if we find survivors they can tell us."

I thought I knew what stone giants could do. They weren't unknown to the army: Mostly they kept to themselves in high, remote places away from people, but sometimes an old or diseased one would come downhill looking for easier prey. A strong channeler and a company of soldiers was more than a match for a sick giant, probably for a healthy one even. An isolated soldier had no chance at all.

I once was the guest of a governor who kept a stone giant caged in his menagerie. The thing was old and blind, most of its jaw eaten away by cancer. Patchy scabs covered it, and it smelled of the decay eating it away from inside. Even so, it had killed and eaten two keepers who had gotten too close, taking it for sleeping. It had almost escaped by tunneling out of its massive cage, disguising the tunnel entrance by sleeping on top of it whenever anyone approached: whether it detected people by hearing or smell I didn't know. The governor had laughed that the tunnel would have been too small for the creature to fit through even if it had been successful, but as soon as I saw the tunnel's trajectory, I knew the creature wasn't trying to escape by crawling through the tunnel—it was undermining one of the walls of its cage.

I still hadn't thought it would have been able to dislodge the exposed supports of the cage, if its plot hadn't been discovered. But when I saw the roof pulled from Lorinhold, I had to admit that I'd been wrong. Given a little more time, that old, blind, disease-ridden giant would have destroyed its cage, and killed everyone in the governor's household while they slept. It probably wouldn't have made it past the palace guards, but they were on the other side of the governor's house and its garden menagerie.

Before that day I had loved zoos and menageries, from the time I was a boy. I still pretended to love them out of love for my daughter, and out of respect for friends and superiors who loved to show off their collections. But from that day forward a part of me sympathized more with the creature in the cage than with the captor, even when the captor was a friend.

Ketya

After his warning, Sperrin seemed to vanish, ghosting across the grass silently and almost invisibly, even in the afternoon brightness. I thought he would head right for the fort, but he actually made for the ruined houses of the village instead, disappearing into the nearest one. After that, I lost sight of him. I kept watching, but if he reappeared, I missed it.

The afternoon sun warmed me. Light playing in the grass looked almost hypnotic. I kept my eyes moving back and forth, from fort to village, trying not to get distracted.

The giant still almost surprised me.

Warned by a whisper of noise, I threw myself to the ground.

A massive arm shot down from the rock above. I rolled as it scraped the ground next to me. Scuttling into the narrow scrape between two huge rocks, I barely dodged a second grab. I almost stood before another whisper warned me. Claws whistled just above me as I forced myself tight against the ground.

Two of them.

Slowly, I eeled forward, far enough into the narrow crack that the first giant couldn't reach in and pull me out. The arms above me kept sweeping down. I dared not risk a glance upward for fear of coming into range.

I wonder if I'll be able to get out of this crack when they're gone? I thought. *Worry about that later.*

I forced down everything but hearing and smell and touch, then focused everything on those senses as I slowly worked my way into the narrow passage. Was this an actual part of the trail, or just a dead end in the rocks? I didn't know. I worried more about the passage ending and leaving me exposed, without enough room to retreat quickly.

Slowly the rocks rose around me. Soon I had room to look up without risking my head. I could hear at least one of the giants above—maybe both for all I knew. I could smell it, faint but musky, slightly cloying like rotting flowers.

I smelled human blood as well. Maybe there had been survivors after all. I hoped Sperrin hadn't walked into an ambush.

The arm swung down again. This time I could see it: Long and corded with muscle, grayish skin. Here and there odd tufts and patches of wiry silver hair dotted the arm. A monster's arm, but sleek and muscular.

I hate that thing. Anger and hate welled up in me, days of frustration and helplessness burning away in sudden fury.

I reached for my knives.

Then I caught myself. Angry still, but I remembered what Sperrin had said. *If you get close enough to use a weapon on a giant, it* will *find a way to kill you.*

I hadn't yelled when the first giant attacked, I realized. I hoped I wasn't leading him into a trap. *Don't be an idiot,* I thought. *He won't miss two giants clambering around on top of the rocks trying to fish me out like a prize tidbit.*

So what could I do that was actually useful?

What would Tenia do in this situation? The thought hurt, but it focused me.

She would want me to be her chancellor.

What do chancellors do? That crystallized things.

I can talk to them. I'm not a soldier but I'm smart. I went to the Academy. I might learn something.

How do you start a conversation with a stone giant? I wondered. The subject had never really come up at the Academy.

"So, uh…nice weather we've been having…" That was lame. In the stories it's always something witty, and the plucky girl always outwits the giant.

The smell got stronger.

A head poked over the top of the rock and looked down at me from the top of the crack, twenty feet above. The giant furrowed its brows, looking puzzled. I probably looked the same way. The giant surprised me: From all the folktales I had expected something more human looking. The stone giant looked no more human than the merrow from the sally tunnels, or the godlings that killed the Empress. The creature looked more fey than anything, with gray-green skin and elfin ears, framing an unnaturally long face. The long face made the stone giant look oddly sad. But huge.

"I smell girl-blood," the creature said. "Tasty, tasty girl-blood." Its voice sounded oddly fluting, like a musical instrument blowing in the wind. Beautiful, if it wasn't coming from a grotesque monster.

"My blood? Really? Are you actually saying that? That's like a quote out of a faerie tale."

The giant furrowed his eyebrows again. "I like blood."

"I'm happy for you. I happen to be *using* mine."

Massive shoulders shrugged. An arm swung down, lightning fast. I flinched, but the arm missed me by two feet.

"Come closer?" An odd pleading tone entered the musical voice.

"I think not."

"But I like blood. Girl-blood I like especially. Tastes good."

"Tough."

A second head peered down at me, as the other giant joined its partner. Two arms reached down, came just short of my face. I slithered as low to the ground as I could get.

What do I do now? They're smart. If I don't do anything they will find a way to catch me. And I haven't managed to find out anything yet.

"Why are you here? Other than to eat me, I mean."

The second giant laughed, throaty and musical, deeper than the first giant. "You piss on a god, the god pisses back on you. We come here to help with the pissing."

"And for blood," the first giant chimed in.

"Someone made a god mad? Mad enough to break the treaty?"

"Gods keep their word. Always. They promised to tell us before they came back. They promised us revenge. And they kept their word. Messengers, they sent."

"Blood," agreed the first giant.

"The gods didn't keep their word to us," I said.

"Do not lie to giants. Gods keep word always. A god was invited to palace, just like treaty. Was invited in to kill. Sent messengers to tell all his friends when magic would die."

"But...not just anyone can invite gods in. The treaty listed who could do it."

The giant's head nodded solemnly. "God followed treaty."

"Was delicious," added the first giant. "Blood."

So the giants seemed sure the treaty *hadn't* been broken. And if one god was breaking the treaty, wouldn't others have gotten involved? But then why would a member of the Ananyan royal family invite their own deaths? It didn't make any sense.

I heard a whisper. From somewhere close, but I couldn't tell where. "You need to move before they start dropping things on you. They prefer live prey, but if they can't catch you alive, they'll kill you and fish you out after."

I had never been so glad to hear Sperrin's voice. Well, not since the palace, anyway.

"Which way?" I whispered back, hoping the giants wouldn't hear.

"Straight ahead. There will be a fork to your left a little way up. You want to take it. If you keep going straight, you'll be caught in a dead end."

I started to eel forward.

"Keep low, especially when you turn. If you stay low, they can't catch you."

I kept moving, painfully slowly. Keeping my eyes ahead, I tried to ignore what I knew hunted me from the rocks above.

A plaintive wail of "girl-blood!" echoed from above as I wedged into the thin crevice to the left. The walls darkened as the crack above narrowed. Soon darkness surrounded me. I found myself crawling; the passage must be widening around me, even as it narrowed above my head.

"You can stand if you like," Sperrin said, from very close by. "Keep a hand against the wall. It stays dark for a while. Unless you happen to see more of those blue runes of yours?"

"I can't see anything."

"That's because there's plenty of rock between us and the giants."

"Good," I said. I still sensed the presence of the giants, much too close. I could feel my heart beating, and imagined I felt the blood pumping in my veins. Knowing that a creature nearby wanted that blood colored my imagination.

"It will be dark for a while. We're taking a roundabout way back to the camp, so that we're not followed."

I remembered why he'd gone ahead. "No one survived in the fort?" I asked. I hadn't really expected him to find anyone, but part of me still hoped that things had gone better here than in the palace, that there had been more warning and an effective counterattack. And, selfishly, I knew more people with us would add a buffer to help ease the tension between my father and Sperrin.

The presence of the giants belied that hope, I knew.

"Not anymore," Sperrin answered. "There had been, but the giants came back for them. I wish we'd been here a day sooner."

"Wouldn't we have died in the fort, then?"

He didn't answer.

We walked in silence, until the darkness grew too oppressive. "Thank you for saving me," I said finally. "Again, I mean. Thank you for saving me again."

"I was glad to have you keeping watch," he answered. "Mostly you saved yourself. I just found you a way out of the place you saved yourself into. With both giants focused on you, I had time to scout."

BY THE TIME we emerged from the rock jumble, high above the fort, it was dusk. Darkness had fallen before we reached the camp. Something in my look quieted my father, however. We ate in silence.

In my dreams, birds talked to me in musical voices like the giants. I awoke unrested to find the rain had resumed outside our shelter.

We trudged onward in a steady drizzle, not stopping till many hours later. Finally we reached the sheltered canopy of a dense thornwood grove. There we burrowed into the dry, pungent needles; I don't know how long we slept, but I awoke refreshed and warm from a dreamless rest, and saw hints of sunlight though the overhead canopy.

Chapter 14

Ketya filled me in on what she'd heard from the giants, first in whispers while we still walked underneath the rocks, and the rest in bits and pieces while we practiced knifework and her father was out of earshot.

The giants had left her with more questions than answers, and some of those questions she addressed to me during our early-morning practice in the thornwood grove.

"Were any of the royal family doing something odd?" she asked me while I stood beside her, adjusting her knife-throwing stance. Apparently, growing up as the chancellor's daughter had left her more innocent than most of her Empress's Academy classmates.

"Probably half of them or so. But not with gods. With cooks, a surprising number of them. The Empress's sisters and a couple of her ladies in waiting seemed to have a thing for cooks. And the usual royal spouse-swapping that you see in any palace. You'd be astonished at what people expect guards not to notice."

Ketya reddened, and her next throw missed the target entirely, but she pressed on. "Nothing at all with gods?"

"I really don't think so," I said while Ketya walked to the edge of the clearing and recovered the errant knife. "The royal family were all potential kidnap targets, so we guarded them pretty closely. Talking to a god would need more privacy, I think. And how many of the Empress's relatives would even have known how to contact a god, or which one might be sympathetic? And none of the royal family lived—you'd think a traitor would have made escape plans."

"And you would have known if another guard had seen something?"

"I would have known. That's not the sort of thing a guard hides from his or her superiors."

"It just doesn't make sense," she said. "Maybe the giants were confused?"

"Fey are what they are, but they're not stupid. Why lie when they planned to eat you anyway? I think the part about the messengers being sent out by the god must have been true. And the rest seems likely."

"I wish I'd thought to ask which god had sent it."

I put a supporting hand on her shoulder. "You did well. You'd never been in that situation before."

"Does it get easier?"

"It never gets easy. You think more clearly when you're not surprised. But you did well. We know more now than we did."

"I guess. I feel like my father would have found a way to find out more."

"He wasn't there. You do the best you can."

"I can do better," she said, shaking my hand off so she could throw. This time she hit the target dead center with both knives.

Ketya recovered the blades in silence, and didn't speak again until she had returned to my side. "My father would know what to make of this," she said. "I just wish he was well enough to tell us."

I looked to the other side of the clearing, where the chancellor slept curled in his bedroll, next to the pile of stones where we had eaten our dinner cold last night.

"Actually, that's what concerns me," I answered.

"What do you mean?"

"You're asking me about what the palace guards might have known. But how did this happen without your father knowing? He was the one in charge of protecting the Talisman of Truce and the one with years of expertise on the gods. Wouldn't he have known about anything going on?"

She reddened again. "I hadn't thought of that," she said. "He's my father so I know better, but I can see how it might look to someone who didn't know him."

"Do you think there's any chance he could have known something was happening?

"No!" she said, loud enough that her father stirred by the rockpile.

She froze until he settled back to sleep, though he would be awakening soon. Then something seemed to occur to her. "I wonder...maybe he realized that, when the god attacked. He should have known and didn't, I mean. Maybe realizing that something was happening in the palace and he didn't know about it is what caused his...breakdown. He knew he should have seen it and stopped it. Does that make sense?"

"Maybe. Something still seems off about it. He didn't miss much that happened in the palace. It's hard to see how someone could have done this without his knowing. And the contact had to have come from the Drowned City. We saw the barrow. Whoever did it broke the seal to let them out."

"Are you saying you think it was my father's fault?"

"I'm not blaming anyone. Your question just made me wonder."

Ketya bristled at my reassurance.

"You just don't like him. You see him as some kind of monster, but he's my father. I know him. The Empress trusted him completely. He would never let anything happen in the palace to hurt the empire."

"You're right. I'm sorry. I don't like him, but you're right: No one ever questioned your father's devotion to the empire. I think he was the only one in the palace who was completely above suspicion, besides the Empress of course. Everyone else was watched and reported on. That's probably why I'm suspicious: I know how much was going on in the palace, even if it was mostly dalliances with cooks and not with gods. Maybe I'm suspicious of something that isn't there."

"You are. My father lost more than either of us. And he devoted his life to serving the empire. It was...it was all he had left after my mother died." Ketya brushed hair out of her eyes. Her long hair tended to stray when she spoke animatedly. "I just wish we could ask him about this. I don't know what to ask giants, and I don't really know what to look for in the treaty. We really need his help. He's the only one alive who knows some of these things."

I nodded, because really I didn't have an answer. Ketya seemed so convinced that I wanted to agree with her, but her words didn't entirely allay my suspicions. The only one who could do that was her father who, whether from madness or evasiveness, wanted nothing to do with our questions.

"I wish I knew how we could help him heal," said Ketya. "No matter what happened, we need his help to figure it out."

That I could agree with at least. Her father stirred again, opening his eyes this time.

"Come on," I said. "Enough knifework for the morning. It's time for breakfast. By tomorrow we'll be halfway to Whitmount."

Ketya
The Mountain Road: Thirteen days after the Loss

The lake stretched clear and silver below us. Mist hid the woods at the far end. We had been following a ridge trail west for the last two days, skirting the broad lake as it opened up in the flooded valley beneath us. From where we stood it would be a half day hike down forested slopes before we could touch water. But with fallen rocks blocking the ridge trail ahead we would need to take at least part of that hike. Detours onto the slopes had become almost routine; while Sperrin told us that channelers usually walked the trail when the snows cleared in late spring or early summer, in order to clear away seasonal rockfalls, that apparently hadn't happened yet this year, and wouldn't for the foreseeable future.

Here and there I could see buildings dotting the lakeside, and docks jutting out onto the water. A string of cable-carriage pylons crested the mountain in front of us and ran downslope, ending at the water's edge with the cable trailing off and submerged in the lake. The pylon across the lake must have fallen from its platform: I could see the flattened hill where the platform had been, but none of the metal supports remained. Scarred and broken trees marked where the pylon had crashed to earth. The dangling cable in the lake reminded me of the cut ferry cable as we left the Drowned City. I wondered if there had been a carriage on those cables when they collapsed.

The water jogged oddly at my memory, reminding me of that glorious family visit to the lake with my mother and father all those years ago. It didn't seem likely that it was the same lake I'd visited, but I really didn't know.

"Was there…was there a resort down there?" I asked Sperrin.

"Just houses, I think. Mostly summer houses, for well-connected people. It's too cold here in the winter to run a year-round resort unless you've got channelers to keep you warm and lit. Once in a while people would come out here in the winter to skate on the lake, but mostly the people who come here in the summer spend the rest of the year elsewhere." He scanned the lake as we talked. I wondered if he was looking for something specific.

"Did you know anyone here?" he asked the chancellor. My father stood aloof on the trail nearby, but as usual he listened to every word.

The chancellor considered. "No one likely to be there now. This time of year it is just servants and attendants and guards, and a channeler to maintain the station and light the houses. It is still too early for the residents to be there."

If he saw Sperrin's sour look, my father ignored it. "Pity. If they had been here, some of them might have lived."

"Some of them *might* have lived," Sperrin answered. "We'll see when we get closer."

He began to pick his way downslope. My father and I followed gingerly after. With no trail to speak of, Sperrin cut over rocks and around trees, moving more quickly than his usual pace. Usually he made sure we kept close, but now Sperrin just seemed to focus on getting toward the lake. Despite the brisk pace, I knew that Sperrin wasn't moving as fast as he could. I still saw him pausing to check for dangers and recent passages. But he moved a lot faster than *I* could. It was all I could do to stay close to my father and within sight of Sperrin's receding back.

We came to a rock face slick with dew. Sperrin scuttled down it like a crab, barely pausing. Stopping, I measured the stone face in my head. *Can I do this with a pack on?* I wondered. *Sperrin could, but he's a lot stronger and more sure-footed than I am.*

"Well? What are you waiting for?" my father said from beside me. I almost stumbled in surprise.

"Go on then," he said. "The overcaptain is in a hurry to see if any servants or soldiers survived in the summer houses below. It will not do to keep a soldier like him waiting."

Scorn dripped from my father's voice. I couldn't tell if he aimed his barb at Sperrin's hastiness or my own indecision.

"I will," I said hesitantly. "I just want to look it over first."

"Move aside then," he said. "You can follow after, when you find your courage. Or if you never find it, I can send the soldier up to rescue you. He likes doing that sort of thing. Whether people want to be rescued or not."

He stepped past me, rolling his shoulders to loosen them before reaching for the first rockhold. His left boot tested a narrow foothold, and he edged outward, reaching for the next rock.

He looked back at me to say something, and his foot shot out from under him, losing the tiny ridge in the stone. His right hand never caught the slick rock he reached for.

My father's eyes widened as he scrabbled for purchase. His left hand and foot barely held, without enough purchase to hold his weight for more than a moment.

I shed my pack and dropped to the ground. Locking my legs around a rough-barked gallowwood tree, I stretched out over the slick rockface until my hand reached my father's. My chest and arms scraped the rock as I added my other hand, holding my father's weight and steadying him until he regained his grip.

"You can let go now," he said. "I have a secure hold on the rock."

As soon as I released my grip, my father began to move steadily across the rockface, more slowly this time.

You could have said thank you, I thought. But I knew that wasn't my father's way. I brushed myself off and checked to make sure the scrapes wouldn't hinder me. Shouldering my pack, I studied the rockface closely, picking out each step. Finally I began to make my way across, slowly and carefully.

Just past the rockface, a rockfall had formed a sort of stairway that led to the remains of a rough track, what had been a wagonroad for the stonecutters who had worked on the lake houses. Sperrin waited for us under a copse of trees at the road's edge, a small lunch for all of us laid out on a cloth in front of him. If he'd seen my father's near fall and my own indecision, Sperrin said nothing about either. My father started to snap at the soldier, then seemed to rethink his words and settled for a growl as he took his portion. I accepted mine in silence, and tried to avoid my father's reproachful look.

Sperrin got up quickly when we had finished eating, wanting to be back on our way. I felt glad for the lack of respite. I needed to be moving, and not thinking about what any of us had done in the rocks above.

Sperrin

I couldn't believe I had let him get me angry. All of those attempts to probe for weakness, and he finally managed to get to me now.

It's not like I hadn't served the same empire he did. I was privileged, too.

That made the second time he'd manipulated me that way. You'd think I would have learned, after the way he twisted all of us at the siege of Davynen.

The only thing was, at Davynen, as much as I hated him, I knew we were on the same side.

The thought bothered me. I didn't want to think the chancellor might have ulterior motives. I preferred to think the chancellor was mad, and painfully self-absorbed. But the madness did seem to come and go conveniently.

Ultimately, it wouldn't be my problem to solve. I would deposit the chancellor and Ketya, alive, with whatever authority held Whitmount. Then I would find a way to return to the fight, in whatever capacity I could be useful. Whether they wanted me to be an overcaptain or a common trooper didn't really matter. I would find a way to return to the thing I was really good at.

Perhaps, sometime between the two, I would be able to find out what had become of my daughter.

Working with Ketya always made me think of my daughter. I had no idea whether they looked at all alike, or had personalities anything like each other. It was just that in my head she represented what my daughter might have become.

I kept getting ahead of the others. My temper made me want to kill, and when I felt that way, I didn't want to be around them.

I wanted to be hunting.

My heart quickened when I saw the dead faerie. Not much more than a woodsprite, dead more than a day from a blow that had almost cut it in half, and left to bleed out on a low, flat rock.

It meant that others had fought back. Someone else survived and fought. Someone else was still fighting, maybe nearby.

Someone good at covering a trail: Besides the dead fey I found no signs of passage.

I doubted I would find anyone in the lake houses. Nothing in them had been built for defense. No one would try to hold them against a determined attack. But I might find the trail of friends.

The last few days had made me fear we might be alone in the mountains. But if soldiers held here, I could be confident they held at Whitmount.

I let the others catch up as we drew closer to the lake, walking on paved roads instead of rough trails. The terrain grew less rocky, and straight-limbed gallowwood trees filled in thickly on either side of the road. High rock walls lined the horizon on all sides: We had climbed far down into the crater.

I heard the first noises as we passed a shattered millhouse. A side wall had crumbled under some sort of assault. Grain carpeted the floor, mixed with pieces of shattered millstone. I didn't see any bodies. Probably the building had been empty when the assault hit. *They're not just killing humans,* I thought. *They are assaulting human buildings, trying to eradicate us from these mountains.*

From somewhere, I heard a high bark, like a dog or wolf. It sounded again, not close. Maybe half a mile? A fight perhaps? This wasn't like the city, where one blade would make no difference on the killing grounds. Here, I might help to win a small fight—might be the difference between winning and losing.

The desire to kill surged through me.

I waved to Ketya and the chancellor. "Hide in there," I said, pointing to the ruined millhouse. "I will return shortly."

Reflexively, I checked my blade. Shedding my pack, I placed it out of sight behind a piece of millhouse rubble. Smiling grimly, I began loping toward the side trail that led behind the millhouse and into the woods, toward the noise.

I wanted a fight. For all those peaceful years in the palace I had buried the joy I took in fighting and killing. I had sought the palace position for that very reason, to get away from my love of killing.

You can never really forget your first love, I thought. *You can bury it for a while, but you can never really forget it.*

Ketya

My father climbed into the millhouse while Sperrin disappeared down the trail. I hesitated for just a moment before shedding my own pack and jogging after Sperrin.

Summer sunbeams lit the trail irregularly, shining through gaps in the thornwood and silver-barked ferrin trees that lined the dirt path. Sweat beaded on my neck and forehead and at the small of my back where I carried the Talisman. Sperrin moved at a steady, long-legged lope, his eyes scanning the sides of the trail as he moved. I didn't want to get too close, but I had to jog faster to avoid falling farther behind.

A low-pitched bark sounded from the woods ahead, followed by frustrated growls. Whatever Sperrin pursued seemed to have lost its quarry.

Abruptly, Sperrin darted through a side-trail I hadn't even seen.

I stopped when I reached the place he had disappeared. I didn't want to rush in too quickly. Kneeling, I removed the knives from my boots. I adjusted my boots, stood up, and started slowly down the side-trail.

The trail opened out into a clearing in the forest. Fallen thornwood needles covered the ground. Half a dozen trails snaked from the clearing in different directions. The air smelled of blood and wet fur and pungent mountainthorn needles.

Sperrin stood with his back two paces in front of a tall, jagged rock. His black sword swung easily in a two-handed grip. Five wolves faced him in a loose semi-circle, their fur bristling. Behind them stood a huge wolf, twice the size of any of the others. Its golden eyes glowed, even in the afternoon light. The wolf's fur glistened, sleek and black like obsidian.

What is that thing?

Sperrin's stance looked loose, his expression relaxed. *He looks a lot more comfortable facing a pack of wolves than he does talking to my father,* I thought.

One of the creatures surged forward, and Sperrin pivoted slightly. His blade flicked. I barely saw the motion before the wolf collapsed against the rock next to Sperrin. Another wolf snapped at him, then pulled back. Sperrin held his stance, waiting for them to attack. They seemed much more coordinated than normal wolves. *Is that huge wolf controlling them?* I wondered. Its golden eyes glittered hypnotically.

Three wolves leaped at once, at Sperrin's face, groin, and calf. The fourth edged sideways toward the rock and the rear of the soldier's leg. Without thinking, I pulled back my arm and launched a knife at the encroaching wolf. The blade buried in the wolf's shoulder. It whimpered and stopped. A second later, Sperrin's blade beheaded it.

All five of the normal wolves were dead.

I pulled back my arm to throw my second knife at the big wolf, but caught Sperrin's look and stopped. "Let it go," he said, as the huge wolf loped from the clearing. "Your knife won't hurt it." He reached down and pulled my other knife from the dead wolf's shoulder and wiped it clean. He handed it back to me, hilt first. "I think we will be having more trouble from that one, though."

"It was fey?" I asked. He just nodded his head, then cleaned his own blade and replaced it on his baldric. Squatting down, I resheathed the knives in my boots. I checked the Talisman as I stood, but it hadn't shifted from its position at the small of my back.

"I told you to stay in the mill," said Sperrin. The words sounded serious, but his face still looked relaxed.

"I wanted to help."

"I can't protect you while I'm fighting. You could have been killed."

I shrugged. "I wasn't."

"I mean it," Sperrin said. "You're not ready for a real fight yet. That's why I told you to stay."

That sounded a little too much like my father to let go. "Do I look like one of your soldiers? I don't have to follow your orders. And I wanted to help."

He looked up from the fallen wolves and slowly scanned the rest of the clearing. Whatever he was looking for he didn't seem to find.

"Was there another person here?" I asked. "What were the wolves attacking?"

"There was. He escaped down one of the paths when I distracted the wolves. Not the same path the fey took when it escaped."

"Are we going to look for him? Or for the wolf?"

"We are going to take you back to your father. When I know you two are safe, I'll scout for other survivors."

He didn't say anything else to me as we walked back to the mill together.

Still, his expression stayed calm as we walked through the trees. In spite of his criticisms, Sperrin seemed happy with me and with my actions. I wondered if I had passed some sort of test.

My father gave us a dark look as Sperrin and I returned. Sperrin seemed to take no notice of my father at all, though. Recovering his pack from its hiding place in the rubble, Sperrin turned back to the paved road, and resumed his walk toward the lake houses.

Chapter 15

Early the next morning I found Sperrin sitting on a wall, by an empty house, looking at the lake. The sun had just risen over the crater's edge, and the surface of the lake glowed orange-red in reflection. A bottle sat on the wall beside Sperrin.

We had spent the previous night in an abandoned mansion, barricaded in the wine cellar against fey attackers that hadn't materialized. I supposed the bottle had come from that cellar.

"May I come up?" I asked. Not waiting for an answer, I climbed up and sat on the other side of the bottle—close, but not too close.

We sat in silence for a while, listening to the morning birds while the sun edged upward past the crater's edge. Sperrin lifted the bottle and took a drink, then passed it to me. I took the bottle and lifted it to my lips. Fire touched my throat, and the taste of fruit. Some sort of yellowfruit brandy.

Finally, I broke the silence. "When I woke up and the door was open, I thought you might have run away from us again."

"I never ran away from you," Sperrin answered, slowly. "It wasn't you I was running away from."

"My father?"

A longer pause. "Not really. I did let him get me angry, but that wasn't it."

"Then what are you running from?" I asked him.

He sat in silence until the sun rose a finger's width higher. Then he took a drink from the bottle and carefully put it down between them again.

"Did I ever tell you about why I asked to transfer from the regular army to the palace guard? What I remember of it, anyway."

"Only that it meant leaving your family behind. You never said why."

"They called it the Battle of Powder Gap, but most of it happened in a thin valley. There was a wall like this one overlooking it." Sperrin's feet kicked the wall as he spoke. "I was in tactical command along with another overcaptain named Nemias. There was a captain-general in nominal command, but I don't think he ever came near the battlefield. Nemias and I ran it. And we did a great job." Sperrin took another drink, then went back to kicking the wall. "We funneled a whole Central Alliance army into that valley. We had set up a killing field with our channelers, and our own army behind to seal the Alliance troops in. We took their channelers down right away, and then they were defenseless. Once the Alliance army was in that valley, they couldn't get out."

He stopped, and finally I prompted him. "What happened then?"

Sperrin sighed. "Nemias and I sat on the wall, and passed around a bottle of yellowfruit brandy, just like you and I are doing. And we watched them die. Even with everything the channelers threw at them, it took a long time, longer than you would think." He took another drink, and passed me the bottle again. It still burned, but I didn't care.

"It sounds horrible," I said, thinking that's what he expected me to say.

He smiled, almost wistfully. "It was the happiest day of my life. I don't think I've ever been so happy. Not the day I was married, not the day my daughter was born. That day, on the wall, watching people die from my plan while I drank yellowfruit brandy and watched. That was the day I decided I needed to leave the army. I was good at it, better than I've ever been at anything else. But I liked the killing too much."

There didn't seem to be anything for me to say. I wondered if there was something more to the story than that. Something he wasn't telling me, or didn't remember yet. But I felt like I needed to say something. We each took another drink in silence.

"How did your wife feel about it?"

He shrugged. "A lot of that part I don't remember yet. If we ever spoke about it, I can't remember it. I don't think she knew that I felt that way. I think that she was proud I was a soldier. The Empress chose us as marriage partners because I was such a good soldier, and she didn't seem to mind that I spent so much time away from her, fighting. I don't think she would have understood."

"Did you try to talk to her before you left?"

"We weren't talking much by then. But I didn't know that I would be leaving her. I wasn't told that until the decision was made. Actually, I was never told it exactly, the Empress just ordered it and it happened." He thought for a minute. "If I had been given a choice...? I don't know. I don't think I could have left my daughter behind, not for anything. But if the kind of soldier I was becoming affected me as a father…" He trailed off, his thoughts elsewhere.

"Thank you for saving me," I finally managed. "I know it cost you a lot to be there, but if you had stayed in your old life I would have died in the palace with everyone else."

He nodded, and stared at the red reflection on the lake.

"Give me a few minutes," he said. "I need to think a bit. I'll be in for breakfast presently." I expected heaviness in Sperrin's voice, but he sounded normal.

I thought I saw the hint of a smile on his face as he sat on the wall and stared out at the blood-red lake.

Sperrin

Somehow, thoughts of the battle had turned into thoughts of my daughter. I wondered why I didn't think about my wife the same way I thought constantly about Lynniene. Why the memories of Lynniene seemed to return so readily, while memories of times spent with my wife remained stubbornly evasive. Maybe because I had resigned myself to my wife's death, while there was a chance Lynniene still lived?

A chance that I could still find her.

A chance that she would still remember me after these long years.

Long odds, I knew. Still, I found myself smiling at the memories of her. She would have loved exploring this lake and the woods that surrounded it, would have insisted we climb to the top of the crater so we could look down from above.

I hoped she had never lost the fearlessness she had gotten from me, and the inquisitiveness that had come from her mother. The two of us hadn't been a good marriage, but our traits had combined nicely in Lynniene. I hoped she had lived.

Ketya

Inside the mansion, I found my father awake and preparing breakfast.

The sight stopped me short when I first saw it. Throughout the trip, my father had rarely helped with the food or other camp tasks, not so much out of his elevated social status, I thought, but as a way of passively resisting what he saw as his captivity.

Something seemed to have passed out of him during the last few days of our journey. Whether defeat or resignation or even some sort of renewed sense of strength, I couldn't say. He looked older, his face a little hollower. But this morning he puttered around the kitchen in a way I hadn't seen since before my mother's death.

The mansion had tins of cooking gel that burned smokelessly. What had been intended for neatness now allowed us to have a hot breakfast without attracting attention. Two pots simmered quietly while water heated in a kettle. I smelled lamb and raisins stewing, and some sort of porridge I didn't recognize. I saw a pantry door ajar behind him, and several sacks open on the counter in front of him with dried meat and ground meal spilling out.

I watched in silence as her father worked, unsure if he wanted help or not and reluctant to ask.

"You need to simmer the bean meal but not boil it," he said, sounding like an expert chef. When had he been in a kitchen in my lifetime? I wondered. Other than to order Mala and her parents expelled from the palace. But some of the anger and resentment of the last weeks seemed to have faded from his voice.

I half listened as he went on with the cooking lesson. In some ways he didn't sound that much different from Sperrin lecturing about throwing knives, although at least with Sperrin I actually got to touch the knives. I tried to relax, enjoy the smell of the cooking food, and listen to what he was saying.

When Sperrin came in, my father had just put the food on the table. "Thank you," Sperrin said, bowing his head toward the meal.

My father didn't respond, and barely spoke again that day as we resumed our trek toward Whitmount.

WE WORKED OUR way slowly around the lake. Sperrin left us for hours at various shelters while he scouted. If he found what he was looking for he never told me about it. Periodically he returned from scouting with the same neutral expression on his face and started us walking again.

Finally I asked him, "You're trying to pick up the trail of whoever the wolves were chasing, right?"

Sperrin nodded. "That's part of it," he answered. "I would also like us to not leave any more trail than we have to for the big wolf. I don't think we've seen the last of that one." He knelt to check his knives in their boot sheaths as he spoke. "And you two may be much quieter than you were, but you're still noisy travelers."

He left again later that afternoon, sheltering us in an abandoned ironworks whose earliest ruins dated back to the Holy Wars. "This may be the safest place in these mountains," he said. "I'll try to be back before dark, but we'll camp here either way." Then he was gone.

Darkness came early in the cold black ruins, and Sperrin hadn't returned. The air chilled quickly as well. We dared not build a fire, but my father had brought tins of the smokeless gel. We set one of them in a small depression where no light could show and warmed water for tea over it. We tried to warm our hands as well, but it didn't cast off enough heat. Sitting next to each other under blankets, we tried to stay warm while awaiting the soldier's return.

Whether because we were alone, or because enough time had passed, or because the cooking lesson had been a harbinger of something, my father was actually in a talkative mood. For the first time since the disaster he spoke more than a few words to me.

We didn't have a conversation exactly, but he told me about a similarly decaying ironworks he had inspected many years ago, before I had been born. I enjoyed just listening: When he was himself, my father spoke mesmerizingly. And tonight he seemed almost himself again.

Later, his tone seemed a little sadder, and when his stories wound down I tried to comfort him. Although I lacked his talent for consoling words, I did my best, trying to remember the tone my mother had used in speaking to him. I told him what seemed obvious to me: No one could have foreseen what had happened. The disaster wasn't his fault. The words seemed to help, at least a little. I saw a grim smile on his face before my father finally curled up in his bedroll and fell asleep, in a sheltered nook near where I sat.

For long hours I sat thinking about my father, and what might save him. If he came back to himself, he might save us all.

I knew he remained unhealed himself despite the encouraging signs, the breakfast, the conversation. Some instinct still kept me from mentioning the Talisman that remained concealed between shirt and tunic at the small of my back.

The moon had nearly set before Sperrin slipped into the silent ironworks.

He sat beside me and seemed about to say something, but I stopped him with a hand held up.

"You should try to be a little fairer to my father," I said. "He's been through a lot. Even more than we have, I think. We need to help him heal." I'd been rehearsing the words all night.

Sperrin didn't even seem to hear me. "Get some rest," he said. "Tomorrow morning I'll be taking the two of you to meet with some other survivors." I saw something in the fading moonlight, almost a shadow behind him. Then it hit me: *He's not alone.*

Chapter 16

When I awoke, my father and I were alone in the ironworks again. But by the time I had water heated over one of my father's tins of gel, Sperrin and his companion had returned.

The girl who shadowed Sperrin looked at least a few months younger than me, maybe a year or two younger. But her thin face showed a confidence that I would never feel. The suppleness of the girl's leathers and fighting harness spoke to a comfort in the mountains. Rather than a heavy blade like Sperrin's, the girl wore a short, curved chopping sword and a small axe at her hips: a scout's weapons. Her brown hair lay braided tightly against her head.

"This is Guthre," said Sperrin. "You almost met her once before, but some wolves intervened. Guthre, these are Channeler Ketya, and her father, recently the Lord Chancellor of Ananya."

The girl bowed her head briefly at each of them. "Sorry for leaving so quickly," Guthre said, her voice pitched lower than I expected from her boyish frame. "My orders were to get back safely, and avoid a fight. I had to report what I saw."

"You did right," Sperrin said. "Getting word back was the most important thing. And I had the wolves handled. My only concern was if they chased you before you got a head start, wounded as you were."

For the first time, I noticed several tears on Guthre's leather tunic, neatly stitched up: a long one on her right arm, and two smaller across her chest.

"My thanks for the time to escape, 'Captain."

Sperrin nodded in response.

The chancellor looked at her appraisingly. "You are very young for a soldier," he said.

"Old enough," Guthre answered, holding herself very straight. "I'm older than I look."

"I'm sure you are," said the chancellor. He looked more closely at her face. "You are very fine-featured," he said. "Do you have fey blood?"

I drew in a breath sharply—even for my father, that was a bit much. The girl just shrugged, though. "I guess you'd have to ask my mother."

I expected more, but my father left it at that.

I shouldn't have been surprised the scout was a girl like me, but I was. I knew women could be soldiers, but almost all of the ones I saw at the palace were men. A lot of what the palace guards did was crowd control, so they wanted big husky men, mostly. Plus the palace was a showplace for the empire—and everyone knew the Empress liked to have processional routes lined with soldiers who filled out their uniforms nicely. Not to speak ill of the dead, of course—and to be honest, once I got to a certain age, I admired the soldiers as much as anyone, even if I would never have said so out loud.

I guess I had some prejudices against women as soldiers. I had nothing against soldiers, and I knew that there were more women in the scouts and other field units where endurance was more important than physical strength. Given how much of the heavy lifting in battles was done by channelers like my mother, that covered a lot of soldiers. But in the world I grew up in, the smartest girls became channelers or bureaucrats. I tended to think of soldiering as something for athletic girls without other options, which I supposed described Guthre. I knew she was brave, and lucky, but a part of me automatically assumed she wasn't smart. Not really fair to someone who had stayed alive through all that had happened, I know.

It wasn't the worst assumption I was going to have to rethink, but afterward I really felt bad about it.

Sperrin

Only a direct order to Guthre saved the chancellor's life on the trail. She would have knifed him for his words and left him for carrion, and I couldn't say I blamed her. Guthre and I took turns scouting while the other kept the chancellor and Ketya moving as quickly and quietly as possible; I suspected that Guthre led the chancellor through thornier brush than he might have encountered otherwise—his own fault if he hadn't learned to avoid it by this time. It wouldn't hurt him to learn to be polite to the soldiers guarding his life, but I doubted the chancellor would ever evolve that far.

We traveled a shaded trail along a ridgeline, with a rock wall to our left and a curtain of ancient grayleafs between our path and a sheer drop. Far below, a river churned over rocks, heavy with runoff. Near midday, I heard a quiet cough and froze: We had reached our objective.

One of the rearguard scouts materialized from behind a cluster of brush. He guided us into the camp while Guthre waited behind in his post. "We'll have a hot meal for you and your refugees before we go, 'Captain," the scout said. "We're glad you're here."

"You've done well enough," I answered.

"I know," said the scout. "The sergeants have saved us a hundred times. And we've done what we had to. But we haven't fought back. Not enough, anyway. Not like you did."

"That was another war," I said, "and you know I had channelers to help."

The scout didn't seemed dissuaded. "The channelers didn't win your battles. Soldiers know. You fought with the tools you had, 'Captain."

"We'll see," I answered. "We'll see."

I had met both sergeants the previous night and briefly heard their story: They'd been on a long patrol with a half-strength company of the Riverhead Scouts, with the rest of the company detached to train new recruits. Long patrols look for poachers and fugitives, make sure the trails are in good repair, and watch for Alliance infiltration attempts—unlikely as those might be in this part of the mountains. They had one young channeler with them, only a year or so more experienced than Ketya and learning the mountains as part of her own training.

What had saved them? Many of the soldiers had grown up in the mountains, as I had. Unlike Ananyans bred in the flatlands, they had never lost their suspicion toward fey, or their sense of an enemy presence in the world around them.

The sergeants had been leading a detachment of troopers on patrol when the main camp had been hit by a wave of nightmares from old legends— wolves ridden by fey who threw magical darts and spears. The scouts in the camp had fought back with no-longer-magical weapons, but been nearly swamped before the troopers on patrol hit the fey from behind and drove them off, at least for that night. The rescuers found the captain and channeler both dead, along with the subcaptain and about half of the scouts. Most of the survivors had been wounded, but the dead channeler didn't have a mark on her.

In the succeeding days they had rescued refugees from the lake region where they had been patrolling and had begun to work their way slowly toward their headquarters at Whitmount, harried by fey but—so far at least—strong enough to fight them off if they kept to defensive ground. In recent days the fey had grown more numerous, and more determined to keep the scouts from the best defensive ground.

The sergeants had been wary when Guthre reported other soldiers near-by, but glad when I found them. None of the scouts knew me personally, but my reputation as a field commander, it seemed, remained known in Whitmount a decade after my departure.

Although as a palace officer I technically had no authority over field soldiers, they took it as a matter of course that I would assume command.

And, I realized, so did I.

I FOUND BOTH sergeants in camp, though Kern, a young man with a thick red beard, was preparing to leave to check on the forward defenders. We clasped hands briefly before the sergeant left. The second sergeant, Talye, was a few years older and the more talkative of the two: She had told most of their story to me the previous night. Although smaller and a little stouter than most of the female scouts I'd known—they tended to be leggy like Guthre, built for long runs—the ferocity in Talye's eyes belied her ready smile.

She seemed to see me as a kindred spirit, or perhaps as a potential mentor.

I wondered what stories they told about me in Whitmount, and how the stories had survived for a decade after my transfer. And then it hit me: *Just because you left your past behind doesn't mean everyone else did. You were a hero, a proven killer. And in their eyes, you've returned when they need you.*

Are you prepared to be that person again? I wondered. *You left once because of what it was turning you into.*

The problems now were more pressing than the war I had mostly left behind, though. *If the price of saving Ananya is becoming a monster, than I suppose I will need to become one.* The words seemed so reasonable in my head. Something I would even enjoy, despite the price. I just hoped I would have a chance to find my daughter before the transformation changed me completely.

After a meal we got underway quickly, even with nearly a hundred scouts and refugees in my new command—a quarter of them injured and the rest carrying packs of food and supplies. Not surprisingly, Ketya made herself useful among the refugees. Even her father didn't actively hinder things. The chancellor had found an appreciative and respectful audience among the older refugees. He pointedly ignored the soldiers, as if holding court in his tower chamber.

I spent the afternoon getting a sense of the troopers: watching them, talking with them, taking my turn with the advance scouts ahead of the column. The last seemed to pain Kern, who respectfully discouraged his new overcaptain.

"Why risk yourself in a common scout's job?" the red-bearded sergeant asked. "You're needed here, alive."

"I need to know the soldiers," I said. "If you want to fight I need to know what your troopers can do."

"You can trust your sergeants," Kern answered.

I nodded. "You and Talye have done very well. I trust your scouting. But I haven't seen any of your troopers skirmish, much less fight. And they need to know me by more than reputation before I ask them to fight."

"Every soldier here would happily die at your order," said Kern.

"I know that. But I don't want them to die. I want them to win."

I didn't think like a scout, I knew. I was a field soldier, trained for battles and ambushes. The finest scouts weren't good for more than light infantry when it came to actual fighting. But without channelers and war-engines to support them, even line infantry couldn't put up much of a fight. Hundreds of years of Ananyan training and tactics had honed a military where the role of most soldiers was to defend and support the channelers while those channelers did most of the damage to the enemy.

That meant I would have to substitute trickery for magic. *I can do that*, I thought, remembering that day on the wall at Powder Gap watching Alliance soldiers stream into my elegantly laid trap. I felt my face flush in spite of myself. The scout pacing me didn't seem to notice. *I can do that again.*

Ketya
The Mountain Road: Eighteen days after the Loss

Over the next couple of days, we settled into a new routine with the soldiers and refugees. In spite of myself, I felt a little jealous of Sperrin, and the easy way he seemed to have taken command. His days were consumed planning with the two sergeants, disappearing for hours with Guthre and the other scouts, coming and going and seeming welcome everywhere. The soldiers lionized him. I wasn't jealous of the way he had taken over the scout troop, which he clearly was suited for. I was jealous because of the way he fit in: Sperrin was back in his element while I had never been farther from mine.

Even my father, gossiping with worshipful headservants, seemed to have settled back into his world. There wasn't really a place for a channeler with no magic in this new and unsettled world.

Although the soldiers seemed much more comfortable with Sperrin than he did with them, everyone else in the camp but me seemed in good spirits and optimistic. Sperrin fit in smoothly, as if he had always been in command.

I missed the times he'd spent showing me how to fight and throw knives. Now that he had real soldiers to work with, I'd been relegated to refugee status, I supposed.

He wouldn't have time to work with me, and I knew it was silly to even wish for it.

He did go out of his way to speak kindly to me. But that didn't make me feel any more useful.

THREE DAYS AFTER we joined the scouts, the wolves returned.

The first time I had heard wolves howl, I thought they sounded incredibly lonely. I no longer felt that way.

Wolves howled all around our camps at night, and harried any scout who strayed too far away from the main column alone. They stayed far enough away to avoid being attacked by the scouts, but close enough to constantly remind of their presence. Now and then we saw the huge black wolf with the golden eyes, staring down at us from commanding ridges. A few of the scouts had slings for hunting small game, but the wolves stayed largely out of range—even if the slings had enough power to do more than annoy a healthy adult wolf.

It felt almost like we were being herded—as if sheepdogs harried us rather than wolves.

Sperrin ordered patrols doubled up, and didn't allow any of the refugees to leave the perimeter of the camp unless we stayed in sight of an armed soldier.

Mostly that didn't bother me, but right now—when I needed to step into the woods to relieve myself while the column made a rest stop—it certainly did. I waved self-consciously to a scout on sentry duty to make sure the woman could see me, then wandered through the trees until a curtain of underbrush gave me at least a little privacy while leaving the upper half of my torso visible to the sentry.

Years worth of fallen brown leaves covered the ground, clumped here and there from the passage of large animals. Unlike the rocky path, the dirt under-foot felt spongy. Something had crushed the leaves in the clearing down, forming a slight depression: I had to glance at he sentry to make sure I remained in view. I found myself nervously glancing around, waiting for wolves to appear at any moment. The clearing had an odd smell, faint but musky, slightly cloying like rotting flowers. Something I had smelled before. Thinking back, I tried to place it.

I froze when the memory hit me.

Then I pulled up my clothes and bolted straight for the camp, not caring if the underbrush scraped me.

I raced past lounging soldiers to the command area at the center of the halted column. Kern stood there going over a guard rotation with an under-sergeant whom I knew only by sight. They both looked up at me as I halted abruptly in front of them.

"Where is Sperrin?" I asked, out of breath. "I need to talk to him. It's real-ly important."

Kern looked at me drily. "He's not here. And he's busy. I can tell him you are looking for him when he has time."

"Where is he? I need to talk to him."

"If you haven't just seen a wolf, it can wait. And even if you have, some-one else will already have told him."

"You don't understand—"

Kern snorted. "I do understand. You're a channeler and you're used to everyone dropping everything for your every whim. Only right now 'Captain Sperrin is working on keeping us all alive, and you don't have any magic to help. So whatever you think is so important will have to wait."

I stamped in frustration, realizing it made me look even younger. "Where is he?" I asked, more plaintively than I meant to.

"I told you—" Kern started, but by then the undersergeant's eyes had given away the answer I needed. I ran for the front of the column, not wait-ing for the bearded sergeant to finish.

Talye yelled something to me when I reached the front of the column, but I kept running. A scout started to lunge for me. Talye's arm stopped the soldier and let me pass.

I never saw Sperrin as I ran forward, but suddenly he stood beside me. He caught me as I stumbled, shuddering for breath. As I sank to the ground I caught a glimpse of Guthre over Sperrin's shoulder, before the scout disappeared. Covering us, I realized.

First I reached to the small of my back to check on the Talisman, and then I caught my breath for a second. I expected some kind of rebuke from Sperrin, but it never came. He squatted in front of me, waiting until I could speak.

"I saw something you need to see," I finally managed. "Well, mostly I smelled it, but I saw it too. You need to see it. Kern didn't want me to come, but I knew you would want to...." I trailed off as my breath ran out.

"Of course," said Sperrin. It seemed an oddly nonspecific answer. "Can you tell me what it is?"

"I think there are giants here. One of them slept here last night, I think. That's what the wolves are herding us toward. There are giants waiting to ambush us."

Unexpectedly, Sperrin smiled. "Show me," he said. Then more quietly, so at first I thought he was talking to himself: "This will be fun."

Guthre murmured an assent from nearby and I knew she had heard the whole thing. "Wait here until I send someone to relieve you," said Sperrin. "Then come and join me. I'll want your eyes on this, too."

"Of course," Guthre said, a lilt in her voice. "You're probably going to need me to bait your trap."

Sperrin nodded. "I may at that. You and Ketya will need to talk. She's been closer to giants than anyone else in this camp that's lived through it."

He strode quickly back toward the front of the column, where Talye waited quietly. The vanguard scouts surrounded her in a loose skirmish line, weapons drawn.

Sperrin sent two of them forward to relieve Guthre, and motioned to Talye. "We'll be here at least an hour," he said. "Deploy skirmishers, but don't let them stray too far until we know the situation. As soon as Guthre returns, I would like both of you to join Ketya and me."

Noticing me struggling to keep up with his strides, Sperrin slowed down. "Now show me what you saw, please."

WHEN TALYE AND Guthre arrived, things began in earnest. While they hadn't had my recent experience with the smell of giants, both of them could read signs in scuffed leaves and spongy earth that even Sperrin hadn't noticed.

I found myself appreciating scoutcraft more than I ever had before, at least in the way the two women practiced it. It reminded me of my dancing days, and the way the choreographer would elaborately map everyone's movements on the stage. This sort of looked like a reverse choreography: like reading the stage to reconstruct a dance after the performers had departed.

"Four giants," Talye finally concluded. "They slept here, left to hunt, and then came back to sleep again. They left this morning before we got too close—long enough for their spoor to dissipate, except in hollows like this one. They're staying close enough so they don't lose contact if we change direction, but waiting for a favorable place to ambush. That wolf-thing is probably keeping them informed about where to find us."

Sperrin nodded his agreement. "You and Kern and I will plan tonight. Likely, we'll start probing at first light. We'll need to find their ambush site without them catching our scouts, and then set up our counter ambush."

Guthre licked her lips.

"Go on," Sperrin said to Guthre. "Pick two others you work with well. Find their position, but don't let the giants spot you, or the wolf either. I know you want to bait the trap, but we need information first. Get back by dark if you can. We'll need the time to plan, and I'll want you well-rested for tomorrow."

Guthre's grin broadened, and then she left the clearing at a sprint. *When she smiles she looks even younger,* I thought. I wondered what could make a girl my age so willing to bait a deathtrap.

KERN DIDN'T APOLOGIZE to me, exactly.

He approached at dusk, while Sperrin inspected the camp's defenses and Talye supervised a work crew. Kern looked tired, his beard and forehead streaked with grease. All the soldiers had been thrown into feverish activity, with the refugees mostly left uninformed for the moment.

That might be for the best, I decided. I hadn't mentioned the giants to my father or anyone else except for Sperrin.

"Do you have a minute?" Kern asked. He seemed reluctant to make direct eye contact. *He's only a few years older than I am,* I realized suddenly. *This is hard for him.*

How do you make it easy for someone to apologize? I wondered. That wasn't a skill I could ever learn from my father.

"Of course," I said.

He fingered the sheath at his belt. "Overcaptain Sperrin tells me that he taught you to throw a knife. He said you had some skill with it."

I blushed. "Really, I'm just a beginner. He taught me what he could in the time we had."

"I understand," said Kern. "Did you want to learn more?"

"I would love to. I know Sperrin doesn't have any time to teach me, though." I may be a selfish channeler like you said, but I'm not *that* selfish. But I held back the words. Kern was trying.

"If you can be up early, we set up a practice target at the south end of camp at first light for the troopers to practice. They rotate, one squad each day, since there isn't time for all of them before the morning meal and the day's march. But you can practice with each day's squad if you like."

"Thank you. I would like that," I said.

"Tomorrow, then." He inclined his head slightly before returning to his duties. In the fading light the gesture made him look almost gallant.

Chapter 17

Guthre sought me out to talk that evening. The young scout had returned just after dark and spent an hour talking with Sperrin and the sergeants.

"May I sit here?" asked Guthre. Her breath steamed a little. Even in summer, nights grew chilly in the mountains.

I sat eating on a low, flat rock at a quiet edge of camp. I'd wanted privacy to think, but for some reason found myself glad the scout had come over.

I haven't actually had a conversation with anyone my own age since Tenia died. The thought hurt. *Only three weeks. It feels like she's been gone forever.*

At my half-smile and nod, Guthre sat on the rock beside me and started eating her own stew.

In the center of the refugee part of camp, I could hear my father holding court. I couldn't hear the words, just the tone of his voice—measured and pitched perfectly, as always—and the laughter of the refugees in a circle around him.

He was doing a lot to cheer them up, I knew. So why didn't I want to be around him? For years I had wanted to have more time to spend with my father and now that he was here I wasn't taking advantage of the time. Once we got to Whitmount he'd be busy with more important things than me. But I supposed that keeping the other refugees cheered up and helpful on the march was also more important than spending time with his magicless channeler daughter.

This was the first hot meal we'd eaten since I had joined the column. Since every enemy in the area clearly knew our location, there no longer seemed much point to avoiding fires.

"Did you find them?" I asked, when Guthre looked up from her bowl.

"I found them," the scout answered quietly.

"How close did you have to get?"

"Close enough," said Guthre. "The others stayed farther away, but I needed to be sure of their positions." She put a hand on top of mine. "Thanks for telling me about the smell. That helped a lot."

"I'm glad I helped. I've been feeling a little useless here. We need more people with your skills, not mine."

I felt oddly relaxed, but tense at the same time.

"We won't always be here," said Guthre. She moved her hand to brush hair from her face, then lay back on the rock, supporting herself on her elbows.

I had to lean back to hear her. I lay on my side facing Guthre, so we could still talk.

"You're going back tomorrow?" I asked.

"Probably," said Guthre. "Overcaptain Sperrin will tell me in a little while, when they're done planning." Her breath tickled me a little. It reminded me of whispered conversations in the old theater back in the palace, when Mala and I would hide in the caves made by the racks of furs in the costume room and tell each other secrets.

I didn't want to move. Guthre and I didn't really know each other enough to be friends, but the illusion felt nice. I missed having friends. I missed Tenia. Thinking of the theater, I even missed Mala, who might still be alive out there somewhere. By sending her away from the palace, my father might have saved her life.

"How did you get to be a scout when you're so young?" I asked. It seemed like a safe question. "I mean, we're about the same age and I only just became a channeler when… you know. But you've been a scout for years, it looks like."

"I had an early talent for it," Guthre said.

"What do you mean?"

Guthre snorted. She looked up at the stars, so she no longer made direct eye contact with me. "I'm good at running and finding trouble," she finally said.

"What do you mean?" I asked again.

I didn't think Guthre was going to answer. I don't know why I asked such a personal question. I just lay on my side and watched the scout thinking. Guthre had a scar on her wrist and the back of her hand where her tunic pulled back. And a crease on the side of her neck that looked like a magical burn.

Finally, Guthre took a deep breath and let out a sigh. "My father wasn't like your father," she said softly. She still looked up, avoiding eye contact, so I had to lean closer to hear her. "My father had been a soldier, though he hated the scouts. Funny how I ended up here." She seemed to want to talk, but had trouble choosing words, like the subject was difficult.

"Anyway, my father wasn't a soldier anymore by the time I was a kid, but he was violent. He would beat and...hurt my mother and me." I noticed the pause. Guthre glanced at me briefly as if making sure I had caught it. Whatever she saw in my face seemed to encourage her, though. "By the time I was ten or twelve I learned that if I could get my father to chase me, he would forget about my mother. So I would run. At first he always caught me eventually, and he would"—that pause again—"hurt me. The longer I could keep away from him, the tireder he would get, and then it wasn't as bad."

Guthre stopped to brush a nonexistent hair from her face. "I had to learn to plan things, even though there was never any time to plan. Just when I was running. I had to be careful not to get too far, or he would give up and take it out on my mother. Too close and he would catch me too soon. The older I got, the better I got at it. Eventually I got to a point where unless I was careless, he couldn't do anything to me I couldn't survive."

I nodded. That part I understood. *You do what you need to survive.* Guthre stayed on her elbows, but turned her head so she faced me more closely.

"Then one day, I got home from school and my mother was gone. I don't know where, just gone. And I should have been sad, but instead I realized I could leave, too." She smiled, not convincingly. "I wasn't one of the popular girls or the smart girls like you, so I didn't have a lot of options that would get me far enough away from my father. And I couldn't take a position where he might have a chance to catch me someplace where I couldn't run." She moved an elbow to brush hair out of her eyes again, and ended up on her side facing me. I wondered if Guthre had ever told this to anyone. *Why is she telling me?* I wondered.

Guthre continued: "So anyway, I went to the local army post and talked to the oversergeant there. I was underaged, but I...convinced him to take me anyway. He had a quota to fill from the province, and I did have scout skills. I never saw my father again."

Like when Sperrin had told me his story on the wall, I didn't know how to respond. "I wasn't one of the popular girls," I finally said. I realized too late that Guthre had probably meant the words as a compliment.

Guthre looked at me dubiously. "You look like one to me."

"I wasn't."

"Did your father ever hit you?" It seemed like a strange thing to ask.

"No," I said. "He wasn't home much, especially after my mother died. But I know he would never have hurt me."

"I'm glad to hear that," Guthre said. "I didn't think he hit you. He doesn't look like the type."

What type is that? a part of me wanted to ask. But mostly I didn't want to talk about my father. I liked lying on the rock, sharing secrets with Guthre. It felt safe somehow, like that last day with Mala.

"Does your father tell you he loves you?" Guthre asked. It seemed like a strange question from someone who didn't know me that well.

"That's not really his way. I don't think he's ever said it in words. Mostly I have to infer it. But I know he would never hurt me."

"Whenever my father used to...hurt me," said Guthre, "he would tell me how much he loved me, over and over again. At first I loved him too, like any kid. But after a while he beat all the love out of me."

"That's sad," I said. It didn't really seem like the right thing to say, but I wanted to say something.

Guthre shrugged. "It's life. But now you know why I don't mind being chased by giants to bait a trap."

I heard the familiar sound of Sperrin's boots approaching. Guthre and I both sat up at once. I felt my face flush, like the adults had caught me sharing secrets in my cave back in the theater. I could see Guthre's face flushed as well.

The scout gave me a regretful smile, slipped off the rock and stood up. "Time to hear about where I'm going tomorrow. Let's talk afterward, please?"

"I'd like that," I said.

I hoped Guthre lived through the day tomorrow.

Sperrin

I wasn't concerned with the bait, I was concerned whether the trap would be there on time, or quietly enough. The Riverhead Scouts were competent enough, but I hadn't commanded them long enough to know how they would handle today's situation.

A squad jogged by me, each group of three carrying a long, iron-tipped pole toward its carefully planned position. I felt relief at how quietly they moved, despite the heavy poles. Most of the soldiers had worked nearly all night preparing components of the trap. I'd left the tiredest behind to guard the camp, while the others put the plan into operation. If all went well, they wouldn't be needed to do actual hand-to-hand fighting, so they could be tired without losing much effectiveness. If the plan didn't go well, light infantry without magical support couldn't stand for long against four giants anyway.

But some things even giants couldn't stand against.

Ketya

Sperrin had left behind Sergeant Talye and a squad of the most exhausted scouts to protect the camp in case the wolves returned. Talye had the guards sleeping in shifts, but even the awake ones didn't seem very lucid to me. I hoped the wolves had other plans for the afternoon.

Right now I stood twenty paces—I had measured them out—from the target that Kern had left out for me, throwing knife after knife then jogging to recover them. My accuracy, pretty good at first, had gotten shaky as my arms tired, but eventually it had started to improve again. Kern had made the suggestion, whether by way of further apology or by way of torturing me I couldn't be sure. But he was right: I needed to be able to hit things with a knife when I was tired, too. The handful of sentries fighting to stay awake at the edges of the camp gave evidence enough of that.

I liked to think of myself as calm under stress, but right now I seethed with conflicting emotions: anger, frustration, even a little jealousy.

I wondered if I would ever get to continue my conversation with Guthre. Would it turn into another conversation I never got to finish, like my last days with Mala and Tenia?

Why is it so important to have a new friend now? a bitter part of me wondered. *Every other friend I've had is dead at the palace or gone. Does it really matter whether I lose another one now? Why even bother to make friends?*

But another part of me really wanted Guthre's friendship. *I wonder why she opened up to me so much?*

Then there was the part of me that was both proud of Sperrin and angry at him. I was excited that he had a plan to save all of us from the giants, and

I hated that I couldn't help with it, or even be there to see it. I was even a little jealous of Guthre's featured role in the trap, although when I'd asked what the role was, everyone's answers had been maddeningly nonspecific. I knew I had no business being near a battle and Guthre was a soldier by trade, but still I felt a bit jealous that Sperrin was ordering Guthre into a fight but not me. And I felt angry at myself for being jealous.

It's frustrating. I remind Sperrin of the ghost of his daughter and he's protective of me—but Guthre is the same age as me and he can order the other girl to her death if need be. It was because she was a soldier, I knew; because she had signed up for it, while I had signed up for a different role in the war and in the empire. But knowing didn't make it less frustrating.

I almost missed the target on my next two throws, which just added to the frustration. I felt tears on my cheeks as I jogged to the target to recover my knives.

Angrily, I wiped the tears on my sleeve, forced my breath back to evenness, and resumed throwing.

Once it was gone, the anger didn't return. I felt calm and empty, and settled into a routine of throwing and jogging.

Talye surprised me a little by stopping to watch me throw. Wordlessly, the sergeant adjusted my release angle. She looked much more alert than the other soldiers, though she had worked as hard as any of them.

It took me a few minutes to work up the nerve to ask the question I'd wanted to ask Sperrin before he'd left that morning. Finally, I just blurted it out:

"I thought you couldn't kill giants without magic," I said to the sergeant.

Talye looked at me appraisingly. "It requires a certain creativity," Talye replied. "A rare kind, but it's the kind Sperrin has."

Suddenly I understood. "Someone who likes to kill, you mean?"

"Oh, I don't think the overcaptain likes to kill. I think he *needs* to kill."

That's not quite what he told me, I thought. Really, I had no idea what to believe.

"Do you wish you were there?" Talye asked me.

"Yes. I really do."

"I thought you might. I do, too. But someone has to stay here and hold the camp. And you're more useful here working on your knife-throwing skills."

"How hard can it be to hit a giant?"

Talye laughed, a little hollowly. "You tell me. You've faced one."

I've faced *two*. But I got the sergeant's point: I would have had no chance at all of harming either of those giants with my knives, even if I'd had the opportunity to throw one.

Talye turned to go, took two steps, then turned back again as I started to throw.

"One other thing," the sergeant said.

"Yes?" I wondered if I'd let my release point get too high again.

"I think you should be very careful before becoming involved with Trooper Guthre. She's not what you think she is."

"What do you—"

"You're not the first person that she barely knows that she's told her life story to. It's hard not to get sucked in."

"It's a sad story," I said.

"Isn't it, though? Trust me, getting involved won't make it any less sad. I don't know what she needs, but you can't give it to her."

"What do you mean by—"

But Talye had already turned and begun walking away.

What does she mean by "involved"? I wondered. *She's my age, and we had a conversation the night before Guthre went off to, probably, her death. What could—*

She couldn't possibly think—

I threw again. The knife hit dead center in the target, for the first time in an hour.

I buried the second knife a finger's width away from the first, then jogged to retrieve them. I realized my face was flushing again.

Sperrin

Guthre beat the giants to the rockface, but not the water.

She reached the fresh rockfall that enclosed the narrow valley and began scrambling up nimbly, climbing between the wicked spikes of the protruding poles. By the time she reached the first safety rope the taunting roars of the giants chasing her had been replaced by a louder roar.

"Ropes up! Ropes up!" I yelled. If any of the giants grabbed a trailing rope all the scouts on the ridge could still die. The troopers holding Guthre's rope paused as she clambered into the loop, but all the other rope crews pulled rapidly.

Then the water hit, slamming her into the rocks.

What had been a beaver pond before it had been released into the narrow valley now hit the rockface in a solid wall, slamming the giants into the spikes.

"Haul her up!" I yelled. The rope crew was already pulling hard, a second crew helping them.

The loop still held Guthre's limp form, scraping the wet rocks on her way up.

"Spikes away!" I shouted as soon as she cleared the edge. Weighted wooden platforms covered with iron-sheathed spikes dropped from the walls on either side, to catch and weight down any giants not firmly lodged on the rockface. The spikes didn't need to kill the giants: The water would do that. All the spikes had to do was hold the giants below the surface for long enough.

None of the giants seemed to have gotten clear. A huge arm broke the surface and thrashed briefly, but I saw no other signs of struggle. A little bit of blood swirled at the edge of the rising floodwaters, but not much. I hadn't expected much to be visible with the force of the water against the rockface.

"Clear the dam," I called as soon as I'd counted off the safe time. It took longer to drown a giant than a man, but the rock wall wouldn't hold for long against the force of the water against it. The scouts gave a ragged cheer as they walked off the dam in small clumps, the last six carrying Guthre on a canvas stretcher. At Kern's instigation they called out my name, but the cheer seemed a little forced. This wasn't the kind of ambush the Riverhead Scouts had trained in preparing—nobody had, really—and every scout on the wall had pushed him or herself to the edge of collapse. Then they had the long wait to see if the decoys beat the giants to the wall, and if their new overcaptain's trap would work.

I scanned the surface of the water again before leaving the dam, waiting for all the surviving scouts to clear first. The water gradually grew still as the pond above emptied. I saw no sign of the two other scouts who had volunteered as decoys along with Guthre. Their job had been to distract the giants and then draw them in the right direction, quickly enough that the creatures couldn't avoid the water, but not so quickly that they reached the wall too soon. The three scouts had worked out that plan together: They knew that part of the business better than I did and I left them to it. I hadn't expected all of them to live, and neither had they.

I smiled as I saw blood seeping to the surface from the impaled giants below. *I wanted to get away from this, and everyone else here would have wanted me to stay and do this. So I wonder why I enjoyed it so much more than everyone else here.*

Chapter 18

Surprisingly enough, it was my father who suggested that I be the one put in charge of Guthre's care. It made a certain sense: I did have some medical training from my time at the Empress's Academy, if little practical experience. I wanted to care for her. And none of the other soldiers could be spared. But probably half of the refugees had more practical experience working with sick and injured people, and I knew Talye and probably others remained suspicious of my friendship with Guthre. In the end, my father's arguments carried the day.

I wasn't sure about his motives. Part of me felt that my father wanted me to fail, as a way of teaching me some inscrutable point. And a part of me wondered if he preferred not to lose one of his audience members to nursing duties. Or perhaps, there was a distant possibility that he had noticed his daughter's friendship with the young soldier and saw some reason to encourage it. Whatever the reason, I felt grateful for my father's support.

Mostly I hoped I could keep Guthre alive long enough to reach better-qualified healers at Whitmount. Guthre had broken ribs and a broken arm, along with gashes on her face and side. Bruises covered her body. New cuts layered over old scars, most of them old enough to predate her time in the scouts. However melodramatic it had sounded, Guthre's account of her father didn't seem to have been exaggerated. I wondered how the girl had survived to adulthood. I wondered how Guthre had survived the newest injuries.

Perhaps I would never understand what Guthre meant when she said she liked to be chased. I would have crumpled and died with injuries like these. I would have stopped running and given up before I'd had half this much damage done to me.

I was glad that my father had never hit me. But I wasn't really sure I knew how to relate to Guthre. One conversation the night before a desperately risky adventure wasn't really enough to tell me how to heal her.

I didn't exactly have what you'd call maternal instincts growing up. My parents were both well-known and successful, but they stressed learning, not helping others. They left that part of my education to my nurses. I don't think that changed a lot as I got older. I don't mean that I was cruel or callous; I think I was nice enough to other people, it just wasn't a trait that was especially valued by any of the people I loved or respected. They didn't mind if I was kind or caring, but no one was going to praise me for it, either.

The Empress's Academy was a pretty cold place in a lot of ways, but the importance of empathy in channelers was at least touched on in a theoretical way. Being a nice channeler could make you a more popular channeler, which was important if you didn't already have the Empress's favor. And being a more popular channeler might mean the difference between an appointment someplace comfortable and an appointment helping to build sewer systems in some disease-infested tropical colony.

As part of that training, and because as channelers we were supposed to be able to help keep our support staff and troops alive in a variety of ways, we were given a certain amount of medical training. Most of it was useless in the face of Guthre's broken body. I knew how to set broken bones with magic, but had no idea how to do it with my bare hands.

I had no idea whether Guthre wanted to live or not. I hoped she did. But how many times could you stand having your body broken before you gave up? I didn't know the answer to that. And I couldn't really ask her friends and fellow soldiers. They did help me bind her wounds and change her bandages for the first time. And they made sure I had clean bandages to do it myself from then on. But after that they didn't come near me or her. I suspected a few might have if it hadn't been for Talye: The sergeant scowled any time she caught me looking near her, and she never came close. But she seemed to always be watching me and Guthre, almost possessively. I wondered what had really happened between the two of them.

In some ways I was glad to be busy, even if caring for Guthre meant my new knife lessons ended again almost before they had begun. It meant I had no time to be jealous or angry or frustrated at my situation. It meant for once I was actually doing something useful.

Sperrin
The Mountain Road: Five weeks after the Loss

Sometimes I needed time alone and scouted ahead of even the lead scouts. Talye and Kern hated the practice, and did their best to discourage me. But I needed time to think, to plan. Sometimes I needed to see the ground ahead of us for myself. While the scouts did their job well, they mostly thought like scouts rather than line soldiers. They could smell out traps and ambushes, but not places to lay traps for others. And three of the scouts whose eyes I trusted the most had been sacrificed in the attack on the giants: Even though Guthre had lived, we would reach Whitmount before she could walk again, much less scout.

It was midmorning on one of those days. Sunlight glittered through the needly branches of a thornwood grove, turning the carpet of fallen needles almost golden when I met the wolf again.

One moment I was alone in the clearing and the next the wolf stood in front of me, eyes gold and luminous. It looked a little smaller than when I had met it before, with a few splashes of gray on its legs that I didn't remember.

"Are you even the same wolf?" I said out loud.

"Yes. And no," the wolf replied. Its voice had a slightly high-pitched canine tenor, halfway between words and yips.

Something about its eyes looked familiar, from before I'd fought the wolf pack. Suddenly it came to me.

"You were a merrow!" I said. "The golden-eyed merrow in the tunnel. Didn't I kill you once already?"

"My kind is not so easy to kill." The wolf bared its teeth, in what might have been a smile or a snarl.

I shrugged. "I killed the giants, I'm sure I can kill you. It just may take a little innovation."

"That was nicely done against the giants. And they will be difficult to replace. But you will notice that I am not a giant."

"So what are you?"

"At the moment, a wolf. Wolves are easy to come by in these mountains. Merrows, not so much."

I nodded in acknowledgment. Some servant of the gods, here to make trouble. It might even be one of the messengers who had alerted the fey to the Empress's impending death. The chancellor might know what god the creature served. Which reminded me of something else that had happened the first time I had met the creature.

"In the tunnel, when you were a merrow. Why were you trying to kill the chancellor?" I didn't expect an answer, but the creature surprised me.

"I made an assumption that was, regrettably, misinformed. I no longer seek to kill him."

"And the rest of us?"

"You, happily, are fair game."

I almost drew my blade, but the wolf seemed in no hurry to carry out its threat. Its shoulders remained relaxed.

"Not yet," the creature clarified. "The hunt is too amusing. You amuse me. You can kill my giants, but you have no idea where to find your own daughter. Not even when she is close enough that I can smell her. Perhaps I will let you search a little longer before I kill you. Consider yourself warned."

The words almost made me relax. For some reason, the creature thought it couldn't kill me now. If it had been confident it wouldn't have given me a warning, it would have attacked. But the other part of what it said annoyed me.

"Does everyone in these mountains know about my daughter's whereabouts except me? Would you like to tell me where to find her, or do you and the chancellor want to have a conversation about it first?"

"Would you believe me if I told you?"

"Probably not. You have a trap to repay me for. You would want to make me pay a price for your giants."

"Fear not. You will pay that price, presently. We will meet again soon. You know better than to think you can hide safely in your fortress of stone and iron." By which, presumably, the creature meant Whitmount, only a day or two away depending on the condition of the trails.

But the wolf didn't stay around to elaborate. With a swish of its bushy tail, the creature turned and almost vanished. By the time I drew breath it had disappeared into the underbrush.

How literally could I take its words? I had always heard gods couldn't lie, but I had no idea about their servants. And the creature had no need to lie to be deceptive.

Close enough that a wolf could smell her? Allowing for poetic license, that might well meant I would find her in Whitmount. That seemed too much to hope for. Assuming she remembered me after so many years.

I shook my head, as if I could banish the unpleasant thought that way. I needed to focus on scouting. For all I knew the creature might not be the only magical wolf in these woods.

Ketya

By the second day after her injury, Guthre regained consciousness for a few minutes here and there, long enough to sip water or broth. Travel along rocky mountain paths, even on a carefully padded stretcher, took a lot out of her, slowing her healing; several more days passed before she could eat solid food or speak again.

The bruising on Guthre's face slurred her words, making them hard to understand at first. Soon, though, I got the hang of it.

"Are you in a lot of pain?" I asked. The column had stopped for a rest break while scouts checked the final route to Whitmount for ambushes. Soon we would be able to see the great fortress looming from the rock face, I had been told. I didn't really care at the moment.

"A little," Guthre answered. "I'm good at pain, remember?"

Gently I wiped the scout's forehead with a damp cloth. I brushed away a strand of damp hair from the discolored edges of the bandage on Guthre's cheek.

Guthre managed a wan smile. "I never told you how I survived the pain when my father hurt me." She squeezed my hand. I squeezed back, at a loss for a response.

Guthre didn't seem to expect one, though. She took a ragged breath and continued.

"From the time I was little I had this fantasy that I had a different father—that my father was really a dashing soldier who would swoop in and take me to exciting places. I've had the fantasy for as long as I remember; I must have made it up by the time I was five or six. I remember him taking me to the most outlandish places, magical gardens and things like that which couldn't possibly have been real. Any time he would catch me and start to…do things to me, I would imagine I was back with my *real* father, and he was taking me on a trip to some exotic place. It was like I could go to another place and not feel the pain so much."

"And that's what you're doing now?"

"I've been doing the same thing since I started waking up. It's funny, I hadn't thought a lot about those fantasies in the last couple of years, until that day with the wolves, when I first met Overcaptain Sperrin. Something about the way he carried himself reminded me of my pretend father." I could see Guthre fighting sleep. She wanted to talk, even as her energy faded.

"I've never tried to be another person," I said, hoping to sound soothing. "I'm glad it helps."

"It does," Guthre said. She looked at me fiercely, as if rallying the last of her energy. "I needed to go to another world to survive sometimes. Sometimes you need to be a different person, in a different place. Some things you can only live through that way. When I was being hurt, it was like I was a completely different person. I even had a different name. Pretty strange, I guess."

"It doesn't sound strange," I said. "I used to have another name, too. Sometime I'll tell you that story." As awful as these weeks had been, I suspected the disaster had robbed my father of the ability to dictate who I chose to tell secrets to, and who I chose to befriend.

"I would like that." Guthre's eyes were starting to close.

"Do you still remember what you used to call yourself?" I asked. I wished I could remember my original name.

Guthre smiled wanly again. "Of course. I used to call myself Lynniene."

"That's pretty," I said.

"Thanks. I don't know where it came from. Maybe something I heard in a story, or maybe I made it up when I was really little. I just know that as long as I can remember, that was what my pretend father called me."

Part IV

The White Fortress

Chapter 19

I walked around the bend, just ahead of the stretcherbearers carrying Guthre, and suddenly stopped. To my right the trees faded away to brush, leaving a sort of narrow plateau, sloping steeply downward into a narrow valley.

Across the valley, Whitmount rose from a sheer rockface. Flecks of crystal in its white walls and towers sparkled as they caught the sunlight. The massive fortress city had been formed out of the living rock in the days of the Holy War. Although modern magic worked in the city—or had until the Empress's death—no channeler could scrape its walls, which were said to be immune to fey as well as the gods' magic. During the Holy War, waves of attackers had foundered at the walls of Whitmount. Unlike the ruin out of which the Drowned City had been reborn, Whitmount wore the scars of past war lightly. The shaped stone of its walls, whitened by magical arts banned in the Talisman of Truce and since forgotten, still remained smooth and polished a dozen lifetimes later. High towers rose above the vertical walls, some of them still containing ancient war machines in armored metal swivel turrets that commanded the valley and surrounding mountains. One turret had been cleared away to form a broad cable-carriage platform, the only outwardly visible sign of the channelers' art. Change came slowly to Whitmount.

I could hear some sort of commotion on the trail ahead. My father seemed to be making a speech. That meant, I supposed, that soldiers from Whitmount had come to meet us and escort us in. Briefly, I thought about heading toward the head of the column to see what was going on. I glanced back at Guthre, who had her head propped up on the stretcher, trying to see something around the obstruction of her burly stretcherbearers. I can wait, I decided.

The whole column had come to a sort of confused halt. From where I stood I could hear Talye calling out orders to send skirmishers to the rear, lest wolves or other mountain creatures try and take advantage of the confusion. Sperrin had seemed to think there would be no more attacks before we reached the fortress—he had told me so himself, while checking in on me and Guthre—but no one wanted to count on that.

EVENTUALLY, SPERRIN CAME looking for me, with a couple of tough-look-ing soldiers flanking him. They carried heavy infantry blades and wore the badge of the Mountain Cougars on their uniform tunics.

"Are you ready to go?" Sperrin asked, a gentle note in his voice. "Time for you to see Whitmount."

I glanced back at the stretcher, now grounded, where Guthre lay sleep-ing. Her bearers had vanished for the moment, probably to get some sleep themselves while officers sorted the slowdown out. "I hate to leave Guthre behind."

"She'll be fine. There's a military hospital in Whitmount. Even without channelers to help, they'll take good care of her. She's one of their own. You can visit her there, probably keep tending her there if you want. But your father wants you with him when he enters the fortress. And I'd like you there as well. There will be a lot of questions about what happened in the Drowned City, and many of them you can answer better than I can."

His tone made it a request, not an order, but I nodded and stepped for-ward. He wanted someone to remind him of his daughter again, I knew. Usually I bristled at feeling like I was a symbol of someone else in the soldier's eyes, but right now I didn't mind. We had reached Whitmount alive, almost entirely because of Sperrin. I owed him anything I could do to make the arrival easier for him. Even if part of me would prefer to remain more anony-mously behind, making sure Guthre received proper care.

Almost without thinking about it I touched my back to make sure the Talisman remained in place. In Whitmount it might finally be useful again. I wondered why I still hadn't told my father I had brought it: Caring for the Talisman of Truce had been one of his primary duties as chancellor, something he had emphasized over and over to me. When his mind was whole he never would have left it behind. Soon, it would be wanted again. Soon the process of repairing whatever had gone so horribly wrong between Ananya and at least one of the gods could begin.

The trailhead had been built up into a small redoubt of precisely cut stone blocks left rough-finished. Where the trail narrowed, soldiers guided a few refugees at a time across a long plank bridge that led to the strongpoint. A wide chasm had been cut across the trail, and far below I could see a forest of iron-tipped spikes. Cables on either side held the bridge in place: strongly enough to withstand winds, but designed so a single soldier could release the cables and send the planks tumbling into the spikes below, along with anyone on them.

Given what we were crossing, the refugees looked glad for the escort across the bridge. Most of the scouts seemed to have gone ahead already, except for the rearguard, which had been augmented by Mountain Cougars. The soldiers I saw looked animated, nearly all of them talking with each other and with the refugees, with none of the aloofness between the different groups I'd observed during their mountain journey. I could make out only snatches of conversation: enough to hear many repetitions of Sperrin's name. That made me smile in spite of myself: My father was used to being the most important person in almost every situation (or second-most important in the presence of the Empress), but here in the shadow of Whitmount, Sperrin's name seemed to generate a lot more excitement. That had to sting.

The redoubt opened onto a broad stairway that led down the steep slope into the valley. I could see the Mountain Road far below, following the broad curve of a river that flowed through the valley. A fortified bridge over the river seemed to mirror the stonework of the redoubt.

After weeks of mountain foliage and spindly trees that grew in the rocky soil, the lush greenness of the valley below took me by surprise. It didn't look much different from the belts of farmland that had surrounded the Drowned City, but those lands seemed like part of a different world to me now.

The stairs down to the valley had been sculpted from the mountain by the same magic that had built Whitmount. From its narrow top at the well-guarded redoubt, the stairway widened dramatically, a flood of glittering white nearly a mile wide where it finally touched the valley. The stone looked newly polished and unworn, despite almost a thousand years of traffic. *I have no idea what sort of magic can do this.* But in a way, I did: When I stepped on the first stair I felt a warmth against my skin, and a slight weight—as if I wore real magical armor beneath my clothes, rather than a stylized Snake Slayer costume. In the long mountain trek I had almost forgotten the armor, as invisibly as it had clung to me. Now the promise of its warmth gladdened me, like the sun emerging from behind a sea of clouds to brighten an overcast day.

As I walked down the stairs, I could see more of the farmland and town beyond, as well as the broad causeway that rose from the midst of the town and led upward toward the massive gatehouse of Whitmount—the main entrance to the fortress as high in the air as most of the Drowned City's towers. Signs of damage marred the edges of the town, even a few ruined houses. But mostly the town remained intact. Whitmount hadn't escaped the attacks that had hit all Ananya after the Empress's death, but here, the defenses had held.

One thing in particular struck me: the sheer number of people working in the fields and on the road to the town. Partly they seemed to be an influx of refugees from destroyed communities, but mostly the extra laborers were needed as a result of the lost magic. I saw forty people struggling to work a haying rig that a single channeler and a driver would have managed easily: I had taken a turn driving a similar rig under the supervision of an experienced channeler while at the Empress's Academy. In other places fields were being worked by lines of people with hand tools—the sort of things people used in backyard gardens but that hadn't been used on farms in generations. Somewhere in the warren of cavernous storerooms that filled the hollowed-out mountain beneath Whitmount, someone had kept a cache of antique farm implements. I wondered how they'd even managed to get people trained to do the work. But there seemed to be no shortage of labor in the valley.

The first hours on the road through the valley passed quietly, but by the time we finished lunch at the river fort that guarded the bridge, a palpable sense of excitement traveled along the road with us.

As we walked along the causeway toward the fortress, passersby stopped. Soon a murmuring crowd gathered, lining the causeway on either side like a parade route. I guess it *was* a parade of sorts. I didn't imagine there had been many triumphant arrivals recently. People followed behind as well, filling the causeway behind us as our route toward Whitmount rose above the town.

The warmth of the Snake Slayer costume had abated after I left the ancient stairway, but as we walked up the causeway the sensation returned, growing in intensity as we neared the gatehouse. The armor never felt uncomfortable; more a protective warmth, like a mother lioness holding her cub very close.

Through the huge gatehouse, I could see troops drawn up in parade formation in the courtyard beyond. A stage had been set up, and I could see hints of a crowd behind some sort of makeshift barriers. Apparently, a celebration awaited us. It seemed a bit out of proportion to our arrival, though by the hint of a smile on my father's face I could tell that he thought it was only his due.

Only a few places are referred to by name in the Talisman of Truce, which is more concerned with nations and gods than with particular locations. Whitmount is one of them. The gods hated the place. Every time my father had me read the treaty that hatred came through clearly, however elegant the language. An older magic had built Whitmount: old as the gods themselves and owing them nothing. Cold iron, painful to fey, filled the stone of its walls. It wasn't just that this fortress was carved out before the war was won: Whitmount was one of the causes of the war. While Whitmount held, humans could not be driven from the mountains, and the fey wanted the mountains for their own.

The gods had wanted it abandoned and leveled as part of the peace, which would have left Ananya's empire reduced to a broad coastal plain wrapped around a hostile mountain range. Ananya refused to yield the point and the gods, worn down by years of fighting their rebellious former worshippers, finally gave way. In return for assuring that control of all magic lay through the bloodline of gods, the gods abandoned their fey allies and retreated back to their own lands. Over the centuries, Whitmount remained as a symbol of Ananya's control of the mountains—and the fey had lost none of their hatred of the place.

Sperrin
The Road to Whitmount: Five weeks after the Loss

Until the captain in charge of the redoubt at the top of the stairs mentioned it to me, I had no idea that Nemias commanded the military forces in Whitmount. I knew my old friend had been promoted to captain-general during my years in the palace, but last I'd heard, Nemias held a combat command at the front lines in the war. For all its historical importance, Whitmount stood deep in the mountains, far from any recent fighting. It guarded supply lines and protected the mountain spine that ran down the center of the Ananyan peninsula—but usually that merited an older commander nearing retirement, mentally able but perhaps lacking the physical strength or stamina needed for forced marches and battlefields.

Whatever political slight had brought about his reassignment, Nemias had apparently taken this posting with the same fierce preparation he brought to the battlefield. I knew the Mountain Cougars by their reputation as under-achievers, but the soldiers here carried themselves like skilled veterans, as good as any of the line infantry units Nemias and I had commanded. And the Riverhead Scouts had certainly pulled their weight and more during the mountain journey.

I wanted to send the wounded ahead, so they wouldn't be delayed by any ceremony on the column's arrival in the city. With no magical transportation and every animal capable of pulling a wagon diverted to agriculture, that proved difficult. Eventually supply wagons were found and diverted, loaded with the seriously wounded, and pulled by whatever troopers from the Mountain Cougars the subcaptain in command of the river fort found stand-ing around. That gave time to rest the column from the long climb down the mountain stairs and get everyone fed—I didn't want anyone passing out on the road. It also let me give answers to a flurry of messengers from the city, so I had some idea of what sort of ceremony to expect when we arrived.

Ketya looked tired and nervous. Her father looked smug, a cat sensing a new supply of mice behind the Great Gate of Whitmount.

And how do you feel? It was a fair question. I really didn't know the answer. I had saved these soldiers, and I had killed our enemies, and they loved me for it. And I loved doing it, I really did. I just hated how much I loved doing it.

Somewhere in this city, if I was very lucky, I might find my daughter. Did I want her to think of her father as a man who loved killing more than he loved her?

AFTER THE WAGONS had passed through the town and onto the causeway, I nodded to the Mountain Cougars captain who'd been staring at me. The captain had arrived at the river fort shortly after the wagons had departed, tasked with escorting me and the refugees and returning scouts into the city. He looked nervous for a captain in charge of an honor guard, but his sergeants seemed competent, and had organized the column smoothly.

In addition to asking Ketya to accompany me, I had asked that Talye and Kern walk with me. Both of them seemed a little uncomfortable being singled out, and Talye had asked to stay with her soldiers.

"Walk with me," I said again. "Your soldiers know their orders, and they're good troops. The Mountain Cougars sergeants are ready if there's a problem.

And I need you with me when I report to Captain-general Nemias. There are events that you know better than I do."

I left my real reason unspoken: It would be easy for others to deny the sergeants the honors they had earned. By their nature, scouts were easy to overlook, even though the two sergeants had saved their detachment when its officers had fallen.

My reasons for asking Ketya to accompany me were more complex, and harder to articulate. Ketya and I had been through a lot together since the fight in the palace, and she had a role to play in helping to rebuild our shattered world. But she was very young, and could be cowed by her father. She would be easy to overlook as well, and I hoped my word could help assure that she remained close to the center of events. Besides, like me she had a knack for surviving impossible situations, something years of soldiering had taught me not to underestimate. And she held Ananya's copy of the Talisman of Truce, which I felt certain would be as important as any battle plans of mine before the crisis ended.

Not surprisingly, the chancellor also walked beside us, although he soon moved to the front, next to the nervous captain. Pointedly, the chancellor ignored me while speaking soothingly to the captain.

As the procession moved forward people began to gather and watch us go by—first in twos and threes, farm workers pausing in their labors to take in the spectacle—but soon the clumps grew larger. By the time we reached the town in the shadow of the mountain fortress, onlookers lined the road almost solidly on both sides. Soon we found ourselves moving through a cheering crowd. Children threw flowers to us like a Memorial Day parade. Unconsciously the scouts smartened their pace and dressed their lines. Even the nervous captain took on a more martial look, with the chancellor beaming beside him.

I enjoyed battles more than the parades afterward. Parades had been something to take my daughter to see. In more recent years, they had been something to protect: The Empress had dearly loved parades.

They're treating us as if we're coming back from a great victory, I thought. *But I guess the way they see things, it was a great victory.*

After the disaster at the palace, any survivors reaching Whitmount would be good news. And the fortress had likely given up on the Riverhead Scouts detachment as lost when the attacks came while it was out of reach of any help.

For that matter, I supposed, you didn't hear of many light infantry victories over giants. I found himself smiling at that thought.

The crowds fell away below us as the procession began climbing the causeway into the fortress. Like the redoubt at the top of the mountain stairs, the causeway had long, bridged sections designed to be collapsed easily, throwing attackers to their deaths. Even with the parade atmosphere surrounding our approach, I saw watchful sentries at their posts. The soldiers on watch in the towers above us focused their eyes outward and upward, not on the approaching parade.

Through the Great Gate, I could see the long gatehouse tunnel and the brightness of the Great Yard beyond. I could see troops drawn up in honor formation and a platform in the center. Loud murmuring revealed a crowd outside my view.

As we stepped off the causeway and onto the flat stones of the gatehouse tunnel, a band began playing "Hemmari's Descant," a lively folk-dancing tune and a staple of soldiers' celebrations. I saw Kern smiling at the music; the song brought happy memories to a lot of soldiers. By contrast, the chancellor frowned slightly: This was a song for soldiers and village dances, not for ceremonial occasions.

We passed slowly through the dimness of the tunnel—now illuminated with charcoal braziers that had been converted into oil lamps. The braziers had been carefully placed beneath each of the now-darkened magical globes that had once lit the tunnel and much of the fortress. The band continued playing "Hemmari's Descant" until I and the rest of the soldiers at the head of the column emerged into the afternoon brightness of the Great Yard. Then they switched smoothly to the jaunty "Memorial Day March," played for returning soldiers.

So welcome back you soldiers to the place where you belong.
Your days on leave are over and it's time to come back home.
They only think you live there but the barracks is your own:
To the road! To the road! To the road!

Is that for the Riverhead Scouts detachment or for me? But I was pretty sure I already knew the answer. It was the sort of thing Nemias would do, making the point that he was glad to see me back in arms without having to come out and remind me that he disagreed with my decision to leave. Welcoming the scouts back with the song added to the festivities, but the returning detachment probably wouldn't have merited the same degree of celebration.

The chancellor seemed a little put off by the choice of music, which amused me for some reason. I had no reason to wish the man ill for failing to prevent the disaster at the palace or for losing his head in the aftermath. But the man had complicated an already difficult situation without adding anything helpful beside his reputation. His daughter had been considerably more useful and resourceful, as well as better company. I hoped that today's arrival at Whitmount meant I could leave the chancellor behind.

Much as the return to killing bothered me, it was more palatable if it meant not having to work directly with that man any more.

A giant carpet woven in Whitmount white had been rolled down the middle of the Great Yard for us to walk across. Guards stood at arm's length intervals, both to show respect and to hold the crowd back from our path. The rest of the honor guard stood in parade formation on either side of the platform at the far end of the yard.

As we started along the white carpet, I found myself wondering where Nemias had found it, and how they kept it clean without magic. The storerooms beneath Whitmount were notorious for containing, it was said, *everything*.

Scanning the assembled blocks of the honor guard, I saw banners of the Mountain Cougars and a second regiment I didn't recognize. The rest of the soldiers seemed to be support troops and odds and ends. I suspected two full-strength regiments could hold Whitmount indefinitely even without magic, but Nemias wouldn't be mounting many offensive operations with this lot. Whitmount could house and feed eight regiments comfortably, but two second-tier regiments seemed about right for support duty and patrols this far behind the front. For our present situation, it felt a bit sparse.

Nemias stood at the head of a small cluster of senior officers and administrators on the platform. The captain-general looked deep in conversation with an administrator that I assumed was the governor-general of Whitmount, the military commander's civilian co-leader. Surprisingly, I recognized the man: I'd seen him in the Drowned City often enough. Burren had been harbormaster in the Drowned City, with forty years of reputation as a canny politician. *What's he doing here?* I hadn't seen Burren lately, but hadn't known the administrator had been transferred. What was such an astute politician doing here in a backwater? It was just as baffling as Nemias's assignment here.

As the band repeated the "Memorial Day March," Nemias and Burren seemed to reach a consensus and their conversation ended. Both had oddly neutral expressions for a celebration; I wondered what last-minute detail they had been trying to iron out.

The nervous captain drew to a halt ten paces in front of the platform, the chancellor beside him. Ketya and the sergeants and I stopped just behind. *If he wants to be in front so badly, there's no use stopping him,* I thought. *Besides, why start another quarrel just when you're almost rid of the man.*

Normally, the governor-general would take charge in a situation like this, but Burren clearly wanted to defer to Nemias today. Odd, since Burren was an entertaining public speaker. After a perfunctory thanks to the band, however, Burren turned things over to Nemias.

Burren had skipped the traditional opening for ceremonies like this, an invocation from the *Book of the Gods*. That made sense, I thought. At least one of the gods didn't deserve any thanks or remembrance today. Instead, Nemias began things with a chant in Old Ananyan, which the soldiers soon picked up on. Usually it was forgotten except for Memorial Day ceremonies, but we all knew it by heart. I smiled as the words of a centuries-old victory chant washed over me, first in Old Ananyan and then in translation, as the whole crowd roared it together.

> *Today the gods are gone forever.*
> *Walk through the ruins of our cities and celebrate.*
> *Leave flowers on the graves of our families and friends.*
> *Celebrate all the things that usually give us sorrow.*
> *Because today the gods are gone forever.*
> *I promised you, child, that this would be the last war*
> *I promised you when you were young.*
> *Now I am old and you are a soldier.*
> *But together we celebrate in all our places of loss*
> *Because today the gods are gone forever.*

Ketya
The Great Yard, Whitmount

Sperrin looked honored and a little embarrassed at the same time by Captain-General Nemias's speech. My father seethed, although you had to know him well to see the anger at the edges of his carefully controlled face. No formal recognition of the Lord Chancellor of Ananya at all, and then a speech lauding the troops with no mention of the high official they had brought all this way. Brought against his will, I had to remind myself—part of me was almost amused at how insulted my father seemed to be that he wasn't accorded proper respect by the people he'd been accusing of kidnapping him for weeks.

What a speech Nemias gave! Part of me still thought of Sperrin as an overaged palace guard with great survival skills. Despite the things he'd confided in me, and the way the scouts had followed him so readily, I had difficulty letting go of the old image. But Nemias had no such image. He lauded Sperrin in front of the assembled troops and crowd:

"This man is the best battle planner since Captain-general Keir, and the fiercest fighter I know," he told them in a booming, battlefield voice. "I've already heard from the Riverhead Scouts detachment that he returned with— and they killed four giants with his assistance. Scouts killing giants! Let's see what he can do with line infantry."

The crowd went wild.

To me the words sounded a little patronizing to the scouts—but they seemed just as enthused as the rest of the audience. I don't really understand soldiers, I decided.

Nemias continued in the same vein, exciting the troops and crowd with the potential for victory that Sperrin brought to Whitmount with him. The scouts and their sergeants he praised generously, if somewhat less fulsomely.

Since I hadn't really played a direct role in any of the "keeping people alive" part of the journey except in having a knack for avoiding death, I found myself watching people and their reactions during the speech. Talye and Kern looked satisfied. Sperrin looked torn, perhaps not surprisingly. I knew the return to killing troubled him, especially with the prospect of so much more killing implied in Nemias's words. But a big part of him loved what he had done, and lived for it.

Sperrin

After the speech the celebration started in earnest. The band started playing again, and when the honor guard was dismissed, there proved to be tables of food and drink behind their line: enough for the whole audience to eat well.

Nemias hopped down from the platform and walked over to embrace me.

"It's been too long, friend. I know it wasn't your will, but I'm glad the storms blew your here. We need you, friend. I need your skills very badly, and your friendship."

"Thanks," I said. "I've missed you. Sorry I couldn't warn you before I left. I never knew—"

"Later," Nemias said. "We'll talk tonight. Tonight we'll toast our friendship and exchange news. But it needs to wait on a sadder piece of business first."

"What—" I started, but with a pat on the shoulder, Nemias turned away. Burren had walked up as well, and with an unspoken acknowledgment the two commanders walked together to where Ketya's father stood, the nervous captain still at his elbow. The nervous captain's sergeants and a few soldiers had rejoined him and stood nearby. They seemed to be waiting on his word before joining the rest of the troopers at the feast tables.

The chancellor watched the two men arrive, a look of displeasure on his face. I assumed he intended to use their snub of him to gain some advantage, and wondered why they had left him the opening. They must have known that not even mentioning him to the crowd would be seen as a deadly insult—it wasn't the sort of mistake that either Nemias or Burren usually made.

Which meant, of course, that it hadn't been a mistake.

Nemias preempted whatever the chancellor planned to say with his own words. Unlike the booming speech he'd given from the stage, Nemias pitched his voice so even I could barely hear it, a half dozen steps away.

"Lord Chancellor, I heard you speak once at Davynen, and then again on your tour of southern military installations. The first time you pushed us into a victory we had no business winning. The second time you spoke for two hours without notes, and you gave one of the most moving speeches I have ever heard. I have never been so proud to be Ananyan as I was when I heard that speech. So you must understand that it is with more than a little regret"—he nodded slightly to the no-longer-nervous-looking captain and his troopers—"that I give the order for your arrest."

They took hold of the chancellor by each arm, and the captain produced a set of irons from inside his tunic and clicked them into place. The chancellor didn't struggle or seem very surprised.

Very few in the festive crowd noticed anything, but I saw Ketya whiten next to me. I touched her hand to caution her but she shook me off angrily.

"On what charge," she said, her voice very cold, "do you arrest the Empress's Chancellor?"

Burren turned from her father and looked at Ketya closely. They had known each other for years, the harbormaster and the chancellor's teenaged daughter, though I doubted Burren had seen her since before Ketya left for the Empress's Academy. Nemias glanced over briefly but deferred to Burren, who seemed to consider his words carefully. Finally, he answered quietly. "If I spoke the charges out loud, that man"—he nodded to her father—"would be torn apart where we stood by this crowd. I will tell them to you later, in private."

Chapter 20

Sperrin
Whitmount: Five weeks after the Loss

We met again that night, Nemias and Burren and I, after the chancellor had been seen to his cell. I had wanted to bring Ketya along, since she would have a role in the events to come. But she remained furious at what she saw as an unexpected betrayal—and I still didn't know the reasons for her father's arrest. But I trusted Nemias, and I knew neither Nemias nor Burren would make such a move without compelling reasons.

So I asked that Ketya be assigned chambers next to mine, where I could tell her what I found out tonight, and where I could keep an eye on her to be sure she didn't try to once again rescue her father. Then I had asked an orderly to escort her to the kitchens for a bit to eat—not surprisingly, Ketya had skipped the feast in the Great Yard—and then escort her to the hospital so she could visit Guthre and make sure the scout was well cared for.

By then a messenger had arrived to tell me that the Governor-general and Captain-general would be pleased to see me at my leisure. Moments later the messenger ushered me into a high tower chamber with tapestried walls and an expansive view of the valley that fronted Whitmount.

A broad oval table topped with polished gallowwood dominated the center of the room, piled high with maps and diagrams. A matching set of straight-backed chairs lined the wall to my right, with two aides standing unobtrusively by them. The people I'd come to see sat near the window in three overstuffed chairs. A low table with sweetmeats and cordial glasses sat in easy reach.

"Over here," said Nemias, waving me to the fourth overstuffed chair. In addition to Nemias and Burren, the man I still thought of as the nervous captain occupied the third seat.

"I believe you've met my aide, Captain Geriald?" Nemias said. The captain no longer wore a Mountain Cougars uniform, but a well-worn Threecastle Tomcats tunic. As an overcaptain, Nemias had commanded that regiment—he'd accepted the command shortly before I had left for the palace. Presumably his aide had been with him since then, and promoted along with him. Geriald looked much more relaxed now.

"I commend your acting skills, captain. The chancellor is not an easy man to fool."

"I was well coached, 'Captain Sperrin," answered Geriald. A short brown beard, neatly trimmed, framed his round face.

Burren laughed. "I took the liberty of suggesting a few mannerisms that might be helpful. It was the least I could do after the way the old schemer out-maneuvered me."

"Outmaneuvered you? Betrayed you is more like it," said Nemias. "Betrayed all of us."

I glanced at the two aides near the door, but Nemias caught my eye and nodded slightly. Everyone in the room could be trusted.

"Betrayed is a strong word," I said, trying to keep my voice neutral. If Nemais said *betrayed*, then there had been a betrayal. But we were still talking about the Lord Chancellor of Ananya, and no evidence had yet been presented.

"A strong word it is," Nemias acknowledged. "Perhaps Burren should explain."

I nodded in agreement.

"Overcaptain, I believe we've known each other for six or seven years, and you know I am not prone to exaggeration," said Burren. He had an odd habit of tugging his red-brown whiskers when he felt nervous. Soldiers' gossip in the palace held that Burren had given up games of chance because of an inability to shed the habit.

"I know your word was well thought of in the palace," I answered. Again, as neutral as I could manage.

"So I thought," said Burren. "I took my job seriously. Perhaps I guarded my privileges and appointments fiercely, but I guarded against waste and mis-chance in my department just as fiercely. No one honest had grounds for com-plaint. They said that nothing escaped me, which perhaps overstated the case. But I kept close watch on all that happened in the harbor.

"When I was transferred it surprised me, especially since the chancellor denied me an opportunity to speak with him about it, and asked me to leave immediately. He wouldn't even allow me to complete exit reports before leaving: He told me to send them later in the cable-carriage packet.

"None of that is evidence of wrongdoing, I know," said Burren, seeing my skeptical expression. "I know the ways of palace politics, and I assumed I had offended the Empress or someone very close to her. The betrayal had probably happened already by that time, but my evidence of it came later."

Nemias reached over and took a sweetmeat. He offered a cordial glass to me, and I sipped it while listening. Yellowfruit brandy warmed my throat as Burren continued.

"My replacement was given two weeks leave before having to report to the Drowned City. So there was no harbormaster at all on the night of the attack. My former subordinates carried on according to standing orders, but without oversight or enough authority if something should go wrong. One of those subordinates, Cerne—I believe you've met her, Sperrin—took it on herself to do the sort of sweep of the harbor defenses that I had done routinely. It troubled her that the entire Home Fleet had been loaded down with fireworks and dispatched on some sea-monster hunting expedition with no harbormaster in place to coordinate between the Home Fleet and the fishing fleet.

"On Cerne's sweep, she found that the harbor guards had been dismissed from their posts. The only people with the authority to do that are the chancellor and the harbormaster. Even the captain of the walls doesn't have that authority. And there was no harbormaster that night."

Burren held up a hand to forestall me. "She saw something more. Cerne saw the chancellor himself ordering watchers from their posts. Following him unseen, she saw him enter the empty Harborgate room and turn the wheel to release the tension on the great chain. The chancellor himself opened the harbor to our enemies.

"Cerne escaped unseen," he continued. "She thought to report what she had seen, but who could she tell? Only the Empress had the authority to countermand the chancellor, and who was Cerne to see the Empress? Even if she had tried, the Empress was in the middle of the initiation ceremony. And before that ceremony ended, the Empress was dead."

Burren reached for a glass himself, and drained it. "So you see, we have reason to accuse the chancellor."

"One question," I said. "How do you know this? I just got here, and I don't think anyone from the Drowned City could have been ahead of me on the

Mountain Road. Anyone moving faster would have been exposed to attack on the road."

Captain Geriald cut in, "Messenger birds."

I looked at him quizzically. Messenger birds had been a staple of the Holy War, long outmoded by the arrival of more modern means of communication. Imprinted with old magic, they could be sent between any major fortress with reasonable speed by anyone who knew the proper commands. For that reason every fortress had kept a coterie of the things until the signing of the treaty and the advent of the Empress's magic had turned them, overnight, from weapon to nuisance. Most of them were released, only to have their descendents infest eaves and foul rooftops ever since. Some of them had been eaten.

"He's right," Nemias said. "Captain Geriald knows messenger bird commands, as do many—I suppose you would call them hobbyists—throughout Ananya. The birds can still be used. Of course, they're only helpful if you want to send to a thousand-year-old fortress, or something sitting where there used to be a fortress. After the disaster, after that first night of fighting, Geriald here had the idea of sending messenger birds to every fortress we could think of and seeing who responded. Whitmount is lousy with the things. We heard back from enough of them that we got a picture of what happened, and we have since been able to reestablish communication between military commands. We are still filling in details, but one of the people we heard back from was Cerne. She survived the fighting and helped organize rescue and repair efforts along with a former dancemaster of all things—a man named Dulcet who'd recently returned to court from the Empress's Academy under some sort of cloud, I gather, although whatever the scandal was likely died with the Empress. But even with their efforts, what's left of the city is in dire shape. I think that unless the magic is restored quickly, they will need to abandon the Drowned City soon."

That all made sense, and I nodded in acknowledgment. "I may be able to contribute some pieces to the story. I was in the palace when the attacks came." I saw Nemias registered my use of the plural. "The chancellor and his daughter were the only two I was able to rescue. Although I am beginning to think I actually only rescued the daughter."

I recounted the fighting in the palace, including the unexpected Alliance soldiers waiting with packs and frames on the landing below the chancellor's room. They had known about the Alliance ships that had entered the harbor after its defenses had been dismissed, but not the purpose of those ships.

Burren took the first stab at putting it all together. "So you think the chancellor had advance warning of a god's attack on the Empress and her family, and arranged an escape to the Alliance for himself rather than try to prevent it? That seems overly complicated, even for him."

"Unless," Nemias said, "he had something to do with the attack by the godservants as well."

I nodded ruefully; they all had much the same reaction. "It's nothing we can prove."

"How would you even do such a thing?" Burren asked. "And why? What could he hope to gain?"

"I don't know," I answered. "I only know one person other than the chancellor who might have an answer to that question, and I don't think you're going to like who it is."

"The daughter." Nemias had already guessed the answer. "But we can't trust her a bit, can we? Her behavior this afternoon…."

"I trust her." They looked doubtful. "Not on the subject of her father, but in other matters."

Burren seemed skeptical. "That would be a big chance," he said. "I agree that she is not a creature of subterfuge like her father, unless the Academy greatly changed her. But he owns her, and has never let her be her own person. She would try to tell you the truth, but in the end she would tell you what he wanted."

"I would have thought so, too," I said. "But I saw her take the Talisman of Truce when he would have left it in the palace, and she brought it all the way here without revealing it to him." I told them what had happened in the mountain hideaway, and how well she knew the nuances of the treaty.

"That's promising, I agree," said Nemias. "But perhaps trust is premature. Let's keep watchful over the next few days; she'll give us grounds to trust her—or grounds not to."

I didn't press the point hard. "The sooner we find out what her father did, the sooner we can start planning how to fix it," I said. "But I agree that a few days of caution may be best. And we may have a battle to plan before that." I told them what the wolf-creature had said to me, which fit with other things that had been seen near Whitmount.

"They will never rest until we are gone from the mountains," said Burren.

"Then they will never rest." Nemias laughed. "Sperrin, we have a battle to plan, and win. Let me tell you what we know of where things stand in Ananya, and what we have available to fight with. Then we can speak of how to put it to best use."

First Burren laid out where things stood generally: They retained a fragile hold on the empire, only because the Alliance attacks and fey attacks were not coordinated. The fey wanted *all* humans out of the mountains. When Ananyan fortresses had repulsed two Alliance attacks on the mountain passes to the north, the same giants and wolves and griffins and other fey creatures that had massacred Drowned City refugees had feasted on retreating Central Alliance soldiers. The Ananyan forts might no longer have magic to aid them, but the fey certainly did. At the same time, Alliance naval forces had sunk or driven off the Home Fleet, its weapons and engines crippled by lack of magic. Alliance ships now harassed the Ananyan coast at will, and it was taken as a given that a fleet was assembling to transport the armies that couldn't fight their way through the mountains. Only in the oldest and strongest mountain fortresses, able to communicate but not support each other, did Ananya maintain her power. And the fey were determined to eradicate those fortresses.

BURREN AND GERIALD excused themselves after the general introduction, mostly to give me and Nemias some privacy to catch up on a decade of separation. They agreed to meet us again the next morning, after I had time to rest.

"I'm glad you're here," Nemias said when the two of us were alone. "These troops will need all the help you can give them."

"Do you think the chancellor was behind your appointment here, the way he was with Burren's?"

"Maybe? Who knows. I don't really care. As it turns out I get to be in the thick of the fighting, and I got to see the miserable old bird arrested, too. Always sure he's the smartest one in the room...we both know the type."

"He helped at Davynen."

"Of course he did. He got to lord it over everyone and watch while that idiot trooper's head got blown off. If the 'general there hadn't been incompetent, we wouldn't have needed him. You and I have never had any trouble getting soldiers to fight."

"Have you had much fighting here?"

"We beat off two attacks on the town the first night, and since then it's been just harassment. It hurts them to come too close to the fort, so they won't do it until they're sure they can win."

"What do you have here?" I asked. "One of the regiments at the review I didn't recognize."

"We have two full regiments and some odds and ends. Not good regiments but they'll do. They follow orders, they fight when you tell them to, and they don't run. They'll be good troops before this is all over. The full regiments are the Mountain Cougars and the Red City Catbears. Elements of the Riverhead Scouts. Four companies of the Whitmount Home Guard. There are also some other scraps and refugees with military experience who have come in, which I've used to plug holes and as replacements. All told, call it eight companies of what you might call line infantry on a good day, and six light companies. Plus I've got about a regiment's worth of engineers who are trying to adjust to the lack of channelers. I have them shoring up defenses and helping with the farms about equally. It's a bit less than five thousand trained soldiers in all. I've been running them through drills on fighting without magic, when the fey give me time."

"How about the civilian population and supplies?"

"We have plenty of supplies in the catacombs, though some of them look like they might date back to the last war. About two years' worth of food if there's a siege, and there might be. As far as people, we have about thirty thousand noncombatants and refugees. A hospital full of wounded soldiers and refugees, and half-dead channelers—"

"Wait a minute." I stopped him. "Did you say *half*-dead?"

"I thought that might surprise you. There aren't many, but some of them survived here—we must have been far enough away from the killing at the capital. The powerful ones all died, and none of them have magic anymore, of course." Nemias shook his head. "It's a waste, really. A few have recovered enough to be useful. But most of them are crippled or mad, or both."

A memory suddenly returned to me. "Nolene?"

His eyes clouded. "She didn't make it. She lasted a day, and I held her hand at the end. She…I don't know what to say, Sperrin. I married late, and I thought the Empress had forgotten me. But I've never been so utterly loved. Never imagined what it could be like. It made me understand, a little, why you would leave the fighting if you thought you might lose Sefa. Not that Nolene was ever anything but supportive of my soldiering."

Nemias refilled his glass and drained it. I was remembering my sword at Nolene's throat the night of her engagement, forcing her to use the engagement token rather than—and then it came back to me. I remembered what I had found out about Sefa that night, about how she had only pretended to care for me. About how she and her sister had conspired to keep her relationship with her first love alive, even while outwardly following the Empress's orders.

So Nolene had escaped punishment. Enough time had passed that I found myself glad of that. I was genuinely glad that she and Nemias had found happiness together.

"Children?" I asked.

Nemias shook his head. "We didn't have any. You know I would have invited you to the namings if we had. For that, the Empress would have let her best guardsman go free for a while."

He seemed to choose his words carefully. "I think the Empress wanted to keep you close and give you a chance to heal. Something happened to you, Sperrin. I don't know if it was just too much fighting for too many years, or if something else happened. But you needed a rest. She knew if the empire needed you, you would be close by."

I nodded ruefully. "Closer than any of us expected, I'm afraid."

"I hope ten years have healed you, friend. There's fighting to be done here. No one but you would have thought of a way to use scouts to kill giants."

"I did enjoy that," I admitted. Nemias refilled my glass and I drained it, letting the yellowfruit brandy sear my throat. Nemias had a look on his face like he wanted to say more but couldn't think of the best way. I filled the glass again and sipped the brandy this time while I waited for Nemias to choose his words.

"There's one other thing," the captain-general said. "I don't know how to tell you this, but your wife is here."

"What?" I had no idea of what to say. Until that last memory had returned, word of her survival would have been happy news. Now, however—dead, Sefa could have been ignored. Alive, what had passed between us would be an unhealed wound. "I thought....I would have thought Sefa was dead. You said that all the powerful channelers died."

"I did," said Nemias. "But...I know you don't know what happened, but Sefa wasn't a powerful channeler anymore. I gather the Empress wasn't happy about her role in your wanting to leave the front. She wasn't a favorite anymore. The Empress arranged a transfer to some sort of menial assignment, the kind they give weak channelers. Her sister told me she was living with someone, someone she'd met before she knew you. I know she never remarried. She and Nolene had some sort of falling out—they went from being best friends to occasional letters. I would have liked to see how your daughter was doing, but they never visited. Then a couple of years ago Sefa showed up here alone and beaten up and without any magic. It was the first time I'd seen her since you left. She talked to Nolene, and then they both asked me to take her in with no questions, in the name of my friendship with you."

"And of course, you did."

"I did."

"What about my daughter?"

Nemias sighed. "I wish I knew. Sefa said 'no questions,' and when I did try to ask later she wasn't very responsive. All I know is she was alone when she got here, and no one has visited her. She's changed, Sperrin."

"We've all changed."

"That's not what I mean." He filled his drink again, and held out the bottle to top off mine as well. "Maybe she'll give you more of an answer than she gave me. I know you two fought some at the end—I didn't know it at the time, but Nolene told me later—but it's your daughter. Sefa might think she owes you some kind of answer. But don't be too hopeful."

"Where is she?"

"In the West Yard, in a cottage near the hospital. You remember Sharret Row from when you served here? It's the fifth cottage from the end."

"I'll visit her tonight."

"You do that," Nemias said. "Then come back here if you need another drink. Geriald will know where to find me. Wake me if you need to."

"It's that bad?"

Nemias didn't answer.

Ketya

Whitmount was about the same size as the palace in the Drowned City, but considerably more vertical. While towers held a prominent place in the palace I had lived in, most of the palace buildings clustered at approximately the same altitude, give or take a few stories above or below the encroaching sea. Whitmount, by contrast, had been literally carved into a mountainside, so all of it flowed between towers and plateaus and steep twisting stairways between levels. Until recently there had been an elaborate system of elevators and freight ramps, all of which relied on magic. So instead I had to take the ancient, heavily worn stairs built into the outer turrets that connected levels.

I hadn't exactly taken the most direct route to my goal, either: I wanted to walk off some of my anger, and losing myself on flight after flight of ancient stone blocks helped a lot.

The aide Sperrin had assigned to show me to the kitchens and hospital seemed relieved when I told him I preferred to walk the endless stairs alone. He gave me precise directions when we left the kitchens and I felt free to storm upward without worrying about losing my composure in front of the well-meaning aide.

Eventually I found the hospital on an upper plateau, a gray stone building set well back from the walls to allow for large windows that let in ample sunlight and the bracing mountain breeze. Neat rows of small cottages surrounded the hospital, mostly facilities for the old and convalescent, I had been told. Unlike the other levels I'd passed by on my way to the hospital, this one had only a small market, heavy on prepared food and children's toys and used books and cut flowers: things you'd want close when you visited a hospital, or had limited mobility.

I wondered how much medicine would even be possible without magic. Care and convalescence, surely. Setting a bone, maybe, though I imagined the pain would be excruciating. But how could you burn out infection or excise a tumor without magic? Short of cutting someone open with a knife and literally butchering them, I couldn't think of any way to do it.

My boots clacked loudly on the smooth stone floor. I entered into a broad atrium, with wide staircases of ginger-colored stone curving upward on each side. Both stairways had been roped off with thick, decorative cords. Apparently only this first level was in use.

A tan-uniformed orderly entered the atrium from a side hall. "Is there something I can help you with?" he asked.

"I'm looking for a soldier who was brought in today. Her name was Guthre." A lot of soldiers were brought in today, I realized. That must have sounded idiotic.

"I think I know the one. Rib injuries, cut on her face, brought in ahead of most of the others?"

"That's her, yes."

"Follow me, please."

I had expected more questions, someone asking why I was visiting, perhaps. I wasn't sure she had a good answer to that, other than *she's my friend*. Which didn't seem enough in this cavernous place in the heart of a fortress. In the palace I would have known what to say.

"She must have done something very brave, to be brought in ahead like that. She was given a private room by order of the captain-general. It's one of the rooms usually reserved for senior officers."

"Yes...yes, she was very brave. She helped kill four giants."

The orderly seemed to expect me to elaborate, but I didn't really have the energy.

"Why is it so quiet here?" I asked as we walked. From the end of the hall, I could hear a sort of murmuring, but otherwise the building seemed strangely free of hospital noises.

"Many of the wards absorb noise, but really it's that the hospital is nearly empty," the orderly said. "You saw how the upper floors are corded off. This place is designed for wars, and there haven't been a lot of survivors brought here yet. A few battle wounded and refugees, and the channelers, of course."

"Channelers? Some of them lived?"

He gave an unfriendly laugh. "If you can call it living. You were a channeler, right?" He looked me up and down. "Don't expect them to be as whole as you. Or even as whole as your brave friend."

He turned around, calling over his shoulder as he left, "Your friend is in the first door to the right. If any of the channelers are friends of yours, they're all together in the ward at the end of the hall." Then he was gone.

I stood outside the doorway for a moment, unexpectedly struck by shyness. Then, steeling myself, I walked in.

"Well, hello you." Guthre's low voice sounded unexpectedly full. She sat propped up on a bed in the sunny room. A table next to the bed held books, a porcelain pitcher and cups, and two bowls, one of dried fruit and nuts and the other containing some sort of mush. The orderly hadn't exaggerated in his description of the room, either. It contained a round table and chairs, a couch against the far wall, rich curtains and a braided rug in bright colors. A dry sink in the corner held a washbasin, with towels stacked on a low table next to it. Battle paintings on the walls added a decidedly un-hospital touch.

Guthre's skin looked brighter, probably less from her continuing return to health than because they had cleaned her. After all, she had only been in the hospital a few hours. I saw that someone had changed Guthre's bandages, more neatly than I had ever managed.

"You look better," I said to Guthre. Suddenly I felt self-conscious about my own unwashed state. On the trail it had stopped bothering me for a while, but now I felt acutely aware of being the least-clean person in the building. On the road, there hadn't been bathhouses. In Whitmount, there were. But I hadn't thought to stop; I'd come here as soon as Sperrin had left for his meeting, after practically forcing me to eat.

"Thanks," Guthre answered. "You look tired, and out of breath. And like you've been angry or crying, I'm not sure which. Why don't you sit and have some water and tell me about it." She gestured to a chair beside her bed, wincing a little as the motion tweaked her ribs. "There's dried fruit if you want it. No fresh fruit anymore with the channelers who ran the hothouses gone, but they tell me they've been hoarding food like squirrels in this fortress since the Holy War days." She picked a shriveled chunk out of the bowl. "They say this piece was picked by 'General Keir himself."

I forced a laugh, then sat in the chair.

For a minute I sat without saying anything. I could feel Guthre watching me, but the scout didn't break the silence. Then I felt tears on my cheeks. I tried to breathe and found myself sobbing uncontrollably.

After a while I pulled myself together. Guthre had a supportive arm on my shoulder—her arm seemed to bother her less than her ribs—but stayed quiet until my sobbing subsided.

"Rough day?" she said.

That almost started me crying again. "I just…I feel dirty and betrayed and I don't know who to talk to. We made it through all those dangers and now suddenly I feel like I can't trust anyone."

Guthre looked puzzled. "You can trust me," she said, a little tentatively. "I don't know what happened, but you can talk to me if you want." She looked around. "I don't think anyone else is listening. I don't know why they would be, anyway. We're not exactly 'generals."

"Thanks," I said with a sniffle. "And now I feel even dirtier. I need to find a bathhouse."

"There's a washbasin in the corner," Guthre said. "Clean up there, then tell me what's wrong. You just got here, please don't go yet."

Nodding shakily, I stood up and walked over to the basin. I washed my face and hands and thought about how filthy the rest of me was. Part of me wanted to sponge off, but I felt strangely self-conscious about undressing in front of Guthre. It wasn't just the nakedness, although I felt unaccustomedly shy about revealing myself in front of the scout. I also didn't know how I would explain the Snake Slayer armor (if it revealed itself) or the cased Talisman of Truce, still hidden between shirt and tunic at the small of my back.

I didn't think my father would get arrested before I could give it back to him. I felt anger surge in me again.

Guthre saw the change in my features, apparently. "Come, sit and tell me about it," the scout said.

"They arrested my father," I said. "Can you believe it? They won't even tell me the charges."

Guthre snorted involuntarily, then caught herself. She seemed to choose her words carefully. "I know your father is very well-known. I'm sure they wouldn't have arrested him without a very strong reason. It's not like they're going around arresting people for soldiers' marriages or anything like that. Especially not now, when everyone is needed."

"There's no reason," I said. "It's just politics. They see he's in a weak position, so they want to get him out of the way."

"They?" asked Guthre. "Does anyone here actually benefit from arresting a popular leader like your father?"

"Someone must think they do."

"Maybe," Guthre said.

"You think he did something wrong, too?

"I don't know him very well. So I really don't know," answered Guthre. "I know you love him, but it's easier for me to believe that fathers can do evil things than it is for you. He never seemed to have a good word to say about you—he wasn't even nice to you."

I brushed hair out of my face. "I know he loved me—he was just busy. And talking about his feelings for people isn't his way."

"I don't know, Ketya. He was pretty open with his feelings about a lot of people. You just never seemed to come up when he talked."

"The empire is in the middle of a disaster. He had much more important things to talk about." I thought for a minute. "Besides, I don't know why they arrested him, but I know they didn't arrest him for not being nice to me."

Guthre shook her head. "Maybe not, but if he'd been a better person he would have been nice to you. Great leader or not, he couldn't see what a wonderful, caring daughter he had."

Guthre took my hand to emphasize the point. Her grip felt warm, and reassuring somehow. I wanted to be angry at Guthre's words, but instead found myself blushing, for no reason I could think of.

Change the subject, I thought. "Guthre, what do you mean by 'soldiers' marriages'? I don't think I've ever heard the term before."

"I guess you wouldn't, in the palace. It's a word for people who are in a relationship not set up by the Empress or her bureaucracy. It's a way to be with someone you love, even if you would never be allowed to marry him or her. That's the term for it in the army, anyway."

"Oh," I said. The idea had never occurred to me before. In my family, the Empress or her agents picked someone for you to marry, sent the marriage blossom that shared memories between you so you loved each other, and that was that. If I'd thought about it at all, I realized, it would have occurred to me that people probably fell in love all the time without magic involved. Mala had told me about her mother's past relationship, after all, but it had never crossed my mind that it might happen often enough to have a name. "Do they really arrest people for that?"

"Sometimes," Guthre said. "It depends on how supportive your officers are, and how quiet you are about it. I don't know how it works outside of the army. I guess the same way. A lot of people live that way for years, until the Empress or her agents pick out a partner for one of them."

I thought of Sperrin and the way his memories of wife and daughter had been lost. Not really the same thing, I supposed, but not so different in some ways, either.

I realized Guthre and I were still holding hands, and felt myself blush again. But I didn't let go.

The brief conversation had visibly tired Guthre. She remained a long way from healed. I held the scout's hand until Guthre's eyes closed a few minutes later and she slept.

Even if I didn't agree with what Guthre had said, her words had calmed me. I remained upset, but much of the forcefulness of my anger had ebbed away while I watched Guthre falling asleep.

STANDING IN THE doorway of the hospital room, I stared out at the empty hall and tried to get my feelings under control. I knew I should ask Sperrin to help me visit my father when I got back, knew I should want to visit my father, but part of me dreaded the idea. It wasn't that Guthre was right about my father—I knew how much my father really loved me, even if saying so wasn't his way. I just didn't have any answers for him. I still didn't even know why he'd been arrested. To me it felt as if the moment had finally come when he really needed my help, and I was failing him—I didn't even begin to know how to help him.

I heard a moaning noise down the hall to my right and remembered the ward of injured channelers. I owed them a visit, too. Some of them might have been classmates, a year or two ahead of me. And if I had shared their talent level, I would have been dead or crippled as they were. Guthre probably would have called me silly for the feeling, but it gave me a sense of obligation somehow.

Or perhaps just curiosity? Either way, I turned to the right, instead of left toward the way I had come in.

A broad set of double doors separated the arched entrance of the east ward from the rest of the floor. From this close, the noise sounded less like moaning than the burbling of a brook. One of the doors stood slightly ajar, and I slipped through it.

High windows kept the room ventilated, and bright in the late afternoon sun, but did little to conceal its grayness. Perhaps a hundred cots were spaced evenly on the gray stone floor. Some of the women lay strapped to their cots to keep them from thrashing onto the floor. Many of them moaned or babbled in their struggles: They weren't struggling against the restraints but with inner demons, like waking nightmares. Others seemed still and unresponsive, breathing but otherwise showing no signs of life. A few looked as if they slept fitfully, at the edge of waking. Here and there a few slept more normally, looking like they might be lucid if only they would awaken. A few of the cots had decorative touches brought by family members—a colorful blanket, a vase of wildflowers—but mostly I looked at a sea of gray.

A few tan-clad orderlies sat at a table against the wall off to my left; one of them approached me now.

"Do you have family here?" the orderly asked. She looked about my age, with a long braid that hung halfway down her back.

"No family, no," I answered. "Maybe some friends. I'm not sure."

"Look around if you like," said the orderly. "It won't bother them. But please don't touch. It agitates some of them."

"I understand," I said.

Wandering through the rows, I saw no familiar faces. Most of the women in the cots looked much older than any channelers I'd known. I wondered if the loss of magic had aged them, draining vitality along with the Empress's magic.

"Do any of them recover?" I asked the orderly after I finished walking the gray rows.

"A few of them have. We move them out of the hospital as soon as we can when they wake. I'm told most of the ones in here will recover at least somewhat, but it will take time."

"Is there anything else that can be done for them?"

The girl shrugged, a helpless look. "We do all we can. We can keep them comfortable and mostly out of pain. But the people who could actually heal them—" she gestured at the cots "—the ones who lived are mostly in those rows."

"How many died?"

"About half. More in places like this hospital, which had the best of the channelers. The weakest ones survived, mostly."

The orderly didn't seem self-conscious about saying it. *She must not realize my training. Or perhaps after so many deaths of friends, she doesn't care anymore.*

I thanked the orderly and left. Utterly drained, I no longer felt angry, just completely purged of emotions. I had many stairs to walk down to return to my chambers, and to find the strength to face my father again.

Chapter 21

Ketya
Whitmount: Five weeks after the Loss

When I was at the Academy I struggled a lot with the theoretical side of how to be a channeler. None of it came naturally to me, and I'm sure that if my mother hadn't been such a great channeler (and one whom many in the Academy still had fond memories of) I would have been encouraged to pursue some other field, no matter who my father was. Maybe I would have understood it better if my mother had lived until I was old enough for her to explain it to me. I understood in theory how channelers could copy memories from one person and give them to another, as they did when making engagement tokens. I more-or-less understood the theory behind how memories could be suppressed, as Sperrin's had been, though I had no idea how to do it in practice. But I didn't understand why you couldn't actually change someone's memories, or implant messages in engagement tokens. Or for that matter why magic couldn't be used to send messages from one person to another, even though it could be used to push cable-carriages across a mountain range or to force trees to bloom in cold climates, or to light palaces. There were good reasons for all those things, stemming, as far as I could follow the explanation, from the nature of the magic that flowed from Senne, the patron goddess of Ananya. Which led me to ask if other gods had different magical abilities and magic in other countries differed from ours. I gather that wasn't a very well-informed question, but I never did find out the answer to it while I was at the Academy.

Some of my questions would be answered later. As it turned out, a little too late to be particularly helpful. And in a more painful way than I really wanted to learn them.

I STARTLED WHEN I entered my chamber. Sperrin sat dozing in an armchair in the far corner, blade across his lap. His eyes opened before I'd taken two steps into the room; he seemed fully awake.

"I'm glad you're back," Sperrin said. "I hope Guthre is healing well?"

I nodded. "She is. They are taking better care of her than I could. I was worried the trip would be too much for her." I tried to look him in the eye. "I hope your meeting went well."

"It…I suppose it did. I found out a surprising thing at the end of it that I was hoping you could help me with."

"Me? My father's under arrest, remember? Why would anyone here trust me?"

"You're not your father," said Sperrin, stretching his legs as he spoke. "Besides, I trust you, and the rest of them trust me."

"So they're leaving me free as a favor to you."

"Basically, yes." He stood, returning his sword to his baldric. I didn't know if Sperrin missed the sarcasm in my tone, or just chose to act as if he had. "I'm certain they would let you join your father if you chose. But no one seems to think that's a good idea."

"Do you know why he's been arrested?"

"I do, yes. Nemias and Burren laid out the evidence for me."

I almost cried out in frustration. He had to be doing it deliberately.

"Can you *tell* me why he's been arrested?"

Sperrin thought for a minute, as if replaying a conversation in his mind. "I suppose I can. No one asked me to keep anything from you. He's been arrested for treason. There is proof he was involved in allowing those Central Alliance soldiers to breach the Drowned City's defenses. There is suspicion that he was involved in the god's attack as well."

"And you believe it?"

"I have a hard time believing it, but I admired your father. Even if I disliked him personally. I'm not unbiased. The evidence is very compelling. He will be given every chance to refute it, I'm certain."

"Well *I* don't believe it. My father would never betray his country or his Empress."

Sperrin said nothing.

"Well, he wouldn't," I said. "No one knows him better than I do. I would know."

"Of course," Sperrin said, but somehow the words didn't actually agree with me.

I shook my head in exasperation. *Unbelievable!* They were blaming everything on my father, a man who had dedicated his whole life to Ananya. Who had thought of nothing but Ananya since my mother's death.

Sperrin waited patiently. I had forgotten he had something else he wanted to ask me.

"What was it you wanted?" I finally asked. "You said there was something else you found out."

"I...it turns out..." It wasn't like Sperrin to struggle with his words. Directness usually came easily to him. He kept at it, though. "It turns out my wife, Sefa, is still alive. The woman the Empress had me forget when she accepted my request to join the palace guard. No one else here seems to be able to tell me where my daughter is, but I'm hoping Sefa will know."

That puzzled me. The pieces didn't seem to fit together. "Wasn't she a channeler? I thought she was powerful, and a friend of the Empress."

"She was very powerful."

"Then how is she still alive?"

"Apparently, the Empress withdrew her friendship with Sefa at the same time she withdrew my memories of her. She may have withdrawn her magic as well. I'm told Sefa isn't well, but she is alive."

"Well, I'm...I'm pleased at that, anyway." It didn't feel like the right thing to say, but I had to say something. "So what do you want me to help with?"

"I would consider it a favor if you would come with me when I visit her."

That surprised me. "Why?"

"We were together a long time. I still have...feelings for her. And the memories I have are very raw. I'm afraid that I don't trust my judgment around her. I might believe her if she lied, or not believe her if she told the truth. Things were unhappy at the end, and I've been gone a long time."

"You just told me you think my father betrayed the empire without my realizing it, but you want me to come with you because you trust my judgement."

He winced, but nodded. "I don't think either of us is a fair judge of your father. I don't know what he has or hasn't done, just the charges which you asked me to repeat to you. But I trust your judgment of my wife more than my own."

The tone of the words came as close to pleading as I'd ever heard from this proud soldier. And I knew I owed him too much to turn him down the only time he had asked for my help, after all of the ways I owed my life to him. But I would still use him to help solve my own problem at the same time.

"I'll go with you, if you agree to come with me when I visit my father."

"Of course." He didn't even hesitate. "You know your father doesn't like me, right?"

"I know," I answered. "But the visit will be easier if he has you to be angry at instead of me."

"Sure. All I did was save his life. Who wouldn't be angry?"

"He doesn't see it that way."

"I know," Sperrin said. "If he did see it that way, it would be a lot harder to believe in his guilt."

Really, I didn't have an answer to that. "When do we go?" I asked, but I had a feeling I already knew the answer.

"If you're not too tired, I'd like to go now. When we get back I'll get Nemias's permission to take you to visit your father, and to bring him anything you think he needs. I asked and was told he was being well cared for. In a fortress as old as this, nothing ever happens for the first time: They have a place put aside to securely hold princes accused of treason—impossible to escape unaided, but luxurious enough that there's less insult given if the charges prove false."

Sperrin

Visiting Sefa meant retracing Ketya's steps toward the hospital. The summer air had grown cool with nightfall in the higher parts of Whitmount, but the walk warmed us.

I wanted to go quickly while I could still force myself to go at all. Much as I didn't want to face my lost wife and the unhappy memories that were most of what I had left of her, I needed to know what had happened to Lynniene. Also, not facing her felt a little cowardly in my mind, for all that I'd faced the giants with less trepidation.

Even Ketya seemed to sense my nervousness, touching my arm in support as we approached my wife's cottage.

I knocked at the door of the one-room cottage, first hesitantly, then louder. No one answered. Trying the door I found it unlatched.

A pair of candles lit the room dimly. A large bed dominated the center of the room. Sefa sat in it, propped up by pillows. She looked older than I expected, aged by more than our decade of separation.

She looked straight at me, her eyes radiating anger and disgust.

"So typical of you to enter where you're not wanted," she said.

"Nemias said you were here and still alive. I thought I should check on you."

"How solicitous of you. Ten years after you ruined my life."

"I am sorry. Leaving was not my choice."

"Liar. It certainly was your choice." She almost spat the words at me. I could feel Ketya just behind me, barely inside the doorway. I wondered why it had seemed so important to bring her along.

Because you never would have made it here otherwise, I reminded myself.

There was no point in defending myself, I supposed, but I had to at least try to make things civil if I hoped to find out what had happened to our daughter. "I didn't choose to leave you behind. I wanted to leave all the killing I was doing behind." I knew that wasn't quite true, now that I had my memories back, but why say now what had seemed too incendiary to say then?

"You made your choice. I don't see how it was any different."

"I had no idea that the Empress would end our marriage. She took my memories, too—I didn't even know I had been married until the palace fell. Did they take yours as well? Did you know what had happened?"

"I knew where you went. Don't you think my sister told me?" Somehow that made me feel a little better, that she hadn't thought I had just disappeared. Even if it seemed to have made her angrier.

"What happened to you then? You were one of the most important channelers in Ananya." I suppose it meant that the Empress had found out about Sefa's failure to use the marriage token and acted on it, even if her sister went unpunished. Angry as I had been the night I held my blade to Nolene's throat and forced her to use her engagement token, I may have been saving her life. At least for a time.

A spasm of coughing wracked Sefa. But she looked at me no less angrily when she resumed talking.

"The Empress's friendship left when you did. According to my sister, she blamed me for your leaving. Said if I'd been a better wife you might not have been so unhappy and forced her to lose your services. My power started fading the day you left. And all of my friends left with it. I was sent out to the provinces, asked to do petty projects that no one cared about, and married off to a widower who beat me for hating him."

That seemed an odd way to characterize our separation. Had she forgotten her own role in what had happened? Or that the widower she lived with—never her husband—was the same lover she'd been visiting for years during our marriage? The same lover she'd risked the Empress's fury to stay in love with, by not opening her marriage token.

I felt Ketya's hand on my back, lightly, for support.

"What happened to our daughter?" I asked. "Where is Lynniene?" For some reason, Ketya's hand tensed at the mention of my daughter's name.

"She's not here. I haven't spoken with her in some time."

"Does she know…?" I couldn't finish the question.

"We told her that you had died a hero's death, the same way you lived. It was kinder than telling her you had abandoned her. And she looked up to you so much. But gradually she forgot you."

"But I—" There was no point in finishing. Sefa would hear what she wanted to. "Where is she? Can you tell me?"

"I can, but I haven't decided yet if I will. She was young when you left, but now she is old enough to know what you cost her. She would have been on her way to being a powerful channeler like her mother if you had stayed. Instead, she lost her chances at a good life when you took them away from me." Sefa coughed again. "She has her own life, without you. She wants nothing to do with soldiers or the army, I can assure you. And she would want nothing to do with you if she remembered you."

I winced at that.

"She would be dead," said Ketya in a whisper. "Both of you would be dead." I don't think she meant to say the words out loud, but Sefa heard them.

"Do you think I would have died like those others? As strong as I was? As strong as my daughter would have been? What do you know about channeling?"

I touched Ketya's arm to keep her from responding again. There was nothing to be gained by picking at unhealed wounds. "I'm sorry for what happened," I said. "I never meant to hurt either of you. I never meant to leave either of you. Please don't hide our daughter from me."

"Right now, it's the only thing I can do to hurt you." Sefa waved the back of her hand at me. "Go away. If I decide I have something to say to you, I'll send for you."

ON THE WALK back to our quarters, Ketya asked me, "Do you think there's any chance she's lying to you?"

"I don't know. I really don't know. I knew she might be angry with me, but I hadn't expected that."

"How could you have known? Your memories were gone."

"I did what I thought was right. I didn't like the person the wars were turning me into. I didn't want to be constantly worried I might lose control and hurt my own wife. I didn't want my daughter growing up with a father who loved killing so much." I sighed. "As it turned out, she didn't."

"Your daughter's name is Lynniene?"

"Yes. It's a family name. Why do you ask?"

"I think I may have heard it before. Is it a common name?"

"No," I answered, "it's restricted. My great-grandmother had it, and three other women in my family before that. But no one else in Ananya has it as a legal name. Maybe you heard it as a nickname?"

"Maybe. That's probably it."

We barely spoke on the rest of the walk back, till we neared our chambers.

"I turn off here," I said. "Nemias asked me to come by and work on some plans with him. I'll get permission to see your father as well. Late afternoon tomorrow? I'll probably be busy with army duties until then."

Ketya nodded.

"Hopefully the visit to my father goes better than tonight did," she said.

"I hope so," I responded, but I don't think I sounded very hopeful.

Ketya

Could Guthre really be Sperrin's lost daughter? It seemed like such a huge coincidence, but could the name really be an accident? I sat at the table in my chambers and wrote down all the details I knew about Lynniene and about Guthre, and tried to match them up.

If Sefa was lying, it seemed at least possible that Guthre and Lynniene were the same person. Only one person in Whitmount could give me a definite answer, though. My father. He'd hinted as much in the barrows. *He knows Sperrin's situation.* That would mean, though, that he knew Sperrin was sending his own daughter on a suicide mission against the giants, and had said nothing.

Speculation will only get you so far, I realized. *You're going to have to ask him. And if you want an answer, he's going to have to think you're on his side.*

And I was on his side, probably more than anyone in Whitmount—not that many people in Whitmount even knew of his presence, of course. But I doubted my father would believe I supported him while he remained captive and I stayed free. I went back to my piece of paper, carefully planning out what I needed to do. Afterward, when I felt confident I had all the details clear in my mind, I neatly folded the paper and dropped it in the charcoal brazier that heated my chambers. I stared at the fire till the heat consumed the paper utterly.

Sperrin

The morning breeze on the battlements felt bracing. Normally I didn't miss the cold, but I had been too long in the moist lowland warmth of the Drowned City. The crisp dry breeze on the heights of Whitmount's defenses refreshed me.

Nemias and I had been walking the defenses together since the sun first crept over the eastern ridge beyond the valley. A small group of junior officers behind us carried rosters, supply inventories, and written notes on all the other information a staff channeler would usually have at hand. Messengers ran back and forth fetching additional information as needed, or carrying requests to shift soldiers or add supplies to particular strongpoints.

The process went slowly; we spent time with the officers of each company as we inspected its position. This had the dual purpose of giving me a chance to meet all of Nemias's captains, as well as building confidence among the defenders: They might be nearly besieged and awaiting a battle with enemies that possessed the magic they lacked, but my reputation for lethal trickery had reached legendary status by the time stories of the scouts' encounter with the giants had spread through the garrison.

I had given particular thought to opposing some of the flying creatures that had attacked refugees outside the Drowned City and had been sighted elsewhere in the mountains. In my eyes, flying attackers would be the principle threat to Whitmount's defenses. By late afternoon, when our inspection tour began winding down, the battlements rang with the clank of metal and shouted orders. Ancient war machines dating back to the Holy War and its aftermath were being hauled up from the catacombs and assembled by soldiers and engineers. I intended to put the antiquated weapons to new uses.

Nemias and I found ourselves alone at the top of an observation platform, staff officers keeping a discreet distance just out of easy hearing.

"So tell me about this meeting you're going to with the chancellor," Nemias said. "What do you think his daughter expects out of it?"

"She's trying to convince herself that she was wrong about him without feeling like an idiot," I answered. "She thinks if she spends time with him, he'll give himself away to her—or maybe prove her right."

"That's all?"

"No, I don't think so. She may not want to admit he was involved, but I know she thinks her father holds the key to restoring Ananya's magic. Which makes some sense, if he was involved in taking it away. I don't know what she's looking for—I'm not sure she does, either—but she's been studying the Talisman of Truce, looking for something. Maybe for what her father did, or even how to undo it."

"You think she'll find it?"

"No idea. She knows the Talisman better than anyone here but the chancellor, I think. So if not her, I don't know who."

"And you said she can be trusted."

"She's still more than a little blind to her father, but otherwise I trust her completely."

"Well, you came around when you saw the evidence. Hopefully she will as well."

"She will. But it may take some time," I said.

"Before the battle?"

"Hard to say. Let's plan on fighting without magic."

"Of course," said Nemias. He put an arm on my shoulder. "I know it's not your choice, but I'm glad you're here. Nobody is better at this than you."

I nodded, acknowledging the truth of Nemias's words without wanting to say them out loud.

"And do what you can with the chancellor and his daughter. We can hold here for a year or two if we need to, but without magic the rest of the empire will starve."

"He'll want us to give him something to tell us what he knows."

"I know that," said Nemias, "and so does Burren. Let's make sure he really *does* know something before we start making choices. I'd love to toss him off this platform and be done with him, but while there's a chance he can tell us how to restore the magic we'll leave his head on his shoulders and keep him hidden away in that cell."

"Agreed," I said. "We treat it like another battle to be fought. But like any battle—when the time comes to act, we may need to act fast."

"I'm sure I'll trust your judgment when that time comes," said Nemias. "But I'll need you to help me win this battle first."

Ketya

"I've been thinking about it, and I think I may need to stay with my father," I told Sperrin as we began the long descent to his cell.

Sperrin didn't seem as surprised as I expected.

"You thought I might say that, didn't you?"

"I had a feeling, yes."

"It doesn't mean I believe him or don't believe him. But I need to find out for myself. He's my father. I'm sure I can figure out the truth." I tried to make the words sound confident, less like wishful thinking.

You'll believe anything your father tells you, part of me knew. But something had changed, at least a little. I still wanted to believe him, but I realized that ever since I had taken the Talisman in the Drowned City, a part of me had been unsure of whether to trust him. I had to at least entertain the possibility that what I had taken for madness in my father was instead deceit.

"Thanks again for coming with me," I told Sperrin.

"You did the same for me," he said. "Not that my wife even noticed you were there until you spoke. I think that would be too much to hope for from your father."

"As you said, he doesn't like you. But that isn't the only reason I asked you to come with me," I confessed. "No one asks you any questions. I would have to explain where I was going to every set of guards at the top of every set of stairs. And I just don't think I can do it. Knowing what everyone thinks he's guilty of, it would just make me feel dirty having to talk about it."

"I understand," said Sperrin.

We didn't speak for another stairway downward, but at the next landing I turned to him. "You think he's guilty, don't you?"

"I didn't at first. But the more I think about it, the worse it looks. I'm not the one who has to judge him. But right now I don't think I would want to be asked to defend him, either."

"I appreciate your not judging him." We went down another flight, the sentries nodding to Sperrin but not challenging him. By now we had almost reached our destination.

"One last thing," I asked as we approached the prison level. "If I do stay, I need to ask another favor."

"If it's in my power."

"It is. It isn't difficult, really. I need you to look out for Guthre."

"I'll visit her. The hospital is caring for her."

"They are," I said, "but it's more than that. I need you to promise to look out for her after she leaves the hospital. To do what you can to keep her safe."

Sperrin raised an eyebrow. "You know she's a soldier, right? None of us are safe."

I sighed. "I know. But at least try to keep her from doing anything stupidly suicidal while I'm not there."

"I'll do what I can," he said. He looked at me inquisitively. Not that I could explain my real reason, at least not until I asked my father to confirm whether Guthre and Lynniene were the same person.

"She's a friend. I'm not very good at making friends, and all the other ones I had died in the palace. It would mean a lot to me to know I have another friend who will be happy to see me return if I have to stay with my father for a while."

"I'm a friend, too," Sperrin said.

Impulsively, I hugged him and kissed him on the cheek. "Thank you so much for helping her, and for being a friend. I really can't thank you enough."

"You're welcome," he said, but his eyes had a sort of knowing look to them. The same look Talye had when she had warned me to avoid Guthre's friendship.

Everyone seems to think there's something dangerous about me being her friend.

"I'll do what I can," Sperrin repeated, and then we had reached my father's door.

Chapter 22

A familiar red-bearded figure stood before the door. "Hello, Kern," Sperrin said to the sergeant. "This is an odd place for a scout, isn't it?"

"Some of us volunteered. There isn't as much scouting to be done with the battle on its way and the fey closing in. I wanted to do something useful. I couldn't think of anything more useful than keeping this god-sucking scoundrel behind bars, except maybe taking his worthless head off his shoulders."

Kern looked at me challengingly, as if daring me to respond. I said nothing.

"We need to see him, sergeant," Sperrin said.

"Why would you want to—" Kern caught himself. "Not my place to ask, sorry."

"No it isn't," Sperrin said, a bit more gently than I would have liked.

The sergeant unlocked the door and let us into the prison suite. "Knock twice to leave," he said. "I'll be here until the watch ends if you need anything."

"Thank you, sergeant," Sperrin said, and we entered. The door shut and locked behind us as soon as I cleared the doorway.

Although clearly a prison—we had traveled deep underground to reach my father's windowless chambers—the room we stood in looked considerably larger and more luxurious than my own. The sitting room contained a low table, three overstuffed chairs, and a charcoal stove for warmth. A narrow side table against one wall held a small library, presumably accumulated by previous inmates. Three rooms opened from the sitting room—two bedrooms and a servants' room.

My father came out of one of the bedrooms, wearing a lounging robe that he hadn't owned before. He looked freshly bathed and shaved. His eyes went to Sperrin, not to me.

"Welcome, overcaptain," he said. "Have you come to gloat at my imprisonment? Be assured that I will not be here long."

"Good evening, chancellor. I don't have any particular business with you tonight. Your daughter asked me to escort her here."

Sperrin gestured to me, but my father's eyes didn't shift. He motioned Sperrin to one of the chairs. "Would you care to join me for a drink, 'captain? I have an abundance of food and drink here and no one to share it with."

Sperrin sat wordlessly. I took the third chair, and the chancellor seemed to notice me for the first time.

"I hope my daughter has come to stay a while," he said to Sperrin. "I can use her assistance here. I will need someone who is not a spy to tend me while I prepare my defense for trial."

"You would have to ask her," Sperrin answered. "And your defense may not be so simple a matter as you think. I have heard the evidence against you, and it is compelling."

My father smiled. He actually looked cheerful. "Bah," he said. "Schemings of political enemies. They will come to nothing. I respect Burren for trying—I might do the same in his place—but of course I will beat him."

"There are many witnesses," Sperrin said.

"There always are when they tell you ahead how guilty someone is. Have you met these witnesses, outside of Burren's imagination?"

"Chancellor, I'm not involved with your case, and I would prefer we not discuss it further. My job was to get you and your daughter here safely. I did that. Now my job is to help defend Whitmount."

"I see," the chancellor said, still smiling. "One would almost believe that my well-being was your primary reason for coming here, if one didn't know better."

Sperrin opened his mouth to reply, then seemed to think better of it. "Is there anything I can get for you and your daughter, chancellor?"

"We have been well provided for. If I need something further for my defense I will certainly ask. As I said, I do not expect any difficulties." My father's smile never wavered. "I suppose I should thank you for your role in getting me and my daughter here alive. It was unneccessary and unasked for, but I must admit that it was well done." He nodded to Sperrin. "I hope your other endeavors in the city go as well."

I had a feeling that my father knew a lot more about the status of Sperrin's relatives than he was saying. But if I wanted actual answers to my questions, I needed to wait until Sperrin left to ask them.

"I think perhaps I should take my leave and allow you and your daughter to enjoy each other's company," Sperrin said, as if reading my thoughts. "I have other duties, I'm afraid."

"Nonsense," the chancellor said. "I am certain you have already worked all day. Whitmount stood without you for a thousand years, and I am certain it will continue standing for a little while. Take the time to enjoy a drink or two with an old man."

You're the same age, I thought. *You even have daughters the same age. Why is my father trying to delay Sperrin? They don't even like each other.*

"It's aged tamindraught," the chancellor said. "It will ease your muscles."

Sperrin did look tired. He accepted the proffered drink and they sat quietly sipping the rust-colored liqueur.

A loud clattering of boots on the stairs outside disturbed us. Someone pounded loudly on the door.

"Overcaptain Sperrin!" came an out-of breath shout. "Overcaptain Sperrin! Come quickly! You're needed urgently. The fighting has begun."

My father bowed his head in farewell as Sperrin strode to the door and exited. The smug smile had never left my father's face.

He couldn't have known, could he? Then I pushed the disloyal thought away. *There's no way he could have known.* I wasn't even convinced of his role in the tragedy at the Drowned City yet. Accusing him of other conspiracies while he sat in a cell deep underground seemed delusional.

And yet, I couldn't help wondering.

Sperrin

Talye had been sent to get me. The excitement of the fight had sent her voice even lower.

"They're everywhere, 'captain. Giants at the gates and flying ones above. Little ones everywhere, getting into everything."

I asked questions as we climbed the stairs, but the answers helped less than I expected. Trained for scouting and light infantry work, Talye couldn't tell me much about how well static defenses were holding against creatures who before a few weeks ago had never attacked static defenses in living memory. I thanked the sergeant and told her to return to Nemias and tell him I would be there shortly.

I had decided to do a quick check of key defensive points on my way to report to Nemias. No point in reporting to him without information I could act on. At the next landing I drew my blade.

The idea of drawing blood had already pushed the bad taste of the encounters with my wife and the chancellor out of my mind. In the distance I could hear shouting, and the clatter of metal on stone. It was going to be a very good night.

Ketya

The bolt on the door clicked back into place before the clatter of feet running upstairs had died away.

"Well, that was a short visit after all," my father said drily. He poured himself a small refill of the tamindraught, only a few sips. "Now that he's gone, and not to imply that I am not happy for your presence, but I begin to wonder why you are here."

"I had some questions that I wanted to ask you in private," I said.

"I am at least heartened that you did not pretend it was simply a social visit."

"It's a social visit too," I protested, "but I know better than to lie to you. It's more than a social visit."

"So ask," my father said. "I am in a talkative mood, and for once we have privacy. Ask before we are hounded by guards and spies again."

"You're not worried about the attack?"

He sipped from his glass of tamindraught. "I am not worried. Captain-general Nemias and Overcaptain Sperrin have many failings, but they are both more than competent as battle commanders. We are deep underground. There may be lapses in their plans that will lead to many deaths, but I am confident they will address those lapses long before the fighting reaches this level."

Putting the glass down, my father leaned back in the cushioned chair. "But surely that isn't what you came here to ask me."

It took me a few tries to get started. "I met Sefa," I finally managed.

"Did you? I'm a little surprised the overcaptain brought you along to what must have been a very painful scene."

"It was painful," I said. "More than he expected, I think."

"Our friend Sperrin is very good at addressing problems that can be solved with that blade of his. He has more difficulty with problems that don't lend themselves to violent solutions. Witness his attempt to leave the battlefield. It made his life worse on every level, and here he is a decade later right back where he started."

"What did he do wrong?"

"He annoyed the Empress. But I think she was more annoyed at Sefa, who should have kept him from doing it. Sperrin, as delightfully naive as he is about some things, performed a number of irreplaceable services on the battlefield for Ananya, and there was every chance he would be needed for the same thing again—witness our present predicament. So he was punished in a way that kept him fully available for use. Sefa was a good channeler, but when a channeler is chosen for a marriage like that, it is with the expectation that she will manage any potential problems long before they reach the Empress's attention."

"So the Empress blamed Sefa?"

"If a dog begs at the table, do you blame the dog or the trainer who failed to break him of the habit?"

"Sperrin wasn't a dog."

"Ultimately, daughter, we are all the Empress's dogs. An important lesson that we disregard at our peril. When the present…situation shakes out, we will all be somebody else's dogs. That's how it has worked in Ananya since the end of the Holy War. Senne's power flows through the Empress, so she—and agents of her choosing—decide who marries, who eats, who lives, and who dies."

"That's a pretty grim way of putting it."

"You are not in school anymore. There's no reason to lie to you. The system is what it is. Our family has benefited greatly by it. So did Sperrin and his family, until they annoyed the Empress."

My father seemed to be enjoying this. It was the most he'd spoken to me in years. I needed to choose my words carefully, though; the flow could shut off just as quickly as it had started.

"I think Sefa may have lied to Sperrin during our visit," I said, a little hesitantly. "She said some things about their daughter's location that I'm not sure I believe."

My father laughed. "And you think you have a better notion of where his daughter is right now than either Sperrin or his wife, correct?"

I flushed, but answered. "Yes. I think I might."

"In answer to your suspicions: Yes, Guthre is actually Sperrin's daughter. And no, her mother hasn't the least notion of where she is. If she told Sperrin otherwise, she lied to him. Sefa finally had enough of the man she let distract her from her marriage to Sperrin—a fairly awful man after his affair with an ex-favorite of the Empress ruined both their prospects—and she abandoned Guthre in order to leave him. The girl left the day after her mother did. I was rather hoping one of them would kill the vile man, but I gather neither one of them had it in her. Maybe the last few weeks of fighting have done it for them."

"You knew Sperrin was Guthre's father the whole time we were traveling with them?"

"Of course I did. It was my business to know. Why do you think I encouraged you to befriend her? That sort of friendship can only benefit you politically."

"But if you knew...why did you let Sperrin send her on a suicide mission?"

My father laughed again. Leaning forward, he picked up his drink and took the last sip of the rust-colored liqueur. He paused to savor the tamindraught before responding. "My dear daughter, Overcaptain Sperrin does not take military advice from me. Besides, it would have been deliciously tragic if she had died, at his hands as it were."

His response left me a bit disgusted. In spite of my best intentions, I couldn't bring myself to respond, and the conversation lapsed.

Sperrin

From the gatehouse overlook I could see what remained of the causeway. One giant lay half-buried in the rubble created when the defenders had collapsed parts of the road. More important, a giant-sized ram intended to shatter the front gate had been lost as well. Three giants remained on the stub of the road outside the front gate, pounding at it with hammers to little effect. Nothing the defenders dropped on them seemed to affect the giants much, but they wouldn't be able to damage the massive gate without help—or at least a lot more leverage than the precipice that remained of the road gave them. The dead giant actually surprised me: After the previous trap, I had expected the fey attackers to be more cautious.

I could see parts of the town burning, but that had been expected as well. Hopefully none of the field workers had been caught outside the fortress. I found himself glad of the night attack: It might have been planned to maximize terror and confusion, but it also meant that very few defenders would be caught in the open.

The signal fires still burned in one of the correct patterns from the redoubt at the top of the stairs. Most likely the fey had gone around the strongpoint, focusing on taking the main fortress first with the intention of mopping up remaining resistance afterward.

The fey might be magical creatures and friends to the gods, but they had no siege train, and no patience for long assaults. To win, they would have to carry Whitmount by storm, and the fortress would not give way easily.

Aside from flying creatures, I expected the biggest problem would be infiltrators. The biggest and strongest fey could be held at bay, but many smaller ones could change shapes, or crawl up sheer walls, or fit into very small spaces. They would look for weaknesses and lightly armed targets, and reacting to those infiltrations would draw off defenders needed elsewhere.

I saw signs of fighting in the outer galleries: splashed blood against the rough stone of the wide passageway, a torn door in the entranceway to one of the turrets, sawdust scattered on the floor to mop up slipperiness and spilled blood. Pairs of sentries stood watch at the entrance to each of the great stone turrets, guarding the engineers and laborers inside who struggled to work the heavy war machines in each emplacement. Brute force was a poor substitute for magic, but the machines had been designed with the thought that channelers might run short over a long siege: Through one open door, I could see a cluster of laborers struggling to adjust the elevation of a massive thrower in response to an engineer's hoarse shouts. Others manhandled barrels of harrowflame with hand-rigged fuses onto improvised wooden rollers that had replaced the magic-powered slideway to the war machine's throwing arms. Almost a hundred soldiers and laborers—grabbed from farm fields or anywhere they weren't needed during the attack—worked a war machine usually served by a crew of six, or four in a pinch.

From behind the next door, I heard a different shout. At my signal the sentries opened the door and entered the turret, blades in hand. I ran forward through the entranceway behind them.

The dark frame of the lightning bear in the turret stood idle on its swivel mount, useless without a channeler to crew it. Inside, three scouts with light weapons fought a ram-headed creature wielding a glittering stillsword. A fourth scout lay in a pool of blood at the fey's feet. A second of the ram-headed creatures was pulling itself through the wide slot in the stone, high up on the mountainside, that the lightning bear normally projected through. The creature had one arm and a leg through the slot; I could see the stillsword slung on its back as it started to pull itself over the edge. My blade struck sparks on the rock as I severed the creature's hand. *No point in going for the head. It's too well armored.* I struck twice to the creature's thigh to loosen its hold on the wall, then smashed its face with the flat of my blade, sending the thing backward off the mountainside.

The scouts had fallen back from the second ram-headed creature, but not before it had scored a deep cut to the arm of one of them. The two sentries, troopers from the Mountain Cougars, circled it warily, feinting and looking for position. I sighed.

"Drive, drive," I called out. "Don't hesitate! It's faster than you are!"

I wanted to let them make the kill for themselves, but I didn't want to lose two more soldiers.

They hesitated. The creature's stillsword flashed, shattering one of the troopers' weapons. He screamed as his wrist broke from the force of the blow. The second soldier tried to drive in, but too slowly. Effortlessly, the creature stepped aside and deflected his blow. Glittering armor covered the creature's midsection and shoulders. As it pivoted to kill the soldier, my thrown knife sank into its buttock, throwing the creature's step off. In two quick strides I closed the gap between us. The creature bent its knees to block a high blow and counter. Instead I sidestepped and swung low. Blood spurted as I severed the tendon at the back of the creature's knee. Its leg buckled. Quickly, the soldier stepped in to finish the creature.

As it hit the floor a squad of reinforcements from the Mountain Cougars poured through the door.

"Clear the wounded," I said, after making sure both creatures were dead. I motioned the two unwounded scouts back to their posts. "You were spotting for the other turrets, right? Get back to it. They need accurate spotters."

Turning to the trooper I patted him on the shoulder. "Nice kill," I said. "Don't hesitate next time."

"Thank you 'captain," said the trooper. "It was your kill. I just finished it."

"The next one will be all yours," I anwered. "If you give them any time they'll go right for your weaknesses. They move faster than you do. So you need to think faster than they can."

"I understand, 'captain."

The soldiers seemed heartened by my appearance on the scene, but I hoped they took the lesson to heart. When the next encroachment came, I wouldn't be there to do the sentries' job for them. They might not have spent much time training to fight fey, but that's who the enemy was. They needed to be prepared to act, not wait for a creature to bring the fight to them.

I detailed a trooper from the roving patrol to replace the injured sentry, and listened to their undersergeant's report while I accompanied the rest of the patrol through the gallery. We were stretched thin in places, he said, but holding.

Hopefully most of the sentries fought better than the two I'd encountered. The Cougars captain whose company guarded this part of the defenses would have formed his best fighters into roving patrols to back them up, but the sentries needed to stay alive long enough for that to help.

NEMIAS'S HEADQUARTERS, IN an upper observation gallery, boiled with activity. Messengers rushed in and out amid the hubbub of staff officers shouting instructions and moving markers on the giant diagrams of the fortress and valley that covered four tables in the center of the round gallery.

The front wall of the chamber formed a giant window into the night, though from the outside it would look indistinguishable from the rest of Whitmount's glittering white facade. Through the transparent rock I could see flickers of large creatures swooping in the night sky, backlit by moonlight. Something—war machine, giant, or other creature—was throwing burning debris from the village. The flaming ruins shattered spectacularly against the walls, showering sparks downward onto the wrecked causeway.

"The walls are holding," Nemias told me, "but they may not be so white anymore when this is all over. We have creatures infiltrating everywhere. The big ones mostly can't get in, but too many of the small ones can."

"I saw that." My encounter with the fey had been duly marked on the chart by a staff officer as soon as I had reported in, along with the Ananyan casualties.

"We're holding well enough against the giants and the others, but the flying creatures are doing some damage. I need you to take care of them, Sperrin."

"How are the machines I set doing?"

"They need a bit of encouragement, I think."

"I am on my way."

"Appreciated," Nemias said. "Once you've got them working, step in anywhere you see a problem. The fey will try to hit where they're not expected, and no one is better at expecting them than you. I'll send a messenger if I need you someplace specific."

I turned to go, before Nemias's touch stopped me. "One more thing."

"Of course."

"Take one of the Mountain Cougars roving patrol squads from the guardroom outside. I don't want you caught out alone with no support, and I want you to have soldiers with you to patch any holes you see. They're not you, but there are some good troopers there. Send a messenger if you need more and I'll find you some."

We clasped shoulders and I strode out. A few words to the subcaptain coordinating the roving squads in the guardroom, and a dozen soldiers soon followed me up the long stairways toward the upper battlements and my improvised air defenses.

The long, sinuous frame of a flying lizard blocked the moon momentarily.

Soon you will die, godling. Blood burned in my veins. *I am coming to kill all of you.*

Ketya
Whitmount: Six weeks after the Loss

Three days had passed in the cell with my father. Whenever he retired to his bedroom I would pore over the Talisman of Truce while he slept. Somewhere, I knew, the words of the treaty could unlock what had gone wrong, and how to fix it. Whether or not my father was involved in the disaster at the Drowned City, the Talisman held the key to the problem. Eventually I returned the Talisman to its hiding place and slept myself.

When I awoke each morning—if I hadn't lost all track of time—new dishes of food would be laid out on the side table. Cold meats and yesterday's bread: Presumably the kitchen staff had more important concerns than hot meals for prisoners and their daughters.

The guard outside changed periodically as well. This morning, through the barred window of the cell door I saw Talye's familiar face.

"I'm glad to see you," I said to Talye as she walked over to the door. "Even if I'm sorry for the circumstances."

"No one blames you for what your father has done," Talye said. Her eyes belied the words, though.

"I don't even know what he's done."

Talye's gaze moved past my shoulder, and I knew my father had emerged from his bedroom.

"I'm not saying he didn't do anything," I said, quietly so my father couldn't hear. "I just don't know. I thought if I came here, I could find out."

"I suppose it saves someone the trouble of protecting you," Talye said. Her eyes looked cold, but most of that look seemed aimed at my father. "You would have been more helpful in the hospital, though."

"I know. I didn't know the battle was about to happen. I hate that I left Guthre there while I'm safe here."

Something in Talye's eyes grew warmer. "Please be careful with Guthre," she said.

This time I had to ask. "That's the second time you've said that to me. And I really don't know what you mean. What is it I need to be careful of?"

"She's a good kid," Talye started. "And a good soldier. I don't mean to give you the wrong impression. It's just that—"

A footstep creaked. Neither of us had heard the approach. Usually boots clattered loudly in the stairs.

"Oh, hello, Kern," Talye said, looking at the red-haired soldier. His eyes looked oddly luminous. "I'm surprised you're awake. What's happened to your eyes, they—"

Talye grunted and spit blood. She pitched forward against him as his knife sunk deep into her bowels, then sliced upward.

The creature that wore Kern's shape stepped aside and let her fall. None of Talye's blood had stuck to him.

"I don't think she's going to answer any more of your questions," said the golden-eyed creature.

"You....I saw you before. You were a wolf then."

"And you let me get away. Pity it cost your friend her life. I hope you didn't like her too much."

"And before that you were a merrow." I said the words in a monotone, talking more to myself than the creature.

"I don't like to stay the same for long," it said. "Yesterday's skin goes out of fashion so quickly."

"What *are* you?" I said.

"You would have to ask your father that. I'm afraid he has neglected your education a bit."

I realized my father now stood beside me, looking out the narrow, barred window in the cell door at the creature in the hall. Something squished when I moved my foot. Glancing down, I saw that my father and I stood in a pool of Talye's blood, which had welled under the door.

"I am hoping he is the one who is going to let us out of here," said my father. "He won't hurt you, don't worry."

"Let you out of here…" the creature said. "Wait, let me see where that's part of your agreement…." He paused in mock thought. "Hmm." He pantomimed flipping through the cards of a treaty. "No, no, looks like it isn't in this agreement. So I'm afraid you will have to find someone else to let you out of that cell."

"Agreement?" I whispered. I felt the blood drain from my face.

"Oh, that's so adorable," said the creature. "Your daughter didn't know."

Chapter 23

Sperrin

The problem with the flying lizards tormenting the upper battlements was they were smart. You could fool one into a trap and kill it, but the next one wouldn't fall for the same trap. I wondered if I would run out of traps before the fey ran out of lizards.

I had started relatively simple the night before. I had the engineers remove the needles from the giant sewing machines—too big to be worked except by magic—that sealed the wagon-sized canvas bags of grain emerging from the grist mills in the valley on their way to the granary. A few hours of work fitted the needles with barbs and adjusted a spear-throwing mechanism so that it could launch a spear—or in this case an improvised harpoon—nearly straight upward. A well-aimed shot speared a griffin under the shoulder, and a crew of fifty rapidly winched it downward. Once they had the creature on the platform, soldiers finished it off with axes and spears, though it still badly hurt several troopers.

We had caught two others over the course of the following day with other stratagems. The great flying lizards no longer swooped in so daringly to scoop up a soldier or tear the roof off a building. And perhaps I should have been satisfied with that, since it fulfilled Nemias's instructions to me.

But I wanted to kill more of them. I just needed to tempt them with better bait.

It took until the second night of the battle before I could dangle that bait in front of the lizards. Another griffin had been injured by a harpoon but had escaped when a dragonet came to its assistance, badly mauling two of the winch crew before they could reach their shelter. The dragonet had made several more harassing passes during the afternoon and evening, always at unpredictable intervals. That unpredictability had made the creature my particular target.

Nemias had sent a few replacements to keep the machines working, and

I had made sure everyone got a hot meal and at least a few hours sleep.

Now, last night's winch crew was rolling barrels of harrowflame into the center arm of a thrower. The side thrower arms, their buckets loaded heavily with iron spikes and old spearheads, had been winched down perpendicular to the center arm. I'd asked the engineers to cut the harrowflame fuses down to almost nothing, so the loaders cleared quickly once they secured the barrel in the throwing arm.

"Go," I said to the sergeant of engineers who nominally commanded the machine.

"What elevation, 'captain?" the sergeant asked, puzzled. "It hasn't been set."

"Don't care," I said. "Just shoot the thing."

"Don't you care what we're aiming at?"

"As long as it clears the fortress, not really. Anything down there isn't in our hands, and I don't really care if it does any damage or not."

"Very well." The sergeant restrained a reaction, and signaled to the trooper on the arm release.

The barrel ignited almost the instant it left the thrower. It left a long, fiery trail in the sky over the fortress, then arced toward the causeway below. I didn't bother walking to the edge of the battlement to see where it hit.

"Again, sergeant."

"No elevation setting again?"

"Where you have it is fine," I answered "Just keep throwing those barrels."

"Seems like a waste," he muttered. A little louder than he should have. I ignored the remark. Once more, the barrel left a fiery trail off into the darkness.

"Again, sergeant. And keep your crew lively. They need to clear the arm the instant that barrel hits, not linger."

The engineer sergeant's heart may not have been in it, but he gave the orders.

On the fourth throw, the dragonet came.

It swooped in just as the barrel settled in the arm and grabbed the harrowflame. In a heartbeat it would soar upward to drop the short-fused barrel on the fortress's defenders.

"Now!" I shouted.

The winch crews released the two side arms. Iron spikes tore into the dragonet. The two arms snapped together pinning the creature just above the center arm, barrel still in its claws. Then the harrowflame exploded, filling the air with the smell of burning dragonflesh.

The creature thrashed hideously. It made piteous noises as its chest and belly burned away. When the harrowflame's intensity had eased to a safe level, I motioned soldiers forward to put the creature out of its misery.

"Sorry about your rig, sergeant," I said, looking at the sagging center arm, its struts bent from the heat of the harrowflame and the deadweight of the dragonet.

"We'll have it back in service tomorrow, 'captain." The skepticism in his voice had been replaced by something closer to wonderment. I would have preferred a little imagination to either, but the engineer had done his job.

"You do that, sergeant. We'll see if we can find you another lizard to kill."

I doubted that would happen. The lingering smell of roasted lizard would discourage the creatures from coming too closely, I suspected. The fey didn't fight like an army, but like a mob of magical creatures. They all wanted to drive the humans from the mountains, but that desire wouldn't be enough to make them coordinate their efforts past the opening hours of the assault. When the defenders won, I knew, there would be no orderly retreat; the attacks would just gradually dwindle as individual fey stopped attacking.

Until then, the attackers could be fierce and creative.

A row of flames suddenly appeared well inside the defensive perimeter. The small houses across from the hospital were burning.

"Cougars, to me!" I shouted. "They're attacking the hospital." I turned to the engineer as the roving patrol formed up quickly. "Get a messenger to Nemias to send help to the hospital. We'll hold it till he gets soldiers there. And keep your crews pushing here."

Before the sergeant could respond, I had vanished toward the flames.

THE ROW OF cottages burned fiercely, an unapproachable inferno. I saw the cottage where I had spoken to my wife, behind a wall of flames. I wondered if she'd been in it. Had my daughter's whereabouts died with the woman I'd been ordered to love and then ordered to forget?

Scanning the area, I saw no sign of attackers or survivors around the cottages. The fight seemed to have moved on to the hospital.

The flames from the cottages reflected on the high glass windows of the hospital—at least from the panes that hadn't been shattered by attackers. The hospital's front door lay on the lawn in two pieces. I could hear sounds of fighting inside, but it seemed to have moved on from the entrance, where the sentries assigned to the building had died quickly. *If the sentries are dead, who's fighting?*

I ran through the door, followed closely by the roving patrol Cougars. The sentries had been killed by thrown darts. Two small fey lay in the rubble with them—pixies or something like them. Small enough to sneak in here and set fires and kill by surprise. But too small to tear a door off its hinges. There would be something else here, too.

Signaling the squad leader, I pointed to the fallen pixies. The soldiers fanned out: No use making an easy target for throwing darts.

Shouting came from the hall to our left. Two troopers took cover near the hallway entrance to act as rear guard and the rest followed me toward the shouting.

A crowd of small fey was throwing darts at a makeshift barricade near the end of the hall. Beds and tables had been heaped to block the passage. The mattresses seemed to be absorbing most of the pixie darts. Defenders behind the barricade threw bottles, jars, and other improvised missiles back at the fey, along with whatever darts made it past the barricade.

A heavy ironwing—not just fey, but an actual messenger of a god—lay face-down near the top of the barricade. An ironwing would have been strong enough to destroy the door, and probably to fly all of these pixies over the walls of Whitmount. But someone convalescing in the hospital had managed to put up a better fight than most of the soldiers defending the palace in the Drowned City had done. I wondered how they'd done it.

We hit the pixies from behind. My blade cut one in half and beheaded another before the fey even realized they were under attack. Within moments the soldiers cut all of them down.

"Save one alive if you can!" I shouted, probably a moment too late. I wondered if they could have told me which god had attacked the palace.

Unless we had acquired a new enemy, the same god was behind our troubles tonight. The ironwing had the same tattoo I'd seen on the ones I'd killed in the Drowned City. I thought of the golden-eyed creature I'd encountered twice already. I'd taken it for fey, but perhaps it was a servant of the gods as well?

With the fighting over, the soldiers moved from room to room checking for survivors and any lurking fey. I topped the barricade, looking more closely at the fallen ironwing. Something had eaten away most of its face and chest. I'd never seen quite that sort of wounds before—did godlings have some sort of vulnerability I didn't know about?

Somehow, I wasn't surprised to see Guthre at the head of the defenders behind the barricade. She had a fresh cut on her face but it looked shallow. Her other injuries didn't seem to be bothering her enough to keep her from fighting anymore, although that might change when the excitement of battle faded.

The rest of the defenders were an odd lot of convalescing soldiers, hospital orderlies, even a couple of emaciated-looking former channelers, armed with whatever came to hand. Half a dozen defenders had fallen, and many hadn't made it behind the barricade before being caught in their rooms, but more of the patients had survived than I expected.

"You're getting good at this," I said to Guthre, pointing at the fallen ironwing. "How did you do it?"

"They use acid to clean wounds and avoid infection," the scout answered. "They dilute it, but they have loads of the pure stuff."

"And you just happened to know where to find it, and how to throw up a barricade in a hurry."

"I like to know all the escape routes. Talye wouldn't approve me to go back to duty so all I could do to fight the boredom was plan for all the contingencies I could think of. And make sure all the orderlies knew the plan. When the battle started they were pretty terrified about what would happen if we got attacked. I guess they hoped some of your trap-making skill rubbed off on me."

"Looks like some of it did," I said. "Why the hallway?"

"Most of the rooms had huge windows where the fey could hit us from two directions at once. The hallway was the only place people could get to quickly where we wouldn't have to defend two sides."

I could see her shift balance. Guthre's wounds bothered her more than she wanted to admit. I sat down on a clear section of the barricade with an unobstructed view of the hall, and motioned for her to sit beside me. I passed my flask to her as she sat, and Guthre took a long pull of yellowfruit brandy. It brought back memories of another wall, watching another battle.

Sitting, and the brandy, seemed to help Guthre regain her equilibrium. She passed the brandy back to me and I took a pull from it.

"So this is what you do all the time?" she asked. "I'm not used to standing and fighting. I'm used to running."

I nodded. "Sometimes there's nowhere to run, though."

I passed the yellowfruit brandy back to her.

"That's true enough," she said.

"You know, I tried to run away once, too."

She looked at me quizzically. "Really? That's not your reputation."

"I didn't do a very good job at it, and it ended badly." I waved at the carnage around us. "I'm a lot better at this part."

Guthre nodded and took another drink. "I'd heard that."

By now my squad of soldiers was starting to reassemble. Any moment reinforcements would arrive from Nemias, and we would be able to get back to other parts of the battle.

"Can I ask you a favor?" said Guthre.

"Sure."

"Can you help me get out of here, and back into action? They won't clear me to return to the scouts yet, and I guess they're right. But I don't want to sit out the battle."

I glanced at the dead ironwing. "You haven't exactly sat out the battle."

She dabbed at the cut on her face. "That's different. They came here. I want something more useful, even if I can't do front-line fighting yet."

I thought for a minute. Ketya had asked for a promise that Guthre was basically asking me to break now. But I did see a potential compromise. "How about this. You can be my aide, until you're fully healed. That should be enough danger for you, and it will free a less-wounded soldier for front-line duty."

She seemed to ponder the idea. "You know I'll be awful as an aide, right? I'm a scout."

"Would you rather stay in the hospital?"

"Hey, I'm a quick learner. Aide sounds good to me."

"Get your stuff if you have any. We'll be leaving as soon as the new guards are ready to take over. If we wait till they're organized, some hospital administrator will want to wait before they let you go."

"Give me a minute to check my room and see if anything survived. Don't leave without me."

BY DAYBREAK, THE fighting had slowed. The battle showed signs of waning. I dismissed my exhausted squad of Mountain Cougars back to their barracks, sent word to Nemias where I could be found, and went back to my own quarters to get some sleep. I put Guthre in Ketya's chambers, next to my own, and left word with the sentry to have me woken in six hours.

When I awoke, I could see the pinks of sunset through my window. Nemias had countermanded my orders to the sentry and ordered that Guthre and I be allowed to sleep. Which meant, I knew, that what remained of the battle was mostly mopping up. Nemias had left word for me to find him after dinner, which gave me a little while to discuss the dilemma of the chancellor with my new aide. I faced, I suspected, some tough choices. Or at least choices I preferred not to make.

"The problem," I told Guthre, "is that we need magic to survive. No matter what it costs to get it. We can win battles like this one, but we can't win wars this way."

"Seems like you're doing pretty well at it. You took on giants, and those flying things."

"But that's only part of a war. We can improvise traps only for so long—the fey are smart and will adapt. Already by the second day of this battle, the flying lizards were adapting and avoiding traps. But even if we could win this war, we lose without magic. The Central Alliance is attacking at the same time as the fey, and even if we beat both of them, most of Ananya will starve without magic to keep the farms and greenhouses going, and to ship the food to where it's needed. Even if the magic came back tomorrow, we'd have famines next winter, I think."

"So how do we get it back?" I doubted any of this was new to Guthre, but she played the role of sounding board willingly.

"That's the problem," I said. "As far as I can tell, the only one who knows exactly what happened is the chancellor, and he isn't telling."

"So we need to make him tell."

"We don't just need the story, we need the truth. He could spin us off in a wrong direction without us even knowing. And even once we do get the truth out of him, we still need to figure out how to undo it."

"Ketya would know how to fix it, I bet," Guthre said. Then her face fell. "But she wouldn't know if her father was lying to her. She believes everything he says."

"That's the problem," I said. "I think we can get him to tell the truth, but not if we leave him here. I think the only way to get the truth out of him may be to give him what he wants, at least in part. And I think he knows it."

"You mean, let him go? How would that help?"

"I mean, bring him with us to wherever the problem can be fixed. Then if we have to, let him go after the magic is back."

"Would he agree to that? Even if he did, wouldn't he just scheme to get us killed so he could escape without having to give us anything?"

"I'm sure he'd try," I said. "Whatever he planned on, I don't think he can do it without help, though." I explained to her about the Alliance soldiers with the packs and frames in the palace, and the Alliance ships that he apparently had planned to escape on during the night the godlings attacked.

"So if I understand correctly," she said, after I had answered her other questions about the massacre in the Drowned City and the journey to where she had met us near the lake, "you are proposing that we free the most wanted prisoner in Ananya from his cell and escort him out of his prison, in return for which we get what, exactly?"

I'd never had an aide who wasn't the least bit afraid of me before.

"It may come to that," I reluctantly concluded. "Prison and the threat of trial are a club—but we may need to offer him a way out, too. We're not letting him loose unless he tells us everything first. And he needs to convince us that he can undo the damage before he goes anywhere."

"And if he doesn't? Or if he says no?"

"Then Burren gets to have the trial he wants, and then he gets to toss the chancellor off the walls. But only the chancellor can give us the information we need. Along with Ketya's knowledge of the Talisman of Truce."

"The problem is getting that information out of him. You have to admit Burren's solution makes a certain amount of sense," Guthre said.

I nodded. "Burren's solution does have a certain elegance, yes. Believe me, I would love nothing more than to kill that man."

"Maybe." Guthre looked skeptical. "Actually, he's the only person I've ever felt like you were reluctant to kill. You would have been happy to wring my neck yourself if you thought it would have bagged you one more giant, and you *like* me. But the chancellor's always been off limits for you."

I started to disagree, then realized she was right. "I suppose he has been off limits. I've known him for a long time. We have a…complicated relationship."

Guthre snorted. "See, that's the problem. This isn't complicated. 'Talk or die.' You need to uncomplicate your relationship with him if you want this to work."

"You know, I think you're right."

"Of course I'm right. That's why you picked me for your aide. I'm a terrible liar and I hate politics. But I'm a good listener, and a good scout."

"Yes, you are," I said. "And I think I know what we need to do now. Get ready to leave."

"Where are we going?"

"Dinner first. Then a visit with Captain-general Nemias. After that, I think we will pay a visit to the chancellor and his daughter."

"Sounds good," she said, turning to the table where her knives sat.

"One more thing," I said as I turned to go back to my own room.

"Yes?"

"Bring everything. We may not be coming back."

THE TALK WITH Nemias went significantly more smoothly than I had anticipated. It was good to have a friend in command, and someone who had known me for years and utterly trusted my judgment.

I had expected to have to lay out the case for what I planned, as I had with Guthre, but that never happened. First Nemias gave me some not-unexpected news when Guthre and I entered his chamber. Geriald and Guthre were there with Nemias, but no one we couldn't speak freely in front of.

"Sefa didn't make it, Sperrin. I'm sorry."

"What a waste." What else was there to say. "I wish the last time we spoke had gone better." I shook my head. "The times before that, too."

Nemias put his hands on my shoulders. "I know you wish a lot of things had gone better. It wasn't your choice to leave. You came back as soon as you could. All the rest was the Empress's doing, not yours."

I noticed Guthre giving me an oddly quizzical look, but she wisely said nothing. It took a moment to compose myself. I hadn't expected Sefa's death to affect me, but it did. Regardless of all that had passed between us, I had loved her and thought she had loved me, and we had shared years and a daughter together.

"That's not why you came here, I know," Nemias said. "You did nice work with the engineers and the hospital both. I think we would have won anyway, at least this round, but it would have cost a lot more lives, and they would have been back sooner than they will now. You've added a bit to your legend, at least here in Whitmount."

I shrugged. "We may have a problem."

Nemias smiled grimly. "Well, you know how to handle problems."

"It's not that kind of problem," I said. "It involves the chancellor."

Nemias flexed his hands. "That *is* a problem. I should try the traitor, but what I really want to do is see him killed."

I nodded. "I may need him. At least for a little while. He has information we need."

Nemias didn't seem terribly surprised.

"Do whatever you need, Sperrin. I'll back you up. I imagine it would be easier for me if I didn't have to put him on trial. Don't tell me the details unless you need my help."

This time I smiled. "You'd only worry."

"Exactly. Don't put me in a position where I have to stop you. If you feel like you have to do something stupid, make sure you're gone before I find out about it. I'll defend you afterward. Just don't ask me to defend you *during*."

"I hope it doesn't come to that."

Nemias laughed. "Me too. But with your history, I wouldn't bet on it. There's no one better at winning a battle, but for such a great captain, you sure have made some bad decisions in other parts of your life."

"That's true enough," I had to admit.

Nemias took a step forward and we embraced. "Just get out of here and do what you need to do," said Nemias. "Take some troopers if they'll help, anything you need. I have a battle to finish mopping up. But one thing?"

"Name it."

"If you have to go, don't take ten years to make it back next time, understood?"

"Understood." I turned and left, Guthre like a shadow two paces behind me.

Chapter 24

I never thought it would be three days before Sperrin returned. I never thought Talye would die while I watched, helpless on the other side of a cell door. I never thought my father would betray all of us.

Somehow I had survived all that had happened in the palace, but I didn't think I could survive this. So much of what had kept me going was not wanting to let my father down, and the whole time he didn't even care.

I just stood there in the pool of blood and I couldn't move. My father said something, but I couldn't understand a word he said. It felt like standing underwater watching someone on the surface try to talk to me. I couldn't even see him clearly. I don't even know if he was talking with me. For all I know he was talking to that…creature who had killed Talye.

I wanted to die. I wanted to never move again. I wanted to stand silent and straight like a gallowwood tree, to die without ever having to move again.

Sperrin

We could hear voices by the time we reached the halfway point of the last stairway. Guthre touched my arm to stop me. Both of us put our packs down quietly. Guthre stepped ahead and took point, moving scout-stealthily.

Gradually the voices coalesced into Kern and the chancellor. The chancellor spoke in heated tones, while Kern sounded almost smug—an odd turn-about from the usual state of things, but perhaps not unexpected given who was on which side of the cell door. *I'm surprised Kern is talking with him at all*, I thought. *He seemed pretty disgusted last time we spoke. Maybe he's having second thoughts about volunteering for guard duty in the depths of Whitmount, far from the fighting.*

"That's not Kern," Guthre said abruptly. "The tone is right, but the cadence is all wrong. And so are the words. They're talking about gods and bargains. Kern talks about hunting and girls."

"You're sure?" I asked, as I drew my sword.

Guthre just nodded. She drew her own light blade and stepped aside to let me take point.

We moved silently down the stairs. Kern—or whatever had taken his shape—stood over Talye's body, talking through the cell window to the chancellor. Guthre startled at the sight of her dead sergeant, but made no sound. We closed quickly and soundlessly.

The chancellor's startled eyes in the cell must have given us away. Kern turned before I could close, stillsword already at the ready.

The luminous golden eyes gave the creature away.

"Pleased to meet you yet again. I see you found your daughter."

Now what is that supposed to mean? No wonder this thing likes the chancellor. They both talk in the same kind of circles.

"Why are you here?" I asked, not expecting an answer.

"It amuses me. But you would probably get a better answer from your chancellor friend behind this door."

"Or I could just kill you both and stop being lied to."

"I can't speak for your friend, but you will find that I am not so easy to kill."

I shrugged. "I killed you once, I can kill you again. If I need to, I'll just keep doing it until it takes."

"Good luck with that. You are very proud. It will come back to haunt you someday." The creature smiled wolfishly.

"Probably. I don't suppose you'd be willing to tell me your name?"

The eyes flashed. "For your book, no doubt. Ask your friend."

I slashed, my dark blade a blur. The blade never struck. The creature vanished.

Putting my back to the wall, I cast around for shadows or signs of an invisible attacker.

"He's gone," the chancellor said from inside the cell. "He will return, but not soon. He can return to his homeland that way, but to get back here he must travel more slowly, through the barrows."

"I think you have some explaining to do," I said. "It's time you told us the truth."

"Why, assuming I had been less than candid with you in the past, would I tell you a different story now?" the chancellor asked.

"Because I can open this door for you if I choose. But I need to know everything if you want a chance at freedom. I need to know what you were doing in the palace and why you were doing it. I need to know the truth."

"And what difference would that make?"

"You hold the key to Ananya's magic. I'm already convinced that you should die for what you did—just for the things I *know* you did, even without knowing all of it yet. But I'm willing to free you if you can help to restore the magic."

"If I agree to do so, will you be willing to promise me an escort to safety? Freedom someplace where Burren can retake me isn't of much use."

"I think we need to hear a full account of what you did before we agree to anything. No more lies."

"And if you don't like what I have to say?"

I hefted my blade. "I'll be happy to kill you right now if I think you've lied again."

The chancellor didn't seem bothered by the threat. "You would lose your last chance to save Ananya if you did."

"It would almost be worth it," muttered Guthre.

Lifting the bolt, I opened the cell door. "Again, I think you have some explaining to do."

"I suppose I do," the chancellor answered. "You would like me to show my cards to you and claim my winnings or accept my loss. It is not an unreasonable expectation. Come inside and we will talk forthrightly, you and I. And then, as you have already surmised, it will be time for us to leave."

Ketya stood just inside the door, still as a wax statue. Guthre went to her quickly, while I entered the room more warily, my eyes never leaving the chancellor.

"Revive her," I said to Guthre, more roughly than I intended. "She needs to hear what he has to say, too."

Ketya

I woke up to the sound of my father speaking. At first I thought I still dreamed, because he spoke clearly and directly, speaking of things he had never talked about, at least not since my mother's death. All of the secrets he said he had never told: It had to be a dream. I lay back and listened, my eyes half-lidded. I was on a couch, my head pillowed in someone's lap. I saw Guthre sitting above me. *I'm supposed to be nursing you back to health, not the other way around,* I thought. Still, I felt groggy and distant, as if I listened to my father's words from far away. Guthre's lap pillowing my head, and Guthre's hands light on my shoulders, felt like the only things connecting me to the same world she and my father lived in.

"You probably know of my wife's death," my father was saying. "Most people would have accepted the loss of a spouse as one of life's tragedies. You did," he said, looking at Sperrin. "But I did not. I knew that only a god could undo what life had done to me—to my wife.

"At the time I was a powerful man, but not yet a part of the Empress's inner circle. Still, I thought I had enough to offer a god. The god did not *have* to talk to me, since I had no standing in the Talisman of Truce, but he did so anyway. We concluded a bargain with certain promises. My daughter's name was included to seal the deal."

"Which god?" Sperrin asked. My father clearly wanted to avoid giving a name, but Sperrin pressed the point. "Which god did you talk to?"

"I am surprised you hadn't surmised it for yourselves. My daughter, at least, should have foreseen it. Only one god had anything to offer me. Only one god had lost as I had."

And then it came to me and I murmured the name without thinking: "Kedessen."

I saw triumph in my father's eyes. I had guessed right.

"Who?" asked Guthre.

A little flush of strength returned to me. "He was the lover of Senne, the goddess who agreed—some say volunteered—to become the source af Ananya's magic as part of the Holy War settlement. She wasn't dead, but she might as well have been dead to him, since feeding her strength to Ananya put her in a sort of coma. There were a lot of sad songs written about their lost love, once enough time had passed after the Holy War for people to think of the gods as exotic and romantic instead of as bloodthirsty killers."

"Oh," said Guthre, glancing at the dead body sprawled just outside the doorway. "I guess they'll have to rethink those songs again for a while."

"So you made a deal with Kedessen," said Sperrin. "That was some years ago. What happened?"

"Yes," said the chancellor. "What happened was that my first approach to the god was...flawed. I was not in the bargaining position I supposed. The god did not feel compelled to keep his word at that time. He brought the old magical abilities in my wife's bloodline back to life, deliberatly misreading a term I had used a touch ambiguously. Why do you think my daughter can see the symbols of the old magic so easily? If there were anyone alive to train her, she could become a sorceror. And Kedessen claimed that technically that bringing to life satisfied our bargain. But he freely admitted that he was cheating me."

"He cheated you?" Guthre asked, incredulous. "And he took your daughter's name? And you went *back* to him?"

"I allowed myself to be cheated," the chancellor responded, stiffly. "I learned from my indiscretion. I did not repeat the mistake."

"Go on," said Sperrin.

"From that time on I worked on attaining a position of real power, one where the god would not be able to break his word or cheat me when I approached him again. I devoted my whole life to it. I did great service for the empire."

"Excuse me if we're less than impressed now," said Guthre.

"You may be less than impressed, but he"—the chancellor nodded at Sperrin—"knows how much I did. My daughter knows how much I did. While I advanced in the service of the Empress, I learned everything there was to know about the Talisman of Truce. Even the most minor-seeming clauses had their importance. I became the foremost authority on the treaty in all Ananya. I used my daughter to test my own knowledge: She probably knows the treaty as well as anyone other than me and the gods. I knew I would need to use it when the time came.

"Finally, I reached the Empress's side as her chancellor, with the power to speak to the gods—and to compel them to keep promises under the terms of the Talisman. Finally, I was ready to return to the land of the gods.

"I chose my time carefully. There would only be one opportunity and it would have to be handled perfectly if I was to avoid reprisal. And their could be no fallback plans, even for me who always planned to turn failures into success; if this one opportunity did not succeed, there would be no other. So I took the Talisman of Truce, as was my right as chancellor, and returned to the land of the gods, this time through the Westbarrow entrance. That also gave me an opportunity to remove the seals that would give the palace warning if the gods returned through that entrance."

He's leaving something out, I thought. I still felt too fuzzy brained to think of exactly what, but somewhere he seemed to have skipped a step.

And then it came to me: the armor that he'd taken from the theater. The Talisman of Truce had a deportment clause, which specified that neither people nor gods would be required to speak to anyone not bearing the Talisman of Truce and clothed in suitable attire, defined in the clause as a formal costume bearing native enchantment of the party's own world. It was further modified by clause 178, with its cryptic references to false costumes and false names. I had never entirely understood the clauses—but presumably they meant what Tenia had thought, that to speak to the gods you needed to wear something made with the old magic, the kind I saw in the runes on the stage of the theater, and in the sally tunnels. And in the Snake Slayer armor that I now wore.

He is trying to trick us into returning with him to the land of the gods, in such a way that the gods will only negotiate with him. Will I also be able to speak with a god? The whole idea seemed so overwhelming, but all of our lives and futures depended on it.

Guthre's hands tightened slightly on my shoulders. She must have sensed a problem.

Should I confront him? I wondered. *Can I confront him?* Probably not, I knew. I would tell Sperrin at the first opportunity, but until then I would have to let my father's words go unchallenged. As far as I knew, he had no idea that I carried the Talisman, or that I wore a costume suitable for conversation with the gods.

Fortunately, my father didn't seem to have noticed my reaction.

"What, exactly, was the bargain you made?" asked Sperrin.

"It was simple, really," my father answered. "My wife's return for the return of Senne to her lover."

"By betraying the Empress and her family?"

"By inviting Kedessen to send his messengers into the palace at a time when the Empress and her entire family would be present, after which he could do whatever he saw fit. The invitation was strictly according to the terms of the treaty."

That didn't seem quite right to me. I would need to recheck the exact wording of a couple of clauses to be certain, though.

"That explains the godlings. What about the Alliance soldiers?"

The chancellor smiled. "That's actually an amusing story. Since I wouldn't exactly be welcome to live in Ananya after my wife returned to me, I reached out to certain members of the Central Alliance leadership who I had become acquainted with in the course of my duties as chancellor. In return for knowledge of the exact time the Drowned City harbor defenses would be lifted and the Home Fleet would be away, they agreed to provide transportation out of the city and a retirement home and income suitable to my rank. Kedessen has by now delivered my wife to that home. She will be waiting there when I arrive."

"If the god kept his promise this time," Sperrin said.

"This time, he had to keep his promise."

Sperrin shrugged. "And how do you intend to get there?"

"You will be escorting me, of course. In return for my cooperation in bringing you face-to-face with Kedessen so you may attempt to convince him to undo this. That's what you want, right?"

Sperrin laughed bitterly. "I wonder what the Alliance thought of your bargain when they realized you forgot to tell them about the sea monsters in the harbor?"

"I forgot nothing," my father said. "The sea monsters were proof against betrayal. If the Alliance kept their word and brought me out of the palace and to their ship, I would have informed them about the sea monsters, and which channel to take to avoid them."

"I suppose it was neatly done," Sperrin said, "up until the point where your daughter lived, and insisted I rescue you. And the point where I killed the Alliance soldiers sent to retrieve you."

The chancellor nodded. "Those were unforeseen developments," he admitted.

Those were the last words I heard my father say. I was still grappling with the idea that he had betrayed our country. To have him admit so coldly that he had planned my death as well was more than I could take. I must have passed out.

When I came to my senses again, my father and Sperrin were talking in low tones near the door, only a few steps from Sergeant Talye's body. Guthre was packing my things for an immediate departure; her own pack already sat on the floor next to me.

Guthre noticed right away when I awoke. "You didn't miss much," she said. "We're leaving now. They've reached some sort of agreement, at least until your father has another chance to betray us."

"We won't let him," I said, trying to project confidence.

Guthre raised an eyebrow skeptically. "Can you get up?" she asked.

I managed a wan smile. "I'm supposed to be nursing you," I said. "Of course I can get up." My legs felt a bit unsteady at first, but after a drink of water and a few ginger half-steps I felt able to walk normally.

"How are we leaving?"

"There are a variety of tunnels and sally ports where we can leave unnoticed," Guthre answered. "I believe Sperrin was questioning your father on the specifics of his protection agreement with the god's messengers and fey helpers, so that we can avoid being killed along the way. He apparently has some sort of protection from them as part of this agreement, but it's not clear how far it extends—at least, he's not making it clear. But as long as he needs an escort out of prison, your father is being somewhat cooperative."

"Are we taking any other soldiers with us?"

"I don't think there are any other soldiers in this castle who wouldn't kill him."

I didn't answer; I just tightened my pack and walked toward the door.

"One last question," Sperrin was saying to my father. "Who was that golden-eyed creature who killed Talye? The same one who attacked you in the tunnels under the palace."

"That was a misunderstanding," said the chancellor. "When he saw me leaving with the two of you, he thought I had contravened our agreement. That creature is Kedessen's half-brother Eury, born of a mortal woman. Eury acts as a sort of emmissary between Kedessen and our world. He isn't a god, but something more like a demi-god. He can change shape and command fey, and when Kedessen chooses, he gives his brother other powers. And my understanding is that he can't be killed."

"We'll see about that," Sperrin answered.

AS SPERRIN MOVED toward the doorway a red-haired figure blocked his path: Kern, the real one this time.

"I was always suspicious of you, Sperrin," he said. "Always the hero, but a little too cozy with the traitor. Are you here to throw away the lives of more scouts? I see you've added Talye to your total."

"That wasn't my doing. The one who did it will pay."

"The one who did it is about to be released, by your hand."

Sperrin frowned. "I wish there was a way to avoid that. I am only doing it out of great need."

"I heard your conversation with him. You're not just letting him out. You're escorting him all the way back to the nightmare place those things came from."

"That is also true, and unavoidable."

Kern's red hair was matted to his head, soaked with sweat. He held a light blade, a scout's weapon. "I knew you were going to release him. Even after everything he's done. Even after that friend of his killed Talye. I can't let him leave."

Sperrin responded in a surprisingly gentle tone. "We need to take him with us. It's for the good of the empire."

Kern spat. "The good of the empire! This traitor is responsible for all the bad that's happened to the empire. But Overcaptain Sperrin, the man who loves killing, is determined to let him live."

"Let us pass, Kern."

"No." The sergeant spat again. "If you want to pass, you're going to have to kill me. And I know you'll enjoy it."

Sperrin's heavy blade flashed, faster than my eye could follow. Kern's weapon fell to the floor with a clatter. The redhead held his mauled sword-hand silently, blood welling between the fingers of his good hand. Fury blazed in his eyes.

"No, I don't have to kill you. Don't tell me what I have to do, sergeant." Sperrin walked past the disabled scout, the rest of us following.

We moved down the hallway quickly. Sperrin and Guthre both knew many ways to get in and out of Whitmount unseen from within the depths of the mountain.

No one spoke for a while, until Sperrin finally broke the silence.

"Unless we get the magic back somehow, he'll never fight with that hand again. It will never heal right on its own. It probably would have been better if I had killed him like he wanted."

"No," I tried to reassure him, "you did the right thing. Most people don't think life isn't worth living if they don't get to kill."

Guthre shrugged. She had started to adopt some of Sperrin's mannerisms, I noticed. "Maybe you're right about Kern," she said to me, "but I kind of see things like Sperrin on this one. I'm not sure I would want to live that way."

Guthre meant the comment seriously, but I had to restrain myself from laughing. *She is her father's daughter*, I thought. *But how am I going to tell them they're related?*

Part V

The Barrow

Chapter 25

We emerged from the base of the mountain a few hours before dawn. I didn't need to point out the blue runes of old magic on the walls of the ancient tunnel; even if the others couldn't see them, we all knew how the catacombs beneath Whitmount had been made. The door clicked shut behind us, leaving no visible seam in the mountain. All the runes were on the inside, I noticed. I wondered if the door could be opened at all from the outside. Not that any of us were likely to be welcomed back to the bloody mess we had left behind.

I wished there had been a way to undo my father's treachery without freeing him, without becoming a party to his treason. I couldn't help thinking that if I'd been more clever I would have figured something out. After all, my father's plan had depended on me remaining blind to his machinations. Although to be fair I'd been a kid for most of them, and away at the Empress's Academy for the rest. Intellectually I couldn't find it in myself to take much blame for my father's actions, but emotionally that didn't make it hurt any less.

Guthre took the lead. I could tell Guthre's wounds still bothered her, even though she barely showed it. Probably Guthre wanted to be alone, and scouting, doing the things that made her useful.

At the moment, having been thoroughly played for a fool, I felt anything but useful.

I'd brought the Talisman of Truce along, had studied its already memorized passages over and over. But I not only had totally missed my father's betrayal—I still wasn't sure how he'd done it, and whether it could be undone.

Sperrin seemed to have a lot of confidence in my knowledge of the treaty. Unless he was just trying to keep me from giving up.

I hoped I didn't betray his faith.

It was hard not to have betrayals heavy on my mind. I barely saw anything around us, my mind just twisting my father's words into shapes, looking for all the times and places I had missed a chance to see him for what he was.

What he was. He was still my father.

He was still the man who had raised me.

Who had, if his words could be trusted, tried to kill me. Or at least had been indifferent to my expected death.

I still couldn't believe it.

Then snap out of it. I heard Tenia's voice in my head.

But I made a mess of things, I protested.

Maybe you did. So figure out a way to fix it. I'm the one who told you to trust him.

But you died because I couldn't see what he was.

I died because I didn't listen to you and I overruled your instincts. I should have listened to my chancellor. Maybe we could have done something about it and maybe we couldn't have. But blaming yourself for being fooled when my mother and everyone else in the empire was fooled too won't help.

I knew it wasn't really Tenia. But I knew exactly what she would have said. And she was right. Maybe I could fix it and maybe I couldn't, but blaming myself for my father's actions and misdirections wasn't going to help. I would need to understand his actions completely to have a chance to help undo them. I couldn't hide behind his lies, and my own illusions, any longer.

Tenia was dead. I couldn't lean on her illusion, either. I would have to solve this myself.

But tonight, in the dimness of the moonlit sunken road that led us by twists and turns toward the Mountain Road, I treasured the memory of those illusions.

I wanted to believe my best friend was still alive. I wanted the comfort of believing my father loved me.

MY FATHER INSISTED that his agreement with Kedessen protected him from direct attack by godlings or fey, and that they wouldn't attack others in his presence, either.

Sperrin disbelieved him, and pointed out the recent example of Talye's death as a counterexample.

"Guarding the door of my cell isn't the same as accompanying me," my father countered. "You only had to fight on the trail when you left me alone so you could frolic with wolves and giants." Whether he lied or not, so far, at least, nothing had slowed our passage back to the mountains.

The truth of my father's statement carried more than a little significance: If we didn't have to avoid fey attacks, we could travel on the Mountain Road rather than side paths, and reach the entrance to the land of the gods much more quickly.

And speed might mean the difference in whether the Central Alliance invasion succeeded. In how many Ananyans starved to death in the coming year.

Sperrin was reluctant to take the risk.

Guthre saw things differently. She looked at the chancellor wolfishly, from across the low fire in our rock-sheltered camp. "So this truce that keeps them from touching you?" she asked. "Does it apply to all of you, or would just part of you be enough?"

He gave her a scathing look, but she seemed unaffected. I suspected that some of Guthre's sarcasm was to mask the pain from her mostly healed wounds. But then a lot of what Guthre did was to mask pain.

I wondered about what Talye had been to Guthre. The two of them had been very close friends once, I gathered. Probably a lot more than that, although maybe not for long. I recalled Guthre's mention of "soldier's marriages" and Talye's warnings about getting too close to Guthre, and wondered what the two scouts had shared together, and what had come between them.

I'd never been that close to anyone. My father discouraged close friendships except for with Tenia, and as close as Tenia and I were, there was always something political about our friendship. I think if she had lived, if the worst hadn't happened, it could have been more. But in some ways I didn't even think I knew how to be a friend. Not the kind of friend Guthre wanted me to be, anyway.

Sperrin

"What sort of guards should we expect when we enter the barrow?" I asked the chancellor. I wasn't at all sure we would even take the same route to the land of the gods the chancellor had used before, but I wanted to find out all I could. We walked on the wide smoothness of the Mountain Road now, so far with no repercussions. Guthre ranged well ahead and often onto side trails, scouting for problems. Ketya walked a little ahead as well, pointedly ignoring her father. That left me to try and find out more about the challenges we would be facing.

"From what I have been told, none of the entrances are guarded," said the chancellor.

"Truly?" I asked. "I find that difficult to believe."

"Who would dare attack? Who do they have to fear?"

That sounded true enough, but I had gradually realized that I couldn't detect the chancellor in a lie. Everything he said sounded true. What a gambler that man would have been! But then, in a way the chancellor already was. Who had ever gambled an empire the way he had?

"What will the entrance look like?"

"I can tell you there will be a stairway down, as if you were traveling underground, instead of to another world. But other than that, each entrance is different, and the same entrance may be different on another day. The world of the gods is just as fickle as the gods themselves are."

"Says the man who sold his daughter's name and his Empress's life to them?"

"Only to one of them. I would have preferred a lesser deal, but I had to take the one available. Wouldn't you have done the same?" The chancellor looked at me for a moment. "I suppose you wouldn't. You left your wife willingly."

"That *wasn't* my choice. The Empress never told me the price before I had to pay it." I knew the chancellor was baiting me, but felt heat in my cheeks anyway.

"Oh, I wasn't speaking of when you left for the palace. I was speaking of last night. You *did* know your wife was in Whitmount, correct?"

A ghost of a smug look crossed the chancellor's face at his small victory.

"She's dead," I said flatly. "She died in the battle. Killed by your friends as part of your bargain."

The chancellor shook his head. "You can't blame me for incidental deaths. Besides, it wasn't a very good match. Both of you were unhappy. Your wife wouldn't follow her Empress's orders and you were too trusting to see what was going on and fix the situation."

"Still no reason for what was done to both of us, and to our daughter."

"You would have to take that up with the Empress. I had only just arrived at the palace when your case came up, so I was not fully involved; The final decision was hers. It did not help that you waited to act until there was no good solution anymore, and all the Empress could do was try to salvage what she could before two useful assets were rendered entirely useless."

Ketya
The Mountain Road: Seven weeks after the Loss

By now Sperrin and Guthre both *had* to suspect they were father and daughter, I was sure of it. If not for the matter of my father's treachery, the matter would have been resolved already.

I couldn't imagine how they couldn't have figured it out. Unless they both just didn't want to confront it. But I knew how important it was to Sperrin to find his daughter: My father might have lied about many things, but I didn't think he had lied about that.

And no matter how much I might not want to think about it, any of us could die in the mountains. Would they want to die never knowing they had found each other, however accidentally? Would they really want to die with that kind of secret? So I looked on it as a sort of duty to tell them, whether they wanted to see it or not.

But I had no idea how. Just blurt it out? What if they looked at me like I was crazy? But my father had told me it was true. The same father who had lied to me until the final confrontation in his cell at Whitmount.

Finally, I couldn't hold it in any longer. It felt like that first river crossing in the darkness the night we escaped from the Drowned City, when I could barely keep from shouting.

The four of us sat more-or-less around a small cooking pit. My father tended a makeshift stew bubbling above a tin of cooking fuel.

"I think you two need to talk to each other," I said, indicating Sperrin and Guthre. My father looked down at the stew, a hint of a smirk on his face.

"About what?" Sperrin asked. "Is there a problem?"

I didn't answer. The tiny clearing descended into awkward silence.

"She's right," Guthre finally said. "There is something I've been wondering. How did you know my mother?"

"Who is your mother?"

"The woman Captain-general Nemias was talking about. Sefa. My mother was named Sefa."

"There must be a mistake. Sefa was my wife. I hadn't seen her in many years, though. Not since the Empress sent me to the palace and made me forget her."

"That was my mother's name," Guthre said. "I hadn't seen her in a while, but I heard about it when she came to Whitmount."

"Guthre," I broke in, "he's your father. Your *real* father. My father knew about it the whole time, but he didn't tell me until after I left the hospital. I swear I didn't know until then."

Sperrin looked a little dazed. "Really? But Sefa said...."

"She lied to you, Sperrin," I said. Now that I had actually said it the words flowed more easily. "She was angry and wanted to hurt you. I don't think she had any idea where Guthre was."

"No," said Guthre. "She left home before I did. I never spoke to her again. She and I didn't talk much the last few years at home."

"So you were Lynniene...?" Sperrin said the words slowly, as if from a great distance.

Now Guthre flushed. "I didn't know the name was real. I thought I'd made it up. Memories of a good father who I'd been taken away from."

"Sefa said they told you I died."

"Maybe they did. I don't remember them telling me anything. I was pretty young. Then when I was older things had gotten so bad that I couldn't believe any of it had been real. I remember a lot of trips with my...I guess my real father. That was you?"

"That was me," said Sperrin. "I was away fighting a lot, but when I was home on leave, we would have lists of places to visit, and we would try to see all of them before I had to return to my unit."

"I remember, I think." The dazed look faded from her face, replaced by a touch of anger. "So that animal wasn't my father? I wish I'd known. I would have killed him."

Sperrin

"I almost killed you," I said. The two of us were scouting well ahead of the others, just close enough to respond to a shout.

Guthre shrugged. "That's all right. It's what fathers do."

"It's funny. I came to Whitmount partly to look for you, once my memories came back. And then I didn't even recognize you in all the time we spent together."

"I *have* changed since I was eight, you know." She spat. "The thing that bothers me is that the chancellor knew about it the whole time. I think I'll kill him."

"We need him to bring the magic back. He knows it, too." The thought pained me a little.

"I'm not an idiot. I won't kill him while we still need him."

"He's very good at being needed. You're not the first person who's been this angry at him."

"I'm sure that's true," she said. "I'm sure it happens all the time. But most of those people have a crazy amount of respect for the man, like you and Ketya do. I just think of him as the guy who betrayed the whole empire because he couldn't handle it when his wife died. It won't bother me a bit if he dies."

"I don't respect him anymore," I said.

"Of course you don't," Guthre answered, but I hadn't fooled either of us.

I tried again. "I don't begrudge his love for his dead wife."

Guthre shrugged again. "People move on. You don't seem real broken up about my mom's death."

"We'd been apart a long time. Even when we were still together."

Guthre nodded. "That's about how I feel. She spent a lot of time angry, but not always at the people who actually hurt her. I don't know if she was always like that."

"Not always," I said. "But sometimes. She loved you when I knew her."

"Maybe. She didn't show it much. She didn't show a lot of feelings by the end."

"She made the best of the situation, I'm sure. My leaving must have hurt her. She'd had a very comfortable life up until then, even if I wasn't in it much."

Guthre spat again. "You're pretty quick to defend her," she said. "But you weren't there to see it when she didn't defend me. Or when I was taking the hurts that beast of a man meant for her. She could have been grateful, instead of pretendng I didn't exist. Instead of running away and leaving me alone with him." She wiped a hand across her eyes, but I saw no tears.

"I'm sorry," I said. "I'm sorry I left you behind."

"It's not like you wanted to. The Empress *made* you leave. Blame her."

"I asked for the palace assignment," I said. "I didn't realize it meant losing my memory."

"And she didn't tell you about it, either. Nobody did. You spent your whole life defending her and fighting in her wars, and she treated you like a pet or a doll."

"She was the Empress," I said. "I'm sure she had her reasons."

"I'm sure she did." Guthre didn't even try to keep the bitterness from her voice. "And now she's dead and I can't say I'm sorry. I'm glad we're getting the magic back, but I hope whoever is the next Empress knows the difference between playing dress-up with dolls and ruining people's lives."

I didn't answer. I honestly had never thought of anything the Empress did as good or evil or just or unjust. She was the Empress. The magic flowed through her. She did whatever she wanted and I had always assumed she had her reasons.

Of course, the chancellor had his reasons too.

THE CHANCELLOR REALLY wanted us to return to Westbarrow and the barrow entrance he had used. His enthusiasm made me more than a little suspicious. Guthre might be right about me retaining too much respect for the man, but that wasn't the same as trustng him. The chancellor had his own agenda; I didn't think it would bother him if we succeeded in restoring the magic, but he didn't care if we failed, either. If he saw a way of returning safely to wherever it was the god had left his wife that didn't require my assistance, the chancellor wouldn't hesitate to betray us again.

"Why are we leaving the trail early?" the chancellor asked me when I turned onto a sidetrack with hours of light remaining in the day. Ketya looked at me quizzically as well. She must not recognize the place in daylight, I thought.

Then recognition colored her face as I turned the key in the lock and opened the hidden stone door. "It's the mountain shelter," she said, "the one where you started teaching me to use a knife."

I smiled. "I hope you still remember those lessons."

"Of course." Ketya looked a little self-conscious about her knife skills in front of Guthre. "I mean, I'm not all that good, but I'll do what I need to."

"You killed a wolf."

"I slowed a wolf down," she pointed out. "You killed it."

They followed me into the mountain hideaway. Not surprisingly, no one had been here since our flight from the Drowned City. I dropped my pack on top of the pallet that hid the passage downward that Ketya and I had followed. It would wait until tomorrow.

"Eat well, and get a good night's sleep," I told them all. "It may be a long time before we get to rest again."

Guthre smiled impishly at me. "Whatever you say, father."

Ketya
The Mountain Road: Eight weeks after the Loss

Sperrin and my father shared one of the barracks rooms, while Guthre and I took the other. With Guthre's help, I dragged a tub into our room and filled it with buckets of water heated on the stove.

"It seems like a lot of work," Guthre told me, bemused. "I thought we were supposed to be resting, not carrying buckets of water."

"We can rest in a little while," I said. "We are going to visit the gods tomorrow, and we are going to be presentable. I am not going to do it covered with trail grime."

"If it makes you happy." Guthre shrugged. "Do you really think it will make a difference?"

"It will make a difference to *me*," I said. "If I have to talk to gods, I don't want to be dirty and self-conscious."

Guthre laughed. "Ketya, you're self-conscious about getting undressed in front of me. How are you going to be more comfortable with the gods?"

I blushed. "That's different."

"Of course it is," said Guthre, but she didn't tease any further. "Do you want me to go in the other room until you're done?"

I took a deep breath. "No. You can stay."

Guthre made a point of walking across the room and sitting with her back to me, so we could still talk while giving me some privacy.

"I'm sorry. I don't know why I'm so shy around you."

Guthre seemed amused by that, but didn't elaborate. "It's all right. Just save me some hot water."

"I will."

"And don't get so shy that you can't check my bandages."

I was glad Guthre couldn't see me blush again.

Why am I so shy around her? I was never this shy at the Academy. Or around Tenia.

I toweled off and got partly dressed, pulling an overshirt over the snake slayer armor so I wouldn't have to explain it to Guthre. Then I relinquished the tub.

Guthre seemed to have no shyness at all; I wondered if she was making a point. Nor did I turn away like Guthre had: I had changed Guthre's bandages, but somehow seeing the scout walking naked to the tub felt different. Unclothed, Guthre looked thinner, too thin to run and fight as long as she had. Even from across the room, I could see half a dozen scars that I hadn't seen before. Guthre stretched once, like a cat, then stepped into the tub. Only then did her eyes meet mine.

I didn't know how to read Guthre's wolfish smile. Neither of us said anything until after Guthre finished bathing.

The scout's wounds seemed mostly healed, even if they still pained her. I checked all of them carefully and changed the bandages on the few that still required them. "Did I hurt you?" I asked, when Guthre jumped slightly at my touch.

"I'm fine," Guthre said, but I pulled back, afraid to hurt her again.

We used the leftover water to wash some of our clothes, hanging them from the shelves near the stove to dry. Then I set a few extra candles near the room's small mirror and started combing out my hair.

"Your hair is so long," said Guthre. "Doesn't it get in your way on the trail?"

"I guess. I hope we won't be spending too much more time on the trail." I thought about it for a moment. "I guess that cutting my hair would feel like admitting that we can't fix the problem. And I don't want to give up on getting the magic back."

"Sure," said Guthre. "I can braid it if you want. Then it will be easier to manage on the trail."

"That would be nice," I said.

Guthre's hands in my hair felt soothing. No one had braided my hair since my mother's death. It brought back memories of a happier time.

When Guthre started rubbing my shoulders, I felt myself leaning back, comletely relaxed. "You're going to put me to sleep," I said.

Guthre sighed.

"Did I say something wrong?" I asked. My brain felt fuzzy. I hadn't been this relaxed for as long as I could remember.

"No, it's all right. You really are sweet and innocent, you know that, Ketya? You deserved a better father than the one you got."

It seemed a strange thing to say. I didn't really want to think. I just wanted to relax and enjoy Guthre's hands on my shoulders. "Thanks, I think. You deserved a lot better than your stepfather."

"I learned from it. Deserve it or not, he made me stronger. I just wish I'd killed him."

Guthre kept massaging my shoulders and neck. Talking about her stepfather didn't seem to disturb Guthre, the way I had trouble talking about my own father.

"Besides," said Guthre, "I have a better father now."

"You always did," I said, drifting almost to sleep. "He just forgot."

"I'm still getting used to the idea," Guthre admitted. "It's weird. I thought I had a terrible father and turned out to have a good one. And you thought you had a good father and he turned out to be terrible."

"I know. It's a little funny." I felt like I was very far away, and somehow that made it easier to talk about my father. "You know, even after everything, I couldn't hurt him. I still feel like he loves me, no matter what he says. I don't know what I would do if something happened to him."

Guthre's hands paused for a moment, then resumed, easing the years of stress from my shoulders and neck. "You know, it's weird," said Guthre. "I think Sperrin feels the same way. Your father might be the one person he can't kill. He doesn't like your father, but he has some weird sort of respect for him."

"My father's not the only one," I protested. "Sperrin wouldn't hurt me. And he would never hurt you. Not now that he knows you're his daughter."

"That will still take some getting used to," said Guthre.

"Have you two talked about it yet?"

The question seemed to baffle Guthre. "Talked about it? Why would we talk about it?"

When I felt so relaxed I couldn't sit upright anymore, Guthre gently laid me on my side on one of the pallets. Then she curled up behind me and pulled a blanket over both of us. Guthre put an arm around my waist and held me close, and it felt nice.

The last thing I heard before drifting into a peaceful sleep was Guthre's voice feather-light in my ear, sounding a little wistful: "Next time we're bathing together, remind me to tell you a bit more about soldiers' marriages."

Chapter 26

Some bridges can't be uncrossed. It was hard to believe just how utterly I had trusted my father the last time we had been in the mountain hideaway. I guess a part of me hadn't trusted him completely, because I didn't tell him that I had the Talisman with me, but even then I told myself it was just until he went back to being his old self.

His old self had been responsible for killing almost everyone I knew.

No one ever said I had great judgment—my father was the one who could read people by looking at them, not me. I just did what I thought he wanted me to, did my best to follow his lead and his instructions.

I'd thought he was teaching me.

The mountain hideout was when I started keeping secrets from him. When I took the Talisman from his room it was only an impulse, and I planned to tell him as soon as he recovered. When I went down the trapdoor with Sperrin, I was deliberately keeping what I was doing secret from my father. I hated lying to him.

Now, we were back, and it turned out he had been the one lying to me all along.

"HOW DO WE find Kedessen?" Sperrin asked as we uncovered the trapdoor the next morning. If the presence of the trapdoor surprised the chancellor, he didn't show it.

"I didn't need to," the chancellor said. "He found me."

"Is that right?" said Sperrin, looking at me rather than my father.

"I don't know," I said, "but I don't think so. I think we need to call on him, at least the way I read the treaty."

"Think what you want," her father said. "We'll see who understands the treaty better."

"Clause 177," I said, and noticed my father didn't meet my eye.

It felt strange. I had been so dependent on Sperrin and others for so long. Now I would be the one they were counting on to know the treaty and to keep all of us out of trouble. As long as my father couldn't be trusted, Sperrin's and Guthre's lives were in my hands.

How did I feel about that? Better than I would have a few weeks ago.

Sperrin deferred a little to me when he opened the trap door again. He took the lead in case of danger, but made sure I had a chance to warn of any hidden dangers or old magic. Guthre protected our rear, her blade drawn.

When we came to the hidden passage, I had to take the lead. Finally, I stood in front of the sealed door.

"Anything we should know before unsealing it?" Sperrin asked the chancellor. "Since you've done this before."

"You would be a lot safer to take the passage from Westbarrow," he said, but mostly he had given up that fight. "I would be surprised if you can open it. There are steps to follow."

Sperrin snorted. "You know the steps, right, Ketya."

"I think so. It will be my first try."

"Do it then."

"You're sure?" Standing in front of the door with its magical bindings, I felt much less confident than I had in the chamber above.

"You're not going to make things any *worse*," said Sperrin.

That seemed true enough, anyway.

Handing my candle to Sperrin, I put my palm against the rune of binding, felt its blue warmth. The rune flashed brightly. My shoulders tingled, as if a spark had shocked against the Snake Slayer armor I wore. As the binding faded, all of the other runes seemed to come unraveled. I stood in front of a blank door of heavy wood. Lifting the bolt, I swung the door open and stepped through.

At first, little seemed to change.

The candle flames flickered at the hint of a breeze ahead. After a few steps, I felt a burning in my calves. I reached down. My knives felt hot to the touch. I pulled them from my boots and dropped them hurriedly, then brought singed fingers to my mouth.

"Oww," Guthre said. "What's going on?"

"I think the gods don't want us to bring weapons," I said.

"Something else your father didn't tell us?" Guthre gave the chancellor a predatory look.

"Do I look like a soldier?" he said mildly. "How would I know if weapons work or not?"

Only Sperrin's heavy black blade seemed unaffected by the otherworldly heat. "This sword is from the Holy War," he said in answer to my questioning look. "It has faced gods before."

"At least one of us has a weapon," I answered.

"We will find others," he said. Removing two thin-bladed black knives from sheaths in his sleeves, Sperrin passed one to Guthre and the other to me. "These were made with old magic as well. Everything else I have is just as unusable as your weapons."

We left the heated weapons piled haphazardly as we moved forward.

"Your father had better be telling the truth about the sentries," said Guthre.

"Why would I lie when my life is at stake, too?" the chancellor answered.

I shushed them both as we moved forward. The Snake Slayer armor had begun to warm against my skin. Not like the heat of the weapons, but a soothing warmth. It felt like the warmth when I had first put the armor on, but magnified. The armor belonged here, I could feel it. It hadn't been made by the gods. *It was made to face gods*, I knew all at once. I felt protected. My arms glowed as the armor shone through my outer clothes. I wondered if the others could see it.

Glancing back, I saw a similar glow around my father. As I had supposed, he still wore the Mouse King suit.

"Why are you glowing?" Sperrin asked the chancellor.

My father shed his overshirt and revealed the Mouse King suit beneath. It glowed a sort of metallic orange in the darkness, its shiny cloth flickering as if aflame. The hood with its mouse ears hung over his shoulders, its glow illuminating his hair.

"It is proper attire for this place," the chancellor said. "The gods will not speak to anyone who is not dressed properly. It is a matter of respect. The treaty is quite clear on the point." He smiled. "Be glad they will speak to one of us. Your hopes hinge on what you can persuade me to tell them."

"Is that so?" Sperrin said. He echoed the same mild tone my father had used earlier. "Perhaps you should look to your daughter."

Moving with deliberate slowness, trying to show the confidence I had lacked in front of Guthre the night before, I peeled off my own tunic, revealing the glittering silver filigree of the Snake Slayer armor beneath. I removed the Talisman from the small of my back and held it inobtrusively.

My father's smile faded, but he said nothing. After a moment we resumed walking.

We found ourselves on stone stairs, winding slowly downward. The rough-hewn walls to either side widened gradually as the cavern grew less close.

Candlelight reflected off the stairs as they grew smoother. Soon we walked on a polished staircase, white as milk. Reaching down, I touched the stone. It felt warm to the touch. The walls held no more blue runes now, as the old magical protections retreated before the land of the gods.

We walked on silently, our boots making no sound against the alabaster of the stairs. The walls faded further to either side. After a while, I saw stars glimmering above: We had passed into the night sky of another world. The stairs spiraled downward through open air, lit by an impossibly full moon. Looking back up, the stairs seemed to spiral into the sky. I couldn't see any signs of the cavern walls that had surrounded us, just a moonlit starscape. Far below, the stairs vanished into woodland. The ground seemed like a patch-work of woods and meadows and hilltop castles. Lights flickered here and there like fireflies, but none of the castles seemed to be illuminated, except by moonlight.

We could have walked two abreast on the wide spiral stairway, but uncon-sciously we stayed single file in the center, as far as possible from the long drop to the woods below.

Lights flickered again.

As if in answer the stars flickered above.

My father threw himself down and huddled close against a stair.

Something swooped toward me. Metal slammed my arm. I yelled in pain. No blood: My armor had turned the blade. It swooped again. I thumped hard onto the stair. Scrabbling wildly, I slid toward the edge.

A hand closed on my wrist.

"I'm not letting you go that easily," Guthre said. The scout smiled at me, then turned back to the fight.

Sperrin held his blade two-handed. Two silverwings climbed rapidly, gain-ing altitude for another attack pass. "Are you hurt?" he called out to me.

"Nothing serious," I said. "Just bruised. I wish these stairs weren't so slip-pery." I gripped the Talisman tightly, glad I hadn't lost it over the edge.

"Stay low. Guthre and I will keep them off you." Sperrin flashed a hand sig-nal at Guthre, who shifted her stance slightly: legs bowed, knife outstretched.

He was being charitable. Guthre had only a slim knife to fight with. The silverwings had curved throatcatchers in each hand, their hilts taped in place with strips of cloth so they wouldn't drop on a bad pass. In the moonlight I could see red stripes tattooed on the silverwings' necks and shoulders.

They climbed together, hovered, then dove. The silverwings picked up speed, banked, and came straight at Sperrin, blades out. Sperrin dropped to his knees, blade overhead. The blade flashed twice as the creatures rocketed overhead.

One of them changed trajectory abrubtly, spraying blood and clutching its bowels as yellow coils oozed out against its bladed hand. With an eerie cry the silverwing lost altitude and plunged toward the wood below.

The second silverwing pitched against the stairs, one of its wing tendons severed. It leaped to its feet quickly to face Sperrin and his blade. Sperrin gave ground slowly before the creature's twin blades. The silverwing hissed and raised its good wing.

Suddenly Sperrin pushed forward. The creature sank to its knees before he reached it.

Guthre withdrew her knife from where she had thrust deep in the silverwing's armpit from behind, in the space exposed by its raised wing. Swinging two handed, Sperrin beheaded it.

"Get the blades," he said. Guthre had already gone to work cutting the bindings holding the throatcatchers in place. Once she had them Guthre pushed off firmly with one foot, sending the creature sliding off the slick stair to plummet to the ground far below.

"Nicely done," said a familiar voice from a few stairs down. This time Eury took the form of a beautiful boy with golden curls. He wore a white tunic trimmed and belted with gold, matching his luminous eyes. A stillsword glittered like diamond dust from his belt, but the demi-god made no move for his blade.

"You again?" Sperrin said. "How many times do I need to kill you?"

"Best get used to it, little soldier," said Eury. "If you want to find my brother Kedessen, you need to come through me first."

"I'm fine with that," said Sperrin, hefting his blade.

"You really think you can beat a god with a blade?"

"Yeah, sort of. I'm willing to give it a try if you're up to it."

Eury laughed. "You will have your chance, little soldier. But not just yet, I think. You have to earn that challenge. I'll see you below, if you live that long." With that, the golden-eyed demi-god leaped easily from the stair.

I looked, but saw no sign of him falling in the moonlight.

From the stairs above us, I heard howling, like the baying of wolves.

"Ketya," Guthre said to me, "take this." She handed me Sperrin's second knife and took hold of the throatcatchers. "Can you tie the straps please? Quickly."

The baying increased in volume. I slid the knife into my boot. Reaching out, I took the ends of the tape from where they clung to the slender needle-points that protruded vertically from the top of the broad slashing blades that enveloped Guthre's fists. As quickly as I could, I wrapped the tape around Guthre's wrists and forearms, securing the blades.

"You can fight with these?" I asked.

"Better than bare hands. I've played with practice blades a little, but this isn't exactly a scout's weapon."

"This is a pretty strange place for a scout," I said, trying to make it sound playful. I gave Guthre's forearm a slight squeeze, then stepped back from the completed bindings. "Fight well."

"Oh, I will. I'm tired of running. I just want to kill them."

She is her father's daughter, I thought, but all I said, again, was "Fight well."

We ended up running anyway. As the baying filled the night, I saw the first wolves loping down the stairs at us. A huge pack of them, black wolves with two heads and bright alabaster teeth the color of the stairs.

Sperrin
Land of the Gods: Eight weeks after the Loss

"You go to the back," I said, pointing to the chancellor with my sword. "I think we'll see if you're telling the truth about them not touching you."

Without protest the chancellor let us pass him and begin hurrying down the stairs, away from the oncoming wolves.

"He knew those creatures were coming, didn't he?" Guthre asked.

"The silverwings? Definitely. He hit the ground when the lights flashed, before we heard them. He saw the signal and didn't warn us."

"Did he know Eury was coming, too?"

"I don't know," I said. "We'll have to face Eury again at the bottom of these stairs. Wolves first, though."

"Where do we fight them?"

"Not here. They can push us over the side just from the weight of them. For wolves we need flat ground."

"Do you have a plan to kill Eury?"

"I'm working on it. He keeps saying he can't be killed, but he's avoiding a fight at the same time. He has *some* weakness. I just don't know what it is yet."

"Maybe the chancellor knows?"

"I don't think so," I said. "That sort of information is currency to him. He would have bartered it to us if he had it. Or used it to get Eury to release him from the cell before we got there."

"Ketya," I called out, "when we get to the bottom, be ready to stand and fight. Sooner, if I signal. Whatever you do, don't run. Wolves are built to take down running opponents. They don't fight well against someone who holds their ground."

"Aren't we running now?" she asked, a little out of breath.

"We're looking for a good spot to fight them, something better than the stairs. If they push it we'll fight here, though."

"I understand," she said. None of us slowed down.

The wolves surged after us, a black mass covering the stairs behind us. Less than a full turn of the spiral staircase separated them from us now.

Quickly, the wolves closed in. Their fur shimmered in the moonlight, highlighted with silver or gray.

"Ketya, keep going," I called out. "Guthre, turn and defend left. Keep moving, though. We need to get down these stairs."

Guthre smiled an acknowledgment and turned to fight.

The wolves surged forward, trying to go around the chancellor. I stabbed randomly to keep them from getting past on the right, not caring how much damage I did as long as they stayed behind the chancellor. On the left, Guthre did the same, poking at fierce snouts to keep the creatures from enveloping us.

"Keep moving," I shouted when the chancellor would have stopped. Guthre and I backed up slowly, matching the chancellor's speed. "Ketya, yell if anything comes at us the other way. And tell us when we get close to the bottom."

"Another four turns," she shouted back, just barely audible over the baying of the wolves.

A wolf got too close. I stunned it with the flat of my blade. A kick to the shoulder sent it sliding off the stairway to fall yelping to the woods below.

Grimly, we kept at it, stair by stair. I hoped Guthre would hold up, injured as she was, but she kept throwing herself at the attacking wolves.

"Save some energy for the fight," I called out. "We still need to kill them when we get to level ground."

"I have plenty of energy," Guthre called back. "Going to be hungry when it's all done, though. What do gods eat?"

"No idea," I said, fending off another wolf. "I hope it's not wolves. Whatever it is, I'll make sure you get the best cut of it."

"I'll hold you to that," said Guthre.

"Almost there," Ketya shouted up at us, after what seemed like forever. "There's some sort of clearing down here, and a bunch of cages. There are paths in the woods, but they keep opening and closing. It's like a maze, but the trees are moving."

The trees felt like the least of our problems. "What kind of cages?" I called back, without turning from the wolves. "Is something in them going to attack us from behind?"

"I don't think so," shouted Ketya. "They're pretty small. I see a cat in one of them. Most of them look empty."

"Looks don't mean much here," I called back at her. "Keep an eye out. And get your back to a tree or something. We'll be fighting these things as soon as we hit bottom."

Another few steps and I could see ground. I jumped off the stairs to the springy ground. Pivoting, I swung my blade and took the legs out from two startled wolves.

The wolves snapped and surged as they hit the base of the stairs. The chancellor fell backward and the wolves leaped over him in their hurry to get to us.

"Just keep them off my back," I said. "I've got the long blade." Guthre and I worked our way slowly toward Ketya, who had her back to a double row of carved wooden cages. She had both knives out and had bloodied a pair of wolves that harried her. One snapped at her arm. The Snake Slayer armor barely held back the wolf's fangs.

Most of the creatures went for me, though. My blade cut through a mass of fur and flesh. A dozen of the creatures lay dead before the wolves started to give ground.

"Are you hurt?" I asked Ketya, once we found themselves alone in the clearing. Guthre walked over to check on the chancellor, who seemed unin-jured except for a few scratches from when the wolves had surged over him.

"I'll be fine," said Ketya. She had cuts and scratches on her legs and hands, but none seemed deep. I wondered if wolfbites in the land of the gods were likely to fester. I supposed it didn't matter: Long before any infection could take hold we would likely either be dead or have access to magical heal-ing again.

Ketya

By the time Sperrin had finished checking my wounds, my hands had stopped shaking. "Sorry," I said. "I was fine during the fight, I think."

"You lived and the wolves are gone. Sounds fine to me," replied Sperrin.

Now that we were free from the immediate threat of wolves, I glanced over at the cages. "It's some sort of crossroads prison," I said. "There's an old folk tradition that magic is stronger at a crossroads. Maybe there's something to it."

"A prison?" Sperrin looked dubious. "A prison for pets, maybe. Why would you build a prison with cages this small?"

He had a point. The cages looked more like elaborately carved rabbit hutches than like cells. None of them had any metal parts, just carved wood with no apparent seams. I supposed they wouldn't use iron in the land of the gods.

Aside from the cat I had seen before, none of the cages looked occupied.

"What's Guthre doing?" I asked Sperrin. The scout walked slowly toward my father, who had regained his feet and dusted himself off.

"I don't know."

Guthre turned her head to look at them as she walked toward the chan-cellor, stopping to kill an injured wolf. "So your father lied to us again. Tell me again why he's still alive?"

No one answered her. Guthre turned and walked past the chancellor, toward the stairs.

My father snorted. "Ketya, I think you had best keep your pet under con-trol, before—"

His eyes went glassy. Guthre slid the thin needle of the throatcatcher's upper blade out from behind my father's jaw, where it had entered his brain.

She wiped it clean on the back of his tunic, just before my father's knees buckled and he toppled to the ground.

"What?" she said, seeing the expressions on Sperrin's and my faces. "Neither of you had an answer for me. I realize both of you have some kind of weird hero fixation on him, and I understand he's your dad, Ket, but to me he's just the evil guy who got the Empress killed. He needed to die."

"Who will speak to the gods? He has the experience, and the armor." Sperrin looked stunned, but not exactly unhappy.

"You mean, besides Ketya? You can. Or I will. The armor comes off, right?" Guthre squatted down, released the tape from the throatcatchers and placed them on the ground carefully, and began expertly stripping the corpse.

"But he—" My face had gone totally white.

"Yeah, I know. Kinda ruins things between us, I'm sure. But he would have dragged you all over the Alliance to rescue your mother, then ditched you once he found her—if he hadn't gotten you killed first. I know he was your father, but he was not a good person."

I didn't reply. I found myself transfixed by the sight of my dead father, now being stripped of his outer clothing and armor.

"So who's taking this?" Guthre asked, holding up the Mouse King suit. "I'll be happy to wear it, but I may not be the most diplomatic person here."

Chapter 27

Ketya

For a moment, all of us stood around stunned. No one knew what to say. My father had been the only one who had any idea of what to expect here in the land of the gods, despite the many times he had lied to us.

Now what? I wondered. How do we even go on? As angry and frustrated as I had been at my father, his death left an empty place that ached in my stomach.

Now what?

An unfamiliar voice from behind me finally broke the silence.

"It really pains me to ask this," said the cat in a low, sultry voice, "but would one of you consider letting me out of this cage?"

I pivoted, and looked at the large, sad-eyed tabby in the cage. "You can talk."

"Apparently."

I took a step back, and found Sperrin standing at my shoulder. "Do you think it's safe to let the cat out?"

"You're our expert on this place," he said, gently.

Our *living* expert, you mean. For a moment anger seethed through me. From the edge of my vision, I saw my father's stripped body at the edge of the stairs. But Sperrin was right. I could be angry later. Just like in the Drowned City when he told me I could mourn later. I wondered when *later* would come. If it would ever come.

First I had to do what I could to restore the magic.

Most of the treaty concerned the human lands where the war had been fought. The sections dealing with the land of the gods mostly focused on dress, decorum, and who had standing to discuss violations or modifications with the gods.

Nothing in the treaty said I *couldn't* release prisoners in the land of the gods. I supposed it hadn't come up in the negotiations. If it had been a serious problem, the gods would probably have used cages with locks, not something any passerby could open. Were there passersby in the lands of the gods? My father had been here at least twice before without harm coming to him, so it probably wasn't always as lethal as today's experience had been.

Impulsively, I stepped forward and lifted the latch of the cage.

The wood flashed as if a magical ward had released. The cat butted the door open and bounded from the cage.

Already as the creature touched the ground it began to change. I reached for my knives, but the woman in front of me held out her hands, palms out.

"I'm not going to hurt you," said the woman. Worn fighting leathers covered her torso. Ancient-style leathers, like the ones soldiers had used in the Holy War. I had seen them in museums and Memorial Day processions, dry and brittle. But these leathers were oiled and supple. The woman looked weathered, especially on her face and around her sad eyes. Red-brown hair hung in a long braid halfway down her back.

"You're a god," I said. I didn't know how I knew it, but suddenly I felt utterly certain of it.

"And your point is?" the woman asked.

"What were you doing in a cage if you are a god? And why are you dressed like that?"

Spoken by a woman wearing a Snake Slayer costume that somehow transformed into real armor, I realized, and I felt myself blushing.

The woman squinted at me, then scanned the clearing. "I don't know any of you. And you don't seem to know me."

"Where should we know you from?" Sperrin asked. I suddenly realized that he had put on the Mouse King armor. It made sense, since he did most of the fighting, but it still hurt to realize.

"Why would you have been sent to rescue me if you don't know me? I didn't think there was a human alive who could make it here safely whom I didn't know. What captain do you serve?"

"My name is Sperrin, and I am an overcaptain in the Army of Ananya, late in the service of the last Empress. And who are you?"

"An empress in Ananya? And overcaptains in her army whom I have never met? How long have I been here?"

I said, "If you tell us your name, maybe we can answer you."

"My name is Juila, sorceress in the central council of Ananya. And I assure you we have no empress. A week ago my sons fell in battle, and I was taken. But we held the field, I think. And you tell me that Ananya still stands."

"Juila…" said Sperrin.

The name came back to me suddenly. "You were married to Captain-general Keir. But you're a god? How can that be?"

The woman looked stricken. "Were married? Has Keir fallen, too?"

"Milady," Sperrin said, sounding oddly formal, as if quoting from a favorite book. "Your husband has been dead for eight hundred years. But all the rest of his days since the day you were taken, he never stopped hoping you would return."

"Eight hundred years…" she said quietly, more to herself than any of them. "Was I forgotten then?"

"Your husband swept the field, after your sons fell," Sperrin said. "He inflicted a defeat so dire that the gods agreed to settle the war. Your body was never found, and your husband always thought you were held prisoner, but the gods swore it was not so."

"They swore falsely then," said Juila. "On what terms did they settle?"

Briefly I outlined the treaty's terms. For the first time, Juila looked amused.

"Really? Senne agreed to give her magic to Ananya as part of the settlement? She always did have a love for the dramatic."

"You knew her?" I asked. It was probably a stupid question, but I had no idea how well gods knew each other. They lived forever, or nearly so, but there were a lot of them, some of whom had apparently fought on the human side in the Holy War. I wondered how many other assumptions I'd been making my whole life were so utterly wrong.

Don't think that way. I pushed the doubts down. I am the one who knows the treaty. With my father dead, what I know is our only chance of saving Ananya. *Focus on what you know.*

Juila smiled wryly. "Knew her? I grew up with her. Senne is my sister. She was the only one who didn't stop talking to me when Keir and I fell in love. I wondered why she didn't make sure I was freed—but if her magic was being drained she would be able to do little more than sleep."

"Her magic *was* being drained," Sperrin pointed out. "Things…changed a few weeks ago."

Again, I explained, this time about my father's betrayal and Kedessen's attack on Ananya. I had thought I would never be able to talk about the things my father had done, the things he had finally admitted to—but when I spoke to Juila the words flowed easily.

Juila immediately grasped the point I had been struggling to see. Even with just a brief knowledge of the treaty she saw what had been eluding me. "So your mother was never actually returned to your father?" she asked. "That would mean the bargain was never consummated. Kedessen took something he didn't pay for."

"That was my thinking," I said, a bit hesitantly. "He can claim that he intended to pay once my father left Ananya, but intent isn't enough. Either he paid or he didn't." Things started falling into place in my head. "Keeping you a prisoner violates the treaty as well, in at least two clauses. We can ask for redress. Whether we'll get the magic back or not, I don't know."

"Who were you trying to get redress from?" Juila asked.

"My father had said he would help us find Kedessen. That the one who took the magic away might be convinced to return it. If not, we could appeal formally to the king and queen of the gods, I think. But we need to talk to Kedessen first or under the treaty he could claim we didn't try to make him aware of the violation."

Juila snorted. "Good luck getting Kedessen to return anything once he gets his hands on it. Part of me wonders of Senne didn't agree to let her magic flow to Ananya just to get away from him."

"They didn't get along?" I thought of all the romantic ballads about the doomed love between Senne and Kedessen. Half the girls at the Academy had written bad poetry about them in composition classes.

"Oh, sweet sorrow, they got along beautifully for a dozen lifetimes. After that, not so much. And Kedessen wasn't one to let go. It would have been worse, but the war distracted him."

"It's odd," Sperrin said. "I've read so many histories of the war, but none of them say anything about gods fighting on our side. I knew your name as a sorceress, but none of the accounts mentioned your heritage."

"In…my time…" Juila shook her head. "That will take some getting used to. Relationships between gods and people were uncommon, but not unknown. The war must have put an end to it with the gods leaving the human lands, but gods and humans intermingled for a long time before the war. When the war for independence came, I wasn't the only god who chose to fight on the human side. And there were humans who fought for the gods as well."

Sperrin nodded, unsurprised. "Wars are always neater in the accounts afterward. I did have another question, though."

"Ask it."

"You were known as a sorceress. Why use the old magic if you were a god?"

"The old magic?" She looked puzzled for a moment before she caught his meaning. "You mean human magic. It wasn't old or rare when I learned it. I'm not surprised the treaty banned it. When I joined the human side, the Court—our king and queen and their attendants—took away most of my powers as a god. So I learned to use the human magic instead. It's not as powerful as the magic of the gods in some ways—for instance, it can't be shared in the way Senne shared her magic with Ananya. And it only works right in human lands, not here in the land of the gods. But it's potent enough in battle on human ground."

"Wait," I interjected. "what do you mean, 'it only works right on human lands?'" I looked tellingly at the Snake Slayer armor I wore.

"Passive magic like your armor will still work. But nothing active, nothing that sends power or moves things."

"Or counters something moving at us?"

"Exactly," said Juila.

"I wonder…" I said, trailing off. "Someone expected something like this to happen, at least when the treaty was being negotiated. I didn't think it would matter, since the old magic was forgotten, but clause 119 where the magic is banned is pretty clear on treaty violations.

If any god shall violate the treaty in a material way
then this clause shall be held in abeyance
even though the remainder of this treaty remain in force.

"So I don't think they will be able to keep you from using your magic. Assuming we live to get back to the surface."

And according to my father, I could learn to use it as well, Kedessen's unwanted payment in return for my name. My father may have lied about many things, but the runes I'd been seeing since my arrival in the palace spoke to the truth of that at least.

For the first time, I started to think we might have a way to survive. Ananya might survive. Without magic people would starve—but perhaps the old magic could be used. Not that I knew much about how it worked or how one learned it, if one wasn't already a god, despite the aptitude Kedessen had given me. But now at least I knew someone who did.

Something seemed to be gnawing at Sperrin. When the conversation went quiet, he finally asked it, in an apologetic tone.

"One last question. A painful one, I'm afraid. Your sons who died. They were demi-gods?"

A shadow passed over Juila's features. "They were," she said. "They fought bravely. My husband trusted them to hold the center at all costs, and they did. He would not have won without them." She looked at Sperrin with sad eyes. "Why do you ask?"

"We have had a few encounters with a demi-god named Eury. Kedessen's half-brother, I'm told. He seems to be under the impression that he cannot be killed, at least not by me."

"If he thinks that, he has been misinformed. It would be difficult, but not impossible."

Sperrin gave her a feral smile. "I am glad to hear it."

For the first time Guthre entered the conversation. I hadn't even seen her since Juila's release. "I'm sorry to interrupt," Guthre said, "But is it safe to talk here? Don't we need to keep moving?"

"Nowhere in this land is safe for you," said Juila. "This spot is as safe as any. But I can take you toward Kedessen's lands while we talk. After a hundred lifetimes spent in this land, I know the way well enough, even with no magic to guide me. Your friend is right; best not to linger."

I winced a little at the word *friend*.

Sperrin

Once the initial shock wore off, I felt oddly liberated by Ketya's father's death. Until now, we had relied on whatever information we could get the cagy chancellor to reveal, and we could trust none of it. Now, for better or worse, we would rely on our own strengths and knowledge: Ketya might know less than the chancellor, and trust herself less than she had trusted his every lie, but at least what she did know I could trust.

My daughter might have destroyed her friendship with Ketya when she killed the chancellor, but she had freed all of us from an unhealthy dependence.

Not that Ketya was likely to ever see it that way.

I saw a sadness in Guthre's eyes that rivaled the sense of loss in Juila's expression. *She isn't even mourning the loss of something real, like Juila is,* I thought. *She's mourning the loss of possibility. Real things she expects to lose, and she armors herself to withstand that kind of loss and pain. It's the loss of possibility that really hurts her.*

I wished I knew my daughter well enough to be able to say something that would make her feel better. Somehow I didn't think the things I'd said to eight-year-old Lynniene in her moments of pain would suffice now. My daughter looked on others to distract her from pain. She jumped into intense friendships that she pushed away from when they became painful as well. I recognized the look from my own youth. My father hadn't known what to say, either.

The trees seemed to shift and part for Juila, forming paths where she wanted to go. We found ourselves walking through what looked like dense forest, though for all we knew the walls on either side might be only a few trees thick. Springy grass covered the path, interspersed with low-sitting wildflowers.

Here and there, openings on the sides of the path revealed tantalizing possibilities: a small pool with a brass mirror hanging above it; a herd of one-eyed sheep, apparently masterless; a castle whose walls shimmered like mother-of-pearl.

Juila ignored them all. She barely even glanced at the side paths.

"If you take us to Kedessen, won't you be imprisoned again?" Ketya was asking her.

I walked behind, close enough to support them without interrupting their conversation. I sensed Guthre moving closer beside me.

"I don't think so," replied Juila. "He may have had nothing to do with imprisoning me in the first place. Even if he did, Kedessen would have trouble imprisoning me again without attracting the attention of the Court. And he doesn't want the Court's attention as long as his bargain is unfulfilled. He needs to either complete the trade or find a way to placate or eliminate you without the notice of the Court."

"I don't see how he could complete the trade *now*," said Ketya. She glanced back reflexively as if checking on her father's body, which we had left at the foot of the stairs.

"He can't, unless he cheats. But he may try to find a way to evade the intent of the treaty," said Juila. "I hope you know the language very well."

"Well enough, I think. But I'm not good at spotting liars and cheats."

"Leave that part to me," said Juila. "To be a god is to be an expert on liars and cheats."

GUTHRE TOUCHED MY hand, signaling me to hang back a few steps, so we could talk without being heard.

For a while she didn't say anything. We walked together on the shifting path through the forest, watching for attacks or sudden movements.

"It's a strange place, isn't it?" Guthre finally said. "If I was a god, I don't think I would want to live here."

I shrugged. "Having magic makes the world different, I think. You want different things out of life."

"Like Ketya?"

"She never really had magic. She tasted it, then lost it. Her mother had it, like my wife...your mother..." I trailed off, remembering Sefa's angry reminder that our daughter could have been a powerful channeler in her own right.

"I don't remember her with magic. I know she must have had it for a while even after you left. But I don't remember ever seeing her use it."

"She was very good at it when I first met her. She was a lot less angry then. At least when I was around. Life got hard for her, I guess."

"Life got hard for me, too," said Guthre. "She could have handled it better."

"I guess she could have. I'm sorry for what happened."

Guthre waved off my concern. "Not your fault. I'd blame the Empress, but she's dead."

"Your mother's dead, too," I pointed out.

"Yeah, but she was alive more recently."

Only by a few weeks, I thought. But I said nothing.

The conversation hit a lull.

"That's not really what you wanted to talk to me about, is it?" I asked.

Guthre shook her head. "No, not really. It's just..." she trailed off, then seemed to gain resolve. "I really ruined things with Ketya, didn't I? You know her pretty well. Do you think she'll ever talk with me again?"

"You *did* just kill her father. Give her a little time to mourn. If you're too visible now, she'll blame you for it—"

"Of course she'll blame me! I killed him."

"Give her time to think about the ways he hurt her and who he really was. Right now she doesn't see who he was, she sees who she wanted him to be." *The way you see Ketya*, I thought. But I would never have said that out loud either.

"I like her a lot," Guthre said.

"I know you do."

"He needed to die." The way she said it sounded almost like a pout.

"I know he did," I said gently. "I think Ketya does too, or at least she will eventually. Try to give her some time. Let's get through this crisis first."

"I'm not good at giving things time. And we may not even live through this crisis!"

"I wish I could help more, Lynniene," I said. "Some wounds take time to heal."

She gave me a determined look. "I'll figure something out. You'll see."

I rubbed her shoulder in support, then returned to scanning the woods for more immediate threats.

WHEN WE STOPPED for a rest break, Juila gestured for me to walk with her, so we could talk in private. Ketya sat on a rock facing away from Guthre, trying not to acknowledge my daughter's existence. While we walked Ketya held up well enough. But whenever we rested and she had time to think, she started shaking quietly.

"You asked about my sons, 'Captain," Juila said. "Remember this: To you they may be just bones in a barrow, children who died centuries ago. But to me they are fresh and real. In my mind I held them a week ago, before we all took our places on the battlefield."

"I understand." And in a way I felt I did. I had lost my wife twice, a decade ago, and again in the battle at Whitmount. And I remembered the fresh pain of finding out a few weeks ago that I had lost my wife and daughter, even though they had both been gone a decade by then.

Evidentally, something in my eyes satisfied Juila, for she went on. "I saw them at the end. The battle went on afterward, but they fell holding the center on the first, desperate day, and I saw their bodies before I was taken."

She paused, shuddering, holding in sobs of her own. After a moment she looked up at me, her eyes sad and empty, but dry.

"Their *eyes*, 'Captain. They took out my sons' eyes. After my boys had fallen, they cut their eyes out."

With that she turned and walked back toward where the others sat, facing away from each other.

Once she could no longer see my face, I found myself smiling. *I had him now. Eury was mine.*

Chapter 28

Ketya

I miss my father. Even now, after time to reflect, I miss him. Even knowing everything he did. Most people can't get past his betrayal, and that's as it should be: To save my mother, he basically sentenced thousands of people to death. But there are parts of myself, things I like about myself, that I know came from him. He was a traitor and a liar and I know now that if our positions were reversed he wouldn't miss me. Part of me still doesn't want to believe it, still wants to believe he always loved me, but even I'm not that blind to my father's shortcomings. But I still miss him every day.

I HAD NO idea that gods fought on both sides in the Holy War. Now, not only had I met a god, I'd met one who could tell me about how to harness the old magic. Again the thought heartened me: With the old magic, Ananya might have a chance of surviving even if I didn't succeed in convincing Kedessen to somehow undo what he had done.

We would need to live to return to Ananya before that would be possible, of course.

But the new possibilities excited me. For the moment, at least, I was able to let go of my father's death and keep moving.

Juila had fallen quiet as she navigated us through the shifting maze of forest paths. The trees all looked alien to me, their leaves a lush dark green that I had never seen in Ananya. Sperrin and Guthre hung back a bit, probably so Guthre could avoid me. Which was just as well. I didn't have anything to say to her right now; looking at Guthre just made me feel empty.

"It's a good thing you know these lands," I said to Juila. "We would have been completely lost without you." The words sounded pointless and superficial, but I wanted to say *something* to restart the conversation.

Juila raised one eyebrow. "I should know how to navigate here. I lived here for hundreds of years, and visited family in this land many times before the war made that impossible. I confess that I do not think you will get what you want by speaking to Kedessen, but I can take you to him easily enough. If he does not find us first."

"Kedessen is the god my father chose to deal with. I'm still not sure how to undo the damage, but I think we have to start where my father did if we want to have any chance of restoring the magic." I didn't know if the treaty was maddeningly ambiguous about reporting violations, or if I was just failing to fully understand some key passage.

"Maybe." Juila sounded dubious. "I can see why you would want to start with him. Kedessen is not the most stable choice, though."

Which is why he was perfect for my father, I thought uncharitably. But I kept the thought to myself.

"You're sure you won't be imprisoned again?"

"I have a lot less to worry about than you do. They cannot kill *me*. And I have a war I am looking forward to helping you win. Since I missed the end of the last one."

I tried to wrap my mind around eight hundred years of imprisonment, even if it had only felt like a few days to Juila. Everyone Juila knew would be dead. *That's not true*, I corrected myself. Only the humans are dead. All of the gods who were Juila's friends and relatives were still alive.

Along with whoever imprisoned her.

Juila noticed my worried look. "Focus on the job you need to do here. Do not worry about your father or about me. I will be fine. No god here can imprison me again without drawing the attention of our King and Queen. Not Kedessen nor anyone else. And there is no way the Court knows about what he has done. They are very scrupulous about treaties. Kedessen follows the letter but not the spirit, but to most gods the spirit is the more important thing."

Now it was my turn to be skeptical. That certainly didn't match most of what I'd read. On the other hand, Juila was living proof that a lot of what I thought of as history was at the very least misleading. She could be right. In which case, she might be right about starting with someone other than Kedessen.

Best to at least ask.

"Juila," I started. "Do you think there is anyone else who can undo this? Other than Kedessen, I mean?"

Juila shook her head. "I do not think it can be undone. But maybe something can be layered on top of it to change the effects."

A smooth voice interrupted us. "Or, you could all be killed and the whole thing forgotten."

Eury had arrived.

His eyes still glimmered gold, but his hair now swept down in a luxuriant golden mane, over a billowing scarlet cape. Eury carried a long blade with a swept golden guard, and flames licking at the steel. A pair of hulking ironbacks accompanied him, heavy stillswords in their hands.

"You looked better as a wolf," said Sperrin.

"If you want my brother, defeat me first," said Eury. He stepped toward Sperrin, waving the ironbacks at the rest of us.

Sperrin held his blade at the ready. "*She* wants your brother," Sperrin said, inclining his head toward me. "I don't care if we talk to him or not. But I do want to see the look on your brother's face when he sees me standing over your steaming corpse."

Coming from anyone else, it would have sounded like bravado, but Sperrin made the words sound sincere.

It's because he really means them, I knew. *For now, at least, he's given in to his love of killing.* Under other circumstances that might have saddened me, given all that he had lost trying to break away from that love, but not while the ironbacks bore down on us.

"Give me a blade," said Juila. I passed one of my two knives to Juila and hefted the other. Not that I had much chance of penetrating the thick skin of an ironback. Guthre lifted her hands to eye level, the throatchatchers once again in her fists.

Sperrin and Eury crossed blades. They circled each other, feinting. Their blades moved almost too quickly to see.

"Not that way," Juila said as she advanced on the first ironback, the knife looking impossibly small in her hand. "You'll need to take his eyes."

She said the words quietly, but I saw Sperrin nod a slight acknowledgment.

Eury took a step back. "Traitor," he said, the words almost a sneer at Juila.

Deliberately, Sperrin took a step forward. "Hold the ironbacks," he said, not loudly. "Don't try to kill them, just hold them. I'll be right there."

Guthre made sure she had the attention of one of the ironbacks and started backpedaling. As it closed on her, she dropped the throatcatchers and scrambled up a tree. From there she tossed small branches and seed pods at the creature, as if taunting a bear and not a messenger of the gods. For its own part, the ironback roared up at her, dropping its blade and shaking the trunk of the tree in an attempt to dislodge Guthre from its upper branches.

By contrast, Juila charged at the second ironback. A quick cut drew blood from behind the creature's knee. Juila sprang back, circling behind it. The ironback's injured knee buckled. It stumbled as it tried to pivot. Righting itself, the ironback lumbered after Juila, limping noticeably.

That left me out of the fight. I tried to watch everything at once, my knife ready to throw if needed.

Eury had knocked Sperrin to one knee. The demi-god moved lightning fast, raining blows that Sperrin's blade barely stopped. As Sperrin tried to regain his feet, Eury laughed and moved in for the kill.

"Not so easy here, is it, 'Captain'? I am closer to the source of my power, and you are far from yours."

"It is a little harder," Sperrin agreed.

"Are you ready to die?" the demi-god asked.

"No," said Sperrin. He swept Eury's leg from under him. Sperrin's blade flashed as the demi-god toppled, slashing across his face.

"My eyes!" Eury screamed.

"The hard part was keeping you from disappearing if you realized you were beaten," said Sperrin. "It wasn't easy to let you think you were winning."

Eury sank to his knees. "My eyes!"

"You can't leave while you're blinded, can you? I think I have to actually cut them out to kill you. I may just do it, too."

Sperrin strode over to where the first ironback was still trying to shake Guthre out of the tree. The creature fell before it could pick up its blade.

I don't think I had ever seen Sperrin look so radiant. The glowing Mouse King armor helped, but the joy he took in the efficient way he killed left me conflicted. I was proud of the way he had killed to save us all, but something about him scared me. And I could see just a hint of pain in his eyes at the pleasure he took from it.

Sperrin killed the ironback Juila had half-crippled, then turned back to where Eury still crouched on hands and knees. The demi-god's powers seemed to have vanished when Sperrin's blade had ruined his eyes.

"O brother, save me! I die!" Eury cried out.

"I wish," Sperrin muttered. Eury was badly injured, but still very much alive.

"Why didn't you kill him?" Juila asked.

"I got tired of walking all over this silly forest looking for Kedessen. I figured hurting his brother would bring him along."

"It won't make him any friendlier."

Sperrin shrugged. "He killed my Empress. We're not here to make friends with him."

"Then why are you here?" a deep voice asked. A radiant form materialized behind Eury. Kedessen looked down on his half brother. "Be healed and begone, fool," he said. Eury's eyes regained their glow as he faded away.

"He is my half-brother and my most loyal servant, but I think he was not contributing to this situation," said Kedessen.

"You mean by losing a bunch of swordfights to me?" Sperrin answered.

"That," said Kedessen, "will not go unremedied."

"Wait," I shouted. "We came to talk."

"Talk all you like," said Kedessen. "I will attend to you presently, after I avenge my brother's momentary loss of vision."

The god stood a head taller than Sperrin, with a mane of golden hair like a lion. He had golden eyes like his brother, but almond shaped, their glow more subtle.

"You can't kill him," Juila said to Sperrin. "You don't want to fight him."

"He doesn't have a choice, dear cousin," said Kedessen. I wondered if they were really cousins or it was a courtesy title between gods. "As for you"— he turned his attention to Sperrin—"you will have the rare privilege of crossing blades with a god."

But he's not carrying a blade, I thought, just as Kedessen reached up and plucked a fiery stillsword from thin air.

He brought it down with incredible force. Sperrin's blade held, but his wrist cracked audibly as the bone snapped. A quick downward slash across the stomach and Sperrin collapsed on his back. The Mouse King armor lay frayed and burned, pulled away from the wound. It hadn't held back the god's blade.

"There," said Kedessen. "I hope you feel privileged."

I threw my knife at the god's face. Somehow a flick of his blade sent the knife flying in another direction.

"Was that really necessary?" Juila asked. She stepped forward, as if to intercede between Kedessen and Sperrin's fallen form. As soon as Kedessen took a step back, Guthre and I both rushed to Sperrin's side. I began tending to the horrible wounds. Guthre picked up Sperrin's sword.

"I thought it was," Kedessen answered. "and he and I both enjoyed it.

Only a moment's diversion perhaps, but most of us don't have the patience to spend a dozen lifetimes in a cage like you do."

So he *did* know about her imprisonment. Did that mean he was responsible, or did all the gods know? It might make a difference, I thought. Not if he succeeded in killing us all now, though.

"It was hardly my choice to be in the cage," said Juila.

"Of course it was. You made that choice the moment you decided to play the hero for the humans against their betters. And here you are, not half a day out of the cage and you are already doing it again. We are going to have to find you a better cage this time. Maybe they will let you keep one of your pet humans in it this time."

Discordantly, the line reminded me of my father's last words. *We're not pets*, I seethed. *That was why we fought the Holy War in the first place.*

Juila didn't seemed bothered. "You have had more dealings with humans than I have these last few years."

"Business dealings only."

"That is not the way I hear it," said Juila. "The way I hear it, you killed thousands of humans rather than admit Senne wanted to be out of your life."

"Senne is the love of my life, the way that long-dead human was the love of yours. That was what made your punishment so exquisite. And that, cousin, is why Senne will return to me."

"Does she even know?" Juila asked. "If anyone saw her awake, they would know instantly that you broke the treaty."

"No one will see her awake," he said, too quickly. "Not until the time is right. The treaty was not broken. As if you would know about a treaty agreed to when you were already locked away."

"Locked away like your Senne, you mean? I don't know all the terms of the treaty, but I know that you made a bargain that you did not complete."

"Nonsense," said Kedessen. "It is a mere technicality, caused by the human's own failure. As soon as he reaches the agreed-on place, the human will have his woman back."

"The human is dead," Juila said flatly.

It took a moment for the implications of that to seep in. Apparently Kedessen had not known about my father's death. *It means he can't fix his mistake.*

Kedessen regained his composure quickly. "A momentary setback," he said. "Inconvenient, but not threatening."

"Only as long as the Court doesn't know," said Juila. "You are only safe as long as the Court doesn't know."

"That is true enough," he said. "But only two of them"—he gestured to me with my glowing armor, and Sperrin, whose armor had faded with the sword-strike—"can face the court, much less talk to it. They will be easily killed. You, cousin, will be a less easy problem to solve, but one that was solved before."

"Solve it, then," she said, hefting Sperrin's knife.

"Oh I will, and gladly. I killed your sons, and I'll kill you." *Steal Sperrin's line, why don't you*, I thought. And then something hit me. Kedessen was lying. *Was he even at that battle? He's just taunting her.*

Kedessen sounded like he really believed his words, though. *He's furious*, I thought. *He really doesn't want to face what he did.* I wondered why not—he was a god, after all. What would the price of breaking the treaty actually be?

Juila danced inside Kedessen's guard, but he parried the attack. *Just a probe*, I thought. That's something I wouldn't have known a few weeks ago.

Kedessen took a few lazy slashes at Juila, testing her defenses. "Do you miss your sons? I enjoyed killing them."

I had never known a god could out-and-out lie. My mother had told me they couldn't and I had utterly believed it ever since. They're gods. They're supposed to be better than us, not just more powerful. But Kedessen felt tawdry somehow—more human than divine.

Now Kedessen and Juila began to fight in earnest.

Their motions looked almost ritualistic: a fight between two immortals with thousands of years of experience between them. I expected Kedessen to have a huge advantage, using a long blade against Juila's slim knife. But she seemed to hold her own easily. Slim and catlike, she evaded Kedessen's dancing blade. The whole thing looked like an elaborately choreographed dance.

I turned back to Sperrin. I had stopped the blood loss at least, and his armor had shed some of the force of the god's blade. But half his ribs had been caved in by the blow. One at least had penetrated his lung. His breath came raggedly, accompanied by bloody froth.

For now he lived. But nobody survived such a blow without magical healing.

I looked up at an odd movement in the corner of my eye.

The sword-dance between the two gods went on in its beautiful precision. But Guthre had crept behind Kedessen on hands and knees. He pirouetted away from Juila's knife, a half-stride away from her. Guthre chopped from her knees, swinging Sperrin's sword two-handed. The blade caught Kedessen behind the ankle. The tendon split and he stumbled. In an instant Kedessen was on his back, Juila astride him. She held her knife firm at his throat.

"You cheated!" He seemed genuinely indignant. *You're a god*, I thought. *Show some dignity*. I knew Kedessen was more angry than crippled. By the time Sperrin's lungs filled up with blood and drowned him, Kedessen's tendon would already have knit itself.

Guthre walked back toward Sperrin with her father's sword in one hand and the god's blade in the other. She spat over her shoulder when she heard Kedessen's words.

"It was an ill blow," Juila said, her blade not wavering from Kedessen's throat. "But you are an ill god. Cousin."

Around us the woods had begun to change.

We have attracted attention, I thought. *Is that good or bad?*

Gradually, the path around us widened into a forest grove. The trees grew taller and straighter. Vines draped over their branches, hung with long strings of flowers. Luxuriant moss enveloped the ground around us, broken here and there by tufts of small blue flowers. Mist filled the woods around the grove, and wisps crept into the clearing here and there.

Last of all, the grove's inhabitants appeared.

Two tall chairs grew out of the ground like living trees. Vines draped them like the surrounding woods. A man and a woman sat in the chairs, beautiful beyond description. I saw gold and radiance and felt the Snake Slayer armor warm my chest and shoulders. Beyond a sense of shining hair and eyes that exuded warmth, I could not have described them, even though I looked right at them.

In front of them, on a bier lined with flowers, lay my father's body.

At the edges of the clearing stood servants with animal heads, silverbacks in glittering livery, and gods dressed in festival finery.

Now this *feels godlike*, I thought. *Nothing at all tawdry here.*

Guthre and I—and Sperrin's dying body, and Juila still astride Kedessen—all found ourselves at the heart of the clearing.

The Court had finally taken notice of our presence.

KEDESSEN RECOVERED FIRST. "Your majesties, I am being assaulted. Humans have trespassed here and freed one who was imprisoned. I beg your leave to destroy them."

A silvery laugh came from the Queen's throne.

"You were waiting for our leave to destroy them, Kedessen? Is that how you explain your present position?"

Juila had pulled the knife back from Kedessen's throat. She made no move to let him up until she caught some signal that I couldn't see. Slowly, Juila stood up, then extended a hand to Kedessen to help him rise.

"There will be no more fighting until the truth of the happenings here has been ascertained," said the King, his voice deep and earthy. "I include in those happenings the dead human we found among your wolves, Kedessen."

"I will be happy to explain, of course," Kedessen said.

"I thought as much," replied the Queen. "Your explanations are always entertaining, Kedessen, and the afternoon palls. We will be glad of some entertainment."

This is going to get bad in a hurry, I thought. *Why are they listening to him?*

Then the answer came to me: *Because you haven't said anything. And it has to be you — your father is dead and Sperrin close to it. Only you are wearing proper attire.*

And if you don't do it now, it will be too late.

"I think the right of explanation is mine," I said. I expected to stumble on the words, but they came out smoothly and crisply. "Under clause 12 of the Talisman of Truce, the party alleging a treaty violation has the right to present a case first. After the violation has been proven, the violater can give his defense."

My words seemed to surprise them.

"You are alleging a violation of the Truce?" the King asked. "That is a serious charge."

"And who is she to bring it?" Kedessen shouted. "She isn't an acknowledged messenger. What gives her the right to speak?"

The King nodded. "That is a fair question, though out of turn. You are attired properly, but are you an appointed messenger? Do you meet the other qualifications?"

"Because of Kedessen's actions, the appointed messenger is dead," I began. I saw the god about to interrupt and speeded up my words. "However, there is an exception to clause 3, which allows a person who has been entrusted with one of the five human copies of the Talisman of Truce to present a case in such times as a messenger may be unavailable."

I pulled the cased Talisman from its hiding place at the small of my back and held it up. *My last link with Tenia.* Taking two steps forward, I knelt and extended my hand with the Talisman in it. One of the courtier gods came forward, opened the case, and examined its contents.

"Your majesties, it is genuine. This is the copy entrusted to the Empress of Ananya."

"But she has a human name!" Kedessan interjected. "Clothed or not, dead or not, she is not a fit messenger. She cannot speak when her name—the source of her power—comes from the old ways."

The King and Queen looked at me silently, awaiting a response. *So that's why my name had power in a trade*, I realized suddenly. *That's why the Empress and chancellor have to give up their names while they serve. The clothes are secondary to the name.*

Which is why, I finally understood, I really was my father's daughter. He might have destroyed my world and not cared whether I lived or died, but he would never in a thousand years have committed the tactical error this god had just made. And he would never have allowed me to make it, either.

Go on, you are my chancellor, I heard Tenia's voice in my head.

Kedessan looked at me smugly, certain he had won the round.

I looked up, looked the golden creatures on the thrones in the eye. "Your majesties," I said. "I have no name. My father traded my name to Kedessan, the first bargain he made that Kedessen did not honor his end of. I do not claim a grievance for that broken bargain, since it did not touch on the treaty." *And because I don't want to mention his paying for my name by giving me a talent for the old magic.* "I merely touch on it so your majesties are aware that Kedessan is in possession of my name. I have only a use-name that belonged to my mother, which is not mine to keep if she has been restored to life as Kedessen claims. As surely as my Empress and my father did, I gave up my name, and by the terms of the treaty and the messenger clause, I hereby invoke my right to argue for redress of the treaty violation."

I took a breath. "I would also ask your majesties, by what right does Kedessan speak here, since he has for years been in possession of the human name that in his claim would have barred me from speaking?"

Kedessan had no reply to that. For a moment, neither did the King. "You may speak," he finally said. "First, please tell me where is the Empress of Ananya, and how did you come to be appointed her messenger?" Which neatly avoided my claim against Kedessan for the moment.

It did cut back to the heart of the argument I needed to make, however. *I am my father's daughter*, I realized anew. Awful as his crimes had been, I was beginning to see a path toward making them right. *Tenia, I really am your chancellor.* All the years I had spent trying to make my father proud, all use-lessly. I was going to win this for the person who really had been proud of me. *I will win this for you, Tenia.*

I could see Tenia's smile in my mind as I answered the King and Queen of the gods.

"The Empress is dead, your majesty, at the hands of Kedessen's servants. This was done at the behest of my father, the lawful messenger, who also lies dead before you." I saw triumph light in Kedessen's eyes and continued before he could interrupt. I wasn't counting on the court upholding my argu-ment about not letting him speak because he had my name. At best maybe they would give me back my name if I won. I wondered what it was—I hope I liked it.

I went on quickly, hoping Juila was right about how the Court felt about keeping their word. "The violation lies not in the deaths, but in the bargain. The terms were never fulfilled, in clear violation of clauses 150 and 154. And since the terms no longer can be fulfilled, we seek redress. Additionally I would like to note that the imprisonment of Juila, which we discovered on our arrival, violates clause 262 in two different places, since she was neither included in the full accounting of prisoners who fought on the human side during the war or any of the addenda, nor was she released at the specified time, or for many centuries afterward. I note also the enforcement mecha-nisms in clauses 119 and 202, which both are brought into force in this case, since the bargain Kedessen made was part of an explicit interference in a human conflict." That last was a stretch, but my father had brought the Central Alliance into the deal, and Alliance soldiers had attacked in concert with Kedessen's messengers. So I had at least a plausible argument.

The King paused to consider. "Let us take up the matter of the god Kedessen first. You have our word that both issues will be settled and the treaty made whole before you leave this Court today."

"That pleases me," I said, the ritual response from long ago.

"Then please proceed."

I laid out the situation in detail, putting everything else—my father's body, Sperrin's horrific injuries, the god waiting to pounce on any rhetorical misstep I made—out of my mind. I began with my mother's death and my father's first flawed dealings with Kedessen, and continued through the bargain my father had made to betray the Empress and how it had played out. I knew the situation better than I realized, once I stopped trying to deny my father's complicity. And I felt oddly confident telling the story. Against all expectations, I found myself *enjoying* it. I wondered if this was how Sperrin felt when he killed someone.

Though an authorized messenger, my father had acted against the interests of the Empress. Before I met Juila that had seemed the heart of the case to me, but by the time I started speaking, I realized that detail barely mattered to the gods. From the standpoint of the treaty, he was perfectly entitled to negotiate a modification. But having negotiated the modification, both parties were compelled to keep their word. My father had broken his oath to the Empress and betrayed his country—neither of which concerned the gods particularly, under the neutrality clause of the treaty—but he had delivered on all his promises to the gods. Kedessen, by contrast, had failed to deliver the principal thing he had promised. Regardless of whether he had intended to keep his bargain—and having just seen Kedessen lie, I wasn't prepared to take the god at his word about it—he had failed to restore my mother to life and deliver her to my father.

I bowed when I finished my summation, and the King asked me a few questions about particulars, and where I felt the Talisman related to them. Each time, I answered succinctly.

"Kedessen," the King asked. "Do you deny any of the case that has been made here?"

The god smiled. He didn't seem worried. I wondered if it was possible he didn't realize the consequences of my father's death, even now. No, it wasn't possible. So he would be laying the groundwork for something else.

"The messenger approached me. I didn't try to tempt him or lure him—he wanted to tempt me. The first time he didn't know the right words, so I was able to cheat him easily enough, to give him something that fit his terms that wasn't what he expected. I couldn't leave him empty handed, after all"—he gestured to me—"this one's name *did* have value. But the second bargain—the second time it was he who cheated me. He seduced me with promises of my lost lover."

From the body language of the King and Queen, Ketya could see they had little patience with Kedessen's argument. He persisted, though.

"I fully intended to fulfill our agreement. He restored Senne to me in exchange for the return of his own lost love. It is not too late to complete that bargain."

I interjected—permitted at this point in the argument. That's why I had wanted to go first, when interruptions weren't allowed. "You try to argue that you intended to keep your bargain with my father"—my mention of our relationship was deliberate—"but given that you both were violating the spirit of the treaty, if not the letter, that's far from evident. Especially in light of the previous bargain, which you did not keep."

"I was not required to keep my word before—" Kedessen started, then realized that he'd said too much.

"Perhaps," I responded. "But that's not a persuasive defense of your intent to keep it this time. Everyone keeps their word when they are watched and compelled. When you weren't compelled you gave your word and broke it. You misled him."

"I wouldn't break it now," he said. "The agreement gave me a means to end my lover Senne's cruel sacrifice."

"But you have already ended it, without fulfilling the bargain. You took your share of the bargain without paying for it. And you ended her sacrifice, which she willingly entered, by imprisoning her." I was actually guessing there, but Kedessen and Juila had seemed to allude to it. And even a denial that he had imprisoned Senne wouldn't exactly make Kedessen look good.

"She is my lover. I will not be parted from her again."

"Does she feel the same way?"

Kedessen didn't answer. The other gods present already knew the answer, just as Juila had.

After that, there wasn't much for Kedessen to say. But he didn't seem bothered.

The King and Queen conferred briefly. Then the king spoke to me. "Very well, we accept your case against Kedessen as proven. What remains to determine is redress."

"I have a suggestion," said Kedessen, a little too smoothly. This was his trap, I knew. "Why don't I bring her father back to life and then complete the arrangement with him? Surely you don't object to my returning your father to life?"

I saw the stricken look on Guthre's face. *They really don't trust me at all,* I thought. *And why should they?* A few days ago would I have taken that deal? Probably. Maybe even a few hours ago. What had changed?

Maybe I'm what's changed, I thought. In any event, I knew what my response had to be.

"Your majesties, under the redress clause of the treaty, it is not the violater's place to suggest the terms of redress. The terms are to be jointly decided by the accuser and the leadership of the other side. They may choose from the specific penalties in the appropriate clauses, or reach an agreement together. Your majesties may suggest ways to fix the problem, but not Kedessen."

"Very well," said the King. He didn't seem surprised that I hadn't accepted Kedessen's bait. "What exactly would redress the problem, in your estimation?"

I had thought a lot about how to answer this question, and still wasn't entirely satisfied. "The violation would be satisfied by the restoration of magic to Ananya, under the same terms as before." That didn't seem like all the treaty would allow—there was room for penalties—but I was not in a strong bargaining position. I didn't think I could push too hard.

"I see," the King said. "That is certainly a reasonable and minimal request." Kedessen looked crestfallen. "But in deference to Kedessen's point, we do weigh his reminder that Senne has sacrificed herself for many of your lifetimes. Does the restored magic need to flow from Senne?"

A look of renewed hope crossed Kedessen's face.

What is the King getting at? I wondered. *When in doubt, follow the exact wording of the treaty,* I decided.

"No," I replied. "As long as the magic flows as it did before, through a conduit acceptable to both Ananya and to your majesties, under the terms of the treaty it doesn't matter what god it comes from."

Kedessen looked smug. *He thinks he's getting what he wants.* But I thought I was beginning to follow the thinking of the King and Queen.

"May I point out that there is a god available for the purpose?" Kedessen looked at Juila as he said the words.

"Under the terms of the treaty she isn't available," I answered. "She must be repatriated as a former prisoner of war, and compensated for her accidental imprisonment." Not that anyone really thought it was accidental, but no need to say it aloud. "Besides, her magic has been stripped from her."

"Kedessen," the King asked, "where is the girl's mother now? The one you restored for the messenger but never returned to him? You *did* restore her, right? Her whereabouts may bear on our decision."

"Of course I restored her," said Kedessen, his tone indignant, as if no one could ever doubt him. "She was placed in the house that the messenger planned to use as a permanent residence following his escape, under guard by my brother until it was clear the messenger would keep his end of the bargain. Once he did, the guard was removed, except for wards placed on the doors to keep her from leaving or anyone without Ananyan blood from entering. The messenger apparently did not fully trust his hosts, and asked me to put those wards on all the entrances until he arrived. Central Alliance guards watch the house now, but she is secure."

"She is imprisoned, you mean," I said.

"Call it what you will, but she is safe."

"Indeed," said the King. "I think we know all that we must. Now we will confer. Please take your ease while we do. I will have food sent so you and your companions may eat. You will have our answer in a night and a day."

"I thank your majesties," I said. "One of my companions was badly injured at Kedessen's hand. I am afraid he may die before your judgment is rendered."

"He will not die today, nor tomorrow," the King said, not unkindly. "And he may yet be healed by the same hand that looked to slay him."

Now what is that supposed to mean? I wondered. But all I said was, "I thank your majesties."

I THINK THOSE first moments in front of the Court were when I became an adult. I had no idea what was about to happen, but it was the first time I ever had to deal with a crisis outside of the shadow of my father, when I couldn't anticipate his disapproval with every word I chose less-than-perfectly.

I thought I would be terrified, that I would forget everything he drilled into me. But that wasn't what happened at all.

You know what I was thinking that whole time I was dueling with Kedessen in front of the King and Queen of the gods?

I was thinking, *This is easy. I never thought I could do this, but it's easy.*

I was always so bad at magic, and always so far below my father's expectations, that I thought I was bad at everything.

But every time I quoted from the treaty and found that I knew exactly what passage to cite, every time I countered one of Kedessen's accusations, I would think, *Is this what my father did?*

I loved it. There I was, with my father's body on a bier right in front of me, dueling with a god. I had never felt so adult, or so alive.

Afterward, part of me felt guilty—I think the same way Sperrin felt guilty when he killed somebody. But while it was going on, I felt the same joy those wolves must have felt when they were chasing us on the stairs, the joy of putting a quarry on the run and then hunting him down.

That isn't quite how things turned out, though.

Chapter 29

Ketya

When I turned from the thrones, I saw three pavilions standing at the far end of the clearing. I had no idea if they'd just been conjured up or had appeared with the rest of the court. The pavilions had colorful fabric structures on them, like giant tents; the tent on the center pavilion had Ananya's crest emblazoned across it.

Not exactly subtle, I thought. But after the intense focus of the negotiations, I needed some time to relax and regroup before the next round.

A pair of goat-headed attendants had placed Sperrin on a broad wooden board, like a small tabletop, which they used to carry him to the pavilion. Guthre and Juila followed, and I entered the tent just behind them.

The inside of the tent seemed far bigger than the outside, with a spacious central room and several openings in the silk, revealing bedchambers. A diffuse light filled the tent, keeping all the rooms at a comfortable light level— like sun shining through fabric, but with no apparent light source. I wondered how it was done. I had plenty of training in magically lighting things, but this light seemed more elegant somehow, even though it drew on the same type of magic I'd trained in.

The attendants placed Sperrin next to a pool of steaming water. The bath gave off a pleasing berry scent as I approached. Guthre knelt beside Sperrin, checking on him.

"How is he?" I asked. Really I didn't want to talk to Guthre right now, but I could hardly avoid it. Guthre *was* Sperrin's daughter.

Guthre looked up at me with a wistful expression. "His bleeding has stopped, and he's breathing more easily. Someone helped him magically, but I couldn't tell you who. None of the gods touched him that I saw."

Juila walked up, and put a hand on Guthre's shoulder. "You should rest. You fought hard. He will be well tended. I have never heard of a guest dying in one of the Court's guesthouses. They are hospital, hostel, and prison all combined."

"Prison?" I asked.

"Of a sort. You can't leave until the judgment of the Court is complete."

"How about Kedessen? Can he leave?"

"No, he can't either," answered Juila.

"Then I'm satisfied," I said.

Liveried servants, looking like men and women with the heads of sheep, entered bearing covered trays of food. Others brought bottles of various chilled juices. They placed the dishes on a low table in the center of the room, surrounded by flimsy looking, diaphanous furniture of the same fabric that formed the tent. The chairs proved sturdier than I expected, and far more comfortable, like reclining on cushions filled with air.

I let myself sink into a chair, and almost fell asleep on the spot. A wave of exhaustion hit me as the energy from the negotiation wore off.

"You should eat," said Juila. "You can rest after, and it will make you feel better. You've never tasted anything like the food of the gods. It's very restoring."

I never imagined I'd have a god trying to convince me to eat.

Trying a morsel, I found Juila hadn't exaggerated: It resembled human food, but the flavors tasted richer and more nuanced, as if everything I'd ever eaten was just a pale shadow of the food served here. Soon I found herself eating with an unexpected appetite.

"What's the magic here?" I asked Juila when I felt more alert. "I thought I understood magic pretty well, but I haven't seen anything like this."

Juila smiled wanly. "All the magic here will be more powerful than you know. It is not really any different, just that you have only experienced Senne's magic split up among thousands of channelers. You can do a lot more if it is concentrated. The nuances get lost the more it is shared."

"Sorry if I hit a sore spot."

"You are not the one who made it sore. It is sore because it is all still close to me, even if it is eight hundred years old to you. I miss my magic with every breath, but I would trade it again for my husband and sons." Juila fell silent, lapsing into memory.

I miss my magic too, I thought, *even though I only had it for an instant.* But I knew my loss paled compared with Juila's.

Guthre sank into the seat next to me. I tried to avoid eye contact, but I couldn't bring myself to be too rude to the scout, after all we'd been through together. I couldn't bring myself to be friendly either, though.

Eventually Guthre spoke, a bit awkwardly. "You were great out there. I was so glad we had you speaking for us."

"You mean because my father, who actually knew what he was doing, couldn't speak to them anymore?"

I had meant the words to wound, but Guthre didn't take them that way.

"Your father would have sold us to Kedessen in return for passage to wherever he left your mother. We both know that. Only you could say what needed to be said today."

She was right, but I couldn't stop myself from defending him. "I'm not my father. He was better at this kind of thing."

"Betrayal came more easily to him. You have honor."

"He—" but then I stopped, because Guthre was right again.

Guthre kept on speaking. "I mean, so many people died because of what Kedessen did. There was nobody but you to make him pay for their deaths."

There was no way for me to respond to that without sounding heartless. Just as well: I wanted to feel heartless around Guthre. It would make things so much easier.

"Guthre, the gods don't care about any of the people who died. All they care about is whether he broke the treaty. He's not going to pay for their deaths."

"But you said—"

"*We* care about them. For the gods it's all about the treaty. So right now that's all I can care about, too."

And then I caught Juila's gesture, silencing us.

"This is not a place for serious discussion," Juila said. "Others are listening. Not just the Court, but many other gods."

"Oh," I said. If I hadn't been so tired I would have known that, of course.

Guthre had a similar reaction. "I should have known that. I'm a scout, I'm used to being the one listening in."

"We're all tired. We should probably sleep," I said.

Guthre managed a smile, only a little bit forced. "I would offer you a back rub but it would be weird with all those other gods watching."

"And because you killed my father," I said. Without turning to see Guthre's reaction, I walked into one of the silken chambers, and settled into the lush bed that dominated the small room. As I sank into what felt like a sea of silk, I regretted my sharpness to Guthre, and wondered if I should get up and apologize. But then I drifted deeper into silk, and sleep claimed me.

"LOOK, THEY'VE BROUGHT Senne," said Juila. "Whatever else happens, you've freed her from Kedessen, at least." The three of us had just emerged from the tent, rested and bathed, our clothes washed and mended by servants we had never seen.

Behind us, servants carried Sperrin, still unconscious but breathing freely now.

I realized I didn't actually know what Senne looked like. All I had seen were festival performances and romantic paintings of her and Kedessen, based on nothing at all as far as I could tell. "Which one is she?"

"The pale redhead," Juila said, indicating with a glance.

Senne looked beautiful and dazed, like a god whose magic had been drained for hundreds of years. She stood far from Kedessen, who emerged from his own pavilion clad in golden finery. I saw Eury in the crowd of onlooking gods as well, rather than by his half-brother's side.

Something else occurred to me. "Is Bayinna here?" I asked Juila. "My mother's family is related to her. If we live through this I'd like to be able to say I saw her."

The thought seem to amuse Juila a little, and she nodded toward a dark-haired goddess with olive skin and striking green eyes.

Not much family resemblance, I thought. But I supposed after forty or fifty generations there wouldn't be. And if she changed shapes like Eury, she might have looked nothing like that at the time.

A murmur passed through the crowd, then silence fell. I steeled myself for what might or might not be another verbal battle.

At a gesture from the King, Kedessen and I stepped forward and stood before the thrones. I bowed slightly in formal greeting. Kedessen did not.

He knows something is coming that won't be good for him.

At the earlier session, the King had done most of the talking, but now the Queen spoke. Her voice sounded like music, like the purest chorus I had ever heard. "Kedessen, this is not your first violation of the Talisman of Truce."

That came as news to me.

"Your previous disrespect for the terms of the Truce must be factored into the price to be paid today. At the same time, you argued poignantly for the price that your lover paid, willingly or not.

"Because all of the direct royal line in Ananya has been killed, the breach is not easily solved. The Truce specifies a very limited number of humans who are entitled to speak to the gods, and the statutory magic must pass to one of them. Additionally, under the terms of the truce the magic must pass through someone who bears the blood of gods in her veins, preferably more than one god. And the human chosen must be native to the region she rules over, so a native-born Ananyan in this case. To choose someone who did not fit all of those conditions would be healing the breach by creating another, which is unacceptable to our Court."

Suddenly I didn't like where this was going.

The Queen looked at me. "Helpful and appropriate it was that you called our attention to clause 119, from which we draw our solution." Before I could react, her gaze shifted to the golden-eyed god.

"Kedessen, you have freed your lover Senne, and it is our will that she remain free." For a moment he beamed, until the impact of the Queen's next words hit him. "You shall take Senne's place. The magic of Ananya shall flow from you, and it shall pass through the messenger before us."

But I can't, I wanted to say. *It needs to flow to someone who's good with magic, not through me.* But even as I opened my mouth to speak, I could feel the power flowing into me. I could see Kedessen, his mouth open to protest, staggering as torrents of power flowed out of him. A pair of lion-headed servants caught him before he could collapse. Angrily, he shook them off and stood erect.

His eyes burned as he stared at me.

"When I return," he said, "there will be no treaty. I will invoke the clause of abrogation, and we will see how you humans fight after a dozen lifetimes with no magic of your own."

"You will not return, this time," said the Queen.

He struggled to hold himself up, but his eyes stayed locked on mine. "The reason you survived the last war is that too many gods wanted you as servants, or as worshipers. They didn't want to kill too many of you. I just want to see all of you exterminated like the rats you are. I just want to see you die."

His strength gone, Kedessen collapsed into the arms of the lion-headed servants. Gently, they helped him back toward the pavilion he'd emerged from.

Many of the gods in the crowd looked shocked, but except for Eury, none of them looked particularly upset.

Could what he's saying be true? I wondered, dazed. Were all of the deaths in Ananya a test for the next war with the gods? If Kedessen had done this before, it could be. What my father had done gave him the pretext, but who knew what other pretexts he'd had over the years. If they were smaller, and no one was able to reach the Court with a protest, who would even have heard of them?

After Kedessen had been removed, the Queen looked to me again. She wore an expression as if she wanted everyone to believe Kedessen had never spoken. "You brought up a second violation of the Treaty as well, the imprisonment of Juila. She has been released and will stay released, but compensation is owed for the breach. Did you have a particular compensation in mind?"

Yes, I thought, *but if I suggest it first you won't agree.* So instead, I said, "You could restore her powers. The ones that were taken from her when she chose the human side in the war."

The look the Queen gave me was about what I expected. "Juila's punishment is separate from her imprisonment," the Queen said. "Even if that were not so, having a full-powered god in the human lands not bound by the terms of the Truce would be profoundly destabilizing, don't you agree? It is enough that she still has the powers of human magic."

I bowed my head in assent. "I have another thought," I said. "You could ask the fey to cease their attacks in Ananya." Even with magic restored, it would take time to pass magic to living channelers and begin rebuilding the ruins of the empire, and the Alliance would be invading at the same time. A cessation of the fey attacks would at least allow the process to begin.

"Very well," the Queen said, "I will agree to this. While you live, the fey will not attack Ananyans. But guard your life well, for at the moment of your death, whatever the cause may be, we will no longer restrict our fey cousins."

Again, I bowed my head in assent. Power boiled inside me, making it hard to focus and speak at first. I forced a measure of control into my voice. "The breach has been healed," I said.

"Almost," replied the Queen. "That settles the formal breach of the treaty, but there is one final matter. When you and your party entered this land, you should have been treated as guests. You and those who escort you were emissaries under the terms of the treaty, and yet you were set upon in our lands. For that, there is a debt owed, but some of it can be made right."

Ever so faintly, the Queen gestured at the platform Sperrin lay on, and I saw his wounds close and vanish. His skin regained its color. A moment later his eyes opened. His daughter knelt beside him and took his hand. Leaning over, Guthre whispered in his ear, and he nodded.

"My thanks to your majesties," he said, sitting up easily.

That's right, he's wearing the Mouse King suit, I remembered. *He can speak here, even if they're not bound to listen. Not that there was much left to say.*

The Queen looked at the chancellor's body lying on the bower, and spoke again. "Your father also died in this land. I understand that some of your people have cause to dislike him, but we have no quarrel with him. He broke no law of ours. If you choose, we can restore him, as Kedessen restored your mother."

I swallowed hard.

I had expected the choice to be difficult. But really it wasn't. As empty as it would leave me, I knew what I had to say.

"Respectfully, your majesties, I must decline. For violating his oath to our Empress, he forfeited his life under our law. Restoring it when so many others have died seems contrary to the spirit of the treaty."

"So it does," said the Queen. "But you spoke of an Empress. You are Empress now." She said the words gently, but despite their musical sound, still I could not absorb them.

She looked over all of us. "Very well. Our business here is complete. I will send guides to escort you from our lands. You may go to anywhere in the human lands where our worlds intersect. You will be safe until you leave this land. And you, Empress, are welcome to return. But you, Juila"—her gaze caught the exiled god and burned—"you had best not return if you value your freedom. Next time the treaty will not protect you."

Juila nodded in acknowledgment but did not speak. Guthre leaned over to whisper in her father's ear again. I saw a look of surprise in Sperrin's eyes, then understanding. He looked at me and I understood the signal. There's something he needs to do. Or that Guthre needs him to do.

"Your majesties, Juila and I will return to the barrow near the Drowned City. If your servants can bring my father's body as well?" The Queen nodded assent.

Sperrin stood. "Your majesties, my daughter Lynniene and I would like to travel to the location where Kedessen left Ket— left the Empress's mother. We would like to bring her home."

"I will send you there, though under the treaty we cannot help you in a way that takes sides in a human conflict. Therefore you will have to find your way back to Ananya afterward without any help from the gods." Sperrin nodded assent and the Queen continued. "I do not know where she is, but I believe there is one here who does."

I almost laughed at Sperrin's expression when he realized who the Queen meant.

Eury, his eyes once again luminous as they had been before Sperrin ruined them, walked up to the soldier and stared him hard in the face. "Be glad you didn't kill me when you had the chance."

"Which time?" asked Sperrin. "Killing you was getting to be an everyday thing for a while."

"Don't think you'll have another chance," Eury said.

"We'll see," Sperrin answered. "We will have plenty of chance to talk of it on the road."

With that, Eury, Sperrin, and Guthre walked from the clearing and disappeared into the shifting forest beyond.

Guthre was just doing it to impress me, I knew. She thought saving my mother would help me get over my anger at her killing my father.

She might be right.

But for now I had to learn to be an Empress. I could feel power swelling within me, seeming to grow at every moment till it threatened to flow out from every pore if I didn't find an outlet for it. And once we were back home, there would be the old magic as well. It could not be forgotten again; as Empress I could not ignore the possibility that Kedessen's threat was more than defeated bluster.

I looked at Juila beside me and at the two lion-headed guides who carried my father's body between them. The Queen and the rest of the court had already faded away, along with the mist and pavilions. We found ourselves on the path once more.

"Come on," I said. "We have a graveyard to visit."

I THOUGHT TELLING Sperrin and Guthre about their relationship would change everything for them, and I guess it did. But as they walked away on that day, I didn't see much difference. They still treated each other the same way, mostly. They both still had a quiet confidence that I knew I would never share. Only now I was an Empress. Now I felt the magic filling me until I felt ready to burst, felt ready to rebuild the world all at once. Now I was supposed to decide who got to channel magic and who didn't, who led armies and orchestras and academies. At first I thought they should have given it to someone better trained, or more knowledgeable, or more grown up. But then it hit me that I was the one who was there, who was knowledgeable enough and trained enough to make a case before the gods and win it. And before it was all over I might have to fight a second Holy War, unless I could become knowledgeable enough and trained enough to prevent it from starting.

A big part of me still felt I was going to be a terrible Empress, the same part of me that always felt I was a terrible daughter. The same part of me that always felt my father was still looking over my shoulder, and critiquing my every move. I guess I was just going to have to get over it, or try to face my demons the way Sperrin was trying to face his.

The first step was to return to the Westbarrow and bury my father, and to bury my fears and perhaps his crimes along with him. And then, with my father a dead statesman instead of a live traitor, it would be time to return to the Drowned City, to the beseiged coast of a beseiged country, and to the seat where the previous Empress had died in my arms.

I was supposed to be your chancellor, Tenia. You were supposed to be Empress.

But the dead girl in my mind laughed easily. *You'll make me proud, Ketya.* She was the only one who could call me that now.

We walked on toward the Westbarrow, where my father's grave would soon join the graves of Juila's husband and sons, and of my best friend.

A few minutes ago the thought would have filled me with sadness. But now, brimming with magic that belonged to the god who had just begun to pay for his betrayal, I felt like I was returning home.

Chapter 30

The smile hadn't left Guthre's face since we'd turned our backs on the King and Queen of the gods and left the clearing for what was almost certainly a deathtrap. Another deathtrap. And I felt more or less the same way, except I wasn't setting myself up for the same sort of teenaged heartbreak that my daughter was.

I had tried to talk to her about it. "You know this can't work, right? Ketya is an Empress now. An Empress can't just have casual relationships the way a soldier can."

Guthre had looked at me like I was delusional. "I thought you said you studied history."

"I did. What does that have to do with relationships?"

Guthre sighed. "Who the Empress is sleeping with *is* history."

"I guess." I felt a little bemused to be having this conversation with my daughter. "Just don't be too disappointed if it doesn't work out."

"Wouldn't be the first time," said Guthre. "But I might as well aim high, right?"

"I'd never really thought of it that way," I admitted. "Marriages were something the Empress arranged, and you fell in love with whoever you married because the magic made you love them."

"That's a terrible system. I hope Ketya doesn't keep that going."

"I don't know what she's going to do. There's so much fighting and rebuilding to do, that I can't imagine matchmaking will be a priority.

"Besides, my brother will kill you all before she has time to start marrying people off," Eury chimed in. We hadn't thought he could hear us.

I snorted. "I see you've gone from threatening to kill me to threatening to have your big brother kill me. I'm not sure that's an improvement."

Eury nodded, unperturbed. "And kill you he will."

"He really meant those threats?" asked Guthre. "I thought he was just threatening the way every criminal does when they're convicted."

"He meant every word," Eury said. "He's been planning it for a dozen lifetimes. I was surprised to hear him talking about it out loud, though. He must have been very angry."

"Why do the King and Queen put up with him if he keeps rebelling?" Guthre asked.

Eury looked at me. "Ask your father. Parents put up with a lot of rebellion from their children."

"The King and Queen are Kedessen's parents? No wonder he thinks he'll get out of the sentence. Does that make the King your father, too?"

"It does," Eury said. "Which is why I know I'll be able to kill *your* father sooner or later."

"We'll see," I said.

We had reached a stairway, a narrow wooden stairwell that wound upward in a tight spiral to the sky.

"It doesn't look very safe," Guthre said. It looked like an old servants' stair, without any handrail.

"You'll be safe enough, at least until we arrive," said Eury. "I want to kill you myself, not have you fall off a stairway."

"I'm sure you'll give it your best shot," I said. I started up the rickety spiral without hesitating.

We didn't talk much, given the steepness of the stairs. We had to walk single file, and as we got higher, the winds picked up. But about halfway up, Guthre called forward to me.

"How much do you know about Ketya's mother? Did you ever meet her?"

"She died before I knew the chancellor. I saw her execute a man at Davynen before she got sick, but we didn't speak. Why?"

"I was just thinking it would be terrible if she was anything like Ketya's father. It would be a shame to come all this way and find out she was just as bad as him."

"Try not to kill her, please," I said.

"I'll do my best. I'm not so good at relationships. But I figure even if Ketya still hates me at the end of it all when we bring her mother back, you and I will have some time to get used to being father and daughter and fighting together. And what better way is there to bond than being guided into the heart of an enemy country by an immortal-unless-you-stab-him-in-the-eyes demi-god who's sworn to kill us both? I ran away from things for a long time, and this feels better. Even if it's insane. I'd rather face the danger for a while. You understand what I mean?"

"I think I'm starting to," I answered. I thought about the way I'd tried to face all the killing I'd done by running away from it, and the consequences it had caused for me and my daughter. I was about to say that I wasn't sure it was the same as what she meant, but by then the wind on the stairs had silenced and I realized we had crossed from sky to earth again.

- THE END -

Acknowledgments

It takes a village to destroy an empire, and I am grateful to the many people who helped me to make life really, really difficult and unpleasant for my characters while angry gods rampaged through their homeland. I especially want to thank Cynthia Manson, who prodded me to write *The Lost Daughter* and pushed me to make it better at every step; Debra Doyle, who expanded my view of the story's scope and how to tell it; and John Betancourt, who stepped up to make sure the book happened.

A longtime editor and book developer, Leigh Grossman teaches publishing-related courses in the English Department at the University of Connecticut while doing work for various publishers. *The Lost Daughters* is his sixteenth book. Originally from the Atlantic City area, he now lives in a sprawling old house in northeast Connecticut with his wife and daughter. (Basically, he's cosplaying the professor from the Narnia books.) Look for him online at www.swordsmith.com or @SwordsmithLRG on Twitter.

CPSIA information can be obtained
at www.ICGtesting.com
Printed in the USA
BVHW07s1211221018
530870BV00002B/108/P

9 781479 418930